Four of the Imperial line-class ship's riggers were on the outside, maintaining the steering vanes and keeping them clear of debris. One of them was spraying foam onto a place near the nose where a burning sac had been blown into the gondola.

Ahle steered her paraglider onto that man – no, a woman, her hair in a tight bun. She looked up in shock and found herself facing a long pistol.

"Detach and depart. If you'd be so kind."

"What – who are you?"

"Captain Karen Ahle, at your service. Now, if you'd please detach and depart? Your crew will be following you shortly, Senior Airshipwoman."

A quick glance back showed that Ronalds, Herrick and the others were kicking off the other riggers the same way. One of them had already jumped, his parachute opening.

"You're pirates? Boarding *us*?"

"We're not the Air Marines your ship, quite conveniently, is presently without. Now, if you *would* please?"

The woman detached – her rig from the safety cable – and looked, again, uncomprehendingly at Ahle. Then she checked the bracings on her parachute, ran to the side and took a flying leap from the airship.

"This is a beautiful ship," said Ahle. "Let's make her ours, shall we?"

Cover art and design by Kriss Morton and Joy Wandrey
Published by Henchman Press
http://www.henchmanpress.com

ISBN-13: 978-1-941620-16-8

Published in the United States of America

Her Majesty's Western Service

Leo Champion

Laura — hope you enjoy it!

Leo Champion

Books by Leo Champion
Legion
The Shark Boats
Her Majesty's Western Service
Highway West
Desert Strike (coming soon)

Dedication

For Markell,
As promised.

...the Great War lasted from 1881 to approximately 1887, engulfing first the European Powers and then the rest of the world. However, it could just have easily run from 1875 to 1882, 1900 to 1905 – or 1914 to 1918.

Given the stage set by the Franco-Prussian War, the era's tensions made such a war inevitable at some point - and given the social turbulence of the industrialized Late Nineteenth Century, its outcome was certain. After years of bloody, costly and inconclusive conflict, Powers began to collapse under the strain; riots and revolution led to disease and famine, while a few exiled remnants watched from remote colonies.

While the United States had mostly stayed neutral in the war, its industry and bankers had financed the Powers heavily. When Europe disintegrated, America was bankrupted; the ensuing Great Panic ripped a nation, already straining under bitter class and regional conflicts, apart at the seams into social apocalypse.

In 1914 a new US Federal Government declared itself, backed by an expeditionary force from the rebuilding British Empire. However, only twelve States were represented in that election - the South, although its slaves were gone, accepted unification only at gunpoint, while new nations had come into being across the Rockies. The west had become wild again...

From the introduction to *A Young Person's History Of The World, Volume VII*; written by W. Churchill, illustrated by A. Hitler. London Press, 1945.

Chapter One

Early March 1963; New York City, New York.

"These machines are destroying our livelihoods! *This* machine is destroying our livelihood!" Marko shouted at the workers. He pounded a shoe on the collapsible table. "This capitalist, imperialist machine – the British Empire, their

1

submissive stooges in Washington, their other puppet governments across the globe – is crushing us!"

There was a roar of approval from the small crowd. Forty or fifty strong, half of them unemployed; the others were mostly union men, Local 404 oilers and 501 shovelers for the most part of those. They waved beer and whisky bottles; two thirds of them were drunk and the rest were well on the way.

In the background, the boilers of the factory floor chuffed loudly and steadily. Intermittent clicks came from the mechanical brain directly behind Marko. Arc lights in the ceiling blazed a misshapen glare across the floor, and the three-inch gold ring in his left ear glinted a hard refractive wink.

"Are we, the workers, going to just stand there?" Marko yelled. He pounded one of the shoes, again. It was a steel-toed workman's boot with a pound and a half of gelignite stuffed inside it. "Are *you* just going to let them take from us our hands? Our *minds*" – he gestured the shoe at the machine behind him – "our *manhoods*?"

"No!" shouted the crowd. Some of them swigged from whisky bottles.

"Fuck them!"

"Traitors!"

"They *are* traitors!" Marko shouted. He was swarthy and dressed in black; six-five but very lean, with a flowing Gypsy moustache. "My friends, my brothers as *men*, they are traitors to us all! Because we are thinking, feeling *men*, not cogs in a machine! When you lubricate the chains, when you fuel the boilers - are the engines serving you? Or are you serving the engines and the plutocrats? As our forebears said–"

"To King Lud!" one man thrust a bottle in the air.

"Gen'rl Lud!" others yelled. Beer sloshed from the cups others waved. The arc lights flickered, and Theron Marko gave a broken-toothed smile.

"The capitalist bastards can burn in hell, I say! We will not serve the machines! We will *not* serve the plutocrats who want us to be no more than subcomponents! Men are free men, and the engines be damned!"

"They can't take our work from us without a fight!" yelled the same man who'd waved the whisky bottle a second ago.

"We're no pieces of a fucking machine!" cried the man next to him.

2

Marko thumbed a switch in the heel of the shoe he'd been pounding, raised its brother in his other hand.

"Men! Real men! We *fight* the machines!" he yelled. "As our forebears did! As *men* did, and *men* will, until we can live as free men!"

He turned, hurled the boots through an oiling port into the cogitator. Immediately it seized up, delicate gears and reactors clamping on the unexpected, hard objects.

Some of the men at the rear of the crowd were already moving, and a lot of the others were looking backwards.

Marko kicked the table over and moved past it himself.

"Men, tonight we strike a blow – for men! Against dehumanization! For manhood, and freedom! Against the machines that are destroying us!"

"King Lud!" somebody yelled. Several voices echoed him.

In the thick of the crowd, now, although they were all running. Some were scattering amidst the floor of the automated factory, amidst machines that processed cotton and the ones that spun it. Defunct already, for the most part.

"We're men, are we not?" the tall, lean Gypsy in black shouted. The short top-hat on his head slanted sideways; the thick-heeled boots gave him more speed as he ran.

"We're men!" the workers yelled, as the cogitator exploded behind them.

* * *

Nikolai Krushschev met him in an alley four blocks north of the factory.

"You're forty-five minutes late," the Russian agent said. He was a short, blocky man in his late sixties, with thick white hair and a heavy grey trenchcoat.

"I was busy." Marko gestured with his head at the scene. A police dirigible was floating over it, its searchlights stabbing down. From this distance they were partly obscured by smokestacks and buildings, but you could see the refracted light, hear the bells of their ground vehicles.

"Quite a ruckus."

"Every little bit helps."

With two fingers, Marko pulled a thin cigar from a pocket, flicked it alight.

3

"Another machine destroyed. Some more encouragement," he continued.

"A few drunken unemployables enthused. Another bullshit trespass rally. You're worth more than that."

"I destroy machines," Marko said. "It's what I do. You've got something more interesting?"

"You've been sidelined here since that Tamil clusterfuck," said Krushschev. "For two and a half years. Of course I have something more interesting. You know that eventually the hunts grow cold."

"For such a *disciplined* bunch of *ordered* people," Marko remarked, "Imperials are remarkably slack about pursuit."

"You complaining?"

Krushchev drew a cigarette, a Virginia Loyal, from his own coat, lit it, and started to walk.

"You're giving me resources," Marko said. It wasn't a question. "Adequate ones, this time. Or you can kiss my ass."

"The Count himself is involved in this," Krushchev shot back. "It's his scheme. You have a blank check."

"I'll believe that when–"

"See it," said Krushchev, and handed Marko a wallet. Marko opened it, glanced at the contents. Blue and green Exchequer negotiables, denominations of two and five thousand.

He flipped through the stack, feeling the quantity. At least a hundred. Squinted at the microleaf and the foil thread. Real, or the very best counterfeit.

"Count Trotsky himself is involved," Krushchev repeated. "This is *his*. You have the resources you need."

Marko halted suddenly, just as they reached the mouth of the alley.

"Then this isn't another insignificant pinprick?" he asked.

His handler stopped, a quarter-pace after Marko, and turned to glare at him.

"You implying the Count dirties his hands with insignificant pinpricks?"

"I'm going to need men, as well as money. For whatever this is."

"You'll have men. You've the gilt to hire others, and there's more where those are from."

"I've heard that before." Marko was coldly serious now. "In

4

Romania. Where that asshole priest abandoned us."

"We came back. Ilescu and his cronies hung. Remember?"

"They should have hung in `52."

Krushchev shrugged.

"They hung in `56. What's a few years?"

"What's a few lives? They shot five hundred men in Unirii Square after that *shithead* reject from a *worthless* Georgia seminary decided it wasn't the time and pulled back."

"You asked the question," Krushchev shrugged. "What's a few hundred men? There was turmoil. Isn't that enough for you?"

"There could have been more. Half the city could have gone up if he'd pushed."

"We're pushing this one. The Count's been planning this for years. You weren't sent to hang out here by a blindfolded dart at a map."

That was news to Marko. He'd always figured the suggestion he go to New York City was that it was a big city where a man could hide, and no more.

"You were taking me somewhere, and you just gave me enough money to outright buy a couple of these factories," he said.

"So put the fucking skepticism aside. You get to burn stuff. Isn't that enough?"

"We were going somewhere?"

* * *

Fifth Avenue was a crowded jam of traffic. Even at two in the morning, the vehicles were packed so tight they could barely inch along; horse-drawn wagons and coaches, steam-cars, a smattering of newer electrical vehicles. They passed a quadricycle, four five-foot wheels around a skeletal frame and a blocky generator; the rider, a goggled man in a brown suit, was pedaling in neutral, using the time to build up charge.

"More and more of the fucking things every year," Marko growled, with a gesture at one of the electricals.

Krushchev stifled a curse as one of his shoes went into a mound of horse manure that someone had pushed onto the sidewalk.

"Some say there's not enough."

5

A group of apprentice-enginemen came past them, stumble-hopping on triple-sprung pogo sticks. One of them landed on the edge of a pool of oil, slipped, had to kick out a brass-adorned rubber boot to steady himself. His buddy behind him gave a good-natured jeer.

Before the Crash, the Upper East Side had been a nice area, home to the mansions of the plutocrats. The mansions were mostly still there, the ones that hadn't been destroyed in the fighting of the late `80s or burned in the Commune that followed, but they were slums now, overcrowded lodgings for the lowest grade of unskilled workers. Here and there was a remnant of vandalized ornamentation, a defaced plaque that might once have held some oligarch's name. Laundry hung from wrought-iron balconies, and off-shift men stood around doorways and entry steps, smoking bad tobacco and drinking from cheap bottles.

A Metropolitan Police patrol came past, two narrow tandem-tricycles with a fifth man jogging behind. The cops zigzagged through traffic, on and off the sidewalk, ignoring the drinking proletarians. One of the tailriders glanced at Marko for a moment longer than seemed necessary; Marko returned it with an even glare. *What the fuck you looking at, goon?*

They crossed Fifty-Ninth, where on the west side smaller factories gave way to the giant industrial estates of Park City. Buildings towered up, nine and ten storeys high, smokestacks jutting a hundred feet above that. A massive freight airship was nested between two of the stacks, unloading by the glare of electrical light. The stack of another building belched, flame and thick soot blasting twenty feet out of its opening.

From a heavy steel ventilation grate came the grinding of the underway chains, massive conveyor belts that rumbled day-in, day-out to haul passenger cars under the city. It took a staff of three twelve-hundred-man shifts to keep them oiled and smooth.

More men serving machines, thought Marko, and spat down the grate.

"Mister? Got a dime?" asked a scrawny waif with a tin cup, as they waited to cross Seventy-Fifth. Steam-driven freight trucks rumbled past in front of them, rubberized tarpaulins covering their loads. "I gotta eat, mister. Got a dime?"

"Go buy yourself a couple houses," said Marko, and tossed

6

him two of the intricately-foiled Exchequer five-thousands.

The urchin studied the unfamiliar bills and spat.

"Thanks for nothing, shithead." He contemptuously ripped them in half, threw them away. "Food *comes* in wrappers."

Krushchev ignored the exchange, and rumbling machinery from the factories obscured conversation for the next two blocks. A cigar vendor wearing the elaborate livery of his brand, a tray against his chest, was good-naturedly bantering with a burly firefighter in a heavy, asbestos-threaded, red-and-black uniform.

A pair of tipsy, middle-aged clericals in dull beige suits staggered up from a dive-bar, one of them tapping his pipe out onto the sidewalk.

"Girls, girls? We got girls!" shouted a pimp's crier in a bright purple peaked-cap.

"Dr. Mephistopheles' Serum," said a coatless teenager with bright green braces and a pouch of advertising flyers. "Cure anything, only two dollars!" He tried to shove one of the flyers into Marko's hand; he pushed the kid away.

A pneumatic mail-tube, six-inch reinforced-glass segments between brass joins, emerged from a sidewalk switching-box into a building of low-grade shops and cheap offices.

For a moment, the kaleidoscope of light, refraction and deep shadow became smoothly bright as the spotlight from an overhead dirigible passed over them.

"Speelys! Speelys!" shouted a man with a pouch of handbills. "Porno speelys, just a buck! Porno speelys, best in the world, just twenty-five feet and a buck from you!"

"One of the great cities of the world," said Krushchev.

"Wouldn't it be wonderful to see the place burn?" asked Marko.

They passed Meer Park, the northeast and last remnant of the huge park that until about forty years ago had ruled the center of Manhattan. A beer vendor – and, doubtless, harder stuff under the flat – was doing a healthy business; a busker with a set of bagpipes played at the ornately-gated entrance.

"More anarchy like this, wouldn't you think?" Krushchev said. "Look. Utter chaos. Everyone out for himself. Fighting" – he gestured at a couple of bruised workers being ejected from a bar by a huge black bouncer –

"Stealing" – at a young man darting across the street,

7

vaulting over the brass-and-chromed rear boiler of a steam-car, a pocketbook clutched in his other hand –

"Whoring" – a pimp, accepting money from a grizzled-looking type in a cheap fedora -

"And trying to raise hell" – a two-bit agitator whose broken-nosed face Marko vaguely recognized, shouting something incoherent outside the entrance to an underway station.

"The more complex, the bigger the explosion," Marko shrugged. "Set this place on fire? The riots of the `80s – let alone the `29 Surge – would be *nothing* compared to how this place would blow now."

"And replace it with dead stiffness. Martial law. The Metropolitans, Guard and Army would shoot on sight. Nobody moved without a permit. They didn't want a repeat of the Crash. I was here in `29. Remember?"

Marko shrugged again.

"Sorting out the pieces is your job. I just break things."

* * *

Past 110th, industrial slums began to slowly ease into a more respectable neighborhood. Cops were on foot, in pairs and sometimes singly. Flashing display lights advertised a kinematograph parlor; a pair of buskers, fiddle and accordion, stood in a doorway with an open violin-case in front of them.

A cop, rather than standing alert as he would have in rougher industrial country, was chatting with the driver of an electrovelocipede, with the checked-black-and-yellow generator-block and passenger-seat indicating a cab-for-hire.

"Where're we going?" Marko asked Krushchev, as they crossed another underway grating.

"To meet some people, I said."

They passed – one looked as though he was going to shoulder Krushchev out of the way – a pair of shaven-headed men in black, the silver double-lightning-bolt insignia on their collars denoting them as German mercenaries, one or another of the units on Federal contract below the Mason-Dixon.

"You get all kinds here," Krushchev noted.

"Which people?" Marko persisted.

Krushchev glanced back; Marko followed his look. One of

the German mercenaries was arguing with a political pamphleteer they'd seen twenty feet back. His friend stood ready, fists already drawn, and a cop was pointedly looking the other way.

"People who're going to fuck things up. People who'll help you fuck things up."

"Then let's get there. There's a reason we're walking, and not riding, twenty-plus blocks?"

* * *

Joe Ferrer looked around the bar with distaste. More pseudos and wannabes, he thought. More talk and noise.

No *action*, although that was what he'd been promised. Tonight was the night he'd meet serious people who were really *fighting* the System. Not pseudo revolutionaries who thought that passing out drivelous pamphlets about the Marxian dialectic, whatever the hell *that* was - a language variation? - constituted rebellion.

Not idiot dilettantes, middle-class children who thought that strumming bad sitar ballads about oppression was the same as a blow against it.

Not drunken industrials, blue-collar cogs who'd finally become aware that they *were* no more than abused cogs, less-educated but no less fucked over than he was, but who saw revolution as no more than a loud excuse to rowdily do what they'd have done anyway.

So far, he was disappointed. The drunken industrials weren't here - this, as much a coffee shop as a bar, on Eighth and 143rd, wasn't their kind of place - but the other types were. A less-than-skilled harpist and a drummer were making loud, electrically-amplified noise at the other end of the room, while a poet declaimed meaningless noise about the 'corporate industrial system.'

Whatever the hell *that* was. All Ferrer knew was that he'd been screwed. Hard. Once too many times. The corporations, with Washington's full legal backing, had ripped him off. A patent, *his* patent, stolen. Millions for them, nothing for him, despite clear paperwork.

Not the first time, the second. The first, he'd accepted it for the sake of his employers; a stable job for Federal Electric was

rth something, right? He'd swallowed it, accepted the
nus, despite the fact that the work had been done on his own
ne in his own shop using his own tools, and allowed them to
ke the application. They'd fired him three months later
iyhow.

The second time, he'd been much more careful about filing
atents and paperwork. And they'd ripped him off anyway,
latantly.

"It'll cost you five thousand dollars to hire lawyers to
contest it," one of FE's lawyers had said. "You don't have five
thousand dollars. You won't find it easily. They won't win in
any case. Thanks for the designs."

Ferrer's fist clenched, *hard*, at the memory.

*I'll stomp those bastards. I will teach them. Once was enough.
Twice is more than enough. I'll see their high-rises burn around their
ears. I'll see their high-rise offices and their whole fucking system
burn around their fucking thieving ears.*

"Mister?" It was one of the waitresses.

"Yes?" Ferrer said.

"They want you in back. Joe Ferrer, right?"

"That's me."

"I bring you another drink? Going to be closed room, they
say."

"Triple Scotch. I'll wait."

The waitress gave him what might have been a Look; *you're
too old to be in a place like this,* perhaps, because Ferrer was forty-
two and not many others in here were above thirty. Or perhaps
it was just the hard alcohol; most of the others were smoking
marijuana or chewing khat, with beer the heaviest drink in
general circulation.

When she came back, Ferrer gave her a buck and headed
into the rear of the place.

"You here to meet - you're Mr. Ferrer?" asked a young man
with streaked black-and-white hair.

"That's me."

"Up those stairs, first on the left."

Ferrer followed the directions, up a tight staircase. The
walls had been pencilled-on with crazy triangular and square
designs, triple-thick charcoal lines added here and there for
emphasis.

It's not engineering. Maybe it's some fucked-up kind of art. Hell

10

if I know.

Ferrer had been hanging around beatie and agitprop circles for far, far too long - two years was *plenty* long-enough in his book - to have much appreciation for that kind of rubbish. Posers, he thought they were. *Posers, pseudos and wannabes the lot of you. Don't want to bring down the system. Just want to ride it, play the cute rebel over shit they - the real System, the Imperials and their Fed corporate puppets - don't give a damn about in the first place, as you all know full well.*

The doorway the man had indicated led to a small room with a rectangular table and a number of chairs. A man in buckskins came in behind Ferrer. They took the last two chairs.

Ferrer glanced around. Most prominent was a tall, very lean, dark-skinned man with a flowing moustache and a big, bright ring in his right ear. He stood at the end of the table. To his right was a stocky, white-haired man in a trenchcoat.

There was a spectacled man in his late twenties with gelled black hair and shifty, darting eyes, a red-haired woman of about the same age who, as Ferrer studied her, lit a new cigarette with her old one and stubbed the old one into a clay ashtray. There was himself, and the man in buckskins, who was tall, brown-haired, well-built and about forty-five.

"Thank you for coming," said the white-haired man. His accent had a trace of Russian in it. "My name is Nick. I'm associated with a foreign government and you wouldn't have passed our screening in the first place if you couldn't guess which. This is Theron Marko. He'll be in charge."

Nods in the direction of the lean, dark-skinned man in black, who smiled.

Needs a dentist, was Ferrer's first thought.

If I'm taking orders from him-

Well, this *was* a break. No loud declamations about the system. People were getting straight down to business.

"You people have been selected," Nick said, "because, one, you're available. Two, because you're *damn* good at what you do, or suited for it. Let me go around the table. Good people tend to be modest. *I'll* do the introductions. Does anyone have a problem?"

If anyone did, none of them said so.

"Pete Rienzi," Nick indicated the shifty-eyed man with the spectacles. "Engineering student turned killer. Spun it as

11

manslaughter, got lucky with the judge and only served five years. Still couldn't get a job out. You've got half a master's in electrical technology, a criminal record, and two more killings since you got out."

"That's me," Rienzi half-waved a hand.

"You're going to be the assistant to Joe Ferrer here. Bachelor's in engineering from Jersey Technical, master's in electrical technology from Columbia, six years at American Kinematograph Corporation and then nine at Federal Electric before they *royally* fucked him over; stole two patents of his, the lesser of which they've made four hundred thousand from. It's a pity it took such a fucking-over to get a corporate drone to see the light, but see the light he did. The first, we hope, of a very great number."

Ferrer nodded firmly. Looked at Rienzi.

In this kind of thing, you have to be ready to kill, he thought. *Knew that when I started to get in. He's probably as much my bodyguard, but he'd better know his work, whatever this is, or be able to learn.*

"Pratt Cannon," the man called Nick gestured at the man in buckskins. "Born in the Republic of Deseret. Did a hitch in their army, sergeant of horse cavalry, before deciding life was more fun on the other side of the mountain. Mercenary scout for Sonora, Texas, the Feds and a dozen private outfits. Killed twenty men in gunfights and dry-gulched three times that number."

Pratt Cannon coughed loudly.

"Dry-gulching implies murder, Mr. Nick. Out where I'm from, bad manners to say that. Sort of bad manners that might get a man killed."

A revolver – Ferrer would have *sworn* he hadn't seen the man move to draw it – was in his hand and leveled at the white-haired Russian.

It didn't escape Ferrer's notice - perhaps in his glance at Ferrer it had - that a flat throwing knife had materialized in Marko's hand. Unobtrusive, but Ferrer could tell from a slight tension in Marko's attitude that it was ready to fly.

"My apologies, Mr. Cannon, but we'll speak plainly here. You began duels on your terms, if that's better."

"Good enough for now, Russki," Cannon said, and lowered the gun.

12

"There are men who know the West better than Mr. Cannon," said Nick, as though nothing had happened. "But not many of them, and not so many still alive."

Nick gestured at the chain-smoking red-haired woman.

"Loretta McIlhan. Of St. John's, Province of Newfoundland. Joined the Imperial Army, armored branch, in `54. Served in the Low Countries, saw action there against Franco bandits, promoted to tank commander and transferred with her battalion to the Hugoton Lease. Made sergeant in `60, involuntarily discharged last year with a rank-reduction to lance-corporal."

"Corrupt bastards," McIlhan said. "Generals rake it off; colonels rake it off, captains rake it off. *Enlisted* woman? *Sergeant* gets some on the side, and there's a court-martial. Like *everyone* doesn't do it?"

Serious people, thought Ferrer. Even if they weren't all the type he much liked.

You put aside those old bourgeois prejudices, he told himself, *when the system fucked you over.*

"You've been vetted hard, all four of you. You may as well know a little about your man in charge," Nick said. "Theron Marko. Born somewhere in Franco country – we don't know whether it's France or Spain, and he doesn't know, either."

Marko showed his broken teeth again.

"Gypsy, Romany. Travels. He's worked for us on four continents, a dozen major jobs. More have succeeded than not. He knows how to light a fire. Speaks six languages and the Imperials have twenty thousand pounds on the head of one of the people they think he was. Assassination of Victoria's eldest, that eight-year-old kid Charles, in Ireland?"

Nick gestured his head at Marko.

"His work."

"Rifle at two thousand yards," Cannon muttered, impressedly.

"Eighteen fifty," Marko said. "Give or take a little."

"Knows his way around a knife, too," said Nick. "Demonstrate?"

"White blotch on the door," Marko said.

Ferrer turned around. So did the others. The paint-blotch in question was maybe an inch at its longest dimension.

"Bracket it at two inches," Marko said. "Learn."

A knife *whick-th*'ed into the door about two inches – *no*, said Ferrer's engineer's mind, *exactly two inches* – above the blotch, burying itself a half-inch into the door. The bare hilt was still quivering when a second hit at the blotch's right, then a third below it, then one to the left.

Marko was smiling. A fifth knife was in his hand.

"I'm in charge," he said. "Let's not forget that, aye? I'm the one running things, after Mr. Nick and his friends."

Even Cannon seemed to be impressed.

"You are here," Nick said, "to meet each other. You'll be working under Marko, with *his* direction. You four are all skilled in your areas. You know specific jobs, fields, capabilities. Not one of you would be here if you had not been vetted to the best of the Okhrana's considerable ability. Marko here knows the big picture."

"What *is* the big picture?" asked Rienzi. "You got us here. What are we going to do?"

Marko shrugged.

"Nothing substantial. Nick told me on the way. We're going to destroy the core of Imperial power and end the miserable pretense of Fed authority on the continent."

"Another Southron rebellion?"

"More than that," Nick said. "Considerably more than that. You'll be operating primarily in the west. The specific details will come later. Federals will die. Imperials will die. Does any of you, despite our screening, have a problem with this concept? Or with doing the killing yourselves?"

It felt to Ferrer as though Nick were looking at him in particular. That impulse made him speak up. He banged his fist on the table for emphasis.

"Never killed anyone but, fuck it, I'm ready to," he snarled. "It's a corrupt system of thieves, and they need nothing else than to be fucking brought down like they were in `89!"

"At this point," Nick said, "you can walk out and forget this took place. This isn't the wading pool, this is the deep water. You'll be dealing with MI-7, Foreign Service, Federal Internal Security and others. This is *not* the wading pool. Speak up and get out, if you're going to."

"I wouldn't have come here in the first place if I thought it was going to be a fucking wading pool," said McIlhan.

Cannon growled an agreement. After a second, so did

Rienzi and Ferrer.

"Good. I'll leave you to Marko, then."

Nick turned to go.

"Wait," said Marko. "I won't be long."

He turned to the others.

"We're going to destroy Federal power on the continent," Marko said, "by destroying the most critical of its props. We're going to destroy Imperial power *globally*, by destroying one of *its* props. Or clearing the road for its destruction, which is the same thing. There's going to be fire and a lot of it, my friends. We're going to have a good time with the burning and the exploding, and there'll be enough for us all to partake in. There's the five of us, and I look forward to furthering my acquaintance with you at Jewell's at four tomorrow. There's the ones we'll work with and you'll direct. There's the tools we'll be using - it's *fun* to use tools, you know, almost as much fun as it is to destroy them."

Marko laughed.

"This is big. Mr. Krusch– oh, I'm sorry, *Nick* - explained it to me on the way here. We have support at the very highest level and we'll be working with people at the very highest level. You should all four of yourselves congratulate yourself for having been selected. If *Nick* calls on you, he speaks with my name. I'll see the four of you when I said. Be packed and ready to travel."

There were a few murmurs. Rienzi began to raise a hand.

"Questions will be answered at the next one," Marko laughed. "Not tonight, my young friend. Tonight, you will head out separately while I head home with Mr. *Nick*, to establish further channels. He knows how to contact you, and you should acknowledge those contacts as well. The plan is set, but it is in flux. As any good plan should be! Now go; go drink, and smoke; chew, imbibe, and inhale!"

Marko paused.

"Because tomorrow - certainly within the week - we *impale*. By year's end, Imperial authority on the continent will have been *spiked*. Through the heart, like the parasitical vampire it is!"

He winked broadly.

"My people came from Romania; I know all about the vampires. We'll talk further tomorrow afternoon."

He's insane, thought Ferrer, as he followed the others out

15

and down the stairs. *He's fucking insane.*

But this Nick man - he'd heard rumors, here and there, of the senior Russian operative in the city, a man who matched that description. Oh, *he* was serious enough.

And so were the others. You could tell that easily enough. And Marko - well, insane was probably a virtue at his level. He'd killed Young Prince Charlie. He'd done - well, God knew what else. He was a serious man.

I've spent two years looking for these serious people, Ferrer thought. He downed the last of his scotch. *Nihil posers and Lud pseudos won't do shit against the fucking system.*

Men like this – plans like this – are what's going to bring it to its fucking knees.

* * *

"What do you think of the plan?" Kruschchev asked Marko as they walked out.

"I like it. You're serious about the backing?"

"Some equipment was brought into the country three weeks ago. It was taken, this evening, to that engineer's lodgings. Details at the highest levels are still being worked out. The Count would *not* have committed the resources he has, if he weren't serious. The other parties are receptive."

"This could be fun," Marko said. "This could be *fun*. And the pyres... you weren't kidding."

"It's not going to topple the Empire in itself," Krushchev warned. "North America is the single most critical point to British influence, but they'll survive even this. In itself."

"The Empire's big. This is a kick to its balls and no question. Might survive this in *itself*, but weakened is good. Weakened at *this level* is plenty good. They lose their basis on the continent, the Feds lose half their revenue - South rises on its own, and that's *all* of North America."

"And could lead quite rapidly to their losing Canada. Even St. John's," Krushchev said. "What do you think of the team?"

Marko thought for a moment before answering.

"Skilled. A bunch of specialists, other than that kid engineer. Sounds fitted, though. What motivates them all?"

"Pretty much what motivates you. They're pissed off. They want action and revenge, maybe some cash. The Rienzi kid's

16

ambitious; he wants glory, too."

"Plenty of that to go around when we're done," Marko said.

They were walking, more quickly, through the dark and quiet streets of upper Manhattan, crossed 150th without incident. The houses here were dense middle-class brownstones, small apartment-buildings becoming multiple-family houses. Ten blocks further north, the multiple-families began to evolve into semi-detached townhouses. Here and there was a livery stable or garage. They passed a brightly-lit Irish bar, a neighborhood place for mid-ranking clericals and low-ranking engineers to hang out. Here and there, parked on the street, were steam-cars and electrovelos.

"Where are we going?" Marko asked.

"Somewhere you haven't been before. Our primary safe house in New York City. You've been introduced to your field team."

"Operational control."

"Yes. You know the basic plan and you have the essential equipment. It's time for you to meet the people who'll be guiding things on the back end. A couple of them will be going out to Dodge City on Wednesday; you'll meet them here so you can recognize them there."

A few blocks later, Marko stopped.

"I have a bad feeling."

"We're on the same block. Come on."

"I have a bad feeling," Marko repeated. He glanced at an all-night diner across the road.

"Something about that place."

"We have security there," Krushchev said impatiently. "Don't worry."

"I told you I have a bad feeling," Marko said. "Go on. I'll be waiting there." He gestured at the mouth of an alley a few feet away. "Come back in five minutes if it's clear. *If.* I recommend we turn around, *right now.*"

"I've heard you get these nerves. What's your problem with control?"

"I don't have a problem with control," said Marko. "We operate in a context. I'll live with that to achieve the ends. I have a problem with getting killed, and *I have a bad feeling.* Something's wrong."

"That building there. Above the news-stand. That's ours," said Kruschchev. "The lit windows. See the lower second pane, green-shaded lamp that's lit in it? Everything's fine. We're not *amateurs*."

"Come in, come out and meet me, then," said Marko. "It'll be three minutes."

"Very well," said Krushchev. Irritably.

Marko shook hands with him. "Good night."

* * *

"He's late," muttered Special Agent Mark Rosen to his partner, leaning across the table of the diner.

"I can read my watch," said the other Federal man, Gonaghy. "Who's the man with him?"

"Can't see," Rosen said. "Looks like they're parting."

"Nobody important. I think. One of those two-bit agitators. Low-level connection; see, he's not being invited in."

"Not invited in," Rosen agreed. That meant something. They were parting half a block away, and it looked like the tall, thin one was turning around completely, had been sent away.

He played through the procedure in his head.

Kruschchev has sent the other man away, indicating he's willing to go this far and no further. If the other man is still in line-of-sight when Kruschchev enters the house - I'm betting he won't be – then Kruschchev will make sure he can't see which house.

It had been a good tip, from a source Rosen wasn't cleared to know; it had been implied that one or another of the Imperial agencies had information from a mole within the Okhrana itself. *All* the key Russian people in New York City, and a couple of their senior continentals, were meeting at this house. Which itself had been something Federal and Imperial intelligence had been searching for: it had already been confirmed that there was a logic machine there, one whose punch-cards would have *invaluable* data.

We're not going to blow it for the sake of another two-bit agit, Rosen decided. As the man on Southern Outer, that was his call to make.

He gestured to the waiter, a young man who had been a waiter for the last week and a junior agent of the Federal Department of Internal Security for the last two years.

18

"Another coffee," he told the kid. Codewords. "Three sugars. And a scone."

"Yessir," said the kid, and headed into the back of the cafe, where the telegraph was.

Rosen's partner smiled thinly.

"Closing it already?"

"Limited window," said Rosen. "My call. Yes."

His palms were sweating.

The waiter came back with another cup of coffee.

"Scone's being made," the kid said. "It'll only be a minute."

That meant the trap was being closed, about to engage.

Rosen felt the small automatic in his coat. His shoe twitched at the valise, where there was a machine-pistol. Just in case. There was a steam-car of four more men ready, but he and Gonaghy were going to be the outer line on this approach. It was entirely probable that the Russians would come out shooting.

"I'm going to get some fresh air," he said to Gonaghy. "Come with."

Gonaghy nodded.

* * *

What the hell is wrong with Marko?, Krushchev thought, as he ambled up the street. Being stupidly resistant - well, he didn't know the man *that* well. Perhaps it was just his way of displaying resistance to the idea of obeying orders.

Nominal resistance; a display like this. Marko was known as a loose cannon, but he was also one who got the job done. A token display like this *would* be just his style: I'll delay you five minutes just to establish that you're not actually my bosses, and then I'm going to obey your orders to the letter.

Still. Irritating.

And what if there *was* something? The man would not have lasted *nearly* as long as he had without damned, *damned* good intuition.

You're scaring yourself.

What if there *was* something there? Would it hurt to go into Angelino's Cafe, make sure that the watch-agents were there as they should be?

Ten feet from the door to his building, Krushchev turned

19

around and headed across the road, toward the cafe.

* * *

"*Shit*," Rosen muttered under his breath. "He suspects something."

There had been a three-man Russian outer security element in the cafe, earlier. They had been very quietly and very rapidly overwhelmed about forty-five minutes ago. Now it looked like Krushchev was going in to check on them.

We've established the pattern. Those people don't get regularly checked on. The Russians don't have the trusted manpower to; three men are supposed to be enough that taking them down would draw noise in itself.

More to the point, the Russian chief of station was heading *directly for them*, and his hand would not be in his pocket like that if it weren't gripped around a weapon.

We want him alive.

Orders had been very specific on that.

We want him.

"We're taking him now," Rosen said to Gonaghy. His own hand went around his submachinegun. The soft leather valise wouldn't slow its bullets.

A steam-truck came down the street, and *oh, shit, we're moving in already?*

It had been, yes, about a minute since he'd given the signal.

The second element, the van, would be moving in now, but on the street corner; a hundred feet away. They would not necessarily get into action.

Krushchev was ten feet away. Heading straight for Rosen and Gonaghy. Something had to be done. Surprise would be eviscerated the second the assault truck deployed.

His thumb un-safetying the gun in his valise, Rosen looked at Gonaghy.

Move.

* * *

One of the two men who'd come to stand outside the cafe, was walking sideways, to Krushchev's left. The way professionals did.

Shit.

He couldn't see any of the three men, the ones who *should* have been in the cafe, either.

"Mr. Krushchev–" one of them began. The smaller one who hadn't moved.

Krushchev's gun, a .475 automatic, was already in his hand, and he shot the man through his coat pocket. Drew properly, fired again, as he stepped sideways.

Shouts and explosions from behind.

Shit shit shit shit, *Marko was right!*

"FIS!" came shouts from behind. "Open up!"

More shouts. Yelling.

The first Fed was falling, collapsed backwards into the window of the cafe. The second one was drawing something, and Krushchev fired at him as he stepped sideways. The first round missed; the second hit the Fed in the side, making him half-step back, and Krushchev's third got him through the throat.

Rapid automatic fire, yelling and explosions from behind. Krushchev didn't want to look back, didn't have the time to. Besides he knew perfectly well about the twelve pounds of gelignite and didn't *want* to.

Besides, there was another steam car turning around the street, a sedan moving at speed, and one of its rear doors was already opening.

The cutoff element. This is a professional operation.

How the hell could this have happened? Only three or four people – *all* of whom Krushchev knew, and knew to be safe and reliable – had known the location of this building until a few hours ago. It was the intelligence processing center for New York City, a secret *very* carefully-guarded.

It had been blown, and the Feds – the Imperials? – had *definitely* had enough time to set up a serious operation.

Very serious. A dirigible came floating across the street, *low*, sixty feet, barely above the rooftops. Engines whined hard as it decelerated.

Figure it out later; run!

Up toward the assault team would be insane. There'd be elements in the alley, too. Down the street, with their southern cutoff coming, wouldn't help. He jacked another magazine into the gun as he ran for the cafe.

Men boiled out of the steam-car.

Behind him, the twelve-pound dead-man charge in the safehouse blew. The front windows blew out; bits of glass, wood frame and burning curtain exploded into the street in a flaming, lethal rain.

In the cafe, people were ducking for cover, hiding under the tables. Krushchev shoved his way through; *back exit. Now.*

A mid-twenties waiter stood blocking the way to the kitchen. Dumbfounded shock, it looked. He shoved the kid out of the way and ran through, past a cowering chef, going for the back exit.

"Mr. Krushchev! Stop now!"

The waiter. He'd drawn a gun.

Fed! I should have known!

Krushchev raised his own weapon, but the waiter's was already aimed. It stabbed flame, twice, and what felt like an iron-toed boot punched Krushchev in the chest. Followed by another.

He staggered back, leaning against the cafe's rear door, tried to fire. His arm sagged. His right shoulder barely twitched.

"Fuck you," Krushchev said. There were papers on him, and he was dead anyway.

"FIS!" the kid waiter yelled. Panicked himself, or close to it. "Drop the gun and come quietly!"

"Fuck you," Krushchev repeated, *forcing, willing,* his left hand to cooperate. It closed around the packet in his left inner-pocket, which was tied to an explosive charge in his coat's lining. Yanked the packet loose, shoved it back. Found the dial, turned it.

One. Two.

He was falling, falling onto his back as the door opened. The kid was moving in.

"Drop the gun! Medic! *Medic!*" the kid screamed.

Three.

"Fuck you to hell and gone," Krushchev snarled.

The three pounds of gelignite in his coat detonated.

* * *

Marko lay flat and motionless on the rooftop, his black coat and pants indiscernible against the tar. He'd seen Kruschchev turn around, go to the cafe, shoot the Feds there–

A Fed car, or Imperials, rolled in. Three men with rifles and submachineguns chased Krushchev into the cafe.

An explosion. A *big* explosion from somewhere inside the cafe.

The safe-house was a mess; explosive charges had gone off there, too, and the place was now burning. Obvious Federal agents were all over the place.

Imperials? Somewhere around, yes. The Feds on their own simply aren't competent to do something like this.

He shrugged to himself. He had the team, the mission, the goal, the equipment and the resources. If this had happened last night, if the Feds had done this then?

Well, the meeting wouldn't have happened.

Imperials must have gotten wind of something from higher-level. Somehow traced it to this from the top down.

Actually not a bad thing. The Imperials close in. Two hours *after* everything was set up. Two hours before would have been much worse.

From the way they were operating – he could see more outer-backup elements coming in now, moving to confer with the command post that seemed to have been set up – they clearly figured they'd gotten everyone.

Except for him, and they didn't seem to know of his existence.

Assume they figured me as a two-bit agitator who Krushchev sent off early.

False confidence on the enemy's part was *never* a bad thing. Ever.

He rolled over onto the fire escape and began to smoothly run down it, with an acrobat's skill and speed. A knife was poised in his hand, just in case.

To use their own filthy technocratic vocabulary, the machine's been fueled, activated and set in motion.

They think they've destroyed the machine, but all they've destroyed was the master governing apparatus.

"Soon," he giggled to himself, "we go west!"

Chapter Two

"The social and economic forces acting on the North American West have been essentially unchanged since the 1840s. They have ebbed and flowed, but their overall balance has remained as constant as the land itself.

The East Coast has changed substantively, California has changed substantively, eastern Canada has changed substantively, Mexico has changed substantively. On this continent alone, in cultural and political terms, the West alone remains essentially the same as what it was a century ago."

Brig. Gen Louis L'Amour, introduction to *Western North America: Plains, Deserts and Mountains; Republics, Technocracies and Anarchy.* Littleton Press, 1959.

Mid-March, 1963; Denver, Colorado.

"Quite a ship, Vice."

Vice-Commodore Marcus Perry nodded, continuing his slow walk around his new command. Around them, six other Imperial Air Service ships were being prepped; the largest of them was a hundred and eighty yards long, a little less than half the size – and a quarter the tonnage – of DN 4-106.

"Line-class," Perry remarked to the other man, an engineering lieutenant-commander in his late twenties. Deputy commander of the Service base here at Stapleton. "Not escort, like the others. They tell you anything about *why* they sent me one of the newest and best? This monster's designed for stand-up fights, not guarding convoys."

"Guarding convoys against stand-up fights?" the base officer suggested, shrugging. "Advanced field-testing, arguably. And it never hurts to *have* the firepower. First of the Denny-Neuvoldt class to be deployed west of the Atlantic."

Perry gestured at the vanes running along the dull-grey aluminum hull, and the center and fore steering fins. Almost all airships had huge aft fins; 4-106 had them front and center, too, and a propeller toward the front, just before the point where the gondola began to nosecone upward, that was supposed to be able to pivot two hundred and thirty degrees.

New innovations; very much new innovations. The ship looked like something out of a rocket-fiction book.

Perry smiled. He'd enjoyed those stories as a young man; they were a part of what had drawn him to the Air Service in the first place.

"I'd be skeptical about flying that, sir. Bluntly."

"Handles like a scout-class, the delivery crew told me." Perry said. "I'll admit it looks strange."

The cabin was long and sectional: front command and observation, double pressure-gun battery below. A hundred-yard catwalk led from there, through a line of rocket batteries, into a bulky engine hall. There, engines fed power to six enormous propellers that stuck from the hall on long struts, three to a side.

"The latest," said the base officer. "Must be a good feeling to be given one of those. A high point in your career, sir, if I may say so."

"You may," Perry said. "And it is. And thank you. And now, we have a convoy to prepare."

* * *

Perry and the deputy base commander walked across the concrete landing pads. Around them, loading cranes turned; airshipmen scampered across steel-netted exteriors, doing maintenance. A balding, bearded Warrant Second in his forties, coveralls filthy with coal oil, approached the two officers and saluted.

"Warrant Morton?" the base officer greeted him.

"Fueling's complete, sir." A nod at Perry. "All seven of the Vice-Commodore's are ready."

"Any issues?" the base officer asked.

"Not a one."

Perry checked his watch; 7:22 am, Central Standard.

"We're on schedule. Good job, Warrant."

"Thank you, sir."

A wind gusted, rocking some of the tied-down airships. Not very hard; each was fastened to the ground by *heavy* steel cable. Someone shouted something anyway; a kid Airshipman Third, perhaps, who'd lost his footing on his rigging.

As they entered the support building, Perry glanced at his reflection in the polished glass of a doorway. Five-nine, built a little stockier than average – but only a little, there were weight regulations. Coffee-colored skin, shaved head and the neat square goatee that was fashionable for Air Service officers of his rank. He wore the standard officer's field uniform; grey shirt, sky-blue trousers and spit-polished, rubber-soled black boots.

On each of his shoulderboards was a single silver wreath, the insignia of his rank; looking at *that* was cause for a slight smile, because vice-commodore at thirty-six was an accomplishment in peacetime; equivalent to Army lieutenant-colonel or Navy commander.

The boards themselves were reason to be happy; the left one had a green border, which indicated a command, and the right-side one had a gold border, which indicated that the command was of a line unit, a fighting squadron.

It was a beautiful morning in Colorado and Marcus Perry was assuming command of a magnificent piece of technology on its operational shakedown run, and in his quietly-analytical way he knew he was happier than any man on government service had the right to be.

* * *

The briefing was short and cursory. The squadron's twenty-eight officers - and seven senior noncoms - knew the procedure; with the exception of the new 4-106, this was a routine convoy run. Large convoy protected by a squadron, even if three of the seven Service ships would be splitting off for Hugoton instead of running with the main group to Chicago. Not a lot of pirates had the nerve or the strength to go after Imperial ships; mostly they preferred unescorted loners. They'd be flying over bad country, still very much the Wild West, but numbers reduced that risk.

Perry had mixed feelings over that. On the one hand, he *wanted* to see how 4-106 would perform in action, and killing pirates was always a pleasure. On the other, he had a skeleton crew, barely enough to handle the ship outside of a fight, until they picked up new men in Chicago.

Weather was about normal, but they were crossing a thousand miles. No known threats, but intelligence over that distance was minimal and it *was* wild country.

"It should be about thirty-six hours to Chicago," he closed the briefing. "Lift in sixty-two minutes."

"Sir," said an enlisted yeoman to Perry outside the briefing room. "Your wife is here."

"Take her to logistics," Perry said.

* * *

"Have you run the checklists I asked for?" Perry asked the senior officer in logistics; the same base XO who'd taken him around 4-106 to begin with.

"Yessir," that man said. In one wall were two of the base's analytical engines, one of them with a mechanitype printer. He handed Perry seven folders of organized papers.

Commander Ricks, who was Perry's XO and would be taking the second wing of the squadron to Hugoton, accepted them one after the other.

"Necessary equipment, final checklist, by category. All seven ships," Perry said.

"Checklist, necessary by category," Ricks confirmed. The thirty-five year-old Ricks was tall, blond and flamboyant, with recruiting-poster good looks. As a personal eccentricity, he wore an ornately-hilted rapier that Perry had seen him practicing with at times. *Born in the wrong century*, was Perry's opinion of Ricks; *competent, but too prone to unnecessary improvisation. The book exists for a reason.*

"All seven, Ricks?"

"Oh, yes. All seven checklists are there."

"Good. Checklists, essential items by on-ship location."

This time Ricks did look through to make sure a list existed for each ship, and not the same list twice, before accepting.

"Checklists, essential items by on-ship location, we have. All seven."

"Checklists, essential items by alphabetical order," said Perry.

"Got them."

"Have two officers and one warrant on each ship go

through and confirm everything," Perry said.

"Yessir." This was standard procedure. Perry's reasoning was that a standard triplicate check might miss something; three different people checking by three different categories would be much less likely to.

Perry drew a notepad from his pocket.

"Very well. Briefing, all aspects, done. Logistics checks, done. I'll be back at nine for a final flight check. Nonessential crew are free as they like; have them report to squadron ready rooms at five to nine."

All of which had been covered in the briefing, and none of which would be new to the enlisted men themselves, who were mostly in their mess, the gym or the ready rooms anyway.

Never hurt to repeat. No such thing as being too precise, too careful, too orderly. The Empire was built on – built *for* – order. Perry did his part.

* * *

"Annabelle." He kissed her.

Mrs. Annabelle Perry was a year or so older than her husband, of African-Indian ancestry; her father had grown up in Sri Lanka, enlisted in the Navy, met her mother in Cape Town. After her father did his twenty-five years – rising to senior chief petty – and got out, they'd moved to London. Like hundreds of thousands of others from diverse sectors of the Empire, pursuing the dream of social mobility in the capital.

Like him, she spoke with about ninety percent of an upper-class British accent; since their teens, like most people of their background and aspirations, they'd been internalizing the tones, vocabulary and speech patterns of Eton and Oxford. She was an accountant, right now on contract as associate CFO for a minerals and ranching firm here in Denver.

"How are the kids? They were asleep when I left this morning."

"They're fine." She smiled. "It's nine hundred and twenty-five miles to Chicago, Ernest told me. Approximately. Is it?"

"Nine hundred and nineteen straight-line, but it varies by how you count it. It was in one of his gazetteers?"

"No, he checked a map with a ruler."

Perry smiled.

28

"He's going to be unhappy when he gets older. The world's already been explored, for the most part. By the time he's grown up, all the maps will have been made."

"By then," Annabelle said, "they'll have a moon rocket, and they'll need explorers there. Or perhaps Venus, exploring the jungles in a pith helmet."

"What about Maria?"

"She just wanted to know when you'd be back. When *will* you be back?"

"I don't know. Orders awaiting in Chicago. It might be another run straight back here; it might be Hugoton, or St. Louis. Or Edmonton."

"Or the South," said Annabelle. "One of the buyers just came from Missouri; he mentioned possible trouble. One of the big German mercenary companies threatening not to renew their contract."

"One or another of the contracting firms is *always* threatening not to renew," said Perry. "It's how they negotiate more money. Nothing ever comes of it."

"Wire me when you get the orders, if they don't bring you back. And take care out there, in that new ship of yours."

"It should be just another milk run, darling," Perry said. "With a new piece of hardware to play with, but I'm not worried. I'll let you know when I get to Chicago. Although I might be back before you get the telegram."

* * *

"Captain on the bridge," reported Specialist Second-Class Vidkowski, and got to his feet.

"Captain on the bridge," said 4-106's XO, Lieutenant-Commander Julian Martindale. The rest of the bridge crew were on their feet, saluting.

"At ease, people," Perry said. He slid the goggles on over his eyes; a formality, but formalities were important. "I have the ship."

"Captain has the ship," said Martindale.

"Captain has the ship," Vidkowski repeated into the electrical telephone.

Perry sat down in the command chair. The bridge was semi-circular at the front of the cabin, clear plexiglass giving a hundred-and-eighty-degree view. In the center was the master pilot's control, a wheel and throttle. Perry's station was to the left of that, the XO's to the right. Both command stations held communications and auxiliary piloting controls, and cogitator-fed tactical boards of the ship. Pairs of heavy binoculars hung suspended on arms above the stations.

Around the edges of the bridge were secondary controls; signals, tactical and engineering on the left, weapons one through three on the right. A presently-closed trapdoor led down into the battery below, where two pressure-guns sat on staggered rotators so that each had a nearly-360-degree field of fire.

The whole setup was crisp aluminum, shiny chrome and black leather. Begoggled officers and bridge enlisteds sat at their stations, ready to issue orders. The pilot - presently, Martindale - stood at his, ready for lift.

A glance at the tactical control wasn't so optimistic. *We're badly undermanned; a ship this size should have seventy-one crew, not thirty-two.*

The weapons stations alone were proof of that. 4-106 had twelve rocket batteries; ten of them were presently unmanned. So was the ventral gun battery, a revolving four-inch cannon.

Engineering, also, was under-strength. Enough men to fly, not enough to fly and fight *too* effectively.

It's a milk run. And we still have more active firepower than West Coventry *or the* Shuffler.

Still. He was looking forward to getting those promised extra crew in Chicago. Flying on less than half your intended complement wasn't going to be easy, and if action *did* happen?

If I'd wanted easy, he told himself with a grin, *I wouldn't have signed up for the Air Service to begin with!*

He checked the chronometer. A shiny digital on his control panel; 9:07 am.

"Very well. Final checks are cleared, First?"

"Cleared, sir," Martindale reported.

"Pilot," he said to Martindale – the man's position on the bridge, this time, not his role – "I want lift in thirty. Signals? Order detached."

"Ordering ground detachment," said Sub-Lieutenant Kent. His fingers twitched on his clicker, sending electrical signals to the flashers. Then He spoke into a tube. "Ordering shipboard detachment."

The Specialist Third next to Kent – one of the crew who'd come over with the 4-106 delivery, Perry hadn't learned her name – leaned over, from her binoculars, and said something to Kent.

"Ground detached has acknowledged, Captain."

There came slithering noises, as the cables were pulled away.

"Shipboard detachment commencing," Kent reported. One after the other, the ship's own anchors – running from the cabin into the landing pads' concrete – released.

4-106 bobbled slightly. The concrete pads moved a little.

"Pilot, lift to one hundred yards in ten seconds. Hold for twenty and then and lift to five hundred. Signals, have *Johnstown* lift. Proceed in wing order."

"Lift to one hundred yards," said Martindale, "acknowledged. Ten. Nine."

"Transmitting signals to *Johnstown* then remainder of squadron," Kent reported, "yessir."

"*Acknowledged*, Sub-Lieutenant, is the proper response. As you well know."

"Yessir. Transmitting signals to *Johnstown* then remainder of squadron, acknowledged."

A short breath. Kent's assistant said something to him.

"*Johnstown* confirms, sir," Kent said. "And sorry, sir."

"Five, Four," Martindale was counting.

"We have a procedure book," Perry said to the sub-lieutenant. "It exists for a good reason, as you will eventually learn. We follow the book on routine matters so that we may think to take better initiative on the less-routine."

"Yessir," said the sub-lieutenant.

"Consider yourself chewed-out," Perry smiled. "And now let's see how our new ship flies!"

"One. Releasing," Martindale said, and pulled a lever.

A hiss. Three heavy clicks. A brief rumble, as the ground weights were dumped from their clutches. And the ground began to fall away.

Around the bridge, there were murmurs.

Martindale flicked the steering wheel from side to side, slightly, and the ship wobbled.

"Responds like a beauty, sir. Crispest steering I've ever felt.

31

And she's holding position well. Monitors are that we've got fifteen mph lateral crosswind and I'm not even *noticing*."

Below, the buildings, and the other airships, were taking a clearer shape as they rose. Pads and warehouses of the base; the plains stretched out beyond there. A cattle-herd moved near the horizon, dark shapes almost haloed under a cloud of faint-orange dust.

The squadron XO's ship, the hundred-and-fifty-five-yard long *Johnstown*, was next to lift. Then the *Plains Eagle*, Perry's personal ship until 4-106's arrival, and *Lady McMurdo*, second ship of XO Ricks' flight, and the *McPanlan*, the *West Coventry* and, smallest of the squadron, a mere hundred and ten yards long, the *Evanstown Shuffler*.

It looked like the mountains were rising, as the vast grey shells in turn lifted. Fins turned, rudders switched; as they rose the dirigibles swayed slightly, propellers churning.

Signal panes flashed behind the bridge of each ship, directed towards each others' bridges.

"Sir, *Eagle* reports lift without incident. *Johnstown* reports lift without incident..." Kent reported, as his assistant spoke into his ear. Her job, her eyes fixed to binoculars, was to read the flashers, mounted behind each ship's bridge, that transmitted coded updates so fast that Perry could barely read them himself. Her own fingers pressed encoding keys, giving one acknowledgement after another.

"Signals, order the assumption of formation." Perry thumbed a key on his own console and spoke into one of the telephones.

"Aft, this is Bridge. Acknowledge?"

A moment, then a young man's voice: "Bridge, this is Aft acknowledging."

"Any sign of our convoy?"

"Approaching from direct east. Big mass of them, sir."

"Approximate ETA?"

The officer on Aft - the commander of the gun battery there - took a moment to confer. His name was Ensign Charles Hastings, Perry knew, with less than six months' experience in the field. He was no doubt conferring with his warrant, a seasoned Senior Warrant named Halversen, who Perry had assigned there precisely so that young Hastings *would* have someone to learn from.

"Bridge, this is Aft. You still there, sir?" came Hastings' voice.

"I am, Aft. Got an ETA?"

"Six to seven minutes, sir. They're making full speed, the Warrant says."

"Thank you, Aft. Cutting in two, one, now."

Aft's connection ended first, and Perry put the handset down.

"Signals, order general spread. We'll close around the convoy."

With more time, a weapons test would have been nice. That 4-106 had relatively few weapons crewed and online... well, that was all the more reason to test-fire those that were operational. But with the convoy having formed over Denver, or around the yards closer to the inner-city than Stapleton was, and coming this quickly as a whole? No opportunity.

The squadron's seven airships began to spread out, moving sideways and forwards in order to encircle the jumbled mass of civilian ships. Unlike the Service vessels, which were a uniform silvery-grey, with darker-black cabins bristling with chromed weapons, the eighty-two civilian airships were a wide range of colors; some plain silvery aluminium, others bright primary colors. Banners hung from a few of them, and – instead of the service identification codes of the Imperial ships – they all had big, colorfully-written names.

Almost all of the ships were bigger than the escort-class vessels of Perry's squadron, and the majority were bigger than 4-106's 350-yard nose-to-tail length. Their cabins resembled small warehouses, mostly not even enclosed; Perry could make out wooden boxes and crates inside the metal grates that mostly covered their cargo holds. Cables dangled loosely, and their flashers transmitted – slowly and clumsily, by Perry's standards - signals that were no more than meaningless social chatter between the various ships.

Well, they were civilians. Their job was to run goods back and forth and make a profit for their owners. Perry expected discipline for its own sake – because you never wanted to get into bad habits, and because the Empire had been built upon organized, disciplined application of force – from his crews and from his fellow Service officers. It wasn't a reasonable expectation for civilians, and he had nothing against them being social or disorganized.

We *exist to serve* them, *after all*, he thought. *There wouldn't be an Empire worth protecting if it weren't for civilian industry and commerce.*

"Signals, flash the nearest and then next-closest of them," Perry ordered, as 4-106 took station behind the vast, colored circus of private ships. "Tell them that Vice-Commodore Perry and Squadron Thirty-One are happy to meet them, and look forward to a comfortable journey to Chicago. Tell them to repeat the signal onwards."

Kent acknowledged.

Perry pulled down the binoculars, found the other ships around his squadron; the closest, *West Coventry*, was almost two miles to his south.

"Signals Two" – oh. No Signals Two, yet; that was something else they were short. "Signals One, then flash the *West Coventry* and tell them to commence circuit position check."

"Acknowledged, sir."

Ahead of them, eighty-two merchant freighters – well, seventy-five merchant freighters and seven smaller passenger ships - bobbled and maneuvered, steering east for Chicago.

"Helm, accelerate to thirty miles per hour," Perry told Martindale. Specs said the ship could do almost twice that, but they were escorting civilians here, and moving at the pace of the slowest of *those*.

"Accelerating to thirty, confirmed," said Martindale. The ship's engines seemed to thrum harder, and the ground moved faster underneath them.

"*Evanstown Shuffler* reports circuit complete," Kent said. "Squadron XO reports everyone maintaining adequate position."

"Very good," Perry said. "Sub-Lieutenant Kent; what do *you* think of our new ship?"

Kent smiled. "First brand-new I've ever flown, sir. We'll see, I suppose, but right now it feels like Newfoundland outdid themselves."

"Specialist First – Assistant Signals, I'm sorry, Specialist, I don't know your name."

"Singh, sir," she said. "Jaleen Singh."

"You came over on this. How did she perform on the trip?"

34

"Admirably, sir. The taxi commander didn't want to hand her over."

"After four thousand miles, that's a compliment. Lieutenant-Commander Martindale, how's she feel to handle?"

"I could run her to Chicago, sir. Most responsive bird I've ever flown."

"You could, but I'm not going to let you; your squadron commander didn't push to make his rank just so he could give lieutenant-commanders all the fun. Lieutenant Swarovski, I know we haven't had the chance to test weapons, but I heard you running diagnostics earlier. What's the word?"

"Undermanned, sir," said the messily-blond-haired Hanoverian, "but she seems good otherwise. Rotates smooth, and the gunners are fine. Hope we do run into something. Killing shit's going to be a pleasure with what we've got."

"I hope it is, Lieutenant Swarovski, but we are Imperial officers on the bridge of an Imperial ship. Please remember to moderate your language to the *Queen's* English in future."

Swarovski smiled sheepishly. As far as rebukes from Perry were concerned, that was a pretty light one.

"Sorry, sir. Will do in future, sir."

"You have the need to curse, go aft to the engine room."

"Engineers will be engineers, huh?" asked Martindale.

Perry grimaced. "I'm a realistic man, First. Speaking of engineers, I'm going to go pay them a visit; take a look at the rest of the ship. Vidkowski, ask Engineering to make sure they don't have any problems? Don't want to distract them if they've got a crisis."

A moment later, the response came back.

"Engineering says everything's good. Engines running just fine. Light on riggers, and they're sweating – this multi-finned design doesn't *completely* operate itself, he says."

"Tell him Lieutenant Swarovski has even fewer gunners than he has riggers, not least because Engineering's *got* half of his department on temp-assign."

"Acknowledged, sir."

Perry stood up. The bridge was rocking slightly, but considerably less than the old *Plains Eagle* would have. Slick and smooth.

"First has the bridge," Perry stated.

"First has the bridge," Martindale acknowledged, without

looking up.

* * *

Mine, Perry thought. *My* beautiful new ship.

He'd served on new ships before, but he'd never commanded one. Things seemed to practically gleam; there were no tarnished fixes, no oil yet trodden into the stamped-aluminum floors. Past the bridge was an empty rocket-battery, then a line of cabins. He looked into his own, briefly; a hammock and his kitbag; a folding desk and chair. Nobody had had the time to fully set up their own cabins yet; they'd all be much like this, if smaller.

He checked out a few of them anyway, on the basis that if nobody had set them up, he wouldn't be disturbing anyone's privacy. Privacy was something you learned quickly to respect, as an airshipman operating in close quarters for, sometimes, months at a time. Single cabins for officers above ensign; two-man ones for ensigns and warrant-grade enlisteds, slightly smaller two-man ones for specialist-grade enlisteds, three- and four-man ones for the airshipman-grades.

Past the cabins, and a small galley whose cook was presently at his rocket station, was another rocket battery. A staircase led up into the infirmary, which was inside the shell itself for better protection. Right now it would be empty, but it held ten beds. Its medic, Specialist Second-Class Rogers, was currently working his backup job in Engineering.

The third rocket battery was manned, or at least half of it was. The stations were like pods, a long nine-inch launcher on each side of the main catwalk; the two launchers were about twenty feet apart. Right now, both gunners on Rocket Three were in the red battery, port-side. On the left of the ship facing forward, to Perry's right as he walked down its spine.

An Airshipman Second and a Specialist Third, another new man, sat in Rocket Three, the Specialist hastily concealing a pulp magazine when the captain entered.

"*Astounding Adventures*," Perry observed. "Anything good in there?"

"Uh – no, sir? I was reading for the moral tone of the crew. Sir. To see if it was a good influence. On Airshipman Second Gilford here. Sir."

"If that's the current one, you're missing a good story by Rod Serling," said Perry. "Or rather, Airshipman Second Gilford is. Your mentoring of your junior crew is to be appreciated, Specialist Third–"

"Rafferty, sir."

"Specialist Third George Rafferty." Perry mentally reviewed the crewman's file, now he had a name to attach. "You saw action in Belgium, didn't you? And over South China?"

"Yessir. Nasty buggers, those Blazing Swords. No technical skill, but they made it up and then some with aggression. Fuckers would ride a blazing hydrogen wing right into you, if you didn't physically blow `em apart."

"So it's not the first time you've handled a nine-inch rocket battery. It's Airshipman Gilford's, I believe. Gilford's been with the Thirty-First for a year now, as long as I've commanded the squadron. Used to the little six-inchers."

"Hell no, sir," said Rafferty. He was a lean brown-haired man with a scar on his jaw, somewhere in his mid-to-late thirties. "Told you, Gil, but I'll brag to the squadron commander any day." He winked hard at his junior man. "Never turn down a chance to get yourself written up for a pay-raise, is what I say. Those senior officers like balls, is what I say, and to their faces."

"I see you're the wise-guy type of barracks-room dodger," Perry observed.

"Do what I can, sir. What I can. Insolent until the drums pound and the horns engage, also, for the record. Sir."

"One who knows Kipling. You were going to brag to me about something? Possibly something that justifies borderline insolence to your squadron commander. Something that, for the record, had better be *good*."

"Well, sir. These Vickers nine-inchers; we had the same, sir, in the 81-284, *Royal Gopher*. Scout-class out of Shanghai, back in `58. Secondment to the Celestials, y'know? Single tube in a three-sixty and that's it. Well, we're running air cover to a brigade of Army holding the line against a bunch of those damn rebels. We happen to be on station, mostly recon. Sub, he flashes base, attack imminent. They say, well, you hold them off until the rest of the flight can show up. We were the scout attachment to a line wing, sir. Big birds like this one.

37

Airshipman First, I was, and I *was* the gunnery officer, sir."

"Go on," said Perry. "What did they have?"

"Crossing the line with ten or twelve steam-tanks. Gotta have been ten thousand men - Chinks, sir, don't know if you've been out that way, they're man-heavy. And about thirty little hydrogen birds. Little, rockets and springs and black-banger two-inchers, but they're still a threat. And, well, our orders were to hold the sods."

"I imagine you did," said Perry.

"Sir, it took twenty minutes for the first of our big boys to come on station, and by then those crazy fuckin' Luds were well and truly engaged with our Army. Sub Donaghan, sir, he's noticed the Army don't have many punchers, so he'll go after the armor first. Air second, and damn the risk. Gave him the George and his second quill for that."

"And what did *you* do, Specialist?"

"Well, sir. They gave me my four back." He touched his shoulderboard, which actually held the twin two-bladed-propeller insignia of a Specialist Third. Airshipman Second Gilford's shoulderboards had a single two-bladed propeller on each, unlike the single four-bladed on a Senior Airshipman. "Killed four of their steam-tanks, sir. We went in low to engage. Sub Donaghan, he said to only open up on their air if directly threatened, and he'd do his best to make sure we weren't. He was firing his sidearm out the bridge window, sir. To dissuade `em."

"You get any of the air?" Perry asked.

"Two, sir. Brought `em down all fiery-like. Then the squadron showed up and took all the fun away."

"Very well," Perry said. "High explosive, third quadrant, *now!*"

"You heard him!" Rafferty yelled at his junior man, who'd frozen. "High explosive, he says!" Rafferty was already opening the launcher's breech-rack, swinging the tube up to the right. "Sir, what range, *sir?*"

"Eleven fifty," Perry said calmly, hands on his hips.

Gilford had finally wrested a rocket, wide and stubby, from the feed. Shoved it into the rack as Rafferty, ignoring the table on the bulkhead, calculated on his fingers.

"Dial her to six-twenty, estimating wind average – sir, we cut and fire?"

"No. And good job, Rafferty. I think you may be permitted to swear and read pulps in my gun bays for a while longer, Specialist Third."

"Yessir, Vice-Commodore, sir," said Rafferty.

"See," Rafferty said to Gilford as Perry left the bay, "I told you there's not a martinet I can't handle."

"Perhaps there is, Specialist Third Rafferty," Perry said, looking back in. "I am not a martinet. I am merely an officer who insists that proper respect be paid to the rules. The rules are what make us effective. Our effectiveness is what stands between pan-Imperial civilization and post-Crash disarray. There is, in fact, no regulation against otherwise-unoccupied missileers entertaining themselves with personal reading material. Enjoy the Serling story, Specialist Third; I rather did myself, the other night."

* * *

There were more - unoccupied - rocket batteries along the catwalk to the engine room, and an – empty - ventral gun battery. The engine room itself was a messy, smoky bulge. In-gondola fuel tanks gave a mixture of petroleum-jellified coal flakes to 4-106's quadruple-burner engines, where they were turned into rotating thrust for the airship's throbbing, driving, six-foot propellers.

The engine-room's crew, past the initial starboard-side control room where a Senior Airshipman in four-bladed-propeller insignia stood at a communications and monitoring station, were wearing duty coveralls and asbestos-shielded emergency parachutes. Their room was hot and smoky, and Perry was glad for his goggles as he went into the acrid gloom.

"Captain in the hall!" Lieutenant Vescard shouted above the chuffing boilers.

"At ease and back to your jobs!" Perry shouted back.

Four masked crew in coveralls, with full-arm rigs covered in asbestos-shielding, monitored boiler temperatures and fuel feeds. Vescard stood at a console next to a plexiglass-shielded computing engine that he wiped every few seconds, scrutinizing outputs. He didn't take his eyes away from it for more than a second at a time. Next to him, a bearded Warrant Second sat at a secondary console, watching buoyancy level and adjusting a lever or a wheel every couple of seconds.

It was these two and their junior enlisteds who kept 4-106 powered and stable. It was from here that buoyancy and weighting were computed, monitored and, when necessary, adjusted.

"Got a drink? Hot as *hell* in here."

An Airshipman First handed Perry a bottle. He took a swig from it. It was cut with *something*, that much he could tell.

"This better not be above one percent vodka, Vescard!"

Regulations said one point five in the engine rooms. Perry had his own standards.

"No, sir! Just enough the men think they're getting something out of it. 'sides, sir, that's not the standard."

He took a bottle from a holder that'd already been welded to the side of his own console. "Here, try this. Mackinaw handed you that one because you're the CO and all, sir."

The Airshipman First had been a new man, one whose face Perry didn't recognize.

"I frown on that sort of thing," Perry told him. "You keep it limited, understood?"

"Understood, sir."

Perry gave the bottle back and drank from the one the engineering officer had given him. That was all water, with maybe a taste of lemon. Lukewarm and sooty-tasting too, though, and a single mouthful was enough.

"How're we so far?" Perry asked. He was getting used to the din.

"Aerodynamics holding up, but the riggers have been busy. We have one half-shift active, another resting. The vanes don't oil themselves, and some issues with the primary steering."

"Martindale said it was smoother than oiled silk."

Vescard grinned.

"Said we had issues, sir. Didn't say we weren't busting them before they got problematic."

Perry clapped him on the shoulder.

"Good job, Engineering."

He raised his voice. "Good job the lot of you. I'll have a bag of ice sent to you from the galley. Or you can go get some yourselves."

"This baby's got an *ice machine*?" asked Vescard.

Another man came up through a trapdoor from the lower

level, his face, rig and coveralls blackened and filthy. Someone handed him a water bottle; he took a swig, spat on the floor – where it hissed – and took another mouthful before he noticed Perry and saluted.

"At ease, Airshipman First. Yes, Engineering, hooked to the flasher batteries."

"*Hell* of a crowler this thing is!" Vescard grinned. "You must be proud as *hell* of her, sir! You boys hear that? We got us an *ice* machine in this thing!"

"Only so long as you can keep that generator running," said Perry.

"Well, then, sir, makes it a hell of an incentive for us to! Screw Chicago, we keep these boilers at prime, boys, and we get *ice*!"

* * *

Past Engineering - Perry breathed relief to be out of the heat and soot, wiping off his goggles with a hand that had itself become dirty - were more unmanned rocket batteries, cabins, then the aft turret, a three-man pressure gun.

Running from a reservoir on the tertiary and quarternary boilers, the pressure-gun was a double-mounted four-inch cannon with a three-hundred-degree rotation. In the same station was 4-106's rear signalman, whose flasher battery was immediately before it.

"Captain in the gun," reported the flasher operator, an Airshipman Second. He stood before Perry waved him down.

Four others were in the relatively spacious gun turret: the gun's crew of Senior Warrant Halversen, Airshipman First Warren Jeppesen, on-her-first-assignment young Airshipwoman Third Carmen Johnston, and battery commander Ensign Charles Hastings. Hastings had been studying the convoy's back-trail through heavy binoculars; Halversen reading some small-circulation tinker `zine, and the other two playing a card game on the auxiliary plotting table.

"Captain, sir," said Hastings.

"Anything of interest though those scopes? Nobody tailing us, I hope?"

"Nobody, sir," Hastings said, as though it had been a serious question. "That I saw. Sir."

"Swarovski said you ran some diagnostics," Perry said, as much to the experienced NCO as the newb ensign. "How's she looking so far?"

"Full traverse, we know. Pressure maxes out, good as it should be. Looks like we can ram ten rounds a minute through each of those tubes," Halversen said. "Wouldn't be shocked if I could jigger it up to twelve. Maybe more, without losing juice."

"You've got permission to take a stab at it, once we're fully-manned."

"Hoped you'd say that, cap," Halversen grinned. He was a stolid, white-haired Greenlander, in his thirty-second year of service. If there was anything about gunnery – spinners, rockets, cannon or pressure-guns – that the Senior Warrant didn't know, Perry had never heard of it.

"How's it holding up, Airshipwoman Johnston? Your first run with the Thirty-First. What do you think of our ship?"

"It's – very nice, sir," said the young woman.

"I'm very proud of it, myself," said Perry. Aware of how personal attention from the squadron commander would be embarrassing the pretty young twenty-year-old. "And don't worry. If your instructors didn't think something of you, you wouldn't have been assigned to a squadron command bird. I'm starting with the assumption that you're good enough."

"Yessir. Thank you, sir."

"Well, I'll leave you to your card game," Perry said. "And you, Ensign Hastings? Your dedication to our backtrail is appreciated, but entirely non-mandatory. If bandits come at us, I don't think they'll try from our six."

* * *

About a hundred and eighty miles in, mid-afternoon, Commander Ricks and his three-ship wing - all of which had been stripped of some crew in order to provide bodies for 4-106 - turned south with seventeen of the convoy's freighters. They were bound for Hugoton, or at least Ricks was; the freighters were going to the civilian railhead at Dodge City.

The main body of the convoy, sixty-five ships protected by Thirty-First Squadron's Primus Wing, arrayed in a loose diamond around the miles-wide bobbing mass, turned slightly north onto a direct course toward Chicago.

42

"Ricks to 4-106, sir," reported Sub-Lieutenant Kent. "I've acknowledged him. See you in Chicago with full crews for us all, he says."

"Tell him I'll buy him a drink," Perry said from the controls. "No – belay that, Signals."

"Yessir."

"Tell him I look forward to seeing him too. Wishes for a safe trip."

"Yessir. Sending now."

"Ricks acknowledges, same to you, he says."

"Thank you, Signals. Off the record, drinks *are* on me, and another round when Secundus Wing shows."

"Haven't seen how Lieutenant Vescard drinks, have you, sir?" asked Martindale.

"I make *Vice-Commodore*'s pay, Lieutenant-Commander."

"Not referring to the hit on your wallet." 4-106's XO tapped his head. "Went drinking with him in Dodge, last month. He and some of the other engineers. I was hurting a week later."

"Vice-Commodore's tolerance, too," said Perry. "How are we doing for schedule?"

"About an hour ahead of where we should be."

Ahead of them, the bobbling mass of the convoy moved, sixty-five joggling airships. Below them, the plains rolled on endlessly, eastern Colorado becoming Kansas. A herd of cattle, perhaps a thousand head, moved past in the distance, kicking up a thick plume of yellow-white dust. On their fringes moved the taller figures of mounted cowboys, protecting and herding the cattle.

The way we are, these freighters, Perry smiled.

"Time to Chicago, First?"

"Eight pm, Central, sir. Like I said, about an hour ahead of schedule. Unless something goes wrong. You expect it to?"

Perry shrugged. "Why would it? You want the controls back?"

"Sir?" asked Lieutenant Swarovski, the weapons officer.

"Yes, Weapons?"

"Mind if I have a turn? Being acting Second? I need the practice. If something happens to you, sir, and Lieutenant-Commander Martindale's asleep."

You want a turn because handling this wizard looks as fun as it really is, Perry thought, but suppressed an unprofessional smile.

"Quite correct, Weapons, and good reasoning. She's yours."

* * *

Near the tail of the dirigible *Karlsbad Streamer*, a six-hundred-yard bulk transport painted in broad, dust-faded red candy-stripes and loaded to capacity with iceboxed beef, two riggers hung on the outside, near the top rudder. They were contract employees and their job was to push the rudder one way or the other when the old dirigible's unreliable control systems failed.

Their *work* involved the aft flasher.

One of them put down his monocular.

"That's it. Butler Lake," he said to his partner. Gesturing at a narrowly V-shaped lake three or four miles away to the south. In the neck of the V was a stockaded cluster of buildings, one of the little fortified ranch-villages that dotted the plains. Big enough to sit on a water source and protect itself from casual raiders.

"You got it encoded? We get one shot at this," said the partner, a stringy red-haired man whose friends called him Red. Sometimes he wished he had brighter friends; he wasn't fond of the nickname.

"I got it encoded," said the man with the monocular, who went by Thick Mick. His name was no variation of Mick, he was of about average build and in fact was one of Red's brighter friends.

"OK. Put the battery in."

Red unslung his backpack. Quickly he pulled leads from the flasher, yanking them free of their connections, and connected them to bolts on the battery in the pack.

"OK. Do as I say. I got this thoroughly encoded. Wait. *Dumbass.* Turn it toward the lake town first, idiot!"

"I was *turning it,* clown."

"Long-off-short-long-off. Long-off-short-on-off..."

Confirmed Service line-class present. Tail of convoy.

"Long-off-long-off-long-off-short-long-off-long-short."

Barely crewed. About half strength. Four escorts total.

"Short-off-short-short-short. Long-long-long-short-short."

90 ships total convoy. Chicago ETA 8 Wed.

"Just one go," Red said, as Mick began to repeat the directions again. "They'll pick it up or not. No need to confirm."

"What the *hell* does anyone in the Black Hills need to know about an Imperial battleship, anyway?" Mick muttered. He eyed 4-106; even from two miles away, its size was scary for a purpose-built fighting craft. Those jutting little nuts along the cabin? *Nine-inch rocket launchers all of them.* Only reason you'd want to know about a killer like that would be so as to *stay the fuck away from it.*

"Jack Kennedy paid us *personally* to transmit that signal. Ride on and transmit it, he said," Red reminded him. "You care *why* the Kennedys want something? Something we're getting a hundred apiece for?"

Mick looked at 4-106 again.

"Not gonna ask why." He imagined that signal being received, being passed on by a chain of temporary heliograph stations, from here to – well, somewhere in the east, he supposed.

* * *

On the bridge of 4-106, Lieutenant-Commander Martindale noticed a series of flashes from the village by the little lake to the southeast. Butler Lake, said the map.

"Sir, take a look over here."

Lieutenant Swarovski was still at the helm.

"What is it?"

"Looks like a heliograph to me. Think it relates to us?"

Later, Perry would curse himself for his not-even-a-decision, forgetting the hundreds of times he'd seen wholly innocuous heliograph flashings that he'd dismissed without a thought. He dismissed this one the same way.

"I wouldn't worry about it, First. You just want an excuse to take that wheel back from Swarovski, don't you?"

Chapter Three

"Like James Curley, Joseph Kennedy and his sons came out of Boston, and in a more peaceful world they might have been only bootleggers - maybe to legitimize in high finance, perhaps even to follow Curley, with his acknowledged early-career mob ties, into politics. Instead of becoming the most notorious raiders to originate in Boston since the time of John-Paul Jones."

From *The Last Hurrah: President Curley's Third Term*. Edwin O'Connor; Little, Brown, 1956.

They came at a quarter past five, out of nowhere and from an abandoned township on the Nebraska side of the old Kansas state line.

"Sir! We have four – no, five, six, eight, nine, *shit, a whole lot* of blacks rising in front of us!" Swarovski cried out.

Late afternoon, dark lines of clouds in the west. Clouds above them, too, at about three through five thousand feet relative.

"Turn to engage," Perry said calmly. He'd have been more shocked if this weren't the optimal time for pirates to attack: it'd be dark in half an hour. For the last half-hour he'd been expecting something. And he'd known, from the more-alert bearings of Swarovski and Martindale – and Halversen, when he'd visited aft again a few minutes ago - that the others did, too.

If it was going to come, it was most likely going to come during the last hour of daylight; time to engage, and much more time in which to run.

"Signals, hit squadron general quarters. Now, please."

"Aye, sir."

"Sir. We have more coming from the north. Little hills, they're rising out," Specialist Second Vidkowski reported. "Sir! We have ten, fifteen, twenty, and sir, I strongly suspect there's some up above."

Ahead of them, the convoy was reacting. Increasing steam, turning to bolt.

In these situations, the captains tended to react like sheep: every man for himself, and the hell with formation or safety. Irrational - he'd audited a hundred lectures where civilian captains had been told not to outrun their escorts, to stay where they could be protected or, if need be, recovered - but a universally-human panic reaction anyhow.

I have to remember that my weapons are stripped for airworthiness, Perry told himself, looking at the ship plot. There was a fully-functional pressure-gun right below him, a fully-functional one aft. There were a nominal twelve missile batteries, of which only two were actually manned.

The missile batteries are not to be considered applicable in this engagement.

"They're ignoring flashes, sir. Definitely hostile," Kent reported.

For the first time, Perry actually looked up to *see* the enemy - or rather, looked away from his consoles and through the window. Little birds, tiny ones, that had been hidden in the township. From the north, to the left, they were powering in on an intercept course to the convoy.

"Signals. Rockets and guns may feel free to engage. Repeat: Free fire is authorized."

"Fire at will is authorized, confirm, sir?"

"Fire at will is authorized, confirmed," Perry said.

The instinctive response, as it always did, calmed him. This was combat; people were going to die. But it was also known and familiar; the protocol, the confirms, the etiquette. Every man on 4-106 had a job to do; every man was doing it. It reduced the visceral, random chaos of combat down to something known and manageable.

Pfung! Pfung! came from down below, the fore pressure-gun battery. Then, irregularly: *Pfung! Pfung!... Pfung!*

"Sir! Fore One reports confirmed hit, one of the fucking bastards is going down in flames!" Swarovski exalted.

"Very good," said Perry. "But Weapons, I did remind you about your language earlier. Please *do* remember that we are officers on one of Her Majesty's ships, not pirate trash."

"Yessir."

"And my compliments to Fore One. Specialist Bronson *was* ready for his own gun, I'd say?"

"Very much, sir."

47

"Sir, more coming from the northeast," Martindale snapped.

Looking around. Yes – more shapes. A *lot* of them.

This just turned serious, Perry thought. The number of confirmed bandits was pushing forty. *We have a real fight on our hands.*

* * *

"General Quarters," Airshipman Second Gilford said. "We got action! Pirates!"

"Yeah," Rafferty said. "Time to kick ass and chew bubblegum." He pulled a stick from his hip pocket. "Want a piece? Strawberry, it's good."

The comm buzzed. Rafferty picked up his handset. "Rocket Three. Yessir. Yessir, understood."

"What's he say, boss?"

"Just got fire at will clearance. See hostiles, take `em down. So put a shrapnel rocket in there."

"Got it," said Gilford, reaching for the ammo feed.

"Pirates didn't figure on us having a ship like this," Rafferty said. "Lot of `em aren't gonna make another mistake like that; not for a while. Maybe not ever."

Gilford hefted the missile into its breech. Rafferty sighted down the bore – *there* was one, a tiny little scout-class, probably spring-powered and held together with glue and frayed rope. Barely a hundred feet long, only semi-rigid; typical expendable piece-of-trash pirate riser.

"Range three hundred fifty," he said, mostly for Gilford's education. "Cut like this" – with a blade, he released the cord that held the stabilizing fins; now, when the missile came out of its tube, the fins would pop up on their springs – "set to three fifty, that's twelve and two, so the fourteenth notch here, hit the timer there – and yank the cap; missile is now live."

"Missile is now live," Gilford repeated.

Crosswind, relative speed, relative height, possible intervening objects during flight time? Rafferty did the math quickly. He'd been a missileer for twelve years, and this had become second nature to him. He understood the variables at an instinctive level, made careful adjustments to the tube in a way that looked like no more than casual fidgeting.

"And, we point it, we sight, we see that he's moving vaguely towards us at a rate that don't count for shit, but where's the little punk gonna be in twenty seconds? Looks about the same, maybe a little ahead. Cone clear!"

"Cone clear!" Gilford echoed, shouting, as Rafferty fired. The nine-inch-wide, two-and-a-half-foot-long missile exploded out of its tube, its backblast flaming in a cone through the bay behind the launcher. Gilford and Rafferty were out of its way, but the shout – and a warning light outside – was for the benefit of anyone walking through the corridor.

Trailing fire, the missile streaked toward Rafferty's target. He watched it with a monocular scope as it struck the pirate high-amidships and blew.

Shrapnel ripped through the pirate's gondola, shredding sacs and releasing hydrogen that the explosion's fire set alight.

Within seconds, the pirate ship was a floating, directionless inferno. Men were bailing from the cabin, throwing themselves loose before they or their parachutes could burn. Flaming debris fell like rain as bits of the gondola detached.

"High explosive, the next," Rafferty said. "Sure you don't want a bit of gum?"

* * *

Three thousand feet above, on the lower edge of the mile-up clouds, a pirate named Karen Ahle looked down at the melee.

"That's it," she said, pointing at 4-106. The line-class airship was heading through the center of the brawl, jinking every so-often, guns and rockets firing intermittently.

"Go, cap'n?" asked her henchman, a big man in his forties named Ronalds. He chewed on a straw as he looked down.

"Go," Ahle said. "Stagger across – left to aft. You know the plan. Go!"

One after the other, Ahle, Ronalds and six of their crew launched from the airship, paraglider chutes opening as they steered for the long bulk of 4-106.

* * *

"Missileers to starboard," Perry directed. "Helm, increase

speed and take us into that cluster."

"Sir!" Swarovski replied, keying a control and reaching for his mike.

"Going in, sir," Martindale said.

A burning hydrogen sac floated past, just below them, attached to a large, thin section of gondola-plate. The air was full of debris, especially the hydrogen sacs. Almost all civilian dirigibles had crude fire-detachment systems; if a sac caught on fire, it could be released – with part of the nets or plating – before the fire could spread. You lost that sac, but you saved the ship.

Of course, you then had to re-inflate a new sac, and you often had to ditch cargo to make up the weight in the meantime. The usual pirate tactic was to force a cargo ship down, land themselves, get the crew off at gunpoint – an unwritten understanding was that the downed crew wouldn't resist, and the pirates in turn wouldn't use any more force than they had to – then re-inflate the dirigible with their own compressed-hydrogen cylinders and fly it off.

That was what most of these trash were attempting to do. Barely-airworthy ships, makeshift contraptions with just enough hydrogen - or, in a couple of cases that Perry had seen, simple hot air - to get aloft and take a stab at something with missiles or crude cannon. This was just a matter of killing them before they could; the pirate ships were easy targets, except that there were so damned *many* of them, and all mixed amidst the bolting, un-coordinated ships of the convoy.

Loose fire – and it was all too easy to hit something you didn't want to, from a swaying airship in an irregular wind – was a bad risk. Airships had a lot of hit points, but nine-inch missiles were designed to inflict real damage. Stray shots into civilian freighters would be doing the pirates' own work for them.

4-106 sped up. The fore guns chuddered, blazing shot and tracers into a larger pirate dirigible, something actually airworthy. The pirate tried to evade, and Perry saw a pair of riggers on the tail, physically forcing it. Another rigger worked with a wrench on a stuck panel, which as Perry watched was released, a burning-from-tracers hydrogen sac lifting out. Two more had caught while that panel was stuck, and those two sacs released a moment later, navigational hazards for the next

50

few minutes.

Martindale turned slightly, so that the starboard missileers and the aft guns could have a chance at that dirigible. Two missiles fired, one of them missing but the second, a high explosive round, blasting the rudder – and the two men working it, unless they'd jumped clear at the last moment – into fragments, along with the aft fifth of the ship. Both of 4-106's batteries opened up on the burning wreckage, pounding three-inch rounds along the length of the gondola, down into the cabin. Men jumped, parachutes opening behind them as they fell.

"Good kill. Excellent job, Swarovski."

"If we only had more *men*, sir."

"Ifs and buts, Weapons. We're doing entirely adequately for what we do have. How about that hot-air job over–"

The aft battery opened up at the hot-air balloon Perry was pointing at, shredding its loose air sac in seconds. Three men jumped from the basket as the thing began to fall from the sky.

"Ensign Hastings is doing quite well, don't you think?" Perry asked. "Pass that on to him, please."

"Will do, sir."

"And Helm, keep going in. Weapons, put one missileer back to a port battery, if you will."

"Sir."

* * *

Four of the Imperial line-class ship's riggers were on the outside, maintaining the steering vanes and keeping them clear of debris. One of them was spraying foam onto a place near the nose where a burning sac had been blown into the gondola.

Ahle steered her paraglider onto that man – no, a woman, her hair in a tight bun. She looked up in shock and found herself facing a long pistol.

"Detach and depart. If you'd be so kind."

"What – who are you?"

"Captain Karen Ahle, at your service. Now, if you'd please detach and depart? Your crew will be following you shortly, Senior Airshipwoman."

A quick glance back showed that Ronalds, Herrick and the others were kicking off the other riggers the same way. One of them had already jumped, his parachute opening.

"You're pirates? Boarding *us*?"

"We're not the Air Marines your ship, quite conveniently, is presently without. Now, if you *would* please?"

The woman detached – her rig from the safety cable – and looked, again, uncomprehendingly at Ahle. Then she checked the bracings on her parachute, ran to the side and took a flying leap from the airship.

The top of the gondola was corrugated aluminum, broken up by the big steering vanes. Ahle ran hunched along them, her rubber-soled boots gripping the surface well, despite the thirty-mile-an-hour backwind and a crosswind. You learned, after a while.

Ronalds and Klefton had already found a hatch; Klefton, a lean man with an assault rifle and a number of ropes, watched as Ronalds jimmied it open.

"Drink, boss?" he asked, pulling a silver hip flask.

"Don't mind if I do," Ahle said, and took a swig of the rum. She passed it to Ronalds, who took a swig and returned the flask to Klefton.

"Time, boss?" Ronalds asked.

Ahle checked the chronometer on her left arm. The clock was ticking up to the minute. "At the sixty."

"Hooked in," Ronalds said. "I'll go first?"

"*I'll* go first, Ronalds," said Ahle, and connected the rope.

Below, a pair of missiles streaked out at a ship a couple of hundred yards away, less than 4-106's own length. One missed, and the other exploded near its aft.

"Sixty. Go!" Ahle said, and leapt down into the gondola.

Inside were structural braces and vast helium sacs. The thing was seventy-five yards in diameter; seventy-five yards down, the height of a twenty-storey building to the cabin area. She rappelled in short bursts, dropping three or four yards at a time. Fore of her was a huge structural brace, a double-triangle shaped like a Jewish star, with big brown helium sacs on either side. A ladder ran through the center of it. Behind, secured in place with narrow girders, were more helium sacs.

Drop, pull, drop. The rope swayed hard, kicking her around as the dirigible accelerated, slowed, turned. Every so-often she caught hold of the ladder to steady herself; every so-often her swinging rope slammed her into the ladder, or into

52

one of the sacs.

After one of the ladder's rungs collided hard with the small of her back, she decided that she preferred the sacs.

A curse came from Klefton, as something like that happened to him. Well within the minute, their footing was stable. A passageway; a door marked 'Medic Bay.'

Ahle un-hooked herself and drew her pistols. One long revolver, in her – dominant – left hand; in her right hand was a pressure-pistol with special ammunition.

"We go in. Klefton, you come with me to the bridge. Ronalds, go through the gondola and link up with Mackinaw at the stern. Boyle's team will be in the engine room. Kick out anyone you see along here. Understood?"

"Got it, boss," said Klefton. Ronalds touched two fingers to his temple.

"This is a beautiful ship," said Ahle, as she kicked open the door to the medical bay. Her guns covered the place, but – as she'd expected – there was nobody inside. She turned back to Ronalds. "Let's make her ours, shall we?"

* * *

"See that one over there? The one firing pressure-guns into that Allied Freighting bird? Helm, take us closer. Weapons, missileers to port and we'll show the gentleman what *real* gunnery looks like. That should put fear of the law into the last of his friends, too."

"Sir," said Martindale and Swarovski.

"Belay that order, please, Vice-Commodore," came a female voice. The accent reminded Perry of upper-class Southern, although terser and less-twangy than the usual drawl.

He turned. As did Swarovski and Martindale, and the others on the bridge.

A woman in brown, with a complex rig, was standing at the entrance, a pistol in each hand. Brown hair tied in a ponytail, a face that was a little too square to be beautiful, green eyes with a pair of lifted goggles above them. Behind her stood a yellow-haired man with an eyepatch and a submachinegun.

"What the *hell*?"

"Vice-Commodore, I'm afraid I'm going to have to ask you

53

and your bridge officers to abandon ship. Klefton, clear out that fore gun."

"You're pirates?" Perry asked. Complete, absurd, disbelief. A pirate was pointing a gun at him *here*, on the bridge of 4-106? Was this a–

"Tell Ricks that this is not an appropriate joke to pull in the middle of a battle. Ma'am, please find an unoccupied cabin; I don't think you realize how serious this is."

"No, Vice-Commodore. I'm afraid *you* don't realize how serious this is," the woman said. "This is not one of your friends' pranks, and these guns are both loaded. I want all of you to put your hands in the air and go to the starboard side. Including you, Vice-Commodore."

"You're hijacking my ship." *My ship!*

The yellow-haired man – Klefton – had opened the bridge access hatch to the fore pressure-guns, was shouting something down. He twitched his gun to the side and fired a shot.

That broke the unreality. A gunshot. *Here. On my bridge.*

One of the female pirate's guns was pointed squarely at Perry's chest. The other, a revolver in her left hand, was sweeping across the bridge crew, covering them.

Slowly, Martindale, Kent and the others were moving to the starboard side.

"I trust that you are all wearing standard Imperial parachutes," said the woman. "You may take backups from their locker, if you see fit." The tone of her voice lowered. "But please *don't* attempt to reach for weapons. I would be very upset if I had to shoot somebody."

"You're *taking my ship?*"

"All three of those gunners jumped, Cap," said the man called Klefton.

"You're *taking my ship?*" Perry repeated.

"That's rather the point of this operation, Vice-Commodore. Now, if you'd please put your hands up and move to starboard?"

They're taking my ship and nobody has even fired a shot and I cannot believe this is happening–

Suddenly Perry's right hand went for his sidearm, an automatic pistol in its holster at his hip. It was covered by a flap, and the double-barrelled pressure gun in the female pirate's right hand went *blurp*, once, twice, and Perry's hand was stuck.

White goo, *sticky* white goo, all over the top of the holster and Perry's right hand. Sticky and hardening, and Perry found himself looking down the muzzle of the pirate's other gun, the long revolver.

Klefton muttered something, covering the rest of the crew with his submachinegun.

"Vice-Commodore, I do *not* appreciate that," the woman said. "Those are gel rounds. That gun is now empty. I will have to use more harmful ammunition if that should happen again. Now, please, put on a parachute and jump."

"You can't do this." Perry glared at the woman. Confident, almost smirky, not even bothering to shoot him with *real* bullets. Not even bothering to disarm him, or the others! Just walking onto the bridge and telling them to jump.

He looked again at his pistol. The whole top flap was covered with the gel; for that matter, it was hardening on his own right hand, becoming a solid crust. The gun wasn't accessible, but *she can't just take my ship!*

"It's getting dark," the pirate said. "I imagine it will be easier for your crew to rendezvous on the ground while there's still light. In any case, I'm going to request that you and your people kindly vacate what is now my bridge."

Some of them – Kent, Vidkowski, Singh – had strapped on parachutes. Others were doing so. Service uniforms did have small backup parachutes sewn into the backs of them, and riggers of course wore proper ones, but nobody really wanted to trust the in-shirt ones if there was an alternative.

"Very well," Perry said. He glared at the woman. "You'll hang for this, you know. You might take my ship, but you won't live to keep it."

"I don't expect to live forever, Vice-Commodore."

"What the *hell* do you want with a line-class warship? Nobody's going to buy it!" *Except the Russians. Or the Franco-Spaniards. Or the Sonorans. Or... but I won't suggest that.*

The pirate's gun tracked him as he put on a parachute.

"That's my own business," she replied. "If it helps, I can give you my word that I will not be selling it to the Russians or the Romantics."

"The word of a thieving pirate. I can take *that* to the bank. You'll hang, bitch. We will pursue you, and we will find you,

55

and we will try you. And we will *hang* you."

She smiled – *she's laughing at me, the bitch!*

"You'll have to succeed in the first of those two before I swing, Vice-Commodore. Now, my apologies, but you really *must* be going. Specialist Second, open the starboard-side door and depart. *Now*, please."

* * *

"You two," came a hard voice.

Rafferty turned to see a large, begoggled man with an automatic rifle, standing in the entrance of his missile bay.

"Who the hell are you?" he demanded, although it was obvious: *pirates have boarded us.*

The rifle was pointed at himself and Gilford.

"None of your business who we fuckin' are. Get away from that tube, open a hatch and jump out. *Now.*"

"You're pirates?" Gilford asked. "You're pirates attacking 4-106?"

"Taking it over, kid," said the man. "Bridge, engine room, you lot. Now, out with you. Cap Ahle said not to kill anyone, but you sons of bitches just give me an excuse and I will. You bastard Imperials been busy *right now* killing my friends."

Rafferty looked at the assault rifle, which was primarily pointed at him and not Gilford. He was standing in the door, fifteen feet away; too far to rush easily. And the only things in immediate reach of Rafferty were missile-setting tools, which wouldn't throw well.

"OK. Gilford, go to the locker and take out two parachutes. He's got a gun pointed at us; do not make sudden moves and do not give him an excuse to shoot us."

The Airshipman Second nodded hard, reached down into the locker.

Rafferty hit the missile trigger and threw himself to the left.

The missile exploded out, in a direction Rafferty really didn't know or care about. The flaming backblast went over Gilford's head, past Rafferty and into the pirate, who turned *just* fast enough to avoid taking the brunt of it in the face.

Then Rafferty was on him, shouldering aside the gun, wrestling the pirate into the ground.

The man had been in his own share of brawls, moved

quickly himself. Rafferty reached for a knife in his boot, but the man saw the movement and an iron-strong wrist closed around Rafferty's forearm.

As good as me, and half again my weight, Rafferty thought, and blew a chewing-gum bubble into the man's face, onto his goggles. It popped and the pirate cursed, orange residue blocking his sight. Rafferty head-butted him in the mouth, *hard,* then kneed him in the crotch. Pounded his head into the deck several times, punched him in the stomach, and banged his head into the deck a couple more times for good measure.

"Gilford, go over the son of a bitch and find the pistol he'll have somewhere," Rafferty ordered, reaching for the man's assault rifle.

Click.

A one-eyed, yellow-haired man with a submachinegun was pointing that gun at Rafferty, a booted foot on the rifle.

"You're lucky I don't like Cooper very much," he said to Rafferty.

"A thug, a boor and he stank," Rafferty agreed.

"Dumb, too. I'm not. Get the hell hands in the air and jump. Junior man, throw senior man one of the parachutes and then the two of you get out *now.*"

"Bastards hit me," groaned the other pirate.

"You deserved it. Now, two of you, get the hell out. Chutes on and jump, *now.* From the catwalk."

Rafferty caught the parachute that Gilford threw to him. Shook his head slightly in response to Gilford's 'do we do anything now?' look.

"OK, OK. We're leaving," Rafferty said.

* * *

"Their personal property," Ahle said to Klefton. "In the cabins; gather it up and throw it out with a parachute."

"Their *personal* shit?" Klefton asked. "Why the hell do we care about that? Some of those guys are gonna have good stuff there. Always a few bucks you can get for spare uniforms and shit."

"We're pirates, not thieves. And that was an order."

"Harvey says we've got the engine room," said a woman named Guildford, coming in. "Thing's firmly under our control. No trouble except the missileers who beat up Cooper."

"Like I said, ass had it coming," said Klefton. He took another swig of the rum and tossed the bottle to Ahle, who took a long drag. "Teach him some humility."

"Guildford, Klefton, gather up the crew's property and throw it out. We're going to need every hand to get this thing to the rendezvous." And – she took another swig of the rum; *traditional and I could use a stiff one* – "good job, everyone. We've taken us a hell of a warship here!"

* * *

Perry seethed, *hard*, as he swung from the parachute in the growing darkness. *Furious.*

That smirking bitch. That fucking goddamned smirking *bitch*. Taking his ship.

"Oh, I'm going to kill you. You'll hang, or I'll shoot you personally," he muttered. "Give me an excuse. I. Will. Shoot. You. Personally. You *bitch*."

The ground loomed; it was almost completely dark. Around him, the other bridge crew were landing. They, and the civilian crews, would have to find their own way back; the rest of the squadron, and the rest of the convoy, would go on to Chicago. He'd meet them there, or at Hugoton or Denver.

Practical considerations had to take priority.

The ground hit him, hard, and he rolled instinctively, began to disengage from the `chute. Flat grass; a cattle herd had been through here not long ago, from how it was cropped. Nearby, Martindale was cutting his parachute loose. Someone – Kent, it turned out – helped Perry up.

"4-106 to us!" somebody shouted. "4-106!"

Not far away – maybe half a mile – a group of pirates were shoving hydrogen into a downed ship, a makeshift airbag.

If we can go after them, get that ship back, re-board 4-106 and take it back...

No. The pirates there would have rifles, and they did have a completely clean field of fire. It would be suicide, even with darkness to cover most of their approach.

As he watched, the captured ship lifted anyhow, discarding boxes of cargo to get off the ground.

"4-106? Captain, that you?" came a man. Four missileers; in

the darkness, Perry recognized Rafferty as one of them. "4-106!"

"That's us, Specialist Third."

"4-106 to us!"

A freighter, a huge one, came over their heads, fifty or sixty feet up. The same that had lifted half a mile away. Someone threw a couple more boxes down; a hissing sound was coming from it, more hydrogen inflation.

Martindale went to one of the boxes, opened it up. Slabs of beef, packed in somewhat-melted ice.

"Well, we've got food," the first officer said.

"4-106? You 4-106?" came a voice from a couple of hundred yards away. Someone with a speaking cone.

"Bring them back, Kent," Perry ordered.

That group – with two dozen civilians – was larger, the engine and rear-gunnery crews, under Vescard. Senior Warrant Halvorsen was the man with the speaking cone.

"Where were our Marines?" the old warrant muttered. "Vice, why the hell did St. John's give us a ship without basic force protection?"

"Their responsibility," Perry growled. "But our problem and the pirates' fault. *They* stole my ship, and Every. Last. One. Of. Those. Bastards. Will. Hang."

"Hey, you 4-106?" asked a civilian coming up. "Some bags for you, strung to a parachute. Marked your number."

"Bags?"

"Yeah, personal shit or something. `bout a mile that way."

"I'll take care of it," Martindale said. "Holt, Lieberman, Jeppesen, and you two, come along."

The indicated crew followed Martindale in the direction the civilian had pointed.

"Any other injuries? Vescard, do a count. We missing anyone?"

"What's the plan, captain?" someone asked.

"We gather all our crew, and any civilians who want to come. Swarovski, do you have our location?"

The weapons officer shook his head. "No, sir. Somewhere in north Kansas?"

"Try Nebraska," said Perry. "About three and a half miles south of us is the Platte River. The nearest town is a place called Kearney, eighteen or twenty miles to the east."

"Everyone's here, sir," said Vescard. "Allowing for the XO and the party he took."

"We'll rest if needed, then march to Kearney. With any luck we'll be able to get transportation from there."

Martindale and his group came back, four of them dragging a parachute that turned out to be full of duffel bags.

"Our shit. They threw down our shit," said Vescard. "What the fuck?"

"That patronizing bitch," said Perry. "She's *returning our personal effects*. Because they're not good enough, no doubt. To rub it in further."

There was a pause, as people went for their bags. Swarovski grinned as he loaded a magazine into a semi-automatic carbine.

More civilians were trickling in, gathering around the Air Service crew.

"The town of Kearney, Nebraska is about eighteen to twenty miles to the east," said Perry. "We're going to go there, and get transport from that point. Civilians are welcome to come, under the protection of myself and my crew."

"What good's that?" somebody sneered. "Couldn't even protect your own selves, let alone my ship!"

"Speak to the Vice with respect, mate," said one of Perry's men.

I am not going to punch that man. I am not going to shoot that man. Because it would be inappropriate to, and illegal. He is upset that he lost his *ship.*

God damn it.

"You may feel free to not come along, if so desired," Perry said coldly. "My crew and I are going."

And when we get back to Chicago, or Hugoton, I am going to find that pirate, and I am going to see her hang.

He'd never been so humiliated in his life. He'd never been this mad.

That bitch is going to pay.

I will track you down, recover 4-106 and put you on the gallows.

Chapter Four

"The US Federal government is primarily focused on holding down their Southern states, and their extensive use of – some might say dependence on – Italian and Germanic mercenary formations is proof that they barely have the manpower to handle *that*.

The Plains, a less troublesome area, is policed by an undermanned Department of the West, whose strength presently consists of seven cavalry squadrons and two of airships, dispersed across an area of approximately 430,000 square miles.

To all intents and purposes, *effective* policing of the Plains comes from local sheriffs' departments, state militias and the Imperial presence based at Hugoton, which assists the Federals primarily by protecting commerce against the pirates that infest the region..."

From a foreign affairs brief to newly-appointed House of Lords members; Parliamentary Communications Division, February 1962.

It was about seven thirty in the morning, and they'd been marching for some hours – after a lengthy meal-and-rest break, cooking beef from the cargo and allowing exhausted riggers to get a little sleep – when they came across the patrol. A steam-car and two riders, one of whom had a shotgun across his lap. The steam-car itself had a light machine-gun on a passenger-door pintel, and the driver steered so that the gun wasn't quite aimed *away* from the group.

"Stop right there and identify yourselves," one of the riders said. He wore a heavy kevlar vest over a white shirt and jeans. On the brim of his cowboy hat was a sheriff's star; another one was pinned to his chest.

Perry was tired and irritable.

"We're downed fucking *pirates*," he snapped at the man,

61

gesturing. His thirty-two crew and about forty of the civilian crew-members. The Imperials were all in uniform; the civilians, from their rigs, goggles and brass-adorned boots, could have been identified at half a mile as aircrew.

"Captain, no need to get annoyed," said the rider. "Just doing my job."

"Vice-Commodore."

"An honest mistake, Vice-Commodore. I'm Deputy-Sergeant Joe Danhauer, Kearney Sheriff's Department. You're from the convoy that was attacked, I imagine."

"Yes. A couple of my own staff are injured, and there are some quite badly-burned crew ten miles to the east of us. I trust there's a doctor in Kearney?"

"We have a whole clinic, Vice-Commodore. I understand you're heading for our town? I'll escort you and your people in."

Danhauer looked over the group.

"You have some wounded."

Two badly-burned civilians had insisted on coming, and their friends had helped them along. Eventually Perry had ordered some of his crew to work as stretcher-bearers.

"Yes," said Perry. Eyeing the steam car, but not wanting to ask any favors of the sheriff's man.

Danhauer turned. "Norris, ride on the hood or walk. And Mikey, I'll have you dismount."

The deputy in the steam-car's passenger seat – a tall, lean kid of about twenty-two – got out. He pushed back the brim of his cowboy hat, and Perry noticed he was quite unshaven for a law-enforcement type.

Not much for discipline out here, he thought.

Danhauer followed Perry's look, and must have noticed disapproval.

"Deputy Norris, *how* did you shave this morning - with a broadsword?"

The kid grinned.

"Sorry, sarge. A broadsword."

"You're walking back. See if any of these gentlemen need help. You can take a couple of their bags. The Vice-Commodore's, to start with."

Halvorsen had offered to take Perry's, but he'd refused; *the least I can do is carry my own bag.* But the twenty pounds had become unpleasant over time, and it was a relief to hand it over to the young deputy.

The burned civilians were helped, one into the steam-car's passenger seat and the other onto horseback. At a slightly faster pace, the group began moving through what seemed to be a more cultivated area, and then onto a packed-dirt trail. Past a fence that looked like it'd been maintained lately, and then a couple of mounted cowboys who watched them pass.

Danhauer dismounted so he could talk to Perry.

"I imagine you'll want rooms for the night."

"I'll *want* to get moving to Chicago as soon as possible. If that's not practical?"

"We don't have the transport, and the nearest railhead would be Kansas City. You can march, or we can send for an airship. I imagine your friends won't be coming back to pick you up?"

"Policy is to go on, regardless. Protect the convoy at all costs."

"Even when - you're about what a lieutenant-colonel is, right? Pretty high-ranking guy to go down."

"The assumption," Perry said, "is that a vice-commodore can take care of himself as well as any lieutenant-commander."

"Makes sense, I suppose. My thought would be that you stay in Kearney overnight. See if you can hire a ship - there's a couple in town, spring-powered scout runners - to send to Kansas City for something that can carry all your people."

"Not viable to hire horses? All I need is thirty-two, for my crew. The ·civilians aren't my responsibility beyond basic physical protection."

"You might, I suppose, but are you carrying enough cash to? Early spring's a busy season around here. They won't come cheap."

"I could write a note - *if* I had official paper. I suppose they wouldn't take payment on arrival in Kansas City? There's a small Service outpost there."

"Possibly, or not," said Danhauer. "I'll arrange bunkhouses for your men just in case."

The deputy-sergeant re-mounted his house and spurred it forwards, riding for the town. After a moment, the steam-car accelerated and followed him.

"I shave with a broadsword," Deputy Norris remarked to

Perry. "That's how badass I am, Commodore. Takes a broadsword to cut *my* beard."

"Uh-huh," said Perry. "How much further to Kearney?"

"Five miles or so?" Norris pointed along the road.

"Then let's pick up the pace, shall we?"

* * *

Kearney was larger than Perry had expected, although he vaguely recalled flying over the place; there were a hundred towns like this on the plains, regional centers of industry and commerce. The advantage Kearney had was its location on the Platte, which had been dammed. There was a power station and what looked like a hydrogen plant, and a scout-class airship hung tethered in a field outside the town limits, whose fencing implied it was normally a cattle yard. From somewhere, an engine puffed.

Danhauer met them on the road in.

"Vice-Commodore, I've arranged rooms at the Grand Junction. Best hotel in the town. A block of a dozen, Sheriff's Department account – don't know how much cash you're personally carrying, but you can have your service reimburse us. Bunkhousing for your enlisted men, at McDonald's."

"Thank you," said Perry. "As soon as I reach a telegraph, I'll have a courier sent with the money."

"Your men have personal cash, I assume? You do?"

"They *should*," said Perry. "Payday was only a couple of days ago. Swarovski's probably gambled all *his* away, though."

"No, sir," said Swarovski. "Won big, the other night in Denver. Hell, I can cover anyone who needs it. Couple of Fed cavalry majors who couldn't handle their liquor."

"Never had much use for Feds myself," Danhauer agreed. "Vice-Commodore, you look like you could use a stiff drink. Why don't I have Norris show your men – and these civilians – to the hotels, and I'll meet you in the bar of the Junction."

"That works." Perry turned to the others. "I think you heard the deputy-sergeant. You civilians, it was a pleasure escorting you in, but I'll leave you to make your own arrangements. My crew, consider yourselves free for now. Behave yourselves, don't get drunk, stay in groups of at least two, and stay in town. Anyone short on cash, see the weapons officer for a loan."

A few sheepish-looking enlisteds approached Swarovski; Perry, with Martindale and Warrant Halvorsen, went in the direction Danhauer had indicated.

The town had wide central streets, paved in brick, with a couple of steam-cars and more than a few horses. Boardwalks ran along each side, a couple of feet above the ground.

They passed a dry-goods store, what looked like a rooming house, a feed store. The directory of an office building indicated a local newspaper, the Kearney Dispatch, a lawyer and a couple of cattle-buyers. Tallest building in the place seemed to be two storeys, although those were common enough.

"Nice little town," Martindale said. "What do you figure the population is?"

"Given the industrial bit on the river? Probably at least a thousand. More houses to the south of us, a lot more," said Perry.

"Local center of commerce. Wonder how soon we can get us a ride out?"

"If there's not one by tomorrow," said Perry, "we walk."

* * *

Rafferty, Gilford and a half-dozen other enlisteds, after being shown to a bunkhouse where they dumped their bags, found their way into the cowboy equivalent of an enlisted bar, a rough, dim place with cheap cast-iron spittoons on the floor.

"Whisky," said Gilford.

"I'll have a beer," Rafferty said. "And he'll have a beer, too. Not a whisky."

"Learning to behave yourself, Rafferty?" asked Vidkowski. The two had served together out of Bermuda as young Airshipmen Third then Second, and then met again in South China some years back.

"Boss can't behave himself if he tries," said Gilford proudly. "You hear what he did to that pirate with the rocket launcher? Would've fried him, too, if he hadn't been all jacketed up."

"I've seen him do worse," Vidkowski said, drinking his own beer. "Only man in the crew to hurt the scabs, though.

65

nember us by anything, it's by what Raff did."

lat Raff did, and what the cap'n's going to do," said
lt Second O'Leary, coming in with Senior Warrant
rsen.

ilford gulped his beer nervously, a bit uneasy in the
ʾnce of the squadron's top enlisted man and another
rant, besides. Halversen ranked equal to a battalion
geant-major. Under normal circumstances even a warrant
:ond wouldn't drink with an airshipman second.

"Double whiskeys for us both," Halversen told the
artender. He and O'Leary, who was a lean red-haired woman
ın her early forties, took the glasses.

"I was under Perry in `56," O'Leary said. "Specialist First
on the *Galway Hawk*. FitzMorrison's division, punching out
pirates in the Mediterranean and running guns to our rebels in
Italy and Greece. Perry was a lieutenant-commander then, just
been promoted."

"Wasn't that when the Frogs made their play for the Suez?"
asked Vidkowski.

"That was what made it *fun*. Well, we're clashing with a
pair of Frog privateers over Cyprus; a nest of the bastards were
somewhere in the mountains, and our wing was hunting it.
Take some hits, and four of the rig crew go down. Three of `em
women. We're moving too fast to rescue, but you know how
the riggers are equipped for that shit."

"Wouldn't do rigging for the world," Rafferty muttered.
"That bonus they get ain't enough."

"You did it for two years," Halversen pointed out.

"Two years too long. Sorry, Warrant."

"They go down. We meet up with some Marines a while
later, pick them up for a ride back to Malta. Turns out they
know what happened to those four riggers. Raped and killed
by those Frog motherfuckers."

"Privateers," said Halversen. "Which is to say, government
ships and government contract but they can be denied. The
Romantics are *assholes* like that."

"Honorable airmen go under their own flag and no other,"
Vidkowski agreed. "I'm not ashamed of the Jack, and I'll
clobber the man who says I should be."

"*Anyway*," O'Leary said, "Perry gets mad. You should have
seen him. Demands permission to hunt them down. Squadron

66

commander – that was Vice Rittenhouse, and a bitch on wheels *she* was – says, well, we got a crisis exploding in the Canal Zone, a rebellion to stop and an Army division to support. But I can live without one escort-class for two weeks, I suppose. You've got that much and no longer to chase down the killers."

"Did you get them?" asked Gilford.

"We didn't sleep," said O'Leary. "Captain Perry wanted to get the scum, and we were operating constantly. Sweeping the hills, landing our Marines to interrogate locals and prisoners. Don't think he was getting more than two or three hours a night of Z."

"You get them, Warrant?" Gilford asked again.

"We got them. Second-last day, and only because Perry was riding the ship so hard. Caught them where they were trying to hide on the ground – we'd learned who it was, a little fuck named Scagnetti and his gang who'd done the raping, in either an escort-class or a scout-class, depending how you measure `em – and the cap says, just open up. No warning, no quarter, no terms. Blow their tanks, blow their ship, blow their buildings, blow them to fucking hell. We have a whole lot of ordnance on this ship, he says, and I don't want to come home with one grain."

"He do it?" asked Rafferty.

"Nothing left of their base but ash and skeletals, and not much of that. Trashed it back and forth, then landed and shot a couple of woundeds we found playing possum in the wreckage. Perry says, you do *not* rape my crew."

"And you know," said Rafferty, "I am *not* planning to!"

"Vice isn't going to be happy about this, was my point," Leary said. "Could've happened to anyone, but I'll bet you ten-two he's seeing it as a personal humiliation."

"Didn't seem very upset, Warrant," said Gilford.

"Of course he's gonna keep his mouth shut about it in front of enlisted types. He'll keep it shut around the junior officers, too. But you better believe he's gonna be seething inside, if I know him right. He'll have taken it personally. Last he took something personally that *I* saw? That wop bastard Scagnetti was dead two weeks later, with every last one of his crew."

* * *

"Excuse me?" It was the young deputy, Norris. He looked up and down the bar – about half of 4-106's enlisted crew was there, in knots and individuals, some of them talking to the local cowboys and a couple of off-shift workers. "Sergeant Danhauer says your captain wants to speak with Airshipman Gilford and Specialist Rafferty?"

"That'll be us," said Rafferty.

"Come with me. Sarge says you fired a missile at one of the pirates."

"More than one, kid," Rafferty said.

"Fired one backwards when they were in your ship," said Norris. "Fried him to a crisp, he said."

"Almost did," Gilford said. "Then Rafferty jumped on him and practically bashed his head in. One tough guy, my gun lead."

"Yeah, well, *I* shave with a broadsword," said Norris, running a hand across the stubble on his jaw. "And, I'll tell you what? When the boogeyman goes to sleep every night, he checks his closet for *me*."

"Uh-huh," said Rafferty.

"Gonna be a Ranger someday," Norris went on, leading them up the boardwalk. "This is just training. They say you've got to have four years doing law-enforcement as well as a military hitch. Three and a half more years, and I'm there."

"You were military?"

"Air Force. Just ground crew," he added, as though he expected the two airshipmen to make a fight of it.

"Hey. Our ground crews are worth more than a damn," said Rafferty. "And your lot aren't too bad either. Sweat themselves as good as any man under the Jack, they do, what I've seen of `em."

"I was with a hard bunch then, I'll grant. Stationed down near my hometown, in Oklahoma near the Tex border. At first. Hey, I got another one. That Charles Darwin guy got it wrong. No theory of evolution, just the animals I choose not to kill!"

* * *

The common-room of the Grand Junction was an upscale place; low electric lighting, polished floorboards, leather chairs. The ship's officers were sitting around, a couple of them talking to civilians; a well-dressed cowboy in his fifties, a pair of men in suits who looked like drummers or cattle-buyers.

Captain Perry was in a booth with XO Martindale, on the same side. Both men had pads and pens in front of them.

"Thank you, deputy," said Perry. "Specialist, Airshipman. Sit down, please. I want you to debrief me on exactly what happened in your missile bay."

"Buy us a drink, sir?" said Rafferty as he sat down. "Tongue moves better after a little oil, y'know, sir."

"You've had an hour in which to oil your tongues already," said Perry. "And I don't want exaggerations here. You put up the only effective fight of anyone on the ship; I heard that much. I want to hear how it happened. Airshipman Gilford, you first."

The XO's pen scribbled as Gilford began to tell his story, Perry asking questions every so-often. When he'd finished, Perry asked Rafferty.

"Very well. You two, tell the bartender you're to have a drink apiece on my tab. *One* drink. Deputy Norris? Would you please find Senior Warrant Halversen and Airshipman First Jeppesen, bring them here?"

* * *

"Thought this man might be of interest to you," Danhauer said about half an hour later.

The guy with him was short and sandy-haired, his square face smeared with grease. About forty, he wore a dirty white shirt under a frayed brown coat, and on his forehead were the goggles of an airshipman.

"Vice-Commodore Perry," said Perry. "Imperial Air Service. What can I do for you?"

"Nolan's the name. Nate Nolan – *Captain Nathaniel* Nolan, at your service. Just winged in half an hour ago, sir."

"A captain of what?"

"*Red Wasp*," Nolan said. "Captain and owner, with my wife. We heard there was a bit of a fight around here, might be some pickings."

Another woman in goggles had come in, her engineer's rig covered in sooty black and a clipboard in her hands. She was talking with the cowboys and businesspeople down the other end of the bar.

"There might be," said Perry. "You might also be looking to take passengers? Can you carry thirty-two people to Chicago?"

"In the hold we could, sir. We might well could. It wouldn't be comfortable, but I can give you a lower rate than any passenger line. You want to give us a few hours to look over where the battle was, see what we can pick up?"

"I'd rather get moving now," said Perry.

"One or two hours, is all I'm asking. You're flying to Chicago. That'll be sixty bucks a head, but I'll cut that down to fifty if you give us until four o'clock."

"That's *five* hours," said Perry. "And you're charging second-class passenger rates for what isn't even steerage. How about four hours, and you get forty dollars a head. Paid on delivery."

"Now, if you don't have the cash down, it might be a little more. How about we say fifty, because a promise ain't the same as a pound."

"Forty-five bucks a head, and you've got until three o'clock to take whatever you can scavenge from the battlefield. And if we're not in Chicago by sunrise tomorrow, you're getting thirty dollars a head. I don't care when we leave; I care when we *arrive*."

"How about fifty a head, and if we don't get to Chicago by sunrise, it's free?"

"That sounds fair," said Perry. "Good luck finding scraps. And be careful, a bunch of pirates also went down. Some might still be out there."

* * *

That thing flies? was Perry's first thought when he saw the *Red Wasp*, anchored at a stockyard near the town's little scout-class. It was a little over a hundred and fifty yards long, small as airships went, and every bit of it looked to have been a battered-apart piece of some other ship, crudely welded onto a frame that itself had started existence as at least three pieces. The aluminum gondola was a multicolored patchwork; pieces had clearly been taken from dozens of other craft, with blobs of color or pieces of lettering joined together in a messy quilt.

The cabin wasn't much better. There was the usual

70

configuration of bridge/cabins then hold then engines; the engines emitted thick smoke just at idle, and the hold wasn't much more than a grilled box. Lines of reddish corrosion streaked the short pathway from the engine room to the hold, and there were frayed streaks of it where the engine room met the gondola. Rusting iron bolts ran along its length, and the entire ship was covered in a film of brownish dust.

"You coming on board, Vice-Commodore?" Nolan asked from the bridge. A gangway had been thrown up, a low ramp going into the cargo hold.

I'm not sure it's safe to, Perry thought. He could hear murmurs from the rest of the crew.

"Chicago by sunrise or it's free!" Nolan yelled.

"Let's get moving," Perry said. "On board."

Perry's crew, carrying their bags, began to file aboard.

The two deputies, Danhauer and Norris, were standing by.

"If you need anything from the Service, Sergeant," Perry said, "let me know. You and your department have gone well out of your way to help us, and we take care of our friends."

They shook hands.

"I've counted to infinity, Vice-Commodore," Norris told him. "Twice."

Chapter Five

Reporter, *Chicago Sun*: Mr. President, you are cancelling your company's push to build a line from Chicago to Lincoln, it having completed the first stage to Madison, but not reached the second stage to Dubuque. Let alone to Lincoln. Why is that?

President Rockingham: We are. And the reason is that it is simply impossible. Until the point where our government can stop wasting resources on attempting to subjugate - sorry, attempting to *integrate* - the former Confederacy and begin to focus them where they are *needed*, on the Plains, we can not build and maintain a railway. We cannot build and maintain a railroad line through unpoliced anarchy.

Reporter, *Springfield Daily News*: The Central Southern Railroad has a line, and a telegraph, clear through to Hugoton. Along essentially similar ground.

President Rockingham: Because the government can be bothered protecting the border with Texas. Because the Imperials, damn their eyes, assist them. If Washington or London decided that the West was *important*, beyond London's precious helium supply, then we would be able to do the same thing.

Reporter, *New York Times*: I simply don't get why it's so hard. We had four transcontinental railroads and three transcontinental telegraph lines at the time of the Crash.

President Rockingham: Because at the time of the Crash, it was not so easy for a band of opportunists in a zeppelin to rip up five miles - and four thousand dollars to buy and lay, I'll add! - of telegraph wire for the value of its copper. Because at the time of the Crash, it was neither easy nor profitable for those same roving thieves to destroy railroad for the fuel value of the ties and the scrap value of the rails. Because the West is infested with those things, and because we as a corporation simply *do not have* the resources to deal with this constant, un-ending, expensive problem!

Reporter, *Boston Globe*: Can't you just sell something and get the resources?

President Rockingham: This press conference is over.

Transcript of Q&A with David Rockingham, President of the Northern and Chicago Railroad; June 22, 1961.

The bridge of the *Red Wasp* was every bit the mess that Perry had expected. A mishmash of rusted control levers, and a helm-wheel that looked like it had come off the axle of a horse-drawn chariot. Captain Nolan stood behind the helm, on the right, and a grey-haired woman in a dress - *a dress!* - and a multitooled rig whose function seemed primarily aesthetic, was in charge of what seemed like the type of balancing station that had been obsolete at Refoundation, in 1909. Spirit levels and long cranks, which would signal mechanically to the riggers.

"What d'you think?" Nolan asked proudly. "My ship. Well, mine and my wife's, and the crew's got shares. Our bird."

"It's... very nice. It's impressive. You've had her how long?"

"Ten years, and a bit. Won her in a poker game down Dodge way. We've been going back and forth across the country ever since."

"Last owner must have seen a sucker and folded," murmured Swarovski.

Perry gave his weapons officer a glare. *We're guests on this ship*, he mouthed, *and don't you forget your manners.*

"Making enough to get by?"

Nolan shrugged.

"Just enough. Scavenging here, high-premium special there. We don't have capacity, but low operating, so... Got to admit, thirty-two Imperials, fifty bucks a head plus whatever our scraps'll bring in Chicago? Sixteen hundred, *that'll* keep us in coal and hydrogen for a bit!"

"Maybe keep the creditors off our heads for a week longer," the grey-haired woman muttered sourly.

"That too, Elise. That too!"

"Made quite a score off of us, didn't you?" Martindale asked.

"Hey, you benefit, I benefit, the ship benefits. And like my bridge engineer said, the creditors benefit. Isn't free trade and mutual benefit what you Imperials are all about?"

"Damned right it is," Martindale grinned. "I was being congratulatory."

"Well, that said, looks like the man on the ground is giving us the signal to lift."

Nolan looked out the window.

"Go!" he shouted, with a thumbs-up for emphasis.

* * *

Cables slid from their hooks, and there was the sound of ground ballast being dumped. The *Red Wasp* lifted, shaking and swaying – *damn*, thought Perry, *does this rattletrap sway!* – into the afternoon darkness.

"Take us north," Nolan said, and turned the helm.

Four or five seconds later, the dirigible began to ponderously turn.

Nolan shouted into his speaking tube again.

"Stop in five. Four. Three. Two. One. Stop turn!" He wrested the helm around in the other direction. The dirigible began to pick up speed.

The grey-haired woman yanked a lever, found it stuck, put weight into it, and ponderously moved it down. Something came through one of her speaking tubes.

"Say it again!" she yelled through her end, and pressed an ear to it.

"I'm going to visit my crew in the hold," Perry said.

"Just down that passageway, Commodore. But you know that. Tell your men I say welcome aboard, if you will! And I'll show you how my baby flies!"

* * *

The hold was a ten-by-forty-foot cage, mostly consisting of a three-inch lattice of bars. They had the silvery tint of titanium, except that in some places they'd broken loose and been replaced by iron ones, welded in. Roped here and there, mostly along a set of struts running down the center of the hold, was various junk: large boxes, pieces of titanium scrap, pieces of aluminum crap. A propeller. Most of a large electrical dynamo. A lot of hydrogen cylinders.

The crew sat, mostly on their bags, along the sides of the

hold, some holding onto the bars for support.

"Everyone doing alright?" Perry asked.

"Sir, I got a question," said one of the riggers, a senior airshipwoman named Hayden. "When we were folding our parachutes after we came down? It was dark."

Perry paused for a couple of seconds, then said, "And? You have a question?"

"No, sir. Just an observation."

"We're flying low, Hayden," said Martindale. That was true; they seemed to be maintaining a height of about six or seven hundred feet. Ground was slipping past under the cage. "So don't worry. You can always jump without one."

Hayden tried to force a smile.

"Thank you, sir."

"Don't worry, people," said Perry. "Captain Nolan's been operating this bird for more than a decade without a serious incident. Should be fine."

"Begging your pardon, sir, but nine serious incidents since `58 when the rigger I spoke with joined," said Rafferty.

"And he survived, so they weren't *too* serious," said Perry.

* * *

The engine hall was even more commotion, thicker smoke from the low-grade crap they used down here. The feed seemed to be – *oh no*, Perry thought, *it is* – linked to a hydrogen cylinder.

That was dangerous. That was extremely dangerous, and none of the three engineering crew - including the woman Nolan had described as his wife - appeared to have the *faintest* idea just what kind of a bomb they were playing with. Hundred-times compressed hydrogen in the engine room? *Linking it through a feed into your boiler?*

Slowly shaking his head, he backed out.

Don't distract them. They've got to know what a jerry-rigged contraption, how barely airworthy a deathtrap, it is they're flying. They're used to it.

* * *

The trouble came around five o'clock. Perry was exercising

the privileges of his rank and hanging out with Nolan on the bridge, where there was at least a functional seat.

From the west, descending out of a bank of clouds about a mile away, came a small civilian airship. Maybe half again the length of the *Red Wasp*, and a glance through his monocular told Perry she was probably a passenger ship.

They also showed her flashes: 'S-O-S. S-O-S. J-R. J-R S-O-S.'

J-R meant Jolly Roger. *Pirates.*

Oh, shit, thought Perry. And then, a moment later: *Oh, good.*

"Pray there's only one of them," Nolan said, putting his own telescope down. "They'll focus on the liner, not us. But if there's *two?*"

"How are you armed?"

"One pressure-gun. A couple of rifles. Oh, and a four-inch cannon we picked up today, no ammo."

"You *do* have a flasher. *Right?*"

Nolan shook his head.

"Just signal flags. Why?"

"Where are they?"

"In that box. What are you going to do?"

"Bear with me. Signal flags. And hook that pressure-gun up."

"What are you doing?"

"You want to save your ship," Perry said. "I'm a Service veteran. Bear with me, captain."

Out of the clouds behind the civilian liner came the pirate. A smaller freight model, perhaps two hundred yards long. Bigger than the *Red Wasp*, and much better-built.

Perry took the signal flags – *hope I'm not too rusty* – and lowered his goggles. Then he went into the hold.

Some of the men were agitated. They'd seen the liner and read the signals.

"We going to do something?" Kent asked.

Perry gave him the signal flags.

"I want you to get up on top, where that pirate can see. And I want you to signal the *freighter* the following: Give Self Up. Protect Our Gold. Will Reward You For Distracting Him. Our Bank Will Reward You And Your Owners. Signal that three times to his flashermen. Clear?"

"We gonna kill the bastards?" Swarovski asked. He stroked the barrel of his rifle.

76

"We *better* kill the bastards," Perry said. "Pirates took my ship. I'm going to take theirs."

* * *

Captain Damon Mack of the *Jolly Rapist* gritted his teeth, trying to make out the signal flags.

"What the *fuck* is that tramp piece of shit saying, Weaver?"

"She's talking to the liner," said Weaver.

"I didn't think the asshole would be hailing *us*. What's she fucking saying to the liner."

"Something about gold. Reward us for. Oh, fuck that. *No way* is that piece of shit carrying gold."

"No way?" asked Mack. "They mine that shit out west, and she's heading east. Same direction anyone from Denver *would* be coming."

"It's a fifth-rate piece of shit," said Lenehan.

"Nobody asked your opinion."

The *Jolly Rapist* was a crew of real men, twenty-nine strong out of the Black Hills. They were tough killers, not the pussy let-them-live Code adherents, and the ship's name was not ironic. Real men – not like Kennedy and his bunch – had only one use for women, and some of them had the same use for men they captured.

"You think it's a bluff. Shitty wreck that nobody like us is gonna waste his time bothering with, so they can sneak gold past," Weaver said.

"Yeah. I think it is."

"So why they fucking scream it out?"

"Panic? Maybe they thought there might be two of us?"

"Bullshit a piece of garbage is gonna have gold," Weaver said, but he sounded less sure. "They going to give their gold courier to someone stupid? It's a bluff. They're trying to let the liner get free. Figure a reward from someone who can operate a *real* ship is going to make up the loss of their garbage."

Mack shrugged.

"Turns out to be a bluff, we'll kill every last one of them."

"I thought we were gonna do that anyway," said Lenehan. "Even their bitches."

That drew a couple of angry noises from others on the bridge.

77

"Once we're done with `em ourselves, morons."

Decisively, he turned the helm into an intercept course with the flying jalopy, which looked to be doing about forty-five.

"We'll get `em in a couple minutes. Hail `em down and tell the fuckers they'll live if they do as we say. May as well take their bird – gonna be *some* asshole who'll pay ten grand for it."

* * *

"You told them *what the fucking hell?*" Nolan demanded.

"That we're carrying gold. And, as you can see by how they'll have intercepted us in about three and a half minutes, they believe it."

"You *bastard*! I know she's not much of a ship, you Imperial son of a bitch, but the *Red Wasp* is *mine*! I've put my life into this bird!"

"Prize law," Perry said calmly.

"What?"

"Prize law. Considering my men and myself to be Marines - we are, after all, only passengers – then six eighths, or three quarters, of the pirate's value will go to the *ship crew*, yourselves as represented by you. The Service is paying you thirteen hundred for our fare. That airship is going to sell, at absolute minimum, for thirty times that, and that's not counting any cargo aboard. There may also be rewards on the individual men. Do you hear what I am saying?"

"You're saying we can make a locker's payload of money if your men can take out this pirate," said Nolan. "I'd like that more if I knew *how*."

Perry had been thinking fast about that himself for the last couple of minutes. The problem was that the pirate outgunned them *badly*, whatever she had. She also had better resilience, more power, better steering and probably less inclination to take them intact - after all, a fall wouldn't damage gold and you could always retrieve it from wreckage.

He had two advantages: One, surprise. The pirates would not be expecting thirty-two Imperials. Two, discipline. His men were almost certainly better at what they did, on average, than pirate rabble were going to be.

Remember. No plan ever survives contact with the enemy, he thought. He needed flexibility and backups, and he needed them *now*.

Martindale was looking at him as well.

"They're going to tell us to go down," said Perry to Nolan. "Comply, but keep them to the lee. What do you estimate the wind as?"

"Ten, twelve?" Martindale said.

"Keep them as close as possible to our lee. When I give the signal, dump ballast. Kent, I want you to gather all seven riggers and six other volunteers. Not Swarovski. Make sure they're all armed."

"We dump ballast, they're going to open fire on us *right away*," said Nolan. "You can retrieve gold from wreckage. They don't need an intact ship."

"But they'll want one, and it'll take them a couple of seconds to respond. My boarding team hits them from above." Inspired by the way the pirates had come onto 4-106. *Two* could play at that, and it'd be easier with a stationary ship.

"We rip out their lift. Engage their safeties, rip open the bags. They can dump their own ballast to an extent, but it'll slow them."

"Immobilize them, you're saying. Then what?"

"Board and attack."

"And what about the rest of us?" Martindale asked.

"Land, spread out, and attack from all sides while they're distracted."

"What if they don't comply with your plan? What if they move faster than expected? What if they shoot this thing down?"

"Then everyone bails and we engage them from the ground."

* * *

"I want to board," Swarovski said as they descended. The pirate was about two hundred yards from them, close enough that through the gaps in the cargo cage they could see individual men. The ship had one rocket launcher that they could see – probably another one to starboard – and what looked like a very crude pressure gun.

"No. You're of more value with that rifle. Shoot anyone, starting with their riggers, then bridge crew and gunners," said

Perry.

"But sir–"

"That's an order, Weapons. We obey orders in the Service, *remember?*"

"Sir. Yessir," said Swarovski. Then muttered "I want the next boarding, though."

"One hundred!" Nolan called out.

The ground below was grass, two or three feet high. It rippled in waves under the wind. Nolan was doing an adequate, if jerky, job at keeping them squarely to the freighter's lee.

Just two riggers aboard the pirate ship, although there was going to be a rig station with possibly another one or two in reserve.

"Fifty," Nolan called.

"You will dump four hydrogen sacs on landing and come out with your hands up," came a voice over the pirate's loudhailer.

"Charming name, sir," Halvorsen muttered to Perry. "The *Jolly Rapist*. Ten to one they're not the Code type."

"Don't tell me you think there's a jot of substance to that Code noise, Warrant," Perry murmured back. "If they respected laws, they wouldn't be pirates."

* * *

"I got a bad feeling," Lenehan muttered to Captain Mack, on the bridge of the ship. "Gonna be hard men aboard."

"Nobody fuckin' asked your opinion, I told you. Fag asshole."

"The balance geek's got a point," said Weaver. "Might be a tramp, but you think they're gonna let gold fly without half a dozen Pinks riding along with it?"

"Thirty of us," Mack said. "I've killed two Pinks singlehandedly. They come out with their hands up, or we blow them to slag."

"Ten grand for the ship," Lenehan said.

"And there might be a hundred in gold. Fuck the ship. She makes a false move, we blow the shithead to hell. Second, remind the guns of that. She *twitches* and we blow her to wreckage."

"I got it," said Weaver.

* * *

"Do we dump the hydrogen sacs?" Nolan asked Martindale. He was uneasy about this, *very* uneasy. This crazy colored Imperial was out for revenge against pirates, but it wasn't *his*, the colored Imperial captain's, stake they were playing with. It was *Nolan's*, and this was insane beyond the standards of what the *Red Wasp* did *normally*.

On the other hand, the size of this potential *score*...

Martindale, who had thrown a blanket poncho over his uniform tunic so that the pirates wouldn't suspect anything, thought for a moment.

"Yeah. We dump them. Your crew ready to dump equivalent ballast and then some? We put them at ease. But we've got to dump that ballast on the *spot*. All at once."

"What's wind, Vidkowski?"

"Ten or eleven."

The ship bumped to the ground, the pirate about a hundred and fifty yards away, just off the ground. Ropes were thrown down, and a couple of men with rifles dropped into the waist-high grass.

Nolan suddenly became very aware of the pirate's weapons. A rocket launcher at a hundred and fifty yards, with fairly low crosswind? And the pressure-gun just aft of the bridge, aimed *right at them?*

How had he allowed the Imperials to talk him into this insanity? Oh. Right. They'd just gone ahead with it.

Well, run!

"Charlie!" Nolan shouted. The code-signal.

"They're not dumping!" came a voice, half-heard through the pirates' loudhailer.

The sounds of ballast, dirt sacks pre-clumped together, moving along the deck. And then suddenly *lift*, and Nolan shouted into the speaking tubes: "Keep us steady over them!"

The wind was pushing them up, fast, hard, as more ballast was dumped and they gained ground.

A rocket fired. Nolan flinched and then screamed as it impacted somewhere aft. *Oh God this thing's going to hell they're better than the Imperials had planned on...*

81

"Fuckers are better than we figured on," Halvorsen muttered to Perry, as the rocket hit the cargo grille and detonated. Only a light one, three or four inches, but enough to send some of 4-106's crew reeling across the way.

"Open the loading!" Perry yelled. They were above the range of the pirate's guns, although she was starting to lift herself.

Swarovski fired his rifle, two quick shots through the cage. "Got one!"

"Attending the wounded!" Specialist Second Rogers - the medic - shouted.

Two of the riggers heaved the ten-foot-wide cargo door open. The grey bulk of the *Jolly Rapist* was coming to be below them, one of the riggers throwing himself flat and raising a pistol. Swarovski fired three times in quick succession, and the bullets sparked off the aluminum surface.

"Now! Go, go, go!" Perry shouted, as the *Jolly Rapist* ditched ballast and leapt up. Only ten feet down, no need for the rope as he fell, just roll and don't fall off the side...

The landing hurt, and he made a dent in the thin plating. Men were coming in behind him. The pirate rigger fired a shot and then took a bullet himself as Specialist Third Rafferty practically landed on top of him, firing down into him.

Blown by the wind, steering around and powering away, the *Red Wasp* was past them now, with only seven of the fourteen-man boarding party aboard.

Halvorsen was already at work with the crowbar he'd brought. He levered off one of the airship's plates and hacked open the hydrogen sac below.

"Get to it, you lot!" Perry yelled. "Cut their lift away or we don't have a damn chance!"

A hatch opened and a man with a submachinegun came up. Somebody fired at him and he ducked back.

One by one, the paper-thin, six-by-six-foot aluminum plates were levered off, the hydrogen bags below ripped open.

The man from the hatch raised his gun through it and fired a wild burst. A senior airshipwoman Perry didn't know yelled in pain and rolled, dropping her crowbar and clutching her chest.

This isn't fast enough, Perry thought. *We're still rising* – four hundred feet now, above the rippling yellow grass, and turning – *and where the* hell *is*–

"Knife," he said to Rafferty, the nearest enlisted man. "Now."

Rafferty yanked a stiletto from his boot and tossed it underhand to Perry.

"Two of you with blades?" Perry yelled, switching the pistol to his left hand. "Take a breath and follow me!"

Without waiting to see if anyone was, Perry leapt into the six-by-six gap that Halvorsen had opened. He fell, about five feet, before landing on the soft silk cushion of another hydrogen bag.

With the knife, he cut open the adjacent ones, ripping wide gaps into them. Hydrogen escaped. Then he slashed the one below, and almost immediately fell; slashing, cutting, opening the bags.

Next to him was Rafferty, slashing away with a long, heavy fighting knife. He cut his way through a hydrogen bag and into another, then lowered his face to breathe from the air between two bags. Hydrogen escaped up, not down; *all* the hydrogen from these ripped-open bags would be going up through the gaps his men were levering.

And I hope to God I don't come across anyone I have to shoot. Or that Rafferty or anyone else does, Perry thought. Breathing deeply himself, as he moved between two layers of hydrogen sacs, past a laddered access area. *One spark and we all burn. Badly.*

* * *

"They're inside his gondola," Martindale muttered. "Swarovski, damn you, hold your fire!"

"They got our steering," said Nolan. "We're fucked. They've got our damn steering, and *they're* just fine."

"No, captain," said Vescard, who'd come to the bridge. "They're fighting for buoyancy. Ditching ballast!"

* * *

"They're *inside* the gondola," someone shouted to Mack.

"And they're *Imperials*! It's an Imperial booby!"

"*Imperials?*" Mack shouted. Not unable to disbelieve – Pinks would never be so aggressive. Fucking Imperial *bastards!*

"Out of ballast!" Lenehan shouted. "We're gonna drop unless we ditch cargo."

"Get the gang together," Mack yelled at Weaver. "Get Biff and the crew, get up into the gondola, and fucking *kill them!*"

"Spark in the gondola and we're dead," said Weaver. "If they're *in* there, they're cutting away and there's loose hydrogen *all over.*"

"Kill them with knives, moron. Knives and pressure pistols whoever's got `em. Now *get rid of them bastards!*"

* * *

Sub-Lieutenant Kent, flat on the surface of the gondola, trained his pistol at the hatch the submachinegunner had come from. The man - sure enough - popped his head out, gun ready; just like the last time, he began a momentary scan for where the nearest Imperials were, so he could fire his burst in that direction.

This time Kent shot him once in the head before he could do more than raise the gun.

I *want* that thing, he thought, as another plate - this one with a hydrogen sac attached - lifted free, floating up into the sky. Before the collapsing man's dead hand could pull the submachinegun back, Kent grabbed it.

It was a one-handed model, obviously; a .400 machine-pistol with a drum magazine that looked about half-full, maybe twelve of twenty-five rounds. He made sure it was loaded and then - as another pirate came up past the corpse of the first one - fired it at that man, a three-round burst at his chest. He fell down the ladder, and there was no third.

They're coming up to get us, Kent thought. He could feel the airship itself, which had climbed to a peak of about five hundred feet, rolling hard, and starting to lose more and more height. *They'll want Perry and Rafferty and those men who went down, first. Won't use guns for fear of sparking the hydrogen. I can fire down at them just fine, though.*

Pointing the gun down the hatchway, he braced himself and waited.

The lower hydrogen sacs were loose and bumpy, and Perry's footing went from uncertain to practically nonexistent. He bounced between them, slashing with the knife, lowering his head to breathe where he thought he could.

The airship was falling. He could tell that. He, Rafferty and whoever the third man was, were definitely getting the work done.

Trying to move forward; he'd been about in the center of the airship when he'd gone down, but he was aiming for the bridge. Take control there...

The ship rocked, hard, and he found himself thrown against a structural vertical. And suddenly, on a ladder above him, was a pirate with a knife.

He saw the pirate first, but only by half an instant. The pirate was a wiry little red-haired man and his knife was long and jagged, and he threw himself down onto Perry with the knife aimed at Perry's throat.

Perry rolled sideways, or tried to. The smooth, unpressured silk had no particular traction, and wanted to lift anyways. What was meant to be a three-foot roll only moved him about six inches, and the pirate adjusted his knife accordingly. Desperately, Perry jerked his head and chest sideways, and the pirate's blade embedded itself in the sac they were on top of.

The pirate's teeth were half-gone, and his breath was foul, as he lay on top of Perry on the deflating hydrogen sac and pulled his knife out for another try.

Perry stabbed him in the kidney, then tried for the throat, getting him instead in the back of his shoulder. That was the pirate's knife-arm, though, and he was already twitching from the wound in his kidney. He screamed and arched, and Perry stabbed him in the throat, again and again, blood fountaining across his chest and face. Breathing hard. Desperate.

Somehow he became aware that they were no longer on hydrogen sacs; they were on hard ground, a walkway at the bottom of the gondola.

The airship was bucking hard, seemed to be tilted at about a thirty-degree angle, although in the confusion Perry had lost his sense of direction. *Definitely* falling, and he had no *clue* as to how far.

I'll get to the bridge, he decided. He had ten rounds in his gun, and that ought to be enough. The further down he was, the safer it was to use the gun.

Thankfully, along the walkway was a mark, in faded white stencil six inches high: "30."

Thirty yards from the nose? He went in that direction, cutting open more hydrogen bags above him and to the sides. 25. An access way, and a hatch.

From somewhere he could hear shouting, then a gargling scream that abruptly ended.

On the hatch was marked, in the same faded white stencil, *Bridge.*

I open it. I shoot. I jump in. I shoot, and I reload, and I kill everyone there, he decided, and braced himself to yank it open.

* * *

"Where *is* that fucker?" Mack yelled. They were falling hard and fast, gods only knew how much lift they were down.

Gods only knew how many *men* they were down. There was fighting going on through the gondola, and for all Mack knew the ship was burning. If the man who would have reported a fire was dead, how could he know?

"Fifty feet and brace yourselves!" Weaver shouted from the balance console. Lenehan had gone to join the fight.

"Turn, damnit!" Mack shouted. Panicked. This was an Imperial trap, and he'd fallen into it, and if there were Imperials aboard his ship and there was that other ship, then they had to have come from somewhere.

There was an Imperial warship about, lying covered somewhere, or just out of sight. There must have been a signal.

Clear those ones off. Kill them. Reinflate, and go.

Reinflation took time, when you'd been hacked to pieces as solidly as the *Roger* seemed to have been from their descent. It would take at least half an hour, and the Imperials would be on them in less than that. Unless he could get a crew together to fight them, six or seven expendable men to delay them on the ground. They'd hang, but Mack and the good ones would – *might* – have enough time to get away.

"Land!" yelled Weaver, panicked, as the ground slammed

them.

Knocking Mack off his feet, and Weaver against a bulkhead.

* * *

The *Red Wasp* touched down about three quarters of a mile from where the pirate ship was about to land, Nolan desperately releasing four hydrogen sacs in order to lose height before they got *too* far away.

"We can't fight from here," said Martindale. "Weapons, you ready?"

"And finally!" said Swarovski.

"Then offload and assemble!" the XO called.

Within half a minute, the rest of the crew was on the ground, standing with pistols and knives.

"We go join the captain," Martindale declared. "We shoot to kill, but be the hell careful not to get any of ours. We're going to secure that thing. Do you people understand?"

"Let's kill the fuckers," said Specialist First Singh.

The dozen or so unwounded crew started running through the waist-high grass, weapons raised.

* * *

"Get your shit together and fight them!" Mack screamed, fighting to get up from the impact of landing.

Lenehan came staggering back, blood streaming from wounds in his side and thigh.

"Got the engine room. They got the engine room. Jags tried to take control – they shot him in the face – we're fucked! We're fucked!"

The balance-man's panic was infectuous, and Mack was *already* on the edge of it.

"I don't *need* this shit!" he snarled, and shot Lenehan through the head. Wounded man. No good to anyone anyhow. Fag asshole anyway.

"Captain?" another man cried from the entrance way, then screamed when he saw Lenehan. "What do we *do*?"

The upper hatch opened. Not *more* people demanding orders he didn't have the information to give them?

No. The man was in Imperial officer's uniform, covered in blood and holding a pistol. He shot Weaver, somehow didn't see Mack, and jumped down.

Mack finally got to his feet. The man from the bridge entrance turned and ran. The Imperial officer, a black man, already had his gun pointed at Mack.

"Imperial Air Service," the man snarled, in one of those effete upper-class Imperial accents. *A nigger posing as a fag aristocrat. How cute.* "You're under arrest for piracy. Maybe you'll live if you answer a few questions."

Mack extended his left hand placatingly.

"Whatever you want. I didn't never kill nobody. Rape nobody, too. Code and all that shit and" – he flicked his left wrist and fired the derringer – "*die,* you fucker!"

* * *

The derringer's bullet hit Perry in the chest, but the chest of his uniform was kevlar and it was a low-caliber round. The shock of the impact made him stagger a half-step back, but he was already firing, emptying his gun into the pirate captain.

"I hoped you'd do that," he said, breathing hard. Taking his spare magazine, shoving it into the automatic. Covering the door against more pirates. The captain was well and truly dead, as were the other two on the bridge. "I very sincerely much hoped you'd try something like that, you pirate *bastard.*"

* * *

"Sir," Martindale reported about half an hour later. "I have the list."

Perry grimaced. Acutely aware that he'd suffered *no* serious casualties during the loss of 4-106.

You didn't join the Service without being ready to put your life down. That didn't make it any easier when your men *did.*

"How bad is it?"

"Three dead, sir. Senior Airshipman Jeppesen, Airshipman First Wold, and Sub-Lieutenant Ross."

Perry sighed, very deeply.

Fuck.

"And wounded?"

"Seven more, three when they got us with the missile in the cargo hold. And a few second-class injuries. Kent and Rafferty both got burned during that fight in the engine room, and Vescard's nursing five broken ribs from where his vest stopped a subgun burst."

"*Fuck*," said Perry.

"On the bright side, we got a pirate ship," Martindale said. "And a nice prize, I must say! Cargo hold full of machine-parts."

"To be returned to their owners," Perry said sternly to Nolan. "For whatever their insurer's deal is, or the twenty-five percent standard fee."

Nolan was grinning widely. His own crew was busily re-inflating the hydrogen sacs from the *Red Wasp*; the pirate, like most, had been loaded with spare sacs and hydrogen cylinders for lifting captured vessels. Perry's people were setting those up, re-inflating the gondola.

"Whatever you say, captain. But the *ship? That ship is mine now?*"

"Seventy-five percent of it is," Perry said.

"The ship. What's the cargo worth? Your quarter can be the cargo and the rewards. The ship?"

"Maybe we'll get enough from the cargo that you can buy the ship at fair value," said Perry. "My men will help bring it in, once it's been floated."

I lost three of my crew, Perry thought. *Now can you please shut up about your big score?*

Nolan and his wife headed away, back toward the *Red Wasp*.

Damnit. He'd been hoping, really, to capture the pirate ship intact. He'd succeeded in doing that. But he'd also hoped to interrogate the captain, or *any* of the crew – none had survived – about where Captain Ahle might be found.

Go to Chicago, check in. Then take a captured pirate ship into the Black Hills, dressed like pirates, with Marines aboard... and *get 4-106 back.*

Next to that, the fact that he was probably a couple of months' pay richer *himself* from this capture – one eighth of the prize, by law, went to Marine officers, and he'd classified 4-106's crew as Marines for Nolan's purpose – was relatively unimportant.

Apprehend Ahle. Get 4-106 back.

* * *

Hands on her hips, Karen Ahle inspected the work that the Dodge City technicians - and her own crew - had done to disguise the airship that the Imperials had called 4-106, and that she'd renamed the *Adestria*, after a Greek goddess of vengeance.

There wasn't a lot you could do to disguise the multiply-finned gondola, short of removing the fore and central steering vanes. Those would be hard to remove and replace, and she didn't know how that would affect the handling. So she'd added a second and third set of dummies, instead; side-vanes at one-third and two-thirds along the ship's length. They consisted of nothing more than aluminum sheeting on titanium struts that'd been attached to the gondola's framework, but they'd confuse anybody looking for a triple-vaned airship.

The rest had been relatively easy. Paint the gondola to an extent - messy streaks did the job, especially on the lower half - and blot out the identification number. People would be looking, and she knew the Imperials well enough to know they *would* search, for a warship, so she had the missile bays and the space between them covered with more aluminum sheeting, painted black. The hold of a particularly sleek high-value cargo ship, whose pressure-guns were pure self-defence.

The best part was that it would all drop away with a couple of minutes' work when she needed to clear for action. Her engineering education said that the dummy fins wouldn't be a major problem anyhow, but if they proved to be? The sheeting could be gotten rid of in under five minutes.

"Good job, people," she said to her crew. The eight who'd boarded with her, the thirty-five who'd stayed on her main ship, the *Aden*, and the forty-two newbies hired to be split across the two. "We accomplished something *impressive* here today. Now, we're not in the Black Hills; this is Dodge City, and you all know what's a ninety-minute ride east of here."

A couple of murmurs: Hugoton. Unavoidable – Dodge was the biggest town on the southern plains, in large part due to Hugoton. It was also the only place within her intended range that you could get repairs like this done. It really didn't hurt that, right now, there were more than forty ships docked amongst the concrete of the pads.

"So, I'm going to stay with the ships. Officers and I, and the new people, will stay with the ships while you go celebrate. We'll walk you through both ships and introduce you to your stations. Tomorrow, the new men can celebrate; my longstanding crew and officers will conduct ground drills with the new ship. And Thursday, I hope you people don't begrudge us captain and officers a few drinks!"

There were a few laughs and cheers.

"Go have fun, people," Ahle said. "Ronalds, Hollis, Petersen, the rest of you, we'll go through the *Adestria* first."

Ronalds, her chief NCO, took her aside. He and Petersen had been off looking through Dodge's plentiful black market while Ahle and the other officers supervised the ship's disguise.

"I found the ammunition," he said. "We should be able to have this thing loaded back up to capacity – and a bit of a reserve besides – by Wednesday. Arranged for fuel, too. How long do you think it will take to get these people ready?"

"I'd *like* two weeks for a comprehensive set of drills. We may not have as long. We may have longer, depending on what happens with those contract negotiations."

"Captain, you're crazy," Ronalds grinned. "You know that, right, ma'am? Stealing a line-class Imperial warship, and hiding it *this close to Hugoton?*"

"I do what I have to do," Ahle said. Deadly serious, all of a sudden. "For justice, for my family. And for a South free of Federal mercenaries and their murdering jackboots."

"Hell yeah, ma'am," said Ronalds, just as quiet and serious. "For a free South."

Chapter Six

Professor: "The Curzon Doctrine was established in 1892 during the early period of Imperial post-collapse exile in Newfoundland. It essentially ended the old imperialism, on the grounds that exactly such behavior had led to the Great War. Instead, Imperial policy going forward was to be that nations, territories and peoples had the absolute right to self-determination, and – if they so chose to be a part of the Empire – fair representation within it."

Student: "That's a crock of crap, professor! Without the Imperials propping them up, the Feds couldn't run their garrisons or their mercenaries through here! What about *our* right to self-determination as free states? The Empire is a bunch of lying bastards!"

Professor: "The Doctrine has been a guiding *principle* of Imperial governance and diplomacy. *Only* a principle. As I was going to say, expediency has caused the Imperials to allow certain exceptions to it..."

From a Politics 110 lecture at George Mason University, September 1958.

They arrived in Chicago, Perry and the two airships, at about ten o'clock the next day, to find the other three ships of the escort waiting. With them were three very scared spies.

"Martindale, take the ship to an agent and process the prize business," Perry said. He'd changed into a clean uniform, but there'd been no chance to shower. He felt every bit of his filth, his body covered in dust and blood. "Swarovski, the casualties, please."

"Already on it, sir," said Swarovski.

Nolan enthusiastically shook Perry's hand.

"You've made me a spiff man, Cap'n Perry! Thank you for all you've done. If you ever need a ride again, you can find me in Dodge City, generally. Or here, Denver, maybe, or the Mississippi ports. Just ask around. I know a couple of agents who line up cargoes, sometimes. They can get a message to me."

"I should be fine," said Perry. Nolan seemed like a nice enough fellow for his type, but that wasn't a type Imperial officers associated with.

Nolan pressed a card into his hand. "No, really, captain. You did me, my wife and the crew a real good turn, sir. *Anything* I can do for you, keep the card. A man never knows."

Something occurred to him. Perry took out one of his own visiting cards, handed it to Nolan.

"There's a telegraph contact number on that, and a mail router. If you know anyone shady, and you hear talk of a Captain Ahle? Pirate, probably from somewhere in the South. Don't push – I don't want her to know anyone's looking for her. But if you do hear anything about her, let me know immediately."

"I'll keep my eyes open in the skeazebars, sir. Your friends are here to see you, and I won't keep you any longer, but thank you again!"

With both hands he took Perry's, and shook it. Perry pocketed Nolan's card, mainly out of politeness, and turned to face his ship captains. With them were two men and a woman in civilian dress.

"Who are these people?" Perry asked.

"Oh," said Lieutenant-Commander Winston, a spare blond woman aged about forty. The senior of the captains with Perry. "Sir, these are Smith, Mathison, and" – the woman – "Raynham. The base commander put them under our protection. They're MI-7. This is Vice-Commodore Perry, our squadron commander."

"Thank you in advance for the ride," Smith – in his forties with deep-set eyes – said. "We appreciate it."

"We're going to Hugoton next, orders say," said Winston. "These people need a ride there to see Fleming. Someone wiped out the rest of their station here."

"Dropped a hydrogen blimp into the building," said Smith. "And a car bomb outside the fire exit. Twenty civilian dead, too. Fucking Russians."

"We'll get them," said Raynham. "But right now we need orders from Fleming. We're all that's left of the station, as your officer said."

"When do the orders say to depart?" Perry asked.

"Originally, two yesterday. I was playing for time, sir. Oh, and the extra officers and men are here. Sir." She looked sheepish. "For 4-106."

"Very well," said Perry. *Trying* to be blase about it. "Are the remaining three ships prepared to lift at midday?"

"Yessir."

"Any civilian escort?"

"No, sir. Just get ourselves to Hugoton."

Which I'd have had to do anyway, to report the loss.

Had attacking that pirate ship simply been a way to play for time, to delay the inevitable humiliation of reporting to Admiral Richardson? Of looking at the other squadron commanders in the group and saying, *I* was the one who lost a brand-new line-class to a pirate boarding?

"My personal crew are going to want a shower and a quick meal," Perry said firmly. "Assemble in the briefing room in an hour. We *will* lift at midday."

* * *

The trip back to Hugoton took about a day, an uneventful trip because *nobody* was going to attack a lone trio of Air Service dirigibles. They were crowded with crew; forty new people had joined the squadron in Chicago, mostly expecting to man the line-class that hadn't made it. They were split crowdedly across Primus Wing's three remaining dirigibles.

Perry seethed as the ships flew south.

* * *

Flight Admiral Richardson was a stern-faced, grey-haired woman in her mid-forties, although she looked a decade older. Her left hand was a prosthetic, as was much of her left arm, and scars on that side of her face indicated skin grafts. The ribbons on the right breast of her day uniform included the Distinguished Service Order, the second-highest Imperial decoration, and the Distinguished Flight Cross, the highest Air Service decoration. She was the second-ranking Service officer in continental North America.

"At ease, Perry, and sit down."

"Yes, ma'am," Perry said stiffly, taking a chair. Her office was as sparse and ordered as she was; no glory photos, minimal decoration. Against a piece of oak on one wall behind her was a scorched piece of propeller, a remnant of the action in which she'd exchanged her hand for a DFC.

"Have a drink, Perry." She poured scotch into two glasses.

"No, ma'am. Thank you."

Richardson poured another finger of scotch into one of the glasses and passed it across the smooth, dark wood of her desk.

"Drink it, Vice-Commodore, and that's an order."

"Yes, ma'am." Perry sipped. It was good whisky, he did have to admit.

"Finish it, please. And then tell me what happened. Here, I'll say, has been chaotic. One of the larger Federal mercenary organizations has been threatening to quit; the Feds are concerned, and I've had to give them the reserve squadron. Just in case negotiations with the Special Squadrons *do* fall through."

"The Thirtieth?"

"Yes; sent them across to Missouri just in case. And intelligence - I don't know if you've heard about the war?"

"The *war?*" Perry asked in shock. He'd glanced at a newspaper in Chicago, nothing of that kind!

"I had dinner with Deputy Director Fleming the other night. He's aged five years in two weeks. In fact, didn't you carry three of his men here?"

"Yes, ma'am." Perry sipped the scotch again. "I heard the Russians, or somebody, wiped out their headquarters. I didn't consider it appropriate to ask further."

"The Scotch is to relax you, Vice-Commodore. So is the small-talk, although it never hurts for you to be informed. No, this isn't classified. That is, of course it is, but we're both cleared. There was an attack in New York City about three weeks ago. The Yanks got some tip, didn't bother to consult us – beyond getting one of the local agents to come along - and wiped out the Russian station there."

"Isn't that a good thing?" Perry asked.

"No, apparently the spies normally tolerate each other. Monitor each others' stations, don't attack them. The Russians considered this an unprovoked attack, thought it was at our bidding – anything the Yanks do in this regard normally *is* – and retaliated by sending a hit squad to our station in New

Orleans. Killed everyone in the place. We responded to the deaths of nineteen agents by destroying their station in Houston. And so forth. Have another drink."

Perry had finished his.

"No, ma'am. Thank you."

"Another glass." She took his, poured two fingers into each of theirs, gave his back.

"Very good Scotch, ma'am. And thank you."

"Fleming and his counterpart *would* have negotiated a peace, but his counterpart – the head of operations in North America, one Lavrentiy Beria – had been killed in the New York City attack. Everything has to go through St. Petersburg, which means it has to go to London first. And meanwhile, our agents and the Russians are busy butchering each other. Fleming's drained dry."

"Those guys in Chicago looked unhappy, ma'am."

"They knew what was happening. All too well. An eye for an eye until Official Diplomatic Things happen, or both sides are blind. They're not going to stop killing us and we're not going to let them. Fleming's pulling his hair out and drinking more than he usually does."

"A *very* unfortunate situation," Perry said. "There are times I'm glad I'm Air Service, not Secret Service."

"A justly-decorated Vice-Commodore of the Air Service," said Richardson. "Now, Marcus, have another Scotch if you like and tell me, exactly what happened. I have the written reports. I want to know what *did* happen."

* * *

When Perry was done, Richardson steepled her fingers and was silent for almost a minute.

"This is going to look bad, Perry," she eventually said.

"Ma'am. I know. Ma'am."

"Not to me. *I* understand these realities. You were steeply under-crewed and actively engaged. The pirates seemed to know exactly what they were doing, and you – and your bridge officers' reports confirm this – made all reasonable resistance. But Whitehall won't think about that. Whitehall will see a brand-new line-class lost to pirates without a shot fired or a casualty inflicted."

"Yes. Ma'am."

Richardson sighed deeply. "A shame. Now, I have new orders myself. One of your wings – I think Secundus, transfer one of the Primus ships over - is to go out on convoy duty. The other two ships, I need here. Lord Charles" – that was Lieutenant-General (retired) Charles Lloyd, Governor of the Hugoton Lease – "wants to enlarge the permanent security presence. Fleming's all but blind, and two more ships here would allay the Governor's fears a bit."

The Squadron's being broken up.

Richardson saw the look in Perry's eyes.

"*No*, Vice-Commodore, this is not a punishment. This would have happened anyway; it's why you were called back from Chicago post haste, without a convoy to guard. Besides, I can read. Implications and body language. Vice-Commodore, you are free to take over Secundus Wing if you so desire, and ordinarily you would either do so or run the squadron's elements from an office here. But if you had complete freedom of action right now, how would you pursue your duty?"

"I'd hunt that pirate down," Perry said, the alcohol making his mouth act before his brain. "I'd hunt her down, retrieve 4-106, and restore the honor of my Service."

"I thought so. Your desire came through clearly in the report, and I'm glad I shared my Glenlivet. Very well. I'm granting you detached duty. You have an appointment with Deputy Director Fleming at one o'clock."

* * *

Deputy Director Sir Ian Fleming leaned back in his chair and reached for his glass. It was empty. Sighing – an old bullet wound, a Frenchman's gift from Jamaica in `43, was acting up again – he reached again for the bottle. He didn't feel like getting up.

There was a knock on the door of his office.

"Come in," he said. It was Agent Connery, a tall, handsome, thirtyish Scotsman on recovery duty after a nasty little incident on the Sonoran-Mexican border. He walked with a crutch.

"Dispatch from M, boss. Marked urgent. Just came out of decryption."

"'M' has a *name*, Connery," said Fleming coldly. He was exhausted and pissed off; one by one his stations and reaction teams were being destroyed.

"Dispatch from Director-General Lord Mountbatten, *sir*," said Connery.

"Thank you. Have a drink." Fleming pushed over the bottle and an empty glass.

Fleming took the telegraph, printed on yellow paper. It was only a few lines, and it said that the Foreign Service was making trouble, wanting to know why *they* weren't being consulted. Mountbatten himself was unhappy, and thought it was a Foreign Service territory game at the expense of – *more than a hundred and thirty, so far* – MI-7 lives. Bureaucratic stupidity.

Do what you can, the telegraph ended, *with what resources you have. Pretend you're improvising in the field again. You have my full authorization to act as you see fit.*

Relevant, that. If unnecessary. Fleming had been a field agent for twenty-five years and, at least in his own opinion, had accomplished more than any other agent in MI-7's history. *Most* of that had been through improvisation.

Fleming's telephone buzzed, the sharp two-tone that meant the front desk.

"Yes?"

"Your one o'clock. Vice-Commodore Marcus Perry of the Imperial Air Service."

"Give me a couple of minutes," he said, and put the phone down. Perry. He knew the name vaguely, one of the squadron commanders based out of here.

"Perry," Connery said helpfully. He produced a couple of files. "Here's his, boss. Here's another relevant one." The second one was labelled 'Pirates, North America; Ahle, Karen.'

Fleming opened them, scanned them both as he finished his drink. It only took a couple of minutes.

"Bring him in, Connery."

* * *

Perry had been into MI-7's offices before, but only to pick up reports. He'd never been into Deputy-Director Fleming's personal office, which was the opposite of his group commander's. While Richardson's was austere, Fleming's was luxurious. Windowless, the walls were covered with heavy, laden bookshelves. The furniture was plush leather and the floor was thickly-carpeted.

Fleming was a thin, rectangular-faced man in his early fifties, wearing a well-tailored black suit that looked as though he'd slept in it. His eyes were lined with stress.

"Take a seat, Vice-Commodore. It's a pleasure to see you again."

Again?, Perry thought, then remembered that they *had* met in passing at various functions.

"Thank you, sir."

"Have a drink?"

"I had four an hour ago with my commander, sir. But thank you."

"Only four? So what'll you have?"

"Really, sir. I'm quite fine."

"Connery, get me a dry martini. And this time, please *don't* shake it? Stir it. *Carefully.* I've told you that enough times."

"Yessir. And one for the Vice-Commodore?"

"If he won't ask for anything else. No? Then it's a martini, Perry."

When the aide had gone, Fleming got straight down to business. He leaned across the table and said "You want Karen Ahle's head. Is that correct?"

"You know her first name?"

"Five foot eight, aged thirty-three, of North Carolina," Fleming said. "Weighs about one thirty. One of those old families. Give us some credit, Vice-Commodore," Fleming smiled thinly. "Spies *do* occasionally gather information. When we're not killing each other."

"I heard there was some trouble," Perry said. "A shame, and my condolences for your men."

Fleming shrugged, reached for a bottle. "Part of why I gave you priority was that I could use some light relaxation. Pirates are *so* much easier to deal with than Russians. Let me give you a rundown on Karen Marie Ahle."

"I'm listening, sir. I'm *very* much listening."

"I'll give you a copy of the file when we're done. Here's the summary: Born in 1930; Wake Forest, North Carolina. One of those old Southern plantation families; one of her great-grandparents was a Confederate general. Family fortunes suffered when slavery ended, as all those people's did, but they held on through the Collapse.

"Stayed more or less on top of things during the anarchy in the South - black guerillas in the countryside, workers' militias in the big cities, renegade Union troops. You know it all. When reunification happens, the Ahles are still a wealthy Southern military family. Her father was an officer in the North Carolina State Militia.

"In 1944. You know what happened in 1944."

"I'm afraid I really don't, sir. I was a first-year at Biggin Hill in `44."

Connery came crutch-walking back with the drinks. Fleming took his, made sure Perry accepted his, and dismissed the aide. Mostly out of politeness, Perry took a sip. Not a bad drink, although his own tastes ran more to the plain and straight.

"Another of their rebellions. A big one. North Carolina went up in flames, and the Feds responded the way they usually do - no diplomacy, just heavy boots. A mercenary unit, the Special Squadrons, commanded by a nasty little Bavarian piece of work named Heinrich Himmler, went through the central part of the state. Federal orders were to execute Major-General Ahle. Himmler and his boys did just that."

"I'm sure he deserved it."

"At the family estate. They leveled it. Butchered his wife and family along with him. As I said, brutal even by Federal-mercenary standards, killing women and children. Their eldest daughter – our Captain Ahle – was off at a technical academy. When she heard the news, she fled to Sonora and somehow got hold of money her father had put in an account for that sort of emergency."

"So she's got a grudge against the Feds. And against the Imperials. And the mercenaries."

"We have every reason to think so," said Fleming. "She finished her schooling in Sonora, was accepted into what they call their Aerospace Academy, graduated two years later, fourth in a class of a hundred and ninety. Six years in their Navy; served under Goldwater in their Californian war. Honorable discharge with the rank of captain. Equates to your rank of lieutenant-commander, fourth on their pay scale. Then got out and went pirate."

"Only for so long," Perry said coldly.

Fleming sighed.

"I have more important things to worry about than pirates, right now. I have a war to fight and this is only a diversion. Your commanding officer called in a favor. Talk with Connery tomorrow morning; he'll advise you. I suppose you should go to the Black Hills; Connery's been up there. My assistant, Senior Agent Moore, also has; you'll talk with him. You can have money to hire a crew; I can give you money. What I *can't* spare is men."

"I understand. Thank you for the information and resources, sir. Deputy Director Fleming, I don't *care* what it takes. Captain Ahle humiliated me and stole an Imperial ship. I am getting my ship back."

Fleming took a long sip from his drink, then sighed.

"I suppose it never occurred to you, Vice-Commodore, to wonder *why* a pirate might want a line-class warship?"

"To commit further crimes."

"That would be overkill. Pirates are in it for the money; they don't begin to need the level of firepower that your 4-106 has, or to want the level of operating cost. You might not care why, but at some level I'm aware that my job consists of more than just wiping out Russian stations and seeing my own men die. It also consists of gathering information - and, in particular, investigating anomalies that might potentially threaten our security on the North American continent."

Fleming drained the last of his martini.

"While you're busy restoring the honor of your Service and whatnot? Find that out for us, will you?"

Chapter Seven

'The Hugoton Lease, in southwest Kansas and the northern part of pre-independence Texas, is an area of approximately 2000 square miles, granted to the British Empire on a five-hundred year lease in 1933. Alongside substantial oil and natural gas deposits – both of which have found to be of use in powering steam engines – Hugoton contains 93% of the world's known helium reserves. Helium being an inert, non-flammable gas critical to the survivability of military airships, this gives the lease immense strategic value to the Empire.'

A Report On Imperial Leases And Bases, Parliamentary News Service, 1953.

"So this is Dodge City," Joe Ferrer said, looking out the window of the slowing passenger car. Not the place of pulp-novel legend; it looked like a cheap industrial town. Shabby two- and three-storey buildings, the occasional four-storey. Higher ones downtown. Ugly hydrogen-cracking plants and slaughterhouses. A *huge* airship park in the northern distance.

"Welcome to Dodge," said Pratt Cannon.

Clicks, as the train was switched onto a different line, and then they passed through a respectably-sized yard; twelve or fourteen tracks. There were long lines of freighters, of tankers, refrigeration and cattle cars.

"Line continues to Hugoton," said Marko. "Eighty-five miles."

"Need a pass to get there," said Cannon.

"Careful about it, too," said McIlhan. "They shoot to kill past the second line. Whole fuckin' area is Imperials Only, Keep Out."

"Always a way. Just got to find it."

The train began to pull into a station.

"Disguise ourselves somehow," Marko went on. "We *got* to scope out Hugoton. Ferrer, you go in back and unload the kinematoscopes. McIlhan, rent us a steam truck. No, buy one. Harder to trace. Rienzi?"

The smirking kid looked up.

"Keep an eye on Ferrer. You're a gunman, he's not. Rough place, eh?"

Rienzi nodded enthusiastically.

"Rough men. I'll show `em."

"Kid," Cannon said quietly. "You're an OK shot. Not too slow, either. In this town there are at least a hundred men who are better at both, and who love to notch their fucking gun just as much as you do. Hear me?"

"Don't start nothing. Yeah, yeah."

"And shoot `em in the back," Cannon grinned. "They'd do it to you."

So this is Dodge, Ferrer thought, as he headed out toward the freight cars at the back of the train. *It's a good thing I'm wearing a gun.*

* * *

Forty minutes later, Marko and his crew had arranged a vehicle - a large, brass-heavy steam truck with the two crated kinematographs inside - and a garage, and rented the whole second floor, six rooms, of a flophouse in the Boot District of northwest Dodge.

Dodge was a violent industrial cowtown, a trading and industrial place where cowboys, airshipmen and oil workers drunkenly blew off steam, but some areas were safer than others. The Boot District was right down at the bottom of the list.

"You keep a gun handy," Cannon warned McIlhan. "Ain't a safe place for a woman. You're gonna get shit."

"I can handle myself," McIlhan said. "Been here before, cattle-rustler."

Cannon grinned. He liked McIlhan; she was a spunky bitch. "No doubt. Boss and I are gonna go sniffing around. See about Hugoton."

"I told you, you ain't getting close without a pass. We *ain't* driving that steam-truck right through without it getting blown to scrap."

"Trail boss says we find a way. Freaky son of a bitch, that guy. But sneaky. I'm gonna bet you he finds one."

"I'll help," said Rienzi. "Always wanted to see a place like

Dodge. Where a man can be a man."

"You can be a man later," Cannon told him. *Stupid kid.* "Right now, you help that engineer man set up those kinny machines."

"He's doing fine on his own," said Rienzi.

"You help Ferrer," said Marko, coming in. "Or you can argue with me."

How long was he outside the door listening? Cannon wondered. Scary son-of-a, that one.

"Got it, boss," said Rienzi.

"Other three of us are gonna ask around and see what we can find. Maybe there's a supply convoy we can get in on. Someone with passes we can buy. Could happen any time. Could be we move out at a dot's note. We're gonna have a problem if you ain't ready with the scopes. It's your fault, *you and I* are gonna have a problem."

"Right away," Rienzi said. He picked up a toolkit and headed out.

Maybe the young punk isn't quite so dumb as he looks, Cannon thought.

"We're also gonna be hiring men. Just in case. See who's in town, who knows what. This clear?"

* * *

Four or five hundred yards away, in a middling-upscale hotel on the edge of the Boot District, Captain Ahle and her inner circle were celebrating. There were twelve of them, as much Ahle's close cadre as her senior officers, and they'd rented a private suite with its own bar. For security, although that had been effectively ignored after the first couple of hours. Trail bosses, pirates, fences and various friends of the officers could come in and out, with their friends, just nodding casually to the guards at the door.

Ahle sprawled on a leather arrmchair, her boots over one of the arms and a crystal glass of port in her hand. Leaning against a wall near her was first officer Jeff Hollis, a lean, tanned, grey-haired engineer who'd emigrated from the South five years before Ahle'd fled as a teen. He threw back his whisky – a good single-malt, they *were* finally celebrating – and gestured to one of the waitresses for another.

"Never figured on this when we left Sonora, did you?" Ahle asked, taking another sip and smiling broadly. Hollis had been a Support Corps major for the Sonoran War Department when they'd met.

"An Imperial ship. I still say you're crazy!"

"We got it. And we're going to use it. Finish the refit, maybe sortie through East Texas for a bit. Little more money wouldn't hurt."

"Oh, we've got enough money, boss-lady," said Maria Sciapella, a native Sonoran who handled the crew's finances. "Stocks, bonds, you name it, as well as liquid cash. The Hermosillo stock market's booming, and we've got nine thousand US dollars handy in Fed banks if we should need it."

"Little more money never hurts," Ahle repeated. "Take down a Texie oil freighter or something? They could use oil in the Black Hills."

"Ma'am!" said Ronalds, coming past. There was a Cuban in his mouth rather than a straw – the straws were just something to chew on when you were sitting in a hydrogen-loaded airship with flames to be avoided - and a glass of heavy rum in his hand. "*Hell* of a ship, we got! A *hell* of a fucking ship! Even you!"

Ronalds slapped Sciapella on the back. The small woman flinched but smiled. Normally the two didn't get along; that was something Ahle had to work on, but for some reason the two *never* had. Lot of people didn't get along with Ronalds. A pity.

She downed the last of her port and gestured for more.

"We're gonna go kill some Germans," Ronalds said. "We're gonna go kill some everyone! Kennedy wants to fuck with us, Joe and Joe? We'll take *them*!"

"Good luck trying," said a handsome fortyish man with light brown hair, coming into the room with a drink in his hand. He wore a jacket lined with silver thread over a waistcoat that seemed to be woven from gold, and a half-dozen pistols were strapped to his waist, chest and thighs.

"Johnny Kennedy!" exclaimed Ronalds. "Good to fucking see you!" He slammed his glass into Kennedy's; somehow, neither of them broke.

"Didn't know you were in town," said Ahle, looking up. "Thanks for coming."

"Something we never did, snatching an Imperial line-class. You're crazy for thinking you can use it, but hell – *our* empire was built on crazy!"

"To the Kennedys!" said Ronalds. "Who can take any of us down, any time they feel like it! Joe and Joe Junior, who made the fuckin' Code! And Jack!"

A waitress with several glasses came over, exchanged people's old glasses for new ones. Kennedy slapped her on the backside as he left.

"Still got an eye for the women, I see, Johnny," said Ahle.

"Hey, I've got a room at the Berkshire. Ask for a Kenneth O'Donnell. Any time you want, Karen. Or how about you, money girl?"

Pete Augustin wandered back, another exiled Southerner. He'd detached from the conversation a little while ago to talk business with a fence he'd spotted. "Hear about Mack Damon, you lot?"

"Who?" asked Hollis.

"Please tell me someone killed that worthless piece of shit," said Ahle.

"Worthless piece of shit," Augustin told Hollis. "The kill-and-rape type. Sort of trash who'd mow down civilian crew for the fun of it, and would've sold `em as slaves into the Dakota mines before Johnny's dad put a stop to that shit."

He turned to Ahle.

"Someone killed the piece of slime. Him and his crew. Guess who."

"Who?"

"Black guy, Imperial, Vice-Commodore whose ship had been taken down Monday evening..."

"The former owner of the *Adestria*?" Ahle asked.

"By all accounts. Riding a little tramp out of Kearney. Somehow baited the son of a bitch in, and boarded him with a full crew of Imperials."

"Assholes like that *deserve* to hang. He hang?" asked Hollis.

"Not enough time, if it was Tuesday," said Kennedy. "Imperials are very law-court about that stuff. No thirty-foot court-martials on their part."

"Killed in the fight, I heard," said Augustin. "Got his bags intact. Buddy of mine's agent, telegraph says; saw it come into Chicago with a tramp freighter whose captain was just as happy as happy can be."

"Mack had a good ship, I'll give him. Fast freighter," said Ahle. She only vaguely knew the man; there were a hundred of that type, and the scumbags didn't mix too much with the more civilized pirates. "Ought to fetch a sum on the market. Of which that Vice-Commodore, usual prize rules? One quarter, personally."

"Sometimes I figure I oughta join the Imperials myself," said Augustin. "Do most of what we do, and sometimes there's *real* chingada dinero if you're an officer."

"Quarter of a ship, in his own pocket," Ahle said. Pirate distribution of loot wasn't nearly as hierarchical, although captains did well enough anyway. "Well, *that* ought to keep that guy and his officers happy enough to not care about losing their first ship!"

* * *

The officers' reorganization meeting had only taken about half an hour; 4-106's excess personnel had been split across the squadron's six remaining – six original – ships, essentially back where they had been. Secundus Wing would be based out of Denver as the squadron had been, and some of the extra crew would be there as a reserve; the rest would be around Hugoton.

The men remaining at Hugoton, manning the two dirigibles left of Primus Wing, had been given three-day passes; so had the officers. In practice that meant Dodge City, although Hugoton had reasonable facilities. Perry had a token drink in the officers' mess and then went back to his quarters to write a letter to his wife.

I am going on special detached duty, the letter said. *I've been briefed, but I don't begin to know what I'm going to be doing. The provisional plan is that I will go to the Black Hills posing as a less-than-reputable merchant who has acquired nine-inch rockets; that may lead me to 4-106, since the new owner of a ship with them will probably be interested in a resupply.*

I have to admit, I'm rather in over my head. Friday and the weekend, one of the MI-7 people will give me an education in basic espionage. I still can't believe this was offered to me, although I can see how a squadron commander would be less than necessary with the squadron split up. And the recovery of 4-106 will be worth any risk to me.

He wrote for a couple of pages and then took an early night; by nine o'clock he was asleep in bed, dreaming of being at the helm of 4-106 again as it lifted from the Black Hills, Captain Karen Ahle a handcuffed prisoner.

* * *

Cannon found Marko in a workman's dive on the edge of the industrial district, juggling a knife, a beer bottle and three shotglasses while he ferociously lectured a bunch of laborers about the evils of the state. He caught the boss's eye and gestured with his head.

Urgent.

"And that, gentlemen, is why we must *smash* the state and its machinery!" Marko flipped the three glasses into the hands of the nearest workers, knifed the lid off the beer bottle – and in the same move, flung the steak knife into the center of a photo of President Agnew above the door – and then drained the bottle in a single long chug.

A couple of the workers applauded.

"Do not serve the machines, my friends! *Destroy* the machines! Destroy their masters and become free again!" Marko slipped through the crowd and went to Cannon.

"What?" he demanded in an undertone.

"I found it. Found our way into Hugoton."

"Talk."

"Imperials lost an airship. To pirates. Friend of a friend heard something about an Imperial ship being disguised. I know where it's parked."

"An *Imperial airship?*" Marko laughed.

"Not going to shoot down their own bird being returned, are they?"

"Gonna try, once they realize it's not returning."

"Fake some damage mid-air. Time they realize we were just overflying with the kinematographs running, we'll be out of their range, and we'll have the intelligence. Fast bird. Could use it later, too. Depending what you got in mind."

"We're go," said Marko. "Airship needs crew. I know some. You know some."

"Rounding up a full crew will take a few hours," said Cannon. "Rienzi and McIlhan are on notice. Ready to start looking for people. Can Ferrer handle a boiler room?"

"Not that kind of an engineer. Besides, he'll be focused on the kinematographs. We'll need a full crew. Eighty miles; we'll have an hour and a half to get them up to speed. Time it so we pass over Hugoton at dawn. Round it up."

"What about the previous owners?" Cannon asked. "Pirates aren't going to give up their prize without a fight."

"I don't see the point in fighting," said Marko. "We'll just kill them all. More questions?"

Cannon shrugged. "None I can think of. I'll get busy finding a crew. Place like this, always going to be bodies available."

"Hire on long-term contract. We'll need them later."

* * *

"I need to see Vice Perry," the man said to the Air Marine guard outside Hugoton officers' quarters. It was two thirty and nothing ever happened on officer shift; the guard had been half-asleep himself.

Confronted by this drunk man in greased coveralls, he was waking up fast.

"Who the *hell* are you?"

"Senior Airshipman – no, Specialist. Spec Third Rafferty, I am. Listen, mate, I *got* to see the Vice. Wake him the fuck up."

"Rip the stripe right off me for waking a Vice-Commodore," said the guard, a lance-corporal. "Bust *you* right down, too. You're drunk."

"Damn right I'm drunk," said Rafferty. "Get me the fucking Vice or it'll be the worse for you. He finds you've kept this from him tomorrow morning, you ain't gonna lose your stripe. You'll get a ten-forty dishonorable."

"Let me get my sergeant," the young lance said. "Stay *right here.*"

As soon as the guard was out of sight, Rafferty glanced at the directory and marched past his station into the hall. Nice place, officer country.

Oh, this was good. This was fucking *good*. He giggled to himself. A part of him wished he hadn't chugged down that

109

flask on the train back from Dodge.

Was there any left? He fished it out of the big pocket of the overalls to check. Yeah, a good-sized stub. He raised it to his mouth and drank the harsh whisky – and there, that was 211, the suite the directory said the Vice lived in at Hugoton. He pounded on the door.

Several hard thumps later, there was a voice.

"What is it?"

"It's me, Vice! Got news! *Important* news!"

From down the hall, Rafferty could hear that young lance and a more mature voice:

"Where'd he go?"

"*There.*"

"What the hell is it?" Perry appeared, wearing blue pajamas and a sheepskin dressing gown. "Specialist Rafferty? You're drunk. And in civvies."

"I'm sorry, Vice-Commodore." A strong hand grabbed Rafferty's arm. A middle-aged sergeant, and he did *not* look happy. Rafferty gave him a shit-eating grin in the hope it'd appease him. It didn't seem to. He turned back to the Vice while he still could.

"I found the bird! I found your lost bird, Vice!"

"Hold on," Perry said to the sergeant. "Rafferty, you're drunk."

"Damn right I'm drunk. But I found the 4-106."

"Sergeant," said Perry, "go back to your station. No. How many men do you have ready right now?"

"Just the regular patrols, sir. And the incident response companies, of course."

"Go to the front and be ready to call the duty officer. I'm going to talk with this man."

The sergeant let go of Rafferty's arm, but didn't lower his glare. *One pissed-off NCO*, Rafferty thought. Well, he was used to the breed.

"Got my thanks, sir," he said. "Listen, boss. I found that pirate, and word is that she's got 4-106 still. They were celebrating, she and her top buddies."

"In Dodge City."

"Right in the Boot District, sir."

"Boot District's off-limits. As you well know."

"It is, sir? I never heard of that."

110

"The list is on your pass. You know damn well it and the surrounding areas are off limits. Everything north of Kliesen Street."

"My mistake, sir. Probably won't happen again. Not too soon. Sir."

"Do you know where 4-106 *itself* is?"

"No, sir. But that pirate would! Airship park in Dodge, not many places you can hide a bird big as that. It's probably in Dodge since all her crew is, and all!"

"And you've got a confirmed location on Captain Karen Ahle."

"Celebrating at the Foster Arms, weren't they? Two and a half hours ago. In Dodge, I know that much, I does. And the place. The Foster Arms. You got any more drinks in your house?"

"No. Stay here for a moment."

Perry went inside, to where a phone stood on a desk.

"Officers' mess? Yes. This is Vice Perry. I want you to make something for an enlisted man named Rafferty who'll be showing up shortly. Fat and calories, whatever best absorbs alcohol. Serve him within five minutes and have him eat it fast. Thank you."

"You want me un-drunk, sir?"

"Go to the officers' mess. They'll let you in. I'll meet you out there in ten minutes. You armed, Rafferty?"

"Wouldn't go into the Boot if I weren't equipped for it, sir."

"Were you with anyone?"

"Yessir. Senior Airshipman Duckworth. Second rigger on the *Shuffler*."

"Where is he now?"

"Off the corner behind the bar. Keeping an eye on things. Sort of figured you'd assemble some men and go for her. That right, sir?"

"That's damned right, Rafferty. Good job. Now go to the mess and sober the hell up, *fast*."

"Yessir. And you'll straighten me out with that sergeant, will you?"

"I'm going to talk with his commanding officer. We're going into Dodge *right now*."

* * *

Perry was reaching for uniform pants when he realized: The Boot District *was* off limits, and any Imperial officer would draw immediate attention long before he and the group reached wherever the Foster Arms was.

He changed it for a pair of workman's trousers, glad he *did* have that set of civvies. A ruffed white shirt and, well, his uniform boots were plain-looking and as good as any. One of Fleming's aides had given him an automatic .40 in a shoulder-holster, telling him to get used to wearing it. He strapped that on, practiced drawing, threw on a black coat over that, and a cowboy hat he'd bought a while ago as a souvenir and never gotten around to taking to the apartment in Denver.

The phone rang again.

"Vice Perry."

"Sir, this is Captain Adrian. Response company, sir. You had an emergency in Dodge?"

"Yes. Two things. One, I need transport there. *Now.*"

"Checked that, sir. Oil train leaving in about ten minutes. Told them to hold for your party. And you'll want some of my men, I trust."

"Give me a platoon. Have them change into civilian clothes, and I need them *now.*"

"Armed, sir?"

"Of course I want them armed!" Perry thought for a minute. The Army captain was correct: rifles would get in the way and be overly visible.

"You're mechanized infantry, correct?"

"Dragoons, sir, yes. First of the Forty-third. Charlie Company."

"The vehicle crews have submachineguns. Your line infantry know how to handle `em?"

"Cross-train all the time, sir. I'll have the platoon draw them from the arsenal and bring personal backpacks, satchels, whatever conceals them best."

"Good job, captain. Meet my men at the station in ten minutes. I'll explain the objective to your officer."

"Heard your squadron lost an airship, sir. Figure you got a lead on getting it back, from what Sergeant Golding said."

"Correct. Get those men ready. Remember, they're to look like civilians. We're going into the Boot District to make an

112

arrest and recover the airship, *not* to start a brawl."

"On it, sir."

* * *

Rafferty seemed at least a little more sober when Perry met him inside the officers' mess; he was chewing on a fried chicken leg. With him was Vescard, dressed in yellow roughnecks' overalls and a cowboy hat.

"Heard from the Specialist here that 4-106's been found, sir," said Vescard. "We're coming along to get it back. With you. If you don't mind."

"We?"

Swarovski came out of the men's room, buttoning a horrendously-bright lime-green shirt.

"Swav and I, sir."

"You armed?"

"Just our service pistols," said Swarovski.

"Speak for yourself, Swav," said Vescard, pulling a massive – eighteen inches long, and *solid* – wrench from a leg-pocket of the coveralls.

"Oh, I've got a knife." Swarovski pulled his issue multitool, which included a five-inch blade.

"That ain't a knife, sir," said Rafferty, taking a Bowie from his coveralls. "*This* is a knife."

"When you gentlemen are finished arguing over the specific definition of 'knife'," Perry said, "we *do* have an airship to recover."

"Right, sir," said Rafferty. "But just so the lieutenant knows, my knife's better than his. Sir."

"Another drink for the road?" The mess bartender produced two beers, pushing them in the direction of Swarovski and Vescard.

"Don't mind if I do," said Rafferty, taking one of the beers and pouring it into his mouth.

Swarovski and Vescard looked at each other.

"Yes," Swarovski told the bartender, and gestured for Vescard to take the other beer.

"*How* drunk are the two of you?" Perry asked.

"Not very," said Swarovski.

"Less than he is," said Vescard.

113

"Then you don't need another one. We've got a train. Come *on.*"

Vescard put the empty beer-glass down. Swarovski took his glass and drank as he walked, putting it down on a table in the mess anteroom.

Halvorsen was waiting outside the mess with Vidkowski. Both were dressed in civvies.

"You're coming along too," Perry said resignedly. At least these two looked sober.

"Ran into Raff on his way here, sir," said Vidkowski.

"Very well." Perry sighed, glanced at his watch. "We're holding up a train. Let's *go.*"

* * *

The supply train was a line of about twenty tanker cars, loaded with oil and natural gas from the Hugoton fields. Near the railyard was a plant where the all-important helium was separated from the oilfields' other products: natural gas and crude oil. Another plant – working three shifts, alongside the oil wells – turned the crude oil into heating oil, which would power engines and heat buildings. More crude was shipped straight to Dodge, where it would be refined at plants there into other products.

Attached to the end, just fore of the caboose, was a third-class passenger car. About thirty-five men in a mix of civilian clothing and carrying a mess of bags – but almost all in their twenties and early thirties, all of them Army – sat or stood inside of it.

A man in neater civilian clothing, aged about twenty-five, saluted the group as they approached.

"Vice-Commodore Perry, sir?" he said to Halvorsen.

"I'm Perry," said Perry.

"Sorry, sir. Lieutenant Harrison, sir. Third Platoon, Second Response. Here to help secure your airship, sir."

"Staff Sergeant MacGreg," said an older man. "Military police." He – and three others – were dressed in dull dark-blue slacks and black shirts. They were all in their late twenties and thirties. "My people here, too. Captain Adrian detailed us alongside Lieutenant Harrison's platoon. Sir."

"Good of him to," said Perry. "That train's waiting on us?"

114

"Yessir, it is. Should have left a couple minutes ago."

Perry boarded, followed by the others from his squadron.

"This is Specialist Third Rafferty," Perry said to MacGreg and Harrison. MacGreg eyed Rafferty unaffectionately; Rafferty gave the MP a broad grin.

Natural enemies, the two of them, thought Perry.

"Rafferty was in the Boot District with a friend of his, when he heard about the pirate who'd stolen my airship."

"Boot District's off-limits," said MacGreg.

"I've spoken to him about it," Perry said. He raised his voice. "This woman is named Karen Ahle. For those of you who haven't heard the story, a line-class airship designated 4-106 was hijacked Tuesday. The pirate has been identified and I was assigned this afternoon to apprehend her and bring the ship back. This is a stroke of luck."

"We're gonna bust a pirate?" an Army man asked excitedly.

"Damned right we are," said Rafferty. "And *hang* the thieving bitch! With a rope!"

"We're going to apprehend her according to the tip Specialist Rafferty gave us," said Perry. "We are then going to find the location of the airship and secure her until a flight crew can arrive to bring her back."

"Fly her back ourselves, perhaps," said Swarovski.

"Probably not," said Perry. Although that *was* a thought.

"You want me to send one section to secure the airship while the other goes with you for the pirates?" asked Harrison.

The train was picking up speed, moving fast. They passed a trio of oil derricks, big and floodlit as their pumps swung up and down. A roughneck on a platform waved, and the train tooted its horn in reply.

"No," said Perry. "One team can accompany - Lieutenant Vescard and Warrant Halvorsen, I think. To identify 4-106 at the airship park. I expect Ahle to offer more resistance. She and her crew may be drunk; they're also pirates and we can expect them all to be well-armed. Piracy is a capital crime, to make this clear. If resistance is offered, shoot to kill immediately."

He lowered his voice.

"Lieutenant Harrison, your platoon has been doing patrols. I understand the protocol is to arrest any civilians trying to get through?"

"Usually just some lost cowboy," said Harrison. "But

there's two fence lines, and it doesn't happen often. We've never had serious trouble."

"Very well. Sergeant MacGreg, please have your men give the Army soldiers basic instruction, in what time we have, in making arrests."

"Wish we had time to get a full MP platoon together," MacGreg muttered.

"We don't," Perry said.

He was impressed it was happening this fast. *Twenty minutes ago* he'd been asleep in bed. Now he was in a train, speeding across the Kansas plains to Dodge City, where - hopefully - he and this platoon would accomplish what he'd expected to take weeks of tricky and unfamiliar spy-work.

This is a godsend, he thought. *Rafferty's discovery.*

I did not *think it would actually be this easy!*

* * *

"We've got a crew," Cannon reported.

"And I found us some roughs. Couple of them have engine experience," said Marko. He was trailed by six of them; industrial ne'er-do-wells, the sort of men he found most useful. He'd have identified with them more if they *were* actually any good at what they did, but each man served Discordia in his own way. Knowingly or unknowingly.

These ones just wanted a quick buck without too much hard work. He hadn't bothered to tell them that they were going to do a reconnaisance flight over one of the best-guarded military bases on the continent. They'd learn that when they got there; if they were unhappy with the fact, hopefully they'd brought parachutes.

"We gonna kill someone?" Rienzi asked. "Hard bunch we got here. Yeah, and we found a third kinnyscope. Fence let us have it for a couple hundred bucks; loot from some ship someone took."

"We're gonna wipe out a pirate crew," said Marko. "Hang back and let me go in first. We kill them all to avoid pursuit, blow their ship just in case they got friends elsewhere. Jack the other ship and go."

"How long you think it'll take to fully inflate?" Cannon asked. "No park's gonna allow a ship to sit parked, gassed-up.

116

Too much of a fire risk. They'll check for these things."

"Helium bird," said McIlhan. "Remember? Imperial warship. No trouble with inflation, just got to get the buoyancy even." She smirked. "*Fuck* it's gonna be good to go back to Hugoton."

"You know how to operate a flasher?" Marko asked.

"Had signals training. Not airships, but ground signaling's the same. I can handle it."

"And read them?"

"Adequately, boss. When do we go out?"

"Men right now are packing and arming," said Cannon. "Everyone's gonna be go in about twenty minutes."

"An *Imperial* ship," Marko giggled. "Fitting."

Chapter Eight

"Dodge City was a messy cattle town and a violent hellhole as far back as 1870. Just goes to show that nothing ever changes. We've got oil and natural gas as well as cattle, now - and we've also got roughnecks as well as cowboys, pirates as well as outlaws. Our department doesn't have a retirement fund, we have a tontine."

Dodge County Undersheriff Pete MacNamara, 1961.

Perry's train didn't stop at a platform. It was a regularly-scheduled freight run to Kansas City, and the engineer simply halted for a minute at a convenient point along the line and allowed the men to pile out. They crossed a couple of tracks and found themselves on a bitumen road in a street of shabby industrial terrace-houses.

The soldiers of Third Platoon spread out, instinctively forming a perimeter around Perry's men and the MPs.

"So one of my fire-teams goes with two of your men to locate the airship?" Harrison asked.

"Locate and identify," Perry directed. "If there are crew aboard or nearby, do *not* engage unless she looks like she's going to lift. The priority is to take the captain and prevent the airship from departing. Do what it takes to achieve that. Take cabs."

"I know where the port is. I *think* I know where we are," said Vescard.

"I know both," said Halvorsen. "I'll take the lead, sir?"

Vescard gave a curt nod.

"Bravo section, Team One. Lance Innis," said Lieutenant Harrison.

"With him, sir," said a blond man. "You heard the flying officer, boys. Follow those two. Permission to depart, sir?"

"Move," Perry gestured. He turned to Rafferty.

"Where's this place?"

"If I got us right, about half a mile from here. It's gonna be dives and shit, and forty of us *are* gonna attract notice."

118

Perry looked at MacGreg.

"He's got a point, sir."

"Very well. Rafferty, you and I will go ahead, with one of the lieutenant's teams. A section will follow at about forty yards with the lieutenant. The last team will go with the MPs forty yards behind that."

"Understood, sir," said MacGreg.

"Bravo second, go with the Vice-Commodore," Harrison said. "Alpha section is with me. Sergeant Charkin, please take Bravo third and accompany the MPs. You heard the lieutenant about pacing yourselves."

"And, Army boys," Rafferty said, "try not to march? I know you lot make a big deal about that, but walk casually. Like you've had a few drinks, right? You boys can't hold your booze, so that shouldn't be too hard to pretend."

Sergeant MacGreg glared at Rafferty. So did Perry.

"Let's get moving," Perry said. "I hope your friend's still there."

* * *

It was late, about four thirty, but Dodge was the kind of place that never completely shut down. Cowboys returning from long drives, and the constant shift workers, men who worked from six in the evening until two in the morning and, consequently, were only about a couple of hours into their after-work drunk.

They walked past sleazy flophouses, a concrete fortress of a sheriff's department building, bars of noisy patrons. For *most* of Dodge City, it was relatively late at night, and the general tone of the drunkenness had gone from the jovial noise of a few hours earlier, to a glassy-eyed sullenness.

They passed a couple of men passed out in the street, one down on his face in the gutter with a stab-wound in his back. There was shouting, and once they had to skirt around a bar-brawl that had spilled into the street. A few times they heard gunshots.

Despite what Perry wanted to think, he could feel they were being watched. Groups of men marching with purpose weren't, he hoped, too rare in Dodge City. Shippers or cowboys out to settle a score for their crew or their ranch. He just hoped

119

that breaking the group up would keep them from drawing *too* much attention.

"Sleazy place," Swarovski said, as they passed a whorehouse. Noises came loudly from the inside.

"Fun, though, sir," said Rafferty. "You ought to come here. Lot of gambling happens."

"High stakes?" Swarovski asked with interest.

"Sometimes. Once saw a man bet five hundred beef on a single hand."

Perry kept the pace up, gesturing for Rafferty to keep them moving. This was a shithole, to him. Most cities had underbellies like this - Dodge was arguably more underbelly than not - but he avoided the places. They were what his parents had worked and self-educated their way out of, and why he had studied so hard himself. They existed, but you didn't need to acknowledge them often.

The sort of trash who'd choose to hang out in places like this - well, Rafferty was a well-intentioned delinquent whose mindset, Perry acknowledged, was still foreign to his own. Lieutenant Swarovski, who was a gambler and a drinker but, when you came down to it, a gentleman, might come slumming once in a while for the novelty of it. But the ones who considered these places their home environment, the men swilling whisky in the bars and getting two-dollar lays in the whorehouses? How *could* you go through life with this as your bar for civilization? Why would anyone not do as his parents had, or as he would have if he'd been born to this kind of environment – find steady work, join a military service, educate yourself, achieve at least the middle class?

The alcohol helped, he supposed. Helped you tolerate it, and hindered your leaving.

They let themselves get trapped, he thought, with a mixture of pity and contempt. *And I guess they get used to it.*

"We got a specific plan for when we get there?" asked the lance-corporal in charge of Bravo section's Second fire-team. Named Turley, he was in his late twenties, with a thin red moustache. On a strap from his shoulder hung a leather attache-case containing a Sterling submachinegun.

"Wait for your main body to secure the exits. Vidkowski, when we arrive, tell the lieutenant that he's to spread his men around the buildings. And rooftops – can't forget rooftops. The

MPs join us, and the other section acts as an outer perimiter."

"Got it, sir," said Vidkowski.

"You want us to go first, sir?" Turley asked. "Trained combat soldiers, we are. And used to taking a bullet or two. Unlike you airshipmen, with respect, sir."

"We fought a boarding action yesterday, Lance," said Swarovski. "It was up close and personal. The Vice here, he stabbed a man in the throat and shot two more at point-blank."

Turley looked impressed.

"Wow, sir? Really? I always thought you airship types fought a more, like, distant kind of engagement. Like the artillery wallahs, you know?"

"Only when things go right, Lance-Corporal," said Perry. "The fact that we're here right now is proof that they don't, isn't it?"

"Ah, sir, but proof they come right eventually," said Rafferty. "And by the way, we're coming up on it. That building to the right, all the green decorations? That's the Foster Arms, sir."

The building Rafferty indicated was an uncharacteristically nice place for the area; clean and neater, with glass windows and bright electric lights on the outside. Gilt letters on a wooden bar, and the front room was bustling even at this hour.

Across the road was a sleazy bar. A man with an expensive frock coat over a set of workers' coveralls, a pair of goggles around his neck and silver-adorned rubber boots, came out smoking a cigar. He staggered as he crossed the road, plucked the cigar from his mouth and raised it in salute.

"Sir!" he said to Perry. "You're outta uniform, sir!"

"Ducks!" said Rafferty. "You OK?"

"I'm more than fuckin' OK, Raff! I'm good! Look what I won." He gestured at the coat. "Fucker was outta money, wanted to raise, put his coat on the table. Nice coat, wouldn't you say?"

"Not the same boots you started the night with," Rafferty observed.

"He raised those, too. After we figured he was my size and I could use 'em. Gave him my old pair. Silver on these!"

"You're hammered," Perry said.

"Am, sir! That's the truth, alright! Fact is, sir, couldn't just hang around and not draw notice. In a bar, I was."

"We can tell, Duckworth," said Perry. "Is our – *friend* still there?"

"Didn't see `em leave, I guess. No bunch of `em."

Lieutenant Harrison and his section caught up with Perry's group. Perry gestured at the bar.

"Ring out and surround the exits. Send a man off to find the Dodge sheriffs."

"Kinley, you heard the Vice."

Perry drew his automatic.

"I'm going in. Those who are coming, follow me."

* * *

The party was still going, although with a more subdued tone. Happy roistering had become a few knots of serious conversation, while some of the other crew and their guests played poker. Hollis and Petersen had tried to drum up a four for bridge, without much luck; they were now playing a somewhat tipsy chess variant, occasionally throwing dice to determine the outcome of a particular move. Ronalds had kept to himself, slowly sipping beer and smoking a chain of Cubans. Every so-often he glanced out the window.

"Look, after this much bad blood, a diplomatic solution *just isn't possible*," Ahle was saying to Pete Augustin. "The Feds *say* they want to integrate the South, but do you see any signs of it?"

"They elect legislators, don't they?"

"And they limit the franchise so absurdly that nobody takes it seriously," said Ahle. "Now, if they were to stop saying that family of anyone who'd been involved in an incident couldn't vote, they might have *respected* delegations. But then the people we'd send to Congress would make deals to let us secede anyhow."

"Or just make it worthwhile for us to stay in the Union. Slavery's *gone*, Captain, and it's not coming back. So what's the fight over?"

"It stopped being about slavery when the Crash hit. This is about our rights as free states," said Ahle.

Suddenly, Ronalds froze.

"*Shit*," he said. "There's people. Outside. Packing something. Spreading out."

"Who?" Ahle asked. She was tipsy – Ronalds didn't seem to be at all drunk, he'd been his usual guard-dog self when she was around – and slowed. "Those little Japanese fellows in black with the swords?"

"None of them this side of the Rockies," Ronalds growled, pacing fast across the room to the front door. The noise in the bar seemed to have abruptly stopped. That wasn't a good sign. "Walk like Imperials. Imperials in civvies."

Shit. She'd feared this. But how could the Imperials have known?

"We get *out* of here, then!" Hollis said.

Ahle – a bit unsteady on her feet, but you couldn't choose, *should have drunk in the fucking Black Hills, should have held the celebration there and had better security when I had to leave the ship!* – drew her own pistols, cocked the revolver and then primed the pressure-gun. A glance at the ticker on that showed gel rounds; good. She'd not kill Imperials unless she was forced to.

Hollis was going through the door that led to the kitchen and the back exit; Ronalds was moving to the closed door to the common-room, getting ready to cover them. Pistol in his hand.

Suddenly the double-doors to the common room were kicked open, the lock breaking. Men with pistols and submachineguns burst in, spreading across the room. Leading them was a black man in plain clothing, two-handedly gripping an automatic pistol.

It took her a moment to recognize him as the Imperial vice-commodore from the bridge of the airship.

"You're under arrest, the lot of you! Pirates!"

From the back came noise and shouting. A burst of gunfire.

"Throw down your guns!" the vice-commodore yelled. "Captain Ahle, you are charged with capital piracy against an Imperial ship!"

"Guns down!" said a moustached young man who looked to be in charge of these soldiers. "Guns down or we kill every last one of you where you stand!"

The vice-commodore walked over to Ahle. His gun was pointed squarely at her head.

Ahle let the pistols fall out of her hands, one after the other, onto the rug at her boots.

"Against that wall. All of you. Hands in the air!"

Against the wall. More men came in, Imperials in plain clothes.

Oh, hell. I knew this had gone too smoothly.

"Cuff them, MacGreg!"

One after the other, the plain-clothed Imperials fitted solid handcuffs tightly around everyone in the room.

"I'm no pirate," said Hollis. "I was just a guest! Not a member of her crew."

A few other voices came up in agreement.

"Wrong place at the wrong time and it was never you, huh?" the black Imperial vice-commodore said.

"That's just right, sir."

"You'll get a fair trial. The British Empire does not conduct summary court-martials outside of emergency circumstances. If you are found to be innocent, you will be released with due compensation."

"Anyone who consorts with pirates is guilty of something," growled another man. "You'll hang."

"Shot while trying to escape, MacGreg? If they give you the opportunity, please feel free," said the vice-commodore coldly. "You pirates hear that? This is your town, but if your friends are looking at springing you, they are invited to try. My men are under instructions to cut you down if you look like you're *thinking* of running. So don't."

This is the vice-commodore whose ship I took, Ahle thought. *Oh, hell. He's pissed.*

Since when have Air Service vice-commodores supervised arrest squads?

Something occurred to her.

"Vice-Commodore," she said.

"Ahle." He pointed the gun at her face again. "How does it feel, *Captain* Ahle, for the gun to be in the *other* hand?"

"It was better the first time, really. But what you really want is your ship back, correct? How about a trade?"

"We don't trade with criminals. You're taking me to the ship."

"What, to sell out my crew?" Ahle sneered. "Hang me and the hell with you, Imperial. I'm not trading my peoples' lives for personal clemency."

"I didn't offer you personal clemency," the vice-commodore said.

"Sir!" came a young man's voice. "Lieutenant Harrison, sir? Sir!"

"Private Rook," said the moustached leader of the soldiers.

"Sir! That warrant sent me from the airfield. Sir, we found the ship but there's fighting! Someone attacking the pirates there! Shooting and everything!"

The vice-commodore straightened up as though he'd been electrocuted.

"Not Vescard. Vescard didn't attack on his *own*, did he?"

"Not your engineer, sir! No! Some other bunch that came in a line of trucks! There's a fight all over the ships, the pirate's one and the one your engineer said was your 4-106. Whole lot of gunmen."

"Pirates robbing pirates? I am *not* losing my ship. How'd you get here?"

"Lance-Corporal Innis told a man to give me his horse or else, sir."

"Take us back there. Quick march! Harrison! Leave one of your teams to guard the pirates. MacGreg, stay and help. Guard them, take them to the sheriff's cells when one of them shows up. Understood, MacGreg?"

"Clear, sir."

"Except for this one." The vice-commodore indicated Ahle. "Their captain's coming with me. Vidkowski, she's your responsibility."

"Aye, sir," said a stringy-looking man Ahle recognized as having been on the airship's bridge.

"Get transport! Commandeer vehicles and let's *move*! Private, which way?"

* * *

Marko carefully wiped the blood off his last knife, concealed it back in his sleeve. The pirates, about sixty of them, had been half-drunk and half-asleep, and it had been far less a battle than a butchery.

That was, of course, after carefully slitting the throats of any port staff who might give the alarm. Which would unhappify the mercenaries, but wasn't that just an incentive for them to stay with him, another option crossed off the list for if they didn't?

125

"Get those kinematographs into the rocket bays!" Ferrer was shouting. Directing a crew unloading the heavy things from their trucks.

"Signed up to fight or steer. Not smash boxes," one man growled.

"You do as the boss says or I'll blow your lazy head off," Rienzi told the man, pointing his revolver at that man's head.

"Captain Caine," Marko said.

A weathered man in his fifties, with short grey hair and a well-worn rig, appeared. He looked rather askance at the butchery that had taken place through the bunkhouse.

"The old crew," Marko explained. "You're in charge of the new crew. Pre-flight this Imperial piece of shit. We're lifting outta here pronto."

"Right, uh, mister. Pronto."

* * *

The drivers of the two steam-trucks they'd commandeered hadn't been happy. Driving a steam-truck was work - you had to keep fueling the boiler via a foot-pump, while steering and maintaining speed - and these two had been nearing the end of their shift of ferrying materials between the freight terminal and an outlying factory.

Perry had thrown some money at one of them and stuck a gun in his ear. Frantic.

"*Now!*" he yelled. "By Imperial authority, I said!"

"Fuck you, mister. Wait, that's a *ten!*"

"That's for your company owner," Perry said, as the man did hit the release and his truck began to roll again. Men were all over the rear of it. "I'll have two more for you personally if you get us there *fast!* I'll also reimburse damage, just *get us to that ship!*"

"Yes *sir!*" said the driver.

Perry turned to Captain Ahle, who was in the crew-sized cab with Vidkowski. Vidkowski's gun, he noticed approvingly, had never been more than six inches from the pirate's back. He knew *exactly* how tricky this pirate was.

"Who might be attacking your crew, Captain Ahle? Or *my ship?*"

"I have no idea," Ahle said. Her own expressions, since

126

learning of the attack, had been shock. Perry believed her.

"Who *might* be? Rival pirates? Do you have any known enemies? Because they're about to get wiped out, if you do; I have a fighting platoon here. Think of it as a small consolation."

"There are always rival pirates," Ahle said evenly. "This sort of behavior is very much against the Code, and will bring down trouble."

"Pirates seek out trouble."

"Not this kind. It isn't profitable."

The truck-driver rounded a sharp corner. Twenty dollars would be about a week's pay for him; making that much in twenty minutes was a *great* deal from the driver's perspective, and he was earning it.

Perry made a note to give the man twenty-five. They were approaching the airship park; various ships' electrical top- and side-lights could be seen, towering high above them. The ground became empty, bumpy dirt.

"This way, sir," said Private Rook, pointing. "Yeah. This way."

The steam-truck rocketed between two freighters, each five hundred yards long and towering high enough to completely blot out the sky. Steel cables held them down, running between deep-set concrete blocks through the keels of their cabins. Past an unlit shanty, half-underground, where crews without money might sleep, or goods might be stored. Then another unlit shanty.

"There!"

In the moonlight, silhouetted, was 4-106. Two extra steering vanes had been added, and so had a lot of bright paint. A casual job of deception, but probably good enough for most.

She was wobbling. Buoyancy adjustment. Getting ready to lift. Still cabled down, but men moving around now.

"Take us in," Perry said. "Take us *right* in. We're going to evict whoever the hell has taken my ship." He glared at Ahle. "Having already arrested the *first* person to."

* * *

"Looks like we got trouble coming." McIlhan gestured, from 4-106's bridge, at the two steam-trucks that were approaching at speed.

"Those pirates' friends?" Rienzi asked.

"None of them got away to give the alarm," said Cannon. "There was that group sorta hovering around the distance near the other ship, though. *Their* friends?"

"Something going on we don't know about?" McIlhan asked.

"Who gives a fuck?" Cannon asked. "You two know how to use a pressure-gun?"

"I'm an engineer," Rienzi boasted. "I can learn *anything*."

"Learn to use a pressure-gun *now*. Get down into that fore turret and fucking kill them, whoever they are. Hey! How's prep going?"

"Engines heating well," came a reply. "Two minutes!"

"Hold them off for two minutes. And then blow the fuck out of that other ship, the pirates' one. But those other people might know something. *Waste them.*"

* * *

The fore pressure-gun mount turned. If Perry hadn't been intently focused on 4-106's bridge, and the people he could see moving about in there, he might have missed it.

"*Guns!*" he shouted instead. "Brake and bail!"

The first burst fired high, missing completely. The truck driver brought the vehicle to a screeching halt, kicking up the hard-packed dust and spinning the truck ninety degrees. Men were thrown around and off.

The second burst of pressure-gun fire, *poum-poum-poum-poum-poum*, riddled the truck, smashing tires and boiler. Perry threw himself out, hitting the dirt ground and rolling. 4-106's cabin was two hundred yards away, and whoever was inside *definitely* did not want visitors.

They were prepping for flight. He could see that now, as a man ran along the stanchions and disconnected one of the heavy cables, then toward another. Boiler going hot.

At best, they had five minutes before the ship lifted.

More pressure-gun fire came, smashing into the truck but missing the men on the ground. One heavy ball ricocheted off a piece of inset concrete and into the air.

"Permission to return fire, sir?" Lieutenant Harrison asked,

128

running over and throwing himself down.

"Do what it takes. We're taking my airship back. Fire and movement. Assault. Whatever."

Harrison nodded harshly and started yelling orders.

"With me, Vice. Leapfrog attack. We're gonna distract that fucking P-gun."

4-106 began to rock slightly, a sure sign that engines were powering. Yes. One of the propellers was spinning. No. All three of the starboard-side ones were.

Some of the soldiers opened fire on the pressure-gun turret. The turret turned, fired back, the balls kicking up thick clouds of dust in the air as they hit dirt. Every third one was a tracer, its abrasive phosphorous surface ignited by progress through the barrel. Those blazed bright orange as they flew through the darkness.

"Go!" Harrison yelled, and leapt up. Perry followed a second later, running forward at 4-106 as the other men fired.

"Fifty yards and *down!*" Harrison said. He carefully aimed at the bridge, fired a burst. The other men from his section did the same. Perry considered helping with a pistol round but no, at a hundred and fifty yards that wouldn't even be a distraction.

These pressure-gunners were not, Perry thought, very good. They didn't know to bounce the rounds, although in dirt that wouldn't have done very much. They were firing randomly and ineffectively; as far as suppressive fire went, it was terrible.

One of the bridge windows opened, and a man with a rifle leaned out. He sighted on one of the other section, running, and fired.

"Shit! Meval's down! Meval is fucking down!" cried one of the soldiers.

"Run!" Harrison yelled.

4-106's propellers were rotating fast now, and lights were on along the length of the ship. Perry leapt up, ran forwards. A pressure-gun ball hit the ground just in front of him, dust exploding up and choking his face. He ran, firing, as 4-106 started to lift.

"Down, Vice," Harrison screamed. "Get fucking down!"

4-106 was lifting. The hell with that. He was *not* going to lose his ship a second time.

"Follow me!" he shouted. "Retake the ship!"

A few men did follow, as he ran for the airship. For the bridge, and the man with the rifle fired twice more, and someone screamed. Dust choked Perry's lungs, but he ran anyway as 4-106 lifted three, five, ten, fifteen feet off the ground, heavy ballast bags being pushed out.

More pressure-gun balls pounded into the dirt around Perry. The fore turret was a pair of heavy guns, built to penetrate armor; even a glancing hit would take his arm or leg off. He'd seen it happen.

He didn't care. He ran, as 4-106 lifted from the ground, ropes dangling, ballast harnesses trailing.

They are not going to take my ship a second time! Those pirates are not going to escape!

He fired up at the bridge as he approached under it, thirty-five feet high now and rising. Grabbed a rope, jumping to grab it, and felt himself pulled up.

His right hand dropped the pistol to take a better hold of the rope. He had a knife in his belt; that would have to be enough.

Gunfire around him, but the world consisted of the rope and the departing 4-106; he felt himself being pulled up above the dark dirt. His other hand pulled, and he began to climb.

"There's one here!" A voice from above, the missileers' catwalk behind the bridge. A man appeared, tall and thin and dressed in black. From thirty feet below, Perry could see that the man's teeth were broken, and that there was a large gold ring in his right ear.

"You'll hang, pirate!" Perry yelled. "You'll all hang, you bastards!"

"Of course. But not today!" The man on the catwalk reached down with a knife and cut at the rope. Perry climbed harder, forcing his strength into it, his ankles kicking and grasping for the tail end of the rope.

"Nice try, my friend. Now scream!"

The rope fell, Perry below it. He snarled a curse before the blackness hit.

* * *

Someone was holding three fingers in front of Perry's face.

130

He blinked a couple more times, shook his head, and looked up.

"How many fingers, Vice?" Rafferty's voice.

"Three. What the hell's going on?"

The fingers became a fist.

"How many now, sir?"

"A fist. None."

"He's *probably* OK."

"Where's 4-106?" Perry sat up. They were just outside one of the half-underground shacks in the landing area. Bodies were stacked nearby, dead pirates by the look.

Ahle was going down the stacks, still handcuffed, Vidkowski's pistol still pressed to her back. She seemed to be examining the corpses.

Perry raised an eyebrow at Swarovski.

"In shock, she is. That's all her crew. Her top ones were at the party. All the others were here. They're dead now."

Pirate scum or not; he had to admit, *he'd* be in complete shock if all his crew had been killed. For a moment, Perry almost felt sympathy for the pirate.

"You OK, sir?" asked a man in a civilian suit with a sheriff's star on the lapel.

"I should be fine. How long was I out?"

"About half an hour, sir," said Swarovski.

"They got away. They got away with 4-106. But they killed *her* crew?"

An image of that broken-toothed man with the earring, cutting the rope.

"All of them," Ahle snarled, whirling. "You took the *Adestria* back and they destroyed the *Aden* and they killed *all* my operating crew. Murdered them. With knives."

"You said you didn't know who," Perry asked, still dazed.

Ahle's wrists strained against the handcuffs. "It's not as though I can do anything now, but no! I don't have the faintest idea!"

Tall, broken-toothed man with an earring. Who stole 4-106.

Perry got to his feet.

"Sheriff?"

"Undersheriff. Vice-Commodore?"

"Yes."

"Your other pirates are in custody. One of your officers has ordered a car for your group on the next train."

"You're not unhappy about our coming into your jurisdiction and making arrests without advance notice? For which I apologize, but there was no time."

The undersheriff shrugged. "It's work off our hands, mister. Besides, Mayor Quentin does what your governor says; we know where our bread's buttered. Crimes out of our jurisdiction, caught inside our jurisdiction, we're not making a fight over it."

"Thank you, Undersheriff."

"We have transport at your disposal whenever you and your men would care to get moving. I also have an ambulance for your wounded. If you need it for yourself?"

"God. How many did we lose?"

"One killed," said Vescard. "Two of them wounded, badly. Those pressure-guns aren't nice to a human body."

"Do you know *who* it was?" The tall man with the earring. "Someone killed *her* crew to get 4-106. Who? Where? Why?"

"Now my crew has been murdered," Ahle said acidly, "and your ship has been stolen by the same unknown third party? Vice-Commodore Perry, don't you think you've accomplished what you came here for?"

Vidkowski jabbed the pirate in the back with his pistol.

"Not a chance in hell, lady."

"I don't know who it was that massacred your crew," said Perry, "although for what it's worth, I'm sorry. I don't begin to know why they stole 4-106. But I know one thing, *Captain* Ahle?"

"What's that? *Vice-Commodore* Perry?"

"I might not have my ship, but I have the bitch who stole it. And she's going to hang."

"At least my men provided the accidental courtesy of giving my name," Ahle hissed back. "Whoever stole your ship *again* never even gave that, did he?"

* * *

They'd timed it perfectly: the sun was rising behind them, the airship designated 4-106 and painted *Adestria*, as they floated over the perimeter lines and into Hugoton at eight thousand feet.

132

"Nose camera, check," Ferrer said. The kinematograph had pride of place on the bridge, pointed down and recording their flight over the installations. Every so-often Ferrer stuck a precisely-calibrated watch in front of the lens for a second or two.

"Starboard camera reports check," said McIlhan from the communications board. "Port reports check."

"Keep them rolling," said Marko. He stood at the front of the bridge, not bothering to give Captain Caine much room to see. He knew the course, that was enough. "We're getting some *good* reconnaissance here. All the lines are sharper at dawn."

"Military headquarters is flashing us," said McIlhan, looking through a scope.

"What're they saying?"

"Asking us to identify."

The first thing they'd done, once airborne, had been to get rid of the dummy vanes. The paint was still there, but – with the sun right behind them – that wouldn't even be too visible. 4-106's engineering was distinctive enough that it should have been identified easily. Probably had been.

"Tell them 4-106," said Marko. "That's us. Rienzi, take two men and man the aft pressure-guns."

"We can man the missiles, too," said Captain Caine. "You gave us enough men, Mr. Marko."

"No. Our role is photography. Missiles only if required."

"You don't mind my asking, why you doing this detailed reconnaisance of the Hugoton Lease anyhow?" asked Caine.

Marko glared at him. It was a frightening look, and the middle-aged captain withstood it for less than a second before turning away and apologizing.

"Because I said to," said Marko. "Now power us along, turn to port once we're past the main installations and then cross those oil facilities. Then, into the Rockies. *Understood?*"

* * *

There had been an exchange of signals – McIlhan saying that the airship had been recovered, claiming to be an Imperial crew, but damaged steering - but that had only lasted so long. After 4-106 had passed over the second large set of oil installations – the Hugoton Lease itself was *vast*, a   two

133

thousand square mile area that hopefully, at this mile-and-a-half of altitude they were getting most of the important parts of – they scrambled two scout-class airships to investigate.

"Your behavior is not consistent with steering issues. Sure you are OK? Land immediately. Cut sacs if needed," McIlhan reported.

"Let them approach close. *Very* close," Marko said. "Then blow them to hell."

The scout-class captains were careless, or perhaps their airships were just shoddy in the first place. Heavy fire from Rienzi at the pressure-guns – at four hundred yards' range, where it could barely miss – destroyed the bridge of one and then the other, and more solid shot from the guns smashed the gondolas and wrecked the scout-classes' airworthiness. Four missiles finished the job, as more pressure-gun fire pounded into the scout-classes' engine rooms and gondolas.

Within a minute of the engagement starting, without their getting a shot off themselves, the scout-class ships were on burning crash-courses toward the grass of central Hugoton.

"Power us up, starboard and *move*," Marko ordered the captain.

"We got a destination?"

"Happens that we have. For now, I want maximum speed. Those Imperial sons of bitches are going to scramble something serious next, and ready to take us. Do *you* want to be there when that happens?"

"Fucking fuck," said one of the hirelings. "We just fucking killed a pair of Imperials!"

Marko waved a finger at Ferrer's kinematograph, which was still recording – in detailed color – everything visible from the nose of the airship, slowly panning back and forth across a ninety-degree arc.

"Time they're done analyzing this into tacti-thingummy maps and using those," Marko said, "whole *fuck* of a lot more Imperials are gonna die."

"You gonna kill someone, kill Feds," said Captain Caine. "Imperials are just goons; Feds are the real jackbooters."

Marko giggled.

"Oh, we're gonna kill us some Feds, too. Worse than kill `em; we're gonna *beat* `em!"

Fleming straightened up in his chair as though he'd been hit by lightning.

"Tall. Black dress. Broken teeth and a gold earring?" he repeated back to Perry. "Are you *sure*?"

"Yes, sir. You know this man?"

"Long, flowing moustache? Although he may have shaved it off."

"I think he had one, sir. And *he took 4-106 over Hugoton?*"

"We have photographic confirmation. Shot down the ready flight of Thirty-Second Squadron, too. They thought he was *you.*"

"I know, sir. I heard the full account of it from Vice Begley. Nine killed. He wasn't happy with me, either. Somehow he was convinced *I* did it until he heard the affidavits."

Deputy Director Ian Fleming leaned back in his chair and steepled his fingers.

"Oh, no," he said. "Someone far more dangerous than you did it, Vice-Commodore. If you're correct. I thought he was *dead!*"

"You know this man."

"Connery," Fleming said to the aide, hovering in the background. "Three martinis, please. Stirred–"

"Softly, sir. Yessir," said Connery. Going over to the liquor cabinet. "Not shaken. Understood, sir."

"Thank you."

Fleming was silent until the drinks had been prepared. When they were, he sipped his.

"Yes, Vice-Commodore. I know Theron Marko."

"Theron who?"

"Theron Marko," Fleming said slowly. "I thought he'd been killed in `58. It was on record that he'd been killed in `58."

"You sound as though you know the man personally." A double-heartbeat. "Sir."

"Years ago. In the `40s. An episode on the Caspian. He has… appeared in our files since then. And before. He's suspected, not confirmed, of being involved with the murder of Her Majesty's first son. Not proven. If he's active, *here*…"

"You're implying a dangerous man." As though any other type could have stolen 4-106 from under his nose.

Again.

"Tell me about him," Perry said. "You have files. Give me his. I'm going to find him. Dangerous or not. *He stole my airship*. And murdered *two* of Thirty-Second's."

"I'll give you more than his file," said Fleming. "I'll give you a partner."

Fleming pushed the phone buzzer on his desk.

Captain Ahle, her hands cuffed in front of her now, came in, prodded by the aide named Moore, who held a sawn-off shotgun to the back of her neck.

"Take a seat, Captain."

"Deputy Director Fleming," said Ahle. "I've always wondered what your office looked like."

"Captain Ahle. Please, take a drink. You can hold a drink when handcuffed; I know from personal experience."

Ahle reached forward, picked the glass up with her handcuffed wrists, and took a long sip.

"Captain Ahle, I'm going to dismiss my aides. May I first point out two things?" said Fleming. "One, there is nothing within two seconds' reach of you that you might conceivably use as a weapon given your handcuffed state. Given that you are not a professional, I would say that there is nothing within *four* seconds' reach of you."

"And the other thing?"

"There is a loaded .45 within half a second's reach of *me*. Connery, Moore, you may leave."

"So what do you want?" Ahle asked. Bitterly. "My crew is dead. My officers are in captivity. My presence isn't necessary for your gloating."

"Your presence is necessary," said Fleming, "if you wish to earn your officers' lives. They are in our custody on charges of piracy. The evidence is compelling. We *will* find them guilty and they *will* hang. Unless."

Ahle was silent.

"Whoever murdered your crew also took photographic reconnaisance of the Hugoton Lease," said Fleming. "Our observers saw at least one kinematoscope. This was presumably the purpose of the flyover, and may have been the purpose of 4-106's theft. I also understand the theft may have been conducted by a high-level Russian field operative named Marko. Him, or someone actively trying to resemble him. The report of the knifework done on your crew implies it *was* him."

"Enemy of my enemy," said Ahle.

"Exactly. I have here a vice-commodore who does not know the scene, who had intended to go underground to hunt you. He is a first-rate line officer but not much else. I have a situation where I *do not have* men available, because I have been using intelligence assets as killers, and even then just barely holding even with the Russians. I have" – Fleming sipped his drink – "a pirate captain whose top confederates we could find guilty and hang. If we so chose. Should I so choose?"

"I cooperate, and you don't hang my people," Ahle said slowly. "That's not good enough. They're not going to rot in prison for the rest of their lives; that's as bad. I'll cooperate within limits if you give them pardons. And me."

"Agreed," said Fleming.

"You can't do it that easily."

Fleming pushed a sheaf of papers across the desk at Ahle. Perry glanced at them; they were carte-blanche pardons, 'all crimes until this date', signed by Governor Lloyd but no countersignature.

What? They're going to pardon her?

"I've done it," said Fleming. "You're a two-bit pirate. With respect to Vice-Commodore Perry here and his personal irritation, you don't matter a damn relative to the man who killed your crew."

"You *know* the man who murdered my crew? Who is he?" Ahle demanded. "Let me loose and I'll rip his throat out." She paused for a moment. "And pardons for my officers, too, of course. And myself."

"I'm low on assets," Fleming said. "Blinded and crippled. Under normal circumstances I would never do this."

"You have a deal to make, Deputy Director Fleming. If it involves saving my officers, if it involves hurting whoever murdered my crew, I'm listening."

"Find Theron Marko. I do not know what he is doing on the Plains. Find that out. I know that the Russians would not activate him – I didn't realize he was still alive! – unless it were something important. He now has a warship and, apparently, a full reconnaissance of Hugoton."

Fleming sipped his drink. Then drained it, in one long chug.

He is not seriously offering her amnesty, Perry thought. *Let alone...*

"You'll work with Perry, who has already been assigned to the recovery of 4-106. You'll complement each other. Perry, do you have any objections to the recovery of 4-106 in this manner?"

You sneaky bastard. How can I say no?

"I have objections to working with a pirate. Sir."

"Overruled. You'll have worked with pirates anyhow, dealt with them as an undercover arms dealer. Do you want 4-106 back or not? Do you want to do your duty or not? You have been seconded to me. Your duty consists of what I say it is. Vice-Commodore, is that understood?"

"Sir. Yes sir."

"Very well. On the successful apprehension or confirmed death – I want his head physically in my hands, Ahle – of Theron Marko, I will have these pardons countersigned. For you and your officers. Otherwise, they will be tried, found guilty and hung."

"I'll cooperate. He murdered my crew."

Fleming looked at Perry.

You can't make me work with this pirate.

Fleming glared at Perry.

"Sir. I will do my duty. Sir."

Chapter Nine

"It continues to be the consensus of both the Royal and Imperial Academies of Science that powered, heavier-than-air flight is a physical impossibility. The laws of physics do not allow an engine to be built that will sustain its own weight to the necessary degree.

The aforementioned group of experimental physicists and rocketeers led by Sir Wernher Braun insist that one may in *theory* be developed, likely involving Sir Wernher's 'air jet' principle.

However, the members of both Academies stand in full unanimous consensus that *actual* powered heavier-than-air craft are, and will be, physically impossible."

- Conclusion of report to Parliament by Royal Commission 131; January, 1963.

The civilian clothes felt uncomfortable on Perry as he sat across from Ahle in a small booth of one of Hugoton's civilian restaurants. For her part, the pirate seemed at ease – although still upset, he gathered.

Losing all your crew will do that to you, he thought.

Then: *She's a pirate. Don't pity her. She chose to live by the sword. So did her people.*

"So, Vice-Commodore. Or are you now Agent Perry? Do we have a plan?"

"The airship went west," said Perry. "Rationally, I suppose we'd follow it. They'll have to put in for supplies somewhere."

"Have you been out there, past the Front Range?"

"A few times." Perry took a forkful of his omelette. It tasted as sour as this whole assignment had become. "Punitive jobs. Against pirates."

"You'd have only scratched the surface. There are a million places they can hide airships. There are more people than you think. Ranching and a *lot* of mining, and the support

139

infrastructure's there. Dispersed but present."

"You sound as though you've spent some time out there."

"Desert Navy. *Don't* tell me you haven't read Fleming's file. And since then. They mine gold out there." Ahle made a smile – or rather, *forced* one, and Perry realized that she must be as bitter about the last couple of days as he was. "Pirates like gold, you know."

"So do the people you steal it from. You don't like my plan."

Ahle raised a hand and began counting off fingers.

"One. We have an identity on the primary suspect. Two. I doubt he arrived in Hugoton with the crew he'd have needed to operate an airship; why bother, when he could easily hire the men here? Three. He *would* have hired the men here. He'd have talked to them. Some might have turned down the job."

"Especially if he'd *told* them the plan was to fly over Hugoton," Perry growled. "That kind of trash aren't for the most part *crazy*, in my experience."

"*If* he told them beforehand. You're assuming everyone's as reputable as I am."

"I'm not assuming you're reputable. Go on."

"Some might have turned the job down, and be around. Others might have overheard."

"We're relying on the word of itinerant pirate scum."

"You're relying on the *assistance* of itinerant pirate scum," Ahle said, gesturing at herself with the three raised fingers.

"Another problem crosses my mind," said Ahle.

"I'm listening."

"You weren't exactly subtle about your capture-Karen operation last night. By now, word all over town is that my officers and I are in Imperial custody. How do you think people are going to react if I suddenly appear, without my officers?"

Perry shrugged. "I doubt they'd recognize *me*."

"They wouldn't, but that's not my point. What do you think the Dodge undercity is going to do when they knew my officers and I were captured, my crew killed, and here am I running free?"

"Probably that you sold them out."

"There's a sense of honor among pirates, however little you want to believe it. Among *some* of us. All of my officers have friends. So do I, although they'd turn their backs if they had good reason to think I'd betrayed my people. So we need an explanation for that."

* * *

Fleming had reviewed the proposal an hour earlier. Now he called Perry in.

"An escape. Good plan. What I'd have thought of, but you're missing a few details."

He picked up a buzzer, spoke into it.

Admiral Richardson came into the room. Clearly having been prepared in the anteroom. She didn't sit down.

Fear rose in Perry's throat. Fleming hadn't offered him a drink this time, either. *This can only be bad...*

"She wouldn't have escaped without assistance," Fleming said. "Such as the assistance that a Vice-Commodore of the Air Service could provide."

Perry looked desperately up at his commanding officer. Her face was expressionless, but Richardson's face was *always* expressionless.

"But a Vice-Commodore of the Air Service would not just randomly provide such assistance," Fleming went on. "Why risk his career to save one pirate, even one he'd fallen for? However, a *disgraced* Vice-Commodore?"

"I'm sorry," said Richardson, her eyes avoiding Perry's. She handed him a printed form.

He didn't want to read it. He forced himself to.

Notice of Military Court-Martial, it said. *Suspicious loss of Airship DN 4-106.*

"This implies that I was in league with her *for my ship to be stolen in the first place!*" Perry exploded. "Fake or not, this is... ma'am!"

"Down, Marcus," Richardson said coldly. "Of course it's fake, but we're going to have to proceed as though it's real. The escape will be staged tonight. You will, unfortunately, have to be pursued. Some very real alert notices will be put out for you. This, for that matter, is a real charge as far as anyone below the level of Governor's Advocate knows."

"Ma'am. This is–"

"Not what you signed up for when you asked to be

reassigned to covert? You should have thought ahead. You got what you *asked* for."

"I told you we should have offered him a drink first," Fleming observed.

"Ma'am–" Perry began.

"You're going to request to be reassigned back to your squadron," Richardson said, and Perry's heart sank. *This is insane!*

"And you can guess my answer. You asked for this. It was important and essential to your duty, you said, and I agreed. Deputy Director Fleming has since convinced me – and the Governor's office – that the loss of 4-106 to a known high-level Russian agent represents a potentially serious threat to the security of Hugoton. This has gone from being a personal indulgence with the hope of a favorable outcome, to an essential duty."

She lowered her voice.

"Vice-Commodore Perry, you would not have risen to your present rank at your present age, without substantial ability. Nor substantial *duty*. The watchword of the Service is *duty*, Marcus. I could order you; I have ordered you. I am also reminding you that you should *know* to do this."

"You will be doing a duty to the Empire," Fleming agreed. He was pouring drinks now, from a bottle that must have been in his desk. "It'll go into your official files, of course. I understand that this sort of detached duty is viewed-upon very favorably by Service promotion boards."

"I have a reputation," Perry said. "I am not a criminal!"

"Your duty to the Empire exceeds personal vanity. *We* know you are not a criminal," said Fleming. "Your commander ordered you, but *I'm* appealing to your better nature and your professional self-interest."

I should refuse further, Perry thought, because this had gone from 'uncomfortable' to 'nightmarish.' Officially a fugitive? His name on watch lists?!

But what would be the point?

Orders were correct; the book existed for a reason.

How can this be correct!?

Stiff upper-lip. Think later. Orders are orders.

"Very well. Sir. Ma'am. I apologize for my outburst, Admiral Richardson. And beg your pardon, ma'am. And

Deputy Director Fleming, the same. Sir."

"Easily granted," Richardson said. She put a hand on his shoulder. "This *will* be favorable to your career, Vice-Commodore."

"Career be damned," Perry muttered. "It's not that I'm concerned about."

"Your reputation as well."

"Especially if he's successful," said Fleming. He looked at Perry. "*Be* successful. I have a bad feeling. If Theron Marko is involved, it is serious business and no mistake. *Damn* those DIS *idiots* for kicking off this war and blinding me right now, of all times!"

"You poured the Vice-Commodore a drink," said Richardson. "I think he needs it."

"I'm fine," Perry said. Shocked and horrified and disgusted, but – duty was duty.

That was the only rationale. Even when duty was –

He'd never imagined *this*. He'd never imagined the Service, the Crown, requiring that he sacrifice his reputation. His morals.

How can this be right?

His commanding officer, and a very senior Intelligence man, were saying it was. The people who defined his duty.

It's wrong and I hate it.

He swallowed. Hard, and again. There were thoughts he did not want to voice. There were appropriate words for this.

"Yes, ma'am," he repeated. "I'm fine. Ma'am." A look at Fleming, hoping it didn't show the shocked hatred he was scared he might be feeling toward the man right now. "And sir."

"Knew you'd come around," Fleming said. "Have a drink to that, then."

"To that, sir," Perry agreed. Took the Scotch, knocked it against Fleming's and the glass Ahle had been offered, and tipped the glass back.

It burned down his throat, but he needed it.

* * *

Two o'clock. Perry had been over the plan, step by step, with Moore. It had to look real. That meant, because enlisted

143

men did go to Dodge City and talk, that the plan had to *be* real.

I hate this. Words cannot begin to describe how much I loathe this idea.

Deputy Director Fleming had said it was necessary. Richardson had made it an order, although he was under Fleming's authority now. The personal tastes of one Vice-Commodore were not relevant to the equation, it had been made clear.

I have to do it. I don't have to like it.

Step one. Go into the cells. Visit Ahle.

He felt the pressure-loaded gel gun in a shoulder-holster under his coat. A fine-tuned item from Fleming's personal armory. Intended for exactly this sort of purpose.

I hate this. In everything but reality, I'm committing mutiny and treason.

* * *

Ahle sat at the door of her her cell, eyes focused on the clock at the end of the hallway. This was a small block of secure cells; the barracks-room drunk types were held on the floor above. Clean but Spartan; a cot, a sink, a toilet and a box for personal property. Almost all of which had been taken away, with the exception of her clothes, and those had been very *very* carefully searched before being returned to her.

At least you could request books. That was one of the privileges they could take away for misbehavior. Ahle's officers wouldn't be too uncomfortable.

Aside from the whole being-in-prison thing. With nooses practically hanging around their necks. If she failed to deliver, they'd all die. At least if that uptight son of a bitch Perry had anything to say about it, although she supposed that if she failed to deliver, he'd be dead himself.

2:05 am, the clock said. 2:06. Behind schedule. She wanted to get up and pace, to the limits that the small cell allowed pacing, but that would have meant taking her eyes from the clock.

A pair of young Army MPs showed up, dressed in neat khaki. One of them had the usual heavy gel gun; both had holstered pistols. The one without the gel gun put a key into the lock.

144

"Captain Ahle. I see you're awake," said the other one. A lance corporal.

"Yes, Lance Corporal. Thoughts of the noose tend to make sleep difficult," Ahle said acidly.

"An Air Service Vice-Commodore wants to see you. He says he has questions to ask. Come with us."

"It's past two in the morning," Ahle muttered.

"Sorry, Captain. Important. You can come nicely or we can put chains on."

"I'll come nicely. What does the son of a bitch want *now*?"

The cell door opened. Hollis, in the one next to hers, gave her a wink. He knew; somebody had to, to give the others an idea in case she didn't come back. May as well know why they were dying.

She shrugged to herself. This happened, when you were a pirate. Part of the deal. You lived or died by it, it and the Code. She'd help Fleming and get that ship back for Perry, if that was what it took. The crew – the *officers*, anyway, the *crew* was already dead and she very much had her own motivation for avenging them anyway – would live.

* * *

Perry was in a small briefing room on the other side of a pair of secure doors. He sat nervously behind a steel desk, focused on his watch. Wearing uniform under a long civilian coat.

Dirt-poor actor, Ahle thought. But the MPs didn't seem to realize anything was up.

"Private Gardner will stay here with you," said the lance.

"I can take care of myself, Lance," said Perry. He touched the automatic on his hip. "And Private Gardner isn't cleared for this conversation. Neither are you."

"She's a dangerous woman, sir. We have orders."

"You also have a security clearance. That does not cover this conversation. You can monitor her perfectly well from the other side of that door." Perry's tone was command; *he is a vice-commodore*, Ahle thought.

Yeah, don't forget that. Senior officer, squadron commander. Mid-thirties; young for his rank, too. This isn't some regular Imperial grunt we're dealing with, Ahle forced herself to remember. This man has seen action, and the son of a bitch would *not* have his present rank if he wasn't good.

"Don't try anything, Ahle. I'd love to kill you," said Perry, as the two MPs left. The door had a small observation window, and young Private Gardner's face was clear on the other side.

"Soundproofed door," said Perry. "And the monitoring is turned off. We can speak freely."

"Are you ready to go?" Ahle asked. A little nervous, although not as nervous as the Imperial.

Perry handed her a notepad. Taped to the underside of it was a two-shot gas gun, a sprayer. Ahle took the attached pencil and began drawing random designs; sketching something for Private Gardner's benefit, schematics or whatever he wanted to imagine. Palmed the gas gun with her other hand and slipped it into a pocket.

Perry drew a sprayer of his own. The things fired a concentrated irritant that set the victim to sneezing and tears. Incapacited for a bit, fine half an hour later. Focused on his watch, they mouthed words back and forth for a couple of minutes.

He's tense, Ahle thought. Out of his element. Well, that was her job, to help him with that shit. He's more competent than he looks.

"We have thirty seconds," said Perry. "Ready?"

Ahle gave a nod.

Perry signaled the man at the door. The two of them got up.

"We're done here," Perry said to the two MPs, as the door opened.

"I told you, I'm not betraying my people."

"Then you'll hang," said Perry. Still focused on his watch.

Suddenly he looked up. Raised the spray gun and blasted first the lance corporal, then a dumbfounded Private Gardner, in the face. Both men began choking and sneezing, the lance-corporal doubling over.

A dull boom, somewhere not far away. Almost instantly, the lights went out.

Perry had an electrical flashlight in his other hand. He turned it on.

"Come on. Spray and run."

The two of them headed out, Perry pausing to bolt the door of the interrogation room with the two MPs inside. Up a corridor, then a flight of stairs. Another checkpoint.

Flashlight beam shone into Ahle's face, blinding her.

"Vice-Commodore Perry, god damn it. Urgent!"

The door opened.

Ahle sprayed the man on the other side in the face. He went down, fighting for breath like the other two MPs.

Down a corridor. Shouts. This was where the petty miscreants were kept, soldiers and airshipmen on seven-, fifteen- or thirty-day confinement.

Halfway, they met another two MPs, with gel guns drawn.

"Stop! Stop right there!"

"I'm an Air Service Vice-Commodore," said Perry. Shone his own flashlight on his shoulders and rank insignia.

The two lowered their gel guns. Perry sprayed one; Ahle the other, squirting the gas hard into the MPs' faces.

And I'm empty, Ahle thought. She bent down and took one of the men's gel guns – he fought to retain it, but he was coughing and sneezing and mostly blinded. Her long fingers felt around the somewhat familiar weapon – not that she'd used this particular model, but physics required all gel guns to be functionally pretty similar.

Damn thing was still on safety. She corrected that – *I think* – and followed Perry.

They were on the ground level. Another security checkpoint, but a cursory one, only a single man. His partner must have run off for help.

"Vice Perry, signing out," Perry told the man there. "Got to run, sign for me."

"Who's the one with you?"

"My assistant," Perry snapped as the door opened. "Sign her out too."

* * *

Outside was dark. The explosion had cut the power to most of central Hugoton, although the inner offices and barracks had emergency internal backups that were starting to come online. A bomb had taken out a vital carrier cable. There'd be an enquiry.

I'll be found guilty as a conspirator, Perry thought, *for things I have no idea how to do in the first place.*

147

No time to think about it. No time to let the bile rise in his throat again. Power wouldn't be down forever; time to run. He had it planned out, had walked through the course; now he led Ahle along it; down a narrow alley between the MP and one of the rapid reaction companies' guardhouses; out the front of that guardhouse, past a trackless steam-tank on a maintenance pad, across a throughway of busy people with flashlights and searchlights.

Power down; everyone went to full alert, yes. The rapid reaction companies were coming out, engaging the electric lights on their eight-wheeled APCs and light tanks; backup power would engage *any time now*. At present nobody was paying him much mind. That'd change.

It would be a disaster to get caught this early. All the trouble, all the consequences from trouble, and *no* gain.

His boots pounded on the dust. Behind another of the rapid-reaction guardhouses, into a narrow gap between the military area and the civilian facilities. On the other side of a – presently powerless – electric fence was a railyard; trains sitting idle, although the closest was powered-up and ready to go, its air brakes hissing.

It would leave, picking up high speed as an express run to St. Louis, in three and a half minutes as of Time. However much of it they had left. Missing it would be another disaster, although there was a backup.

How long before somebody discovered the disabled MPs? Probably already happened. No time to worry. His boots stamped as he counted off paces; four, five, six, seven, *eight*, and yes, the slight bulge on the ground of the bags Fleming had left. Next to the slit cut open in the fence.

"Good to see you. You've got just under seventy seconds," said Fleming himself, stepping out from a shadowed recess.

"I tear-gassed our own MPs," Perry growled, not thinking *superior officer*. "You bastard."

Was that a grin on Fleming's face? Hard to tell in the darkness.

No time to think too much. Well, maybe a little time, a minute was more than he'd hoped for at this point.

An electric alarm went off from the direction of the prison. Heavy *braang-braang-braang*.

No. No time. He scooped up one of the sacks, Ahle taking

148

the other. Ducked to fit through the slit in the wire; Fleming had cut two of the three detection wires. As soon as power went on, those cuts would be noticed and there'd be a patrol on the way.

"Open boxcar one away on the left," said Fleming.

Ahle fit through the wire after Perry, turned left.

"You've got forty-five seconds," Fleming said. He extended a hand and yes, that *was* a grin on the bastard's face. Polite reflex made Perry shake it anyway. The train's airbrakes began to hiss louder, and from up ahead came the sound of a steam-engine heating up, the chuff-chuff-chuff that said it'd be moving *very soon*.

"Good luck out there. It'll stop in Dodge City for a bit; don't get out. Go on with it to St. Louis; it'll be about a day. Food in the bags. Downtown bar named the Green Gables. Ask for Josiah and tell him you're with Methuselah."

"Sir," said Perry, remembering his manners.

"And something for you." Fleming pressed something hard, cold and metallic into Perry's hand. A flask.

"Traditional to drink in boxcars," he said under his breath. "Sainsbury Estate 40 from my personal stock. Enjoy."

He's thinking about alcohol at a time like this?

Perry dropped the spy's flask into his coat and turned. Ran for the boxcar, pulled himself in; Ahle extended a hand.

Inside was dark and greasy, like an engine hall without the moving parts. A lot of empty cardboard boxes filled half the boxcar, and there was matted straw on the stamped-metal floor.

"Looks like a comfortable one," said Ahle. "Your man arranged it well." She pulled the heavy door closed so that only a slit remained.

The train jolted into motion; a sudden, hard jerk that would have knocked a less experienced airshipman off his feet. Perry could barely make out anything in the darkness, but Ahle was already going through her pack.

"Yours, I think. Has the civvies in it," she said. "Now give me my guns back. What did Fleming want, anyway?"

Perry handed her the pack and the flask. Ahle unscrewed the lid of the flask, took a deep sniff.

"Sainsbury Estate," she said. Took a sip. "Damn, forty-year. I like your deputy director. He's classy."

"Ian Fleming," Perry said, "is a scheming *bastard*."

"He's an Imperial spymaster," said Ahle dismissively as the train accelerated out of Hugoton. "Of course he is. But he's got *excellent* taste. Makes up for everything."

"You don't understand duty," said Perry. He couldn't believe it. MPs were order *personified*, internal order. And he'd tear-gassed four of them. He, a respectable and honorable Vice-Commodore of the Air Service. There was time for that to sink in now, and he didn't like it.

"You don't understand detached duty," said Ahle. "Or piracy." Ahle took another sip of the rum and passed it back. "Your education starts now. Have a drink."

Chapter Ten

MACARTHUR DISMISSES TEXAN INAUGURAL PROVOCATION

In response to newly-elected Texan President Lyndon B. Johnson's inaugural-address challenge Monday, United States Secretary of War Douglas MacArthur made a statement yesterday of contempt and dismissal.

"Johnson has done us the favor of declaring himself a nuisance," MacArthur said, "but if Texan history for the last half-century shows, he is – in his own words – 'all hat and no cattle'."

MacArthur's response follows an angry inaugural address by Johnson, believed to have been directed mainly at his political base of exiled Southerners.

"The Republic of Texas has been pushed around enough by the United States," Johnson's address included, "and it is time we asserted ourselves against them. Washington thinks they have the strength; Washington will learn that Texas, too, can be as strong as they are – if not stronger. Washington will shrug this off; Washington will learn a painful lesson."

When asked at the press conference whether the United States intended to take Johnson's threats seriously, the Secretary of War gave a blatant dismissal.

"Texas has been causing trouble since we recognized them. But they're outclassed by Sonora, as they learned to their detriment in 1958. Johnson's talk is just talk, but if he wants to bring it, he can feel free."

The notoriously grudge-holding Johnson has not yet given a reply to MacArthur's response…

From the *New York Daily Herald*, January 23rd, 1960.

The line-class military airship formerly named 4-106 touched down in a certain narrow, doglegged box canyon in the Rockies, a location Pratt Cannon knew of as safe. The canyon walls were only about eighty yards apart, with buffeting crosswinds, and the airship bumped several times against them as it uneasily descended.

151

The bottom was sand and spots of grass underfoot, made dark by the bulk of the airship filling the space above. Hisses came as helium was pumped back into its compression tanks, reducing buoyancy.

"Make camp," Cannon's voice came. "It might be a few days."

Over the course of the flight, Cannon and Rienzi had polled the crew for those with woodsman's experience, combat experience, military skill. They were a rough lot of trash, in Ferrer's eye, these new crew – fifty or so pirates, mercenaries, criminals and general ne'er-do-wells – but there was a surprising amount of competence between them. Not just in their primary skillset as airshipmen, but most knew their way around weapons, and quite a number claimed to have some skill as woodsmen.

Talking with Captain Caine, it made sense. Airships went down *all the time* over the Rockies; not just the general lawless frontier environment, but the high altitude's thinner air and the mountains' turbulent air currents – and crews, including downed pirates, often had to walk a bit to civilization, foraging as they went.

Now, eight or nine with hunting skill were given rifles and told to bring back food; deer or wild cattle, whichever. The others were divided into watch squads.

"Mr. Ferrer, Mr. Rienzi and I are going to go for a little walk," said Marko to the assembled crew leaders now, in the dark shadow of the huge airship in the small canyon. "We'll be back in a day or two. Mr. Cannon is in charge while I'm away, with Ms. McIlhan his second; they speak with my voice. Captain Caine is responsible for the airship; he speaks with my voice, too, on those matters. You'll be visited by friends soon; the officers have their passwords. Anyone else comes along, kill them and make sure they don't get away."

"Settle yourselves and the men in, boys; we're going to be here a bit," said Cannon.

* * *

"What's he want with the kinny tapes?" Rienzi asked Ferrer, a few minutes later as they packed. The two shared one of the officers' cabins of the airship, although neither had a

152

whole lot of personal stuff in the first place.

"He wants us," Ferrer said, "to keep them safe. Carry them safely. He'll cut your throat if those are damaged."

"Right over Hugoton," Rienzi exalted again. "Blew away two fuckin' Imperials! And this is just the start, he said. *We flew right over Hugoton and shot down two Imperials and it's just the start!*"

"Just the start," Ferrer agreed. He could see the purpose of shooting down the airships – they'd have *been* shot down, otherwise – but there'd been people aboard them, and the fire would probably have killed at least a couple. That was still distasteful to his visceral mind, no matter how he tried to rationalize it.

The Collapse didn't just happen. The old oligarchs had to be brought down. And killed.

"So pack the speely tapes good," Ferrer said. "In amongst the spare clothing. We're going to be trekking over mountains."

"You know exactly where we are in the first place, anyway?" Rienzi asked. He was wearing a pistol on each hip, and a round-magazined submachinegun was slung over his shoulder.

"No, and I don't want to. Boss knows where we are, that's good enough for me."

"No, you don't," agreed Marko, appearing in the doorway. "Rienzi, exchange that subgun for a rifle. Now. Get one for Ferrer, too. Ferrer, why aren't you armed?"

"I am, boss," said Ferrer. He tapped the .38 in its shoulder holster, under his jacket and vest.

Marko sprang; a blur of motion and pain. Suddenly Ferrer was face-down on his bunk, arm twisted into a pain-imminent hold, one foot off the floor. Marko twisted his arm; pain, *agonizing* pain, ran up Ferrer's arms and shoulder into his neck.

"Couldn't draw that fast enough, could we?" came Marko's cold hiss in Ferrer's ear. "When I said I wanted you armed at all times, I said I wanted you *armed* at all *times*."

Marko stepped back, got up. "The two of you be at the nose in five minutes with those speelies. We have a meeting arranged."

* * *

Thirty-First Squadron's day room was chaos, the next morning. Only Senior Warrant Halversen and a couple of the older engineers were silent, standing in the back watching the other officers' disarray.

Near the front, Commander Ricks was talking with Swarovski. The handsome blond squadron XO was sitting jauntily on the desk at the front, his non-regulation sword hanging to one side. Swarovski, who liked the XO and was thinking of getting a sword of his own, sprawled on a seat he'd pulled up.

"I'm telling you," Ricks was saying, "love can make a man do crazy things. It's always the uptight ones who crack first."

"He's married," said Swarovski. "You haven't heard him on the bridge. He loves that wife of his."

"His wife's cut from the same cloth he is," Martindale put in. "Haven't you met her? Accountant. Tax codes and rulebooks just like the old man. Close couple."

"And he broke," said Ricks. He touched the hilt of his sword. "Always helps to have a little fun. XO never did any of that, and look what happened. Vice Rulebook blows up a power line and runs away with some pirate captain."

"I don't believe it," Swarovski repeated. "The pieces don't fit together. Something else is going on."

"How do you know?" Martindale asked. "You had a drink with Director Fleming or something?"

"Maybe I did. Look, the man's an airship commander, but I *saw* him in action with those pirates we killed. He's no more an espionage agent than you or I am. Best airship commander since Rivington, but outside a ship? He's as much basic training and luck as anyone else. If he rigged the bomb himself, I'm a hex-pushing Luddite."

"So who did?" Ricks pushed. "If *he* didn't do it all on his own?"

"He *couldn't* have done it all on his own," said Swarovski. *Can't these idiots see the obvious?* "Martindale just named the guy. Fleming did. Using him for something. Here you've got a redundant Vice who, let's be frank, is obsessed with getting that ship back, when everyone knows there's a spy war going on. Fleming's using what he's got handy."

"I still don't believe it. I'm going to ask the Flight Admiral,"

154

said Ricks.

A cough came from behind. The three officers turned to see Flight Admiral Richardson standing in the doorway, her adjutant – a spare Kenyan commander named Sophie Ojibwa – behind her.

A rustle as the room came to order. The officers and senior warrants got to their feet, saluted, as Richardson came to the front of the room.

"Acting squadron commander Ricks, you were going to ask me something?" Richardson asked. Her flat green eyes swept across the room, covering it like a Marine with a submachinegun.

"Ma'am. Yes ma'am," said Ricks. "We were wondering—"

"Of course you're wondering," said Richardson. "Understandable and justified. I'm here to do two things, ladies and gentlemen. The first is to confirm Commander Ricks as the acting commander of Thirty-First Squadron until such time as a replacement for Vice-Commodore Perry is appointed. Hereby you are, Commander. The second is to illuminate you regarding the matter of Vice-Commodore Perry. At ease and sit down."

The room settled, people taking their seats. Ojibwa had a pen and notepad out, ready to take something down.

Scary bitch, that one, Swarovski thought. Perry was alright, but the Flight Admiral had seen some *real* shit and it had left a mark on her more than physically. Mid-forties was young, in peacetime, for a rank that equated to Army brigadier or Navy commodore, and you didn't get that high that fast by being nice. Or normal.

"Regarding Vice-Commodore Perry; Sophie, the papers, please."

"Ma'am." The adjutant passed her boss a sheaf of papers. Swarovski was close enough to read the print on the wanted poster when Richardson held it up. A blurred black-and-white photo – something from file, Swarovski thought, the magnification was badly off – of Vice Perry, with a physical description. Reward of five hundred Imperial pounds – *damn*, that was more than what Swarovski made in five months. Wanted for desertion, assault, gross property destruction and attempted murder.

"Your former squadron commander is a wanted criminal,"

said Richardson. "Pass these around and take a close look. He has committed – you know what happened last night."

Ricks, next to Swarovski, very much looked as though he wanted to say something, like he was straining to keep his mouth shut.

"Vice-Commodore Perry is a deserter and a traitor," Richardson said. "I know you have other questions; I am not going to answer them. I'm aware of the speculation; I am not going to comment on it. Acting squadron commander Ricks, what is the philosophical foundation of our Service?"

An Academy question, and one that the XO answered as promptly as the cadet he'd been at Biggin Hill fifteen years ago.

"Reason and logic, ma'am."

"What is the tradition of the Air Service?"

"Duty and service, ma'am."

"And?"

Jeez, thought Swarovski, *she's going to ask for Admiral Fisher's birthday next.*

"Nothing else, ma'am," responded Ricks like a cadet. "The Air Service was created from whole cloth out of reason and logic, to serve the Empire through the Great War and beyond."

"Reason and logic," Richardson transparently pretended to muse. "And the evidence is precisely what you see in front of you. Vice-Commodore Perry has betrayed his country and his Service. Full stop. Now, I am specifically prohibiting further discussion of the matter. Is *that* understood?"

"Yes, ma'am," came murmurs.

Richardson raised her voice.

"I don't think I made myself understood, Thirty-First Squadron. I am *specifically prohibiting* speculative discussion regarding your former squadron commander. Is that *understood?*"

Much louder: "Yes, ma'am. Understood, ma'am."

* * *

"Specific prohibitions my ass," Rafferty said to Duckworth at lunch in the enlisted mess. The two were off by themselves in a booth, half-eaten corned beef sandwiches in front of them.

Duckworth took another bite of his and thoughtfully chewed it.

"Men crack, Raff."

"Not that one. I was with him on that pirate ship. He's a spy, I'm a fuckin' Lud bomber. Don't have the skills to. May be a fine airship commander, but he just don't have the jack skills to do what they say he is."

"Hush up, Raff," said Duckworth. "You heard what the hag lady told the officers this morning. Offence even to discuss it."

"And how about that for a sign? Don't tell you it's a crime to discuss a regular bust-up, do they?"

"Rafferty," said Vidkowski, sitting down with a plate, "shut up. You don't know the hag lady. I've been in her division for years. Don't fuck with her. Don't even *think about* fucking with her. Shut up."

"Bullshit," said Rafferty.

"Rafferty." Vidkowski's voice was raised. "Shut. Up. And that's an *order*."

Rafferty's mouth curled in a snarl.

"Yes *sir*, Admiral fucking Vidkowski. Since when did you become such a straight-edger?"

"I don't want to see you on the third floor," Vidkowski said. He lowered his voice. "Of *course* something's fucking going on. Do you think the rest of us don't know it, too? We don't *talk* about it. We pretend that what the hag lady wants us to believe is true. Fake it and keep your fuckin' yap shut when drunk. *Understand?*"

"Yes *sir*," said Rafferty with a bit less malice. Thinking.

* * *

"He's *what?*" Annabelle Perry asked the MP lieutenant at around the same time. He'd come into her firm's offices with a submachinegun-armed squad of Air Marines, throwing the entire operation – outside a couple of executives who'd come up from field mining operations and were taking the entire thing in full stride – into complete disruption. 'Duke' Marion, the CEO, was standing by impassively.

"Yes, ma'am. Your husband has taken off with a pirate and is now a wanted fugitive. On orders from the Governor of Hugoton Lease, you and your children are being taken into protective custody."

"You can't just take my second-ranking financial away like that," Marion objected. He was a big man of fifty-five, a self-made company founder who'd started as a prospector and then a miner, and wasn't ready to take shit from any kid lieutenant. "In case you haven't been informed, *Lieutenant*, the city of Denver – the State of Colorado – is *not* the Hugoton Lease. You have no jurisdiction here."

"Staff Sergeant Kawa?" the lieutenant said.

A man with stripes on his arms produced a document from a folder.

"The Colorado State Rangers *do* have jurisdiction here," the lieutenant said. "This warrant authorizes the operation. Would you like me to put you on the line to the man who signed this, Mr. Morrison?"

Marion looked at the warrant and snarled.

"I know Colonel Taylor."

"You can't just – what *happened?* It doesn't make any sense!"

"Ma'am, my orders come directly from the Governor," said the lieutenant. "Your children are presently being taken from school. Now, if you'd come with us to Stapleton?"

This is insane. Marcus can't have done this. Can't *have.*

Not hurt. Too shocked and confused to be hurt. Yet. Maybe there'd be pain later. *For now,* Annabelle told herself, *just go with it. Do what the nice man says.*

"You can't give me any explanation at all?"

"*I* could use an explanation, too," said Marion.

"I don't know any more than what I've told your associate CFO, Mr. Morrison," said the MP lieutenant. "Now, Ms. Perry, the ship is waiting for us."

* * *

At Stapleton, Annabelle met the two children, who'd been taken straight out of school. They weren't upset; they were military children, used to the uniform and to obeying orders. For them it was an exciting adventure with an airship ride.

"Wow," said ten-year-old Ernest, looking at the ship they were about to board. MPs had come by their apartment as well, packed clothing. "That's a warship! An escort-class warship! Is Daddy on it?"

Annabelle thought for a moment. How much to reveal to them? The MPs apparently hadn't said anything.

"Daddy's going to be away for a while," she said.

"We're not going to see him at Hugoton?" Ernest asked.

And why are we being taken to Hugoton in the first place? Protective custody just doesn't make sense.

But the highest-ranking officer they'd seen so far was the lieutenant XO'ing the ship, which – Annabelle had been around her husband's service long enough to know – was a streamlined escort-class, built for speed and not fighting capability. She had the feeling it was a very high-level taxi. With the exception of a pair of scout-classes being refueled, it was the only Service ship at Stapleton, which was unusual as well; escort-classes normally operated in two-ship flights.

What is going on?

She didn't believe the story about Marcus falling in love with a pirate and running off with her, not for a moment. They'd been married twelve years, known each other for fifteen, and Perry simply wasn't that type. It didn't make the slightest bit of sense, which meant that something else had to be going on.

The lieutenant clearly didn't know; he was your typical Army MP who saw his job as being to obey orders, not think about them too much. Maybe they'd find out at Hugoton.

She hoped.

"If you'll come along and board, ma'am," said the lieutenant. "We'll be at Hugoton by six."

* * *

The train had been going all night and all day, and on into the next night, stopping only briefly to onload more coal and water, perhaps to change crews. They crossed sparse Kansas plains, occasionally seeing airships, once a flight of Service vessels and, another time, a low-flying Federal escort-class, the whole of it painted a bright Union blue, prominent stripes and stars so big he could count all thirty-four of them.

Egotistical, aren't we?, he thought, not for the first time, as the boxcar trembled along. They were maintaining a steady pace that amounted to about thirty miles an hour, through territory that had been slowly growing more developed and

159

civilized. Of course, this was the Texas border, most definitely a hostile border, and the railway line to Hugoton was under Imperial protection.

Thirty-four stars, of which Texas was most definitely not one. Neither were the seven Western states of Minnesota, Iowa, North and South Dakota, Nebraska, Kansas and Colorado, although the Federals had enough of a presence in that last one.

Sonora and Deseret were respectable countries but not especially hostile; Sonora was dynamic and ambitious, but her ambitions lay more to her north than her east; she'd gobbled up southern California a few years ago – Ahle had been involved in that, hadn't she? – and everyone expected her to move north when she'd finished assimilating that, probably war with the Free City of San Francisco before long. Deseret had military strength and was no friend of Sonora, but the Mormons were insular to the point of paranoia, not even trading very much with outsiders.

Still, Federal authority maintained a claim over the entire state of Colorado, and in practice that claim was respected only so far as the Department of the West had the troops to enforce it. Nobody but pirates contested the rest of the West.

More troops here, down along the Texas border. Texas had successfully seceded during the Collapse; there'd been a short war over it in the early `20s, which the Empire had negotiated an end to in what Parliament had called the Southern Compromise. Washington could stomp on the rest of the South all it wanted – at best a very limited respect for the absolute-right-of-self-determination Curzon Doctrine, for diplomatic reasons – but Texas would go free.

Washington had eventually come to accept the deal – the same negotiations had given the Empire the Hugoton Lease, and Washington a huge stack of money with which to fund its Reconstruction of the South – but the results had included a steady stream of disaffected, pissed-off Southerners emigrating to Texas.

In theory, that was supposed to be an outlet. But London hadn't considered how strongly these people would still consider themselves to be Southern. Texas didn't have the military strength to be a real threat to the United States, but they certainly had the motivation to be a prickly-bad neighbor.

Not my problem, Perry thought, as the train rumbled on through the darkness. He'd eaten earlier – Fleming had included a couple days' worth of ration tins – and now he lay back on a pile of the cardboard boxes and attempted to sleep.

I broke the law. God knows what the squadron's going to think. God knows what Annabelle is going to think. Dear God.

The sleep didn't come easily.

* * *

Ferrer woke from an uneasy sleep to a bad feeling. Marko was standing over him in the darkness, a knife in his hand.

Is he going to kill me? was Ferrer's thought. His role was almost done, wasn't it, and it would save the Russians the price of a nice farm if Marko simply cut his throat. Perhaps he knew too much anyway. Fear slipped through him.

"They're coming," said Marko. "Get the speelies ready."

Ferrer got to his feet, pulled his boots on. They'd been waiting all night – did Marko *ever* sleep? – but now a small dirigible was coming into sight; a sleek, streamlined vessel that couldn't have been more than a hundred yards long, flying very low up the narrow canyon. Just the shape of it; no headlights, no running lights, navigating by moonlight. Double fins; maneuverable as well as sleek.

It slowed as it approached the small campsite, and for a moment a blazing searchlight stabbed out from the bridge, covering the three men. Rienzi moved his hand across his pistol menacingly, feeling threatened, and Marko backslapped him hard across the face.

A rope dropped, and three men rappelled the fifteen or so feet down to the ground. They approached the campsite, one of them carrying a briefcase. They wore civilian clothing, but Ferrer could tell from their bearings that at least two of them were military.

"Mr. Skorzeny," said Marko to one of the military types. "I've heard about you."

"I've heard about you, too, Marko," said that man in a Germanic accent. He was sixtyish, with a prominent scar dividing the right side of his face. "Do you have the tactical information?"

"We have it. Maps and scopes. And a little bonus."

161

"Hugoton," mused the other man with a military bearing. Lean and rangy, and his accent was clear Texas. "Skorzeny's coming back to Houston with me." A head-gesture at the third man, who held the briefcase. "The Third Department could use copies as well. Just for general reference."

The Third Department. Ferrer had heard whispers of those guys; an intelligence service that rivaled the Okhrana, reporting directly to Count Leon and the Tsar. Smaller than the Okhrana, but feared more.

"The Third Department," said Marko. Thinking. Musing. He smiled. "Very good. Tell the Count well played."

"I'll tell him directly," said the agent. "He's in Houston for the final negotiations. He sends his regards, by the way."

Marko turned to Ferrer. "The recordings."

"Yessir." Ferrer stepped forward with the case.

The man from the Third Department stepped forward, and they exchanged briefcases. Skorzeny and the Texan watched coldly. The case Ferrer took was smaller and much lighter than the one containing the kinematograph tapes of the Hugoton reconnaissance.

"Your orders are in there," the Third Department man told Marko. "As well as more money, should you need it."

"You should know that I have an Imperial line-class," said Marko. "The Denny-Neuvoldt type. Crewed by a bunch of trash, and the Imperials know it's in unfriendly hands. The specifications as I've been able to gather are in there, too."

"Specifications for the Denny-Neuvoldt. I don't think we have those," said the man from the Third Department.

"We heard about your little overflight," said the Texan. "Killed a couple of them, didn't you?"

Hugoton bordered Texas, and there was a respectably-sized Texan garrison in Fort Guymon, on the Texan border just to the south of the Lease.

"Only a couple," said Marko. "Plenty of fun left for you guys."

"Plenty of fun for you to have, too," said the Third Department man. "See the new orders. We're scheduled to move into final execution two weeks from now. You're going to be busy."

Behind them, the dark, streamlined scout-class lowered. The Texan, the man from the Third Department and the

Germanic named Skorzeny turned their backs and headed back to the gondola, from which a staircase had dropped.

There was excited fire in Marko's eyes, and a new vibrancy to his movement, when he turned to look at Ferrer.

"The Third Department," he said. A wicked smile on his face. "It was the Third Department. You know, I *really* didn't think the Count was that ruthless."

"What do you mean?" Ferrer asked.

Marko's eyes glinted in a way that Ferrer had found exciting before, but that was before the killing, before he'd personally seen Marko cut the throats of fifty sleeping men with the enthusiasm of a young child. Now a shiver of fear went down him.

"Oh, you probably don't want to know. Not if you want to retire and enjoy your ten thousand pounds. But there are some clever men afoot here, engineer."

"And some more killing yet to be done, I hope," said Rienzi. "Only got to notch it three times so far this operation."

Punk, thought Ferrer. A third-rate engineer and a bloodthirsty goddamned punk to boot. Marko was fear and respect, but Rienzi was nothing but disdain and contempt. How the kid had ever gotten into MIT to begin with...

"Oh, there'll be a lot more killing before we're all done." Marko's broken-toothed mouth spread in a wide, wide smile. "We'll see what the orders say next, but I can assure you they'll involve a lot more killing. Now, shall we get back to that beautiful ship we've borrowed?"

Chapter Eleven

Name: Special Squadrons
Founder: Heinrich Himmler, 1933
Type: Armor/mechanized
Present station: Western Missouri (since 1959)
Strength: 14,000, including 230 tanks and approximately 600 other combat vehicles. Quasi-independent logistically.

Notable accomplishments: Successful suppression of Raleigh-Wake Forest area in 1944 secessionist insurgency. Continuous operations suppressing insurgencies in Missouri since 1949.

Overview: The Special Squadrons, an almost entirely Germanic unit, is one of the larger mercenary units on longstanding contract in the Southern States. They have a record of zealous accomplishment; some, including more liberal New England and Midwestern Congressmen, have in fact accused them of being overzealous.

It has been the consistent position of successive Administrations, however, that there is no such thing as over-zealous when it comes to retaining our hard-won victory in the Civil War, and the Squadrons are considered a valued addition to our strength there.

From the *Federal Registry of Foreign Auxiliaries*, Washington DC, 1962.

In the first half-hour of the morning, clear light and a chill, the train rumbled slowly into a railyard that Ahle identified as St. Louis.

"You know the place on sight?" Perry asked.

"Hardly the first time I've been on a train. But I don't know the city. We're going to have to ask directions to your place. Come on, and be careful. Rolling stock can kill you without noticing."

The train hadn't stopped moving – maybe it wasn't going to, just slowing down – when Ahle bailed out, landing on her feet between two sets of tracks. Perry was an experienced airshipman and therefore agile, but he stumbled a bit on the

164

hard rocks.

"This way. When we get there, keep your mouth shut and be polite. We need these people."

"What people?"

"Just come on."

Ahle led Perry across one set of tracks then another, until their way was blocked by a stationary train, a long line of oilers that might or might not have come out of Hugoton. She paused for a moment and then climbed over the back of one, Perry following. That led to a couple more lines of tracks. Perry froze as they saw a yard worker signaling with a pair of flags to someone further up the line, but the yard worker – who clearly saw them – didn't appear to give a damn. Around another line of flatcars, and over to a chain-link fence. On the other side was scrubby light forest.

"Always a hole in these things somewhere," Ahle explained, turning right along the fence. "It'll lead to a jungle."

"Why'd that guy ignore us?"

"Line workers are just grunts. Don't care either way about the hobos."

Indiscipline, thought Perry. No wonder that man was still a grunt at the bottom of the food chain. But he was a part of this world now, at least temporarily.

Get 4-106 back. Redeem myself. Everything else had to be secondary to that. Including trusting this damn pirate.

Still. She was behaving herself, and Perry had to figure she had her own code of ethics. The Code might have been PR-driven malarkey or a power play on the part of the legendary, apparently-invulnerable Joseph Kennedy, but it *was* also a code of ethics of sorts, that he supposed some people might adhere to. She had reason to be trusted; from her perspective, she was avenging the death of her crew and saving her officers. He'd have done the same.

Except that I work for the law. I live by the law.

Yeah, which made present circumstances all the more difficult. He'd told the Service that he was prepared to give his life, but his *honor*? If he failed, if he lost, he'd be remembered not as a man doing his duty, manipulated by a bastard spymaster into risking it all, but as a fugitive and a traitor. Annabelle would know the truth, but who else would? What would his parents, retired in Bournemouth, think? What would his friends from the Academy think? The officers and warrants of the squadron he hoped would still somehow be his when he returned?

About a hundred and fifty yards down the line – they passed another disgracefully negligent yard worker, who saw them and kept going with his flags as though he hadn't – Ahle found her hole in the fence. On the other side was a loose trail that might have been made by deer; she headed down confidently.

Perry wanted to draw his pistol, but restrained himself.

A very short walk later, they came to a clearing where several men slept around the remains of a bonfire. Various trash and debris was strewn around, and a lean man dressed in black sat on a log absently strumming a guitar. He looked up as Perry and Ahle appeared.

"Well, well, well," he said.

"If it isn't the money man," said Ahle.

Money man?, thought Perry. The thirtyish guy didn't look like he had a nickel to call his own.

"Cap'n Ahle, *ma'am*. How you doin', boss?"

"Doin' just fine, Johnny. How you been?"

"Well," said Johnny, "I ain't been back to Folsom. That's saying enough, ain't it?"

"Good enough for me, Johnny. The black man here's Mark Perry, late an officer of the Air Service."

Johnny gave Perry another look. Strummed a couple chords on his guitar.

"Running with Imperials now, cap'n?"

"Sprung me out of Hugoton. We're hoping – you been around St. Louis, haven't you?"

"I been here. I been there. When you get right down to it, I been everywhere."

"Hoping you might direct us to a place. Maybe we can buy you a drink when we get there."

The 'money man' got to his feet, swung the guitar on its strap around to his back.

"Always up for a drink, cap'n Ahle. Where's it you're looking to buy me one?"

"Green Gables. You know the place?"

"Downtown. Near the Arrow, hike from here. You'll owe me two drinks."

"We can do five if you want," said Ahle.

"Five might be about reasonable," said Johnny. "I hear what happened to your last crew. Like to know, if you wouldn't mind explaining, although that man next to you says a bit, maybe."

"They were killed by a son of a bitch we're going to track down and execute," said Ahle flatly.

"Hold on," said Johnny. He bent down, shook one of the sleeping men until he came to a wakeful grunt. Johnny said something to him that Perry couldn't quite make out.

"Telling him I'll be back in three hours," said Johnny. "And if I ain't, he'll know who to look for. So'll the others. No offence, cap'n, but I hear what happened to your last crew."

"I *know* what happened to my last crew. The bastard's going to pay."

"He better. But Bobby here's just to make sure. Cap, you were a good boss, but those rumors they swirl, hear me?"

"I hear you," said Ahle. "Just take us to the damn Green Gables, will you?"

* * *

A walk. Through industrial streets, then a nicer neighborhood, then into downtown, where the giant silvery St. Louis Arrow – a four-hundred-foot-high tourist attraction pointing west – was visible between lines of skyscrapers. It was early in the morning, but the first clerks and data-punchers were making their way in, men and women in bowler hats and trilbies, some with fashionably fake airshippers' goggles around their foreheads.

To them, Perry thought, *the frontier is romantic and exciting.*

How little they knew.

They stopped at an automat for coffee; quarters went in, the – amplified, fake? – sound of gears clanked, and coffee poured out in cups. The drink was light and fluffy by Service standards, where squadron messes and ship cooks vied with each other to brew the harshest, most burned and brutally caffeine-loaded coffee that they could.

But the clericals around them were treating the stuff like harsh 'Dimers brew, and Perry pretended to do the same. It did have caffeine, and he ordered another cardboard cup to walk

167

with before they left. He was tired; the cardboard had insulated some of the damn boxcar's shaking but not all of it, and between that and his uneasy nerves he hadn't slept well. The coffee helped.

* * *

"So you escaped," Johnny was saying as they walked through tenement streets on the other side of downtown, loosely following the river. It seemed to be a dockside district.

"He got me out," Ahle motioned at Perry. "They were cashiering him already. He decided, what the hell."

"Fuckin' Service," Perry put in for plausibility.

"Uh-huh. So what you looking to do now? Lost your ship, lost your ossifers, lost your crew."

"Got my money. Bank of Sonora. We'll get my officers back."

"Bust them out of Hugoton?"

"Do something," said Ahle. "They're my people. Might need a new crew before then. You looking for a job?"

Johnny thought for a moment.

"Maybe. Music's good, but I could stand to be on a ship again."

"You were in the hobo jungle. Where you headed?"

"North. Figure might be someone hiring in Minnie. Failing that, get a ride for the Hills."

"The Black Hills," Ahle explained to Perry.

"So we're going pirate, are we, Mr. Imperial Officer?" Johnny addressed Perry directly for the first time in a while.

"They cashiered me. Got to go somewhere," Perry said. "Gaol isn't my idea of a fun time."

"So off you run with this pirate lady."

"Right."

"Still uncertain, huh?"

"A bit," said Perry.

"You'll get to like it. Ahle, she's Code through and through. Ethics, just like your Service rules. Don't kill. Insurance companies cover it all anyhow. You're not *really* doing a whole lot of harm. Even shoot up the bad pirates who are, rob the robbers."

"Honorable pirates don't rob other honorable pirates,"

Ahle said to Perry. "Anyone else is fair game. How do you *think* the Code got established."

Perry wanted to say he didn't give a damn for that publicity-driven Code bullshit, but it would have been tactless given the circumstances. Besides, this was a new aspect he hadn't considered.

"Uh-huh," he said. "How far are we from this place?"

"It's on the docks," said Johnny. "Just a few more minutes."

* * *

Shady, but Perry had expected that; the sub-basement of his expectations had been mined the night before last, and he hadn't expected anything above the most utterly dismal. The Green Gables was a vile bar on a street that overlooked the docks, a place where disreputable riverboatmen got wasted. The bouncer was a four hundred pound Samoan with a spiked club who eyed the three of them with utter contempt as they entered.

The inside was dark and greasy, and populated even at seven in the morning. Dockhands – pirates and thieves no doubt, too – drinking whisky and beer. A couple of bindlestiff hoboes lounged in one corner.

Ahle approached the bar with reasonable confidence.

"Johnny, what d'you want?" asked the bartender, a small mousy man with a face of stubble.

"I want a rye whisky. These two have business here."

"Business, huh? What'll you have?"

"Just a beer. Whatever you have," said Ahle.

"I'm good," said Perry.

Ahle elbowed him.

"Two of those," said Ahle. "One for him, too."

The three sat down at the bar. Johnny downed his shot of rye, signaled for another.

"You owe me a buck besides this, Cap'n Ahle."

"Have five and get out of here," said Ahle. "And pass the word. I got out, maybe I could use new crew."

"Maybe I'll see you in the Black Hills." Johnny downed his second rye and headed off, probably – Perry thought – to spend the five bucks getting hammered elsewhere.

"So he showed you here, you two. What do you want?"

asked the bartender.

"We wanted some drinks," Ahle said. "What's it to you?"

"Don't ordinarily see a nigger and a bitch together," said the bartender indifferently. "Especially you, Cap Ahle."

Ahle raised an eyebrow.

"Oh, yeah, we heard of you. Stole an Imperial line-class and then got jacked yourself. Came over the wire last night. Looks like the nigger's the same Imperial vice they got wanted for treason and a bunch a' other shit."

"You heard?"

The bartender poured their drinks, savoring it. Perry took a taste of his beer; awful crap. One sip was enough.

"Yeah," said the bartender. "I hear things. So what do you want?"

Perry had been over the lines enough times to rote-memorize them. "We're here for Josiah. Said to say we're with Methuselah."

The bartender looked sharply at them.

"With *who*?"

"Methuselah, I said. You want to get Josiah or not?"

"Why didn't you say so?"

"Hey, I ordered a fuckin' beer two minutes ago!" one of the other patrons shouted as the bartender headed for the back room.

"You can wait," the bartender yelled back. "This shit's *important*."

* * *

Joseph Capdepon the Second was a heavy-set, burly man, with a full beard that was greying already; he was only thirty-three. His first act when the bartender shook him awake was to reach for the .44 revolver under his pillow. His second was to ask what was going on.

"Man comes in asking for Josiah," said the ratty little bastard. Privately, Capdepon suspected him of palming money, but he didn't have the evidence and Fred *was* good at keeping his yap shut. "From Methuselah. You said that was a big deal."

Josiah from Methuselah. Fucking right that was a big deal.

"Drinks on the house to them while I get dressed."

170

Ian Fleming. Bastard should have died years ago; Methuselah, the old man of the Bible, was fitting enough.

He had some idea of what the asshole might want, too. Anyone asking for Josiah specifically? That was good.

Meant he'd be rid of them faster.

He rolled out of bed, pulled on pants and boots and a kevlar vest underneath his coat. Any connection with that scheming bastard Fleming, you couldn't be too careful around.

* * *

The bartender ushered them, drinks in hand, into a back room. It looked like an office; there were old beer kegs stacked in one corner, but bills were pinned to a noticeboard on one wall, and the desk was crowded messily with papers.

Capdepon, a big bearded man, came in through a door behind the desk and sat down at it. He eyed Ahle and Perry like they were poisonous snakes.

Perry eyed the bar owner – he was obviously that – the same way back.

"So. You're from Fleming."

"Maybe we are," said Ahle.

"Maybe you can prove it. There's a rum bottle."

A rum bottle?, Perry thought.

"The flask that rum came in," said Ahle, thinking faster.

Right. Nice silver flask. He hadn't thrown that away. He fished in his bag for it and handed it across the desk into the bar-owner's thick, grasping fingers.

Capdepon held it up to the single flickering light in the room. His eyes widened slightly as he inspected the crest on it, some thin engraving Perry had felt but not given a moment's thought to.

"Miss L. Shit. Fleming's cashing in his chip with *her*?"

"Who the hell," Perry asked, "are you talking about?"

"Miss L," Capdepon repeated. There seemed to be relief in his voice. He reached down to his desk, opened a drawer, rummaged for a moment and pulled out an obsidian chip the size of a playing card. Pushed it across the desk at Perry, who took it. Engraved in the chip was lettering that might have been Viking runes but wasn't English.

"What's this?"

171

"Give it to her man. He knows what it is. You need transport?"

"We could use it," said Ahle. "Miss L, huh?"

You know this woman, whoever she is, Perry thought. Probably be time to ask questions later.

"Barge going south in twenty minutes. Fred'll get you on board. Get out of here."

As they got up, so did Capdepon. "And tell that shady bastard Fleming, if you see him again, that I'm done with him. It's over. Hopefully the spider will kick you right out on your asses. Give her my regards, by the way. Joseph Capdepon's highest respects and regards."

Now *that*, Perry thought, is interesting. Doesn't give a damn for Fleming, but respects this woman in New Orleans like, unless he was very wrong, not much else.

Interesting person to meet, he decided. New Orleans seemed like the wrong direction, but – given the context – probably not.

"Take us there," he said. "I'll pass it on. And to Fleming, too."

* * *

Perry had seen – from ground-level and from two thousand feet – some of the pretty steamers that cruised up and down the Mississippi, colorful boats with names like *Delta Queen*, *Natchez XII* and *Belle of Cincinnatti*. Elegant vessels that played to wealthy people and tourists, and the *Memphis Darling* was absolutely not one of them.

She was a gunmetal-grey hulk whose noisy engines belched thick smoke as she warmed up. An industrial ship whose only passenger class was steerage, and not even much of that; her main function seemed to be the pushing of a pair of barges, each her own eighty-foot length and twenty-foot width. They were loaded with grain, piled under tarpaulins that still spilled enough to keep a flock of circling birds interested.

"Tickets," said a late-twenties crewman in a frayed white jacket. He was very good-looking, with the fashionably slicked black hair of the younger generation. "We'll be in Memphis tomorrow morning, Orleans midday after. Welcome aboard. Take any empty cabin."

The cabins were tiny two-bunk things that wouldn't have

172

gone amiss on an airship, except that they stank of old cigarette smoke. Perry wondered aloud just how *many* people seemed to be crammed into this ship.

"More than you figure. Migrant workers, traveling mechanics, probably a downed airshipman or two," said Ahle. "Everybody meets in New Orleans."

Perry considered dumping his bags here – but no, this was the only change of clothes he had, and he wasn't leaving some of the gadgets Fleming had given him. Traveling workers probably included their share of thieves, and he wasn't about to take chances.

Only about a half the *Darling* was devoted to passengers, two dozen cramped cabins below decks and a small common room with a cash bar. Most of the stern was devoted to cargo – crates stamped 'Machine Parts' – and powerful engines that resonated through the entire ship. Back above decks, they left the common room – a poker game was already starting up – and found a quiet space on the deck. For certain low values of quiet, as the engines bumped and shook.

A large, sleek passenger airship passed overhead, following the river south, and Perry wished he were aboard it. *Was* there a good reason they'd taken steerage on a freighter as opposed to train or airship, or at least one of the nicer riverboats? It wasn't as though they didn't have the money; Ahle was carrying several hundred, and Perry several thousand, dollars from MI-7's operations account.

"Never did the ocean type of piracy," mused Ahle. "A couple hundred years ago, it might have been fun. White sails and cannon booming."

"Robbing and stealing," said Perry. "Not to mention murder."

"True, those pirates never had a Code to speak of. And their victims never had insurance. You can tell the insured ships, you know. Most of them. Always a bit cocky. The other ones will jettison their cargo rather than be taken, and we'd let them go. The crews of the insured ones never cared. Owner-operators we tried to leave alone."

"Even when they had money?"

Ahle shrugged. The steamer was moving slowly, enormous rear paddle wheel churning spray. They seemed to have reached full speed, and by Perry's eye that full speed wasn't much more than ten or twelve miles an hour. No wonder it was going to take them almost three days to reach New Orleans!

"If you have money, you can afford insurance," said Ahle. "We're just skimming a little bit off the top." She paused. "You know, I never killed anyone as a pirate. Ever."

"I find that hard to believe. You stole enough."

Ahle's lip curled in a slight snarl. "You know, I have to work with you to keep Ronalds, Hollis and the others alive. I don't have to *like* you, Imperial, and I don't. I'm going to the common room for a drink. Alone."

Ahle stormed off.

Loyal to her people?

Well, pirate scum. Loyal to her people meant loyal to scum, even if it meant denying they *were* scum. For a moment he'd almost felt sorry for her, with her officers' lives held to ransom over a mission she wasn't guaranteed to succeed at.

Bastards deserved to hang, of course.

Worry about yourself, Marcus. Worry about Annabelle and what the children will think if you don't succeed at this and you're a fugitive, not a respectable Imperial airshipman, for the rest of your life.

Which won't be long.

* * *

Eventually night fell. A couple of hours after sunset, they stopped by a rickety pier at Cape Girardeau to offload a few passengers and onload a few more. Ahle cooled down, possibly after a few drinks, and got Perry to buy her one – "and one for yourself, we may as well spend Ian's money" – in the common room.

The steward with the slicked-back hair was joined by the other steward, a tubby blond kid who couldn't have been older than seventeen, and who'd given them their tickets at the St. Louis pier. Now the older steward had a microphone, fritzing faintly through a speaker in one end of the common room, and the kid had a sax. The thirty or so traveling workers aboard the steamer gathered in an appreciative crowd in front of them.

"And this evening we have the Albinos; Slick Willy over here out of Little Rock on the saxophone and E.A. Presley – that's me, ladies and gentlemen – on vocals as always. You all got your drinks, because we got a new song for you this trip! The Southern boys' blues, and I think you'll know what we're talking about."

Despite himself, Perry found himself smiling and raising his beer. This was where jazz *came* from, although a couple of stewards on a Mississippi rustbucket couldn't be very good.

He took a sip from his beer and nodded as the kid named Slick Willy opened with a blare on his sax. The other man began to sing:

Dark night, falls over Memphis
Feds they're on the prowl
We're not the Klan, there's not a man
But the Feds, they're on the prowl.

The Feds, they have the khaki
Their Germans wear light grey
Like my great-granddaddy wore
Before he went away

Me, I'm wearing blues
Got the Southern blues
Real bad

The Feds they got the cuffs on you
The mercs they'll simply shoot
All the work my parents did
It goes northeast as loot

I got the Southern blues, man
- Sing it, brother –
Got the below-the-Mason-Dixon blues, real bad.

It went on for a while in that vein – Southern blues singers, it seemed, got a whole lot of material from the Federals' behavior. *And they* are *jerks*, Perry thought; heavyhanded and abusive, while the Imperials looked the other way in total defiance of the Curzon Doctrine.

Then, the Doctrine didn't say anything about Imperial allies, just that the Empire *itself* would respect the absolute right of nations and regions to self-determination. Pieces of the

175

old Empire – most of the Russian Empire now, and the Franco-Spanish Romantics did some pretty atrocious things in Africa and south Asia – had been held in place by force.

Pieces of the post-1909 Refoundation Empire could leave any time they saw fit; they stayed for the benefits and had a voice in its governance. But the United States was an Imperial ally, and treated its South the absolute opposite way; not even trying to win hearts and minds, holding down the territory through brute force. And the Imperials looked the other way, sometimes actively assisted...

They'd argued this sort of thing as cadets at the Academy, and as junior officers. As he'd gotten older and been promoted, abstract philosophical bullshitting became less important; you discussed practicals, not hypotheticals.

But the workers here, the bullied smallholders and dispossessed landholders of the South, the blacks who were abused from both sides, the traveling migrants with him on this boat as it slowly made its way down the black Mississippi – these weren't abstractions or hypotheticals. The people who'd created an entire musical genre were right here, right around him, and he was *working* with someone whose family had been wiped out by mercenaries who completely ignored the Geneva Conventions but had been paid, when you came down to the real source, with Imperial money.

We're supposed to be the good guys, the Empire. But we look the other way at some pretty damn shady and disgusting behavior.

It was confusing and disconcerting to think that people like Ahle might have a point, might have valid grievances.

As the two stewards segued into a new song, about a woman who'd left, as the engines of the heavy steamer thrummed resonantly through the boat, as the *Memphis Darling* pushed her barges slowly down the wide, dark river, Perry headed over to the bar again.

"Scotch," Perry told the off-duty crewman in filthy coveralls, who was filling in as the stewards played. He pushed over a dollar. "And make it a triple."

Chapter Twelve

...also present at the 1875 signing of the Hanoverian Alliance, as part of the British and German entourages respectively, were two officers who, it is known, met. Then-Commander Jackie Fisher, and then-Colonel Ferdinand von Zeppelin.

Fisher was already well-regarded in the Royal Navy for his work on torpedo development, and it is understandable that he at first saw Zeppelin's dirigibles as a means to deliver those. His own diaries, however, show that he was quickly saw other military possibilities in airships, and was determined to add them to his Navy.

In March 1877, four years before the outbreak of the Great War, Fisher was promoted to captain and put in charge of the newly-established Royal Navy Aerial Arm, precursor to the Imperial Air Service that the great military innovator would go on to father...

From *The Air Service: An Abbreviated History*, Chatham Press, 1941.

Karen Ahle loved New Orleans. The Free City, they called it, because it sat on the border of Texas and the United States, looking onto the Gulf of Mexico and its coastlines with Mexico, Yucatan and Spanish Cuba, itself a gateway to vibrant Central America and the teeming Caribbean. There was room for a trade town – trade in goods proper, illicit and stolen – at that intersection, and teeming New Orleans with its thousand fences fit that space as though it had been built for the purpose.

Lake Pontchartrain, as they slowly exited the canal leading to it, was filled with hundreds of airship support barges, more of them loaded than empty. Water taxis and motorboats ferried people around between the barges, or back and forth to the city whose flood-barrier walls rose on their right. The channel was thick with shipping and a breeze blew in their faces, light soot mixed with thick salt, as Perry stood with Ahle and a dozen of the other traveling workers.

"How are we going to *find* this woman once we land?"

177

Perry asked. He seemed to have warmed since their clash, possibly due to seeing first-hand on the ground what the Feds were doing. The boat had been brutally searched in dock at Memphis by a platoon of yellow-uniformed mercenaries, jabbering at each other in fast Italian while occasionally barking an order in broken English at one or another of the stewards.

They hadn't paid much attention to Ahle or the heavily-sweating Perry, but they'd roughed up a couple of the other workers and shaken down a ten-dollar bribe from Perry, who'd simply handed it over without trying to negotiate down. They'd gotten smaller bribes from others of the better-dressed passengers – six fifty from Ahle, after first trying to extort ten – and something from the boat's captain, probably after indicating they'd keep the boat in Memphis indefinitely without it.

That kind of shit could and did happen; for that matter, some of the units – such as the damned murdering Special Squadrons – were known to simply confiscate boats, airships or whatever they could get their hands on.

But they'd made it out, and the experience seemed to have maybe given the Imperial some context. Or perhaps the blues the stewards had been playing; it might have been artistically lacking, but it was genuine, more genuine than the smoothed-up performers at upscale clubs in Dodge and Denver played. Those performers were just making a buck; these guys *felt* it, and maybe some of that had come across.

She looked back at Perry.

"We're not going to find her."

Perry seemed bemused.

"What's the point of this trip, then?"

"You've never heard of Miss Lynch, have you? She knows *everything*. We won't find her; she'll find us. We'll check in at the nearest hotel, get a drink, and wait. It shouldn't take long."

It didn't even take *that* long. They were met at the dock by a well-built, crew-cut man of about thirty who introduced himself as Johnny Unitas. There was a twinge of northerner to his accent, but that didn't surprise Ahle; people of all kinds found their way into New Orleans. Looked unarmed to a casual observer, but Ahle could see the tell-tale bulge of a pistol under his silver-trimmed brown leather jacket, and would have bet he had at least one hideout gun plus a few knives.

"If you'll come this way, Captain; Vice-Commodore?"

He led them off the docks and to a waiting car.

"I trust you have the chip?"

Perry reached into his jacket and handed over the obsidian chip. Unitas inspected it closely, then put it into his own jacket and nodded.

"Take a seat," he said. "The boss will see you after lunch."

New Orleans, at the height of noon in late March, was busy and crowded. The open back of the steam-car made a walking pace through the dock district, past loaded freight trucks and colorfully dressed pedestrians, toward and into the dense, crowded French Quarter. Ahle was aware – Perry probably wasn't – that they were being led and tailed by narrow two-man electro-quadripedes that weaved in and out of the traffic but always kept about the same fifty-foot distance.

Unitas, riding shotgun, was maintaining a degree of alertness himself. They passed a bronze statue, thirty feet high, of Governor Huey Long, at the center of a rotary, and then the streets became a lot denser and the buildings a lot older. The traffic only increased, though, and even Ahle – a Southerner, used to it normally – was feeling the heat and the humidity as the car inched through crowded traffic.

* * *

Eventually they stopped outside a discreetly upscale cafe with a couple of loitering men smoking cigarettes around it. As Perry watched, one of them ambled off, only for another passer-by – in an expensively fake airshipman's rig, thigh-high leather boots and a begoggled top-hat; urban trash with money – to take up station a few feet from where the first man had been.

He wasn't as familiar with this business as Ahle clearly was, but his few days of accelerated training with Agent Connery had taught him a few things. One of them was that these men were obviously guards, and another was that if a professional like this Miss L apparently was, had two guards visible, there were going to be at least four in the windows and rooftops. A lot of security for a brothel.

"Welcome to Denard's Cafe," said their guide, the man

called Unitas. "Why don't you come in and have a couple of drinks? Miss L will make herself available to you presently."

This is a lot of rigamarole to deal with a two-bit information broker, he thought.

Then corrected himself. Her man had known – *she* knew – that he was an Imperial Vice-Commodore. He hoped nobody had noticed the chills that ran down his spine at that; he'd never imagined the underworld having resources, information like that implied.

Surely any intelligent person would focus their efforts through legitimate channels, rise honorably as his parents had, as *he* was – or hoped he still was – doing?

The outside of Denard's was discreetly upscale, but the inside wasn't the slightest bit discreet about it. They passed through a couple of extravagant anterooms and into an – airconditioned! – room that stank faintly of expensive cigar smoke. The furniture, including the long bar that ran down one side of the long room, was expensive mahogany decorated with what seemed like real gold.

At midday, it was about half-full, two thirds women in expensive frilly dresses of bright silk; one or two of them carried parasols, indoors. The men wore suits, for the most part, black and white, a few in white-vested black suits. There was none of your trashy wannabe-airshipman fashion here; pure class, through and through, with about fifty percent more class added on for emphasis. It *felt* like a bordello.

Unitas guided them to a table at one side.

"Drinks while you wait?"

"Rum."

"Of course." A liveried flunky had followed them to the table. "Rum, for the captain. For the Vice-Commodore?"

"Just iced water, thank you."

"Something we don't serve, I'm terribly sorry to say. How about Scotch on the rocks?"

This wasn't a place to get drunk, or even buzzed.

It probably wasn't a place to make enemies, either.

"Heavily watered."

"Very well, sir."

Unitas left them as the drinks arrived. Perry took a cautious sip. Well up to Fleming's standards, and past Flight Admiral Richardson's; this was close to the best Scotch he'd ever tasted.

A single-malt with a light, peaty flavor. He took another, appreciative sip. From the look of her, Ahle was enjoying her rum just as much – more, because she was at ease here. She'd been here before, she'd said, but never been granted an audience with the infamous Miss L.

A heavily-tanned man in a tricornet – a *tricornet!* – appeared, came over to the table. The rest of his dress was as idiosyncratic as his hat: double-buttoned red coat, bright white pants, knee-high boots with wholly unnecessary buckles that could only have been solid gold. A cutlass hung by his side.

"If it isn't Karen Ahle," he said. His accent was Australian. "And her renegade Air Service Vice-Commodore. It's good to see you alive, Captain."

Ahle rose, extended the back of her hand. The man flamboyantly kissed it.

"If it isn't Captain Brian Carbin," she said.

"Her renegade Air Service Vice-Commodore," Carbin addressed Perry. He'd been carrying a glass, and he raised it. "To true love, Vice-Commodore. And to the wrong side of the tracks.

Manners required Perry to touch his glass to Carbin's, which contained a bright pink concoction with an umbrella.

"To true love," he agreed, thinking of Annabelle. "A wonderful thing."

"A lot of people are wondering how you escaped Hugoton but your officers didn't make it," said Carbin. "One might have thought you'd have brought at least *one* along with you."

"I tried," said Perry. "But the place is an Imperial stronghold."

"In the same cells as they were, no doubt." Carbin was a lot more serious now. "And yet, none of them escaped. While your crew was wiped out by, shall we say, *unknown assailants.*"

"And?" Ahle asked.

"Your accounts in Sonora don't have to be split so many ways as they had, did they?"

Ahle became equally cold.

"What are you implying, Carbin?"

"I'm not the first to speculate. I'm the first to see you, though, and raise the matter."

Unitas coughed discreetly behind Captain Carbin.

"Captain, Vice-Commodore? The madam will see you

now."

* * *

From what he'd heard of her, and gathered, Perry had formed certain expectations of Miss Lynch. From what he'd experienced so far working for Fleming, at some level he'd expected to be proven dead wrong yet again. It was almost disconcerting that this time, his expectations of Miss Markell Lynch had been absolutely dead right.

She was a blonde woman with an elaborate hairdo, dressed *very* expensively in a corset and light jacket. Attractive and in her early forties, her high-heeled boots lay crossed over one another on the top of a broad oak desk in an office that rivaled Fleming's for luxury. She waved an ostrich-feather fan in front of her face as Ahle and Perry entered.

"So Fleming finally saw fit to call on me, did he? Sit down. Drinks?"

"No, thank you," said Perry, before Ahle could ask for more rum.

"Captain Ahle?"

"Another rum, thank you."

"You heard the lady," Lynch said to one of the elaborately-carved wooden panels.

The door behind them opened – had Unitas really closed it? – and another flunky came in with a glass of the same color of rum Ahle had been drinking in the entrance room.

"So, Ian Fleming sent you. I'm not remotely surprised that he did at this time; I've been expecting it ever since that spy war began. What specifically can I help you with?"

This woman was probably very good at playing the back-and-forth game, thought Perry, better than he was and probably better than Ahle. You didn't play to an opponent's strengths; he'd get straight to the point.

"We're looking for a stolen line-class airship designated DN 4-106," said Perry.

A smile came across Lynch's face.

"For a moment," she said, "I was afraid you were going to ask me something hard."

You know where it is?

How *could* this woman in New Orleans, *however* excellently-

182

informed, know where his ship had vanished to? That was insane!

"I can also give you the last known location of Theron Marko, the man who stole it. I imagine Mr. Fleming would be *very* interested to learn that."

"He would be," said Perry. "Are you going to tell us, already?"

Lynch smiled.

"Certainly. But I need a small favor from you first."

"What kind?"

"Nothing substantial. I simply need you to obtain important documents from one of the better-organized mercenary units in the South. Events have piqued my curiosity."

"Buy them?" Perry asked.

"I could buy them myself if they could be bought. The Special Squadrons have vices; they have rather a lot of vices. Those vices do not include corruption on any substantive level."

"Plenty of fucking other ones, though," said Ahle.

"Technically," said Lynch, "rape and murder are sins, not vices. I know they wiped out your family; I was in Raleigh then. You *do* know what they call Heinrich Himmler, correct?"

"The Butcher of Raleigh," Ahle muttered.

"What they did to Wake Forest, they did far worse to Raleigh," said Lynch. "I was there at the time. But one depersonalizes and allows the memories to pass. Are you willing, Captain Ahle, to engage these people?"

"I was already planning to," said Ahle.

"Vice-Commodore, do you want your airship back? Do you want your airship back sufficiently as to go to Missouri and get me what *I* want?"

"This wasn't the deal," said Perry. However nasty these Special Squadrons guys were, they were still employees of an ally! How far did things have to *go*?

"It's the deal I'm offering you," said Lynch. "Satisfy my curiosity and I'll satisfy yours."

"You owe Fleming a favor already."

"He must have misspoken. I owe him a *hearing*; that's what the black chip means. I'll talk to his people, which I'm doing now. I'm offering you a quite reasonable deal. Center place in an already-planned operation where I could just use a couple of experienced people to execute the meat of. Do you want to or not?"

"I want to," said Ahle immediately. "Hadn't expected to mix pleasure with business."

"Hold on, Ahle," said Perry.

"No. This is the best deal we're going to get from her."

"I'm said to be honorable," said Lynch, a faint smile on her face.

Documents. Documents could be replaced.

Who would this woman in turn sell them to, though?

What kind of secret plans would the Special Squadrons *have*, though? They were a mercenary unit whose job was regional counterinsurgency, an ongoing task you rarely needed specific major plans for. Something about the negotiations they were involved in, nothing too substantial. Important to the shady underground, not to anyone else. Blackmail, not treason...

"You swear you'll give me the location of 4-106. That you know it and you'll give it."

"It's in a certain canyon in Colorado, at present," said Lynch. "I'll give you a map when you give me the Squadrons' plans."

"You'll hand over the map first."

"We have a deal, Vice Commodore," said Lynch. "You'll head for Missouri tonight."

Chapter Thirteen

Interviewer: Your name and rank at the time of the action, please.

Subject: Jason Cordova, mister. Commodore – they called me a colonel – of the Republic of Texas Air Force. I commanded my Armadillos.

Interviewer: Who were the Armadillos?

Subject: *Cordova's* Armadillos, baby.

Interviewer: Right. Who were they?

Subject: Are they. We're still around and kicking ass.

Interviewer: Right. Who?

Subject: My ship, the *Lone Star*. Jennifer Atkinson and the *Squeeze*. Bill Snider on his *Scimitar of Silence*. Paula Handley on *The Vorpal*. Shirley Meier on the *Pith and Vinegar*. Richard Evans on the *Dread Wyvern* and Peggey Rowland with her *Five Speed*.

Interviewer: And what happened in the incident we're referring to?

Subject: First I'm going to have to give you an overview. We'd been on service to Texas for the last couple of years, and at the time they were balls-deep with Sonora in the territory the old USA called 'New Mexico.' They'd taken Santa Fe and General Houston was trying like hell to withdraw his Second Army from Alberquerque before it got encircled, too. The damn Sennies knew it and were pressing hard.

Interviewer: So what were you facing?

Subject: All the Tex ships had withdrawn, leaving just us. Expendable, they obviously figured. Mercenaries. So we had our seven and shit-else. The enemy had at least twenty line-class ships over Alberquerque, and a dozen more escort-classes.

Interviewer: So what happened?

Subject: You know perfectly well what happened. They made two films about it. We whipped 'em but good. Four times our weight and we wiped 'em out. Completely. Your troops didn't have to surrender; they withdrew in good order and whupped some Sennie ass along the way.

Unitas and eight other men were in the airship's cabin with them, a small, sleek private ship named the *Marlyville Zephyr*, that was right now speeding through the afternoon at two thousand feet over Louisiana. Bayous unfolded below them, but Ahle had more important concerns than the scenery.

She was finally getting a crack at the Squadrons! She'd waited her entire adult life for this; it was what she'd hoped to do with 4-106, hit the bastards with *real* force, take out a measurable amount of their strength and ideally their top officer, the man who'd killed her family, Heinrich Himmler.

Only a minor crack, but *still!*

Perry was a lot less happy, but screw him. He seemed to dig that Lynch did have the whereabouts of 4-106 and would give it to him. His mission would be complete, sooner rather than later.

That Lynch clearly considered this job too dangerous to trust to her own people – Unitas and his squad would be the diversionary element, not the main attack taking the main risk – was irrelevant to Perry. Air Service officers were promoted on brains and skill, not dumb courage – it was what made the Imperials so damn dangerous – but they didn't lack courage either. And Perry was the driven kind; he'd rather die than lose honor.

He's already lost his honor, Ahle corrected herself. *But he'll die to regain it.*

The plan was simple. A couple of high-ranking SS emissaries were coming from Texas, heading for SS HQ in Colombus, Missouri. The SS had a base in Joplin, in the southeastern corner of Missouri, where the emissaries were right now, and they'd be going to the main headquarters in Kansas City.

If past behavior was to be repeated, the SS emissaries would land in Joplin and ride from there in the ground vehicles they were more comfortable in. Heavy armored vehicles that a direct attack simply wouldn't work on; that was what they were *used* to. The SS had an incredible amount of institutional knowledge at dealing with asymmetrically-fighting local insurgents, which they'd been doing for a solid third of a century now.

But a high-ranking SS emissary – Lynch had told them that the principal was a full colonel in his early sixties – would not want to sleep in the field unless he had to. They wouldn't want to drive through the night either; that was the best time for ambush from an ambushers'-survivability standpoint, since there was darkness to melt their way into.

So it was almost certain that the colonel and his entourage would stay in Joplin until dawn, and only then move. That was an opening.

Unitas and his squad would link up with local Klanners – who she'd always considered distasteful, and she could see from the look on Perry's dark face that he *hated* the association for more than one reason – and attack. Meanwhile, she and Perry would paraglide in from an airship, get into the guest quarters, find the plans and escape into the other direction from the ambush.

A simple plan, the good kind.

* * *

Otto Skorzeny got out of the airship at Joplin, Missouri, or rather the base a safe couple of miles south of that town. The sight of the heavy armor was reassuring; three steam-tanks, hulking grey Tiger IIbs with their double five-inch rocket launchers. Light armor, too, a trio of eight-wheeled support carriers; light tanks with wheels and speed, to all intents and purposes. There should have been four, but he'd been informed that one was in the shop.

Special operations had been the start of his career, in Poland and then the early years of the Special Squadrons; death from above, the airborne assault tactics that had been pioneered in the Great War and developed extensively since.

But as he'd gotten older and – *be realistic, Otto,* he told himself – slower and heavier, he'd become rather fond of having a heavy tank to carry him around, not to mention having its two inches of frontal armor between himself and incoming fire.

Of course, he told himself, returning the salutes of the men he passed as he headed toward the base's guest quarters, *we're going to be facing a whole lot more than insurgent fire before this is done.*

He'd been back to homeland Prussia on sabbatical a few times, sabbatical for him meaning more fighting in different environments. He'd *seen* what a Polish nine-inch rocket could do to the armor on a Tiger II. For a lot of the Squadrons' younger men, grunts who'd come from fractured Germania seeking fortunes, or at least a stable income and some land to confiscate for their own, it would be new. A lot of them wouldn't survive the experience.

He pushed those thoughts from his mind and turned to address the leader of his escort, a promising young first lieutenant named Schierbecker.

"Your men can take quarters," he said. "Schierbecker, speak with the base commander regarding security and report to me when done."

Schierbecker gave the arm-out, palm-forward salute the Squadrons used.

"Jawohl, mein Oberst."

"English, please," said Skorzeny. For the benefit of the Third Department man on Skorzeny's heels, a man with the – acquired, as Skorzeny well knew, and this man had acquired it well – knack of making himself seem invisible from three feet away.

"Yessir, Colonel."

"Thank you."

Joplin was a small base, home to one light and one heavy mobile platoon, plus an infantry detachment for local security. The base itself consisted of two buildings; the main quarters, a heavy three-storey building with a watch tower reaching into the sky, and an auxiliary building with garages below and the guest quarters above. Sitting in the open plains, it was all ringed with thick razor wire, heavy pillboxes at the corners and the main entrance. Not the best of security, not when the plans under Skorzeny's arms – as he entered the best of the guest rooms, secured the valise and lay down on the room's only other item of furniture, the bed – were so important.

He wasn't getting any younger. Neither was the commander, General Heinrich Himmler, or his deputy, Brigadier-General Sepp Dietrich, or any of the other top officers who'd been with the organization from its start. This plan was going to be their retirement; a final big operation for the top officers, with enough payment that they'd be able to retire in comfort to somewhere pleasant. Maybe South America, where they weren't known.

With that in mind, Himmler had sent half of one of the mobile reserve battalions down to meet them, traveling at night despite the danger; no small group of Klanners would be insane enough to attack two full armored companies traveling at night, and there wouldn't be time for a large group to assemble. They were due for arrival a couple of hours before dawn.

They were relatively unprotected *now*, but as of tomorrow morning they would be very, very well protected indeed.

Skorzeny put his hands behind his head, lay back on the hard bed and tried to relax. This time tomorrow he and the plans would be safe in Columbia.

* * *

Perry felt the gas gun, then handed it back. Produced his own, a much finer weapon, from the bag of goodies Fleming had given them.

"I'll take your magazines, though," he said. Accepted four of them, clipped them onto his belt.

"Do you want a little insurance?" Unitas offered him a .45. "Just in case things go badly wrong and they're wearing masks or something?"

"I have my own gun."

"I'll take one of those submachineguns," said Ahle. They were in the *Marlyville Zephyr's* arms closet, a room hidden toward the tail of the airship's rigid structure. A shaft ran through the roof of it, intermittently drawing back and forth as it controlled one of the steering vanes.

"Here you are."

Ahle inspected the weapon, which had a short barrel perforated with penny-sized holes for air cooling, and a big forty-round drum magazine.

"More ammo," she said, ignoring Perry's glare and slinging the gun over her shoulder. Around her neck – and Perry's – hung black facemasks for use with the gas guns.

"You are *not* going to kill Imperial allies," said Perry. "That's where I draw the line. Attacking with nonlethals is one

189

thing. You're not going to kill them."

"I'll treat them just as they treated my family," Ahle said. "Out of courtesy to *you*, I won't kill them unless forced. If it's them or me..."

"If it's them or you," Perry began, but stopped. Obviously she wasn't going to surrender. For that matter, neither was he, if you *really* came down to it.

Ahle grinned at him.

"Thought so. How long do we have?"

Unitas pulled out his watch, a plain silver model. Checked it. "We drop in just under an hour, at midnight. Rendezvous with the Cyclo—" A look at Perry, who had made no secret that he *hated* working alongside the Klan – "with the leader of our local auxiliaries. This ship goes back up. Attack commences at four am, time when the human body's normally most tired and they're going to be the least effective. You guys drop from your gliders at the same time. Guide yourselves in and engage the man with the documents. We'll keep up the distraction for as long as we can then withdraw to the north. You withdraw to the south and fire a flare to get picked up. Clear?"

"Clear," said Perry flatly.

"Been waiting years to take a crack at these bastards," said Ahle happily. "Whenever you guys are ready."

* * *

Nerves in Perry's throat as the *Zephyr* sat above the clouds a mile up, two miles to the windward of the Joplin base. It was a light wind and a dark, overcast night; there'd hopefully be just enough light to make out their objective, which would be in the second building. Unitas had shown them a map; guest quarters were presumed to be above the garage, a low two-storey building.

Perry hoped Lynch's intelligence on this was as good as it seemed to be on everything else.

He hoped it *was* as good on everything else as everyone seemed to think. What if they went through all of this – attacking allied mercenaries, for God's sake! – only to find she'd been wrong or lying about 4-106?

Think on the good side, he told himself. *We've got a well-planned operation. Go in, grab whatever documents they have, spray*

190

anyone who gets in our way, and escape out the back. It's not rocket science. Then come back, get the location of 4-106, retrieve my ship and fly back to Hugoton with honor. Sooner than I'd expected.

"One minute," said Ahle. They were in the ship's cargo hold, strapped into the long detachable gliders.

"Pilot says to tell you we're still on station," said a crewman.

"Fifty seconds. You ready?"

"As I'll ever be."

No time to worry about what might go wrong. Hadn't enough things gone wrong already?

"Thirty seconds. Opening door," said the ship's crewman. He pulled a chain and the cargo hold's wide door swung downwards with an oiled clank. Perry could see the shape of clouds moving, not too far below.

I've done the cross-training. I know how to handle an assault glider.

"Fifteen seconds," said Ahle. Was that bloodthirsty idiot *grinning?*

"Ten."

"Five." Ahle dropped her watch back into the pocket of her jacket. Pulled the mask on. Perry was already wearing his.

"Four," came Ahle's heavily-muffled voice through the mask. She adjusted it slightly.

"Three. Two. One. Launch."

Ahle, then Perry, took a short run and then leapt out of the hold. For a moment the heavy wings were nothing but drag, as they fell, but then the edge of the hang-gliders caught the air and they were flying. Exposed under the raw aerodynamic wing of the glider, they swept through thick misty clouds and then down under them.

Ahead and to their right, pinprick flashes and tiny cracks of gunfire. A klaxon wailed, faint from this distance but probably deafening up close. The dark compound looked much as it had on paper; the two large fences, surrounded by a ring of barbed wire and stolid pillboxes. Two searchlights came on, pointing north, sweeping. One of them went out mid-sweep.

Ahle, eighty or so feet ahead of him, turned and gave Perry a thumbs-up. Angled her glider slightly to the left.

Perry returned the thumbs-up and angled his glider the same way.

The wind swept past them, the ground rushed below them, as they lost height. The sounds became more audible, gunfire gaining strength, the klaxon wailing further.

From the locations of the muzzle-flashes, Perry could get an approximate idea of the direction the fighting was taking. The attackers were spread out in an approximate half-circle focused on the base's front entrance; the SS was shooting back from pillboxes and their heavy main building. As Perry watched, the headlights and then the shapes of one, two, three of their tanks appeared, moving in single file toward the gate.

Immediately below, two gouts of flame from something. Mortars, it seemed, as the shells crashed into the base. More fire opened up from that direction.

Draw them out against the frontal attack. and then enfilade 'em. The Klan were smarter than he'd given them credit for.

Perhaps not too much smarter. The enfilade fire was only coming from one side, not the two that it *could* have come from. Perry felt relief despite himself; it was good to know that those race-hating bastards weren't too competent.

Down to within a few hundred yards, a couple of hundred yards up. The ground was racing past now, loose scrub and trees, and then they crossed into the two-hundred-yard perimiter the SS had swept clean around their base. Low grass, regularly cut. Stubs that might have been mines. Inside the base, men were still running, and the gunfire now was a din; incoming rifle rounds, outgoing machine guns stammering lengthily at every muzzle-flash.

Perry aimed his glider at the roof and hoped, prayed. Unhooked his feet as they passed across the barbed-wire fence, feeling the glider tilt and slow. Ahle was already landing on the secondary building's sloped wooden roof, shrugging off the glider.

Perry joined her a moment later, his rubber-soled boots crashing into the roof. The glider wanted to go further, and he wrestled it to the ground. Pulled the nailgun from its upper strut and fired one, two, three, four, five, half a dozen nails into it, to keep it from tumbling to the ground and immediately warning people.

A glance around. They were below the level of the main three-storey barracks building, but that was to their north and all their attention seemed to be focused that way, or to the

192

enfilading fire from the northeast. The secondary building that they were on was south of that.

Ahle already had her crowbar out, was working at the hatch set tightly in the door. Perry went over, gas gun raised, pointed it down at the hatch as Ahle got the bar placed and began to apply pressure.

The door came open with a crack., and Perry stared straight into the face of an assault rifle. A flash of an instant; a bowl-helmeted SS man who must have heard Ahle at work, or had a bad feeling or *something*–

His fingers closed around the trigger of the gun he'd already aimed down. A thick stream of gas poured down into the man's face.

The man pulled the trigger of his own gun, and rounds whistled up into the air, but he was already choking. The rest of his automatic burst thudded into the ceiling; he could feel the rounds impacting under his feet. Ahle was already dropping through, fired her gas gun at something else; Perry braced himself and followed.

They were in a barracks bunkhouse, triple bunks spaced tightly together. They were made and looked unoccupied; definitely guest quarters. The place smelled of piss, unwashed bodies and old tobacco.

Ahle gestured toward the place's one door, stopping for a moment to give one of the two disabled SS men a vicious kick to the ribs. Then another burst of spray to the face, which caused him to redouble his choking. Through the mask Perry heard her mutter something about Raleigh.

"No time for that shit," Perry snapped at her. "Let's move."

They'd already gassed two men. At some level he'd hoped to accomplish this totally cleanly. Well, they were in it now, in more than one way. Only one way out, and that was through.

Mission confirmed. Engage. Time later to worry about the morality of it all.

Gun raised to his shoulder, he ran forward to the door, stopped at either side. It looked onto a corridor; the big bunkroom seemed to take up about half the building. On the other side of the corridor was a line of doors that seemed to be private rooms.

Which one was the man with the documents in?

Ahle arrived next to him.

"Cover me," Perry snapped, and headed for – not the nearest door, which said 'Washroom', but the next one, about ten feet further down the corridor. Stepped back, braced himself, booted it in.

Bed and dresser. No people.

Wished he'd brought the crowbar down from the roof. Kicking in every last one of these doors...

"Use this," Ahle said, moving toward him with one of the fallen SS men's automatic rifles. Long barrel and a banana clip. Then dropped it, raised her gas gun, squirted a long burst at a man who'd come through one of the doors with a drawn pistol. The man fell backward against the wall, dropping the pistol to clutch at his face.

"Or there. Oh shit."

A man emerged from the same door with a submachinegun. Bullets spat. One of them slammed into Perry's chest, a horse's kick despite the thick kevlar he was wearing. He threw himself sideways through the door he'd just kicked open, his chest screaming pain.

Don't think about the pain. Or the busted ribs. We've got an armed one ready for us.

* * *

Skorzeny ducked back into his room, changed magazines. Two confirmed, but he thought he'd gotten one. Maybe not – that had looked like a *controlled* dive, like a man in armor might make.

Two against one. The rest of his escorts – Lieutenant Schierbecker and one man had gone out to see what was going on with the attack, which *had* seemed too well-timed to be truly coincidental. The sergeant, with him, had been the sacrificial lamb for the benefit of Skorzeny getting a picture of the situation.

He had that now. Two attackers who'd come in through the roof, probably by glider. His two men guarding the roof hatch had been taken down, and the other two at the front entrance were out of reach. They wouldn't hear his calling above the sound of the gunfire and the light mortars that seemed to be landing randomly in the compound.

So it was two to one. He'd faced much worse odds than

194

that in his life. And they were using, for some insane reason, nonlethal gas guns. A competence/qualification exercise?

He hadn't been notified of that. If that bastard Interior Secretary Hoover wanted to pull shit like that on him at this time?

Well, the *Wichser* would be down two agents.

Pulling the mask on over his face, Skorzeny drew his pistol. When you were outnumbered, only one course of action. It had served him well throughout a long life. Attack.

* * *

"He's wearing a mask!" Ahle shouted to Perry, and dropped the now-worthless gas gun. Threw herself back into the bunkroom. Her back pressed against the wall, she unslung the submachinegun and prepared to reach out.

Bullets smacked at her. She pressed herself back. Shit. Shit, shit.

Perry would hesitate. And the bastard would get them both. She was fairly sure that this one was the ranking SS emissary.

Ranking SS meant he'd probably been active twenty years ago. Probably had rank then, too.

Probably been in Wake Forest.

Wish I had a usable grenade, she thought, glancing out and ducking back again. A bullet chewed splinters from the doorway an inch from her face.

* * *

Skorzeny advanced down the corridor, his ears focused, listening. His submachinegun was trained on the door the man he'd shot had fallen into; he was going to go in, spray the room with lead while keeping the other one pinned, then take the pinned one down. Another shot – and another – served to keep that one pinned.

Wish I had a couple of grenades, he thought.

Advancing. Another shot at the door, keeping the one in there pinned. And – on the ground, a boot and a heavy shape.

I did get you!

He threw himself into the room, emptying fire into the

195

shape, realizing as he lunged over it that it was two-dimensional and empty –

* * *

Perry, in socks and shirtsleeves, launched himself at the man in a punishing rugby tackle. His shoulder crunched into the bastard's stomach, slamming him once then – half a second and three feet later – again, as the momentum slammed the already-dazed man against the facing wall.

He heard, rather than saw or felt, weapons clattering to the ground, but there was no time to do anything but press the advantage. Punched him in the stomach, then a hand found the man's forehead – he was turning his head, trying to bite, one hand reaching already into his belt – and slammed it against the wall, once, again, three times.

He straightened up, kept slamming the man's head against the wall until the man stopped moving. Then Perry let him slump to the ground.

"Bastard," he hissed, recovering his breath. The last five or ten seconds had taken more out of him than the entire operation until that point.

Ahle appeared, saw the unconscious SS man. Looked to be about sixty, maybe late fifties. Prominent scar on his cheek. Shoulderboards had some organizationally-unique insignia that Perry couldn't read – a U-shaped pattern of stripes – but there were a lot of them. High-ranking guy. That and his age almost definitely made him the emissary.

"That's Skorzeny," said Ahle. She turned back to the door, covering the corridor with her submachinegun. "Shit, Vice. You took down Otto Skorzeny." She glanced at his feet. "With your boots off."

"*Never* thought I'd use rugby once I got out of the Academy," Perry gasped. He picked up his gas gun, gave the unconscious man a burst in the face for good measure. Couldn't be too careful. He let the gun drop on his sling and reached down for his boots.

"I could do him more permanently. *Please* let me do the bastard more permanently."

"No."

"He might get up. Men like that can take almost anything.

196

If we don't take him down, he'll be a problem in future. If he lives, he'll be a problem in future."

"For someone else."

"For *my* people. I have an account in Sonora, Vice. Successful pirate. I'll give you two years' worth of your pay, write you a check as soon as we're back in New Orleans, if I can just cut his throat. Please."

"No. Not going to kill a man who's down. Thought you had your Code?"

"The man's a war criminal. Member of a criminal organization."

"He's gassed and unconscious," said Perry. "You're going to cut the throat of an unconscious man? Would your Kennedys approve of that?"

Ahle mouthed something pissed-off – she'd lost the mask when she pulled the rifle – and turned back toward the corridor.

"Didn't think so. Get that mask back on and we'll grab the documents and scram."

Perry carefully behind Ahle – he was fairly sure she wouldn't turn around and try to kill Skorzeny, but he *knew* how much she hated these guys and their senior officers especially – they headed down the corridor for Skorzeny's room.

Inside was a rumpled bed, a duffel bag and a compact briefcase chained to the radiator.

"*Shit*," Perry muttered. "Give me that rifle."

"Could be chips in there," said Ahle. "Cover me. There'll be more."

"What are you doing?"

In answer, Ahle reached for a thigh pocket and showily palmed a set of lockpicks.

"Didn't you once call me a thief?" she asked.

* * *

From the gunner's seat of his command car near the head of the half-battalion that had been sent down from Columbia to escort Colonel Skorzeny back, Major Brent Roeder looked at the sky on the horizon. There were flashes and flickering, coming – he confirmed on his compass and map – from the exact direction of the base at Joplin.

That meant a firefight. The flares had been sent up by the local garrison, which he knew wasn't very big.

His vehicles had been moving slowly, at about fifty percent of the Tiger II and IIb tanks' safe maximum speed – *twenty* percent of the light Cheetah armored cars' maximum – for the sake of saving fuel and not inflicting needless damage on the roads.

Now, the garrison seemed to have come under attack. Roeder was an experienced soldier in his early forties, a man who'd come up from the ranks and had his share of skirmishes in the violent Silesian borderlands even before joining the Squadrons. You didn't win battles by hesitating.

And you *definitely* didn't win battles by pretending there wasn't one happening.

"Full speed ahead!" he shouted. Leaned down to his driver. "The hell with fuel and we don't have an hour. Get us to the Joplin base *now*."

* * *

It was a tense few minutes, the sound of the firefight going on outside. Perry had to remind himself that although it *felt* like half an hour since they'd landed, it had really been – he checked his watch to confirm; less than quarter of an hour past four – yes, barely five minutes. Unitas' men and the Klan wouldn't last forever, but they'd hold on longer than *that*.

Tense moments. The second-hand of Perry's watch, as he stood with mask on and gas gun pointed down the stairs, clicked painfully slowly. Ahle muttered something about a bitch of a lock.

Eventually it came open with a click. Triumphantly, Ahle opened the still-chained briefcase. It had taken more than three minutes.

"You've got a bag," she said. "Get that shit in there while I cover you."

Perry nodded, and they changed places. Inside were several small cases that could have held either decks of playing cards or, much more likely, chips for an analytical. They were numbered, and he scooped them into the bag. Underneath that were folders, and Perry froze.

He didn't read much German. The under-text on the label of the top one, he couldn't read. Teil eins von sechs something-something-something.

The label, he could clearly read. The last words of it struck him like a hammer to the face:

Karten, Hugoton Lease.

Hugoton?

Hugoton?

What in God's name would Federal mercenaries want with maps – and *chips* – of Hugoton?

A unit that's talking about not renewing its contract, mind...

"Perry! Perry, damnit!"

"Hugoton. These are maps of the Hugoton Lease!"

"Who *cares*? Just get them into the bag and we'll go! Worry about content later!"

The sound of stamping boots on the stairway. "Because it looks like we've got friends coming."

Hugoton, Perry thought, and shoveled the rest of the material – folders and then more chip-cases – into the backpack. A scan for interior compartments – no, nothing – and then picking up the gun.

"Oberst? Mein Oberst?" shouted a man, half-appearing at the top of the stairwell. Perry sprayed him in the face and he tumbled backwards, rolling down the stairs.

A shout came from below.

Oh, fuck, thought Perry, *that's torn it.*

"Move! Down, and we'll *find* a way!" Ahle snapped. "Before they mobilize!"

Down the stairs, which led into a garage with a hulking eight-wheeled combat vehicle parked under a refueling chute. The door leading out – he could taste the fresh air, see the darkness – was a few feet away.

A figure ran through it, blinked to deal with the light and shouted something. Ahle shot him – not with a gas gun, with the *real* submachinegun she'd never put down, fired a burst into him.

Shit, shit and *shit*, thought Perry; *we'll never be able to pass this off as a training exercise now.*

The man had friends, too. They were gathering on the other side of the door, talking in fast German.

It was obvious that they were preparing to storm the door;

they had no idea how many people were inside and were being hesitant. As soon as an officer or NCO showed up...

"Into the vehicle!" Ahle shouted, already stepping up the ladder on its side.

He followed her. It was the only hard cover, yes. And – he took position behind the thing – it had a gun.

Benefits of being a counterinsurgency organization. An Imperial vehicle in the shop would *never* have had live ammo in the hopper for its turret-mounted chaingun, but these guys weren't behind safe lines; they were an isolated garrison in the middle of territory that collectively hated them.

He began to chamber a round into the gun he was behind, then thought better of it. Raised the gas gun instead, pointed it at the door. Maybe he could gas the first ones to come through, but the others – they *did* carry masks. They'd be impervious.

Shit. Shit. And Fleming was going to be *very* interested in why this mercenary organization had an emissary coming from Texas – Texas, with no love for the United States – with maps of Hugoton.

Maps that, he realized in a jolt of shock, *they must have obtained from 4-106 when it flew over the place!*

These people had a connection, although it was impossible Miss L could have realized it, with the bastards who'd stolen 4-106!

He put down the gas gun and racked the bolt of the chaingun back.

Ahle was in back, doing something. He heard something clank. She moved forward, took position below him, in the driver's seat. Muttered something.

"Was that for me?" Perry asked.

Somebody had arrived outside the door, was barking orders. Perry aimed the chaingun – it worked the same as an airship's weapons turret, pedals turning the turret by air compression – at the door and gave them a warning burst.

"Pressure gauge in the vehicle," she said, louder. "Warming up. Let's see if these controls work as they should."

"You know how to drive one of these?"

"You don't realize, do you? I've *studied* the Special Squadrons. I've seen a spec sheet for this vehicle. Cheetah IV, and the crew hasn't done too much personal modification to this particular one. Just keep these assholes off us for a few minutes while the boiler warms and we'll get *out* of here!"

"The garage door's closed!"

"And?"

"With your hands up surrender!" one the SS men – the officer? – outside the door yelled.

Perry considered saying something back, then swept the door with another burst. These people weren't going to be insane enough to charge, would they?

No. But they had heavy armored vehicles – more of this particular type, and three much *larger* tanks, at least one of which was operational. With bigger guns.

"How's that boiler coming?" he called down to Ahle.

"Just a couple more minutes."

* * *

The lights – not many of them – of the small town of Joplin, Missouri, drew closer to Roeder's bouncing command car, which was pushing sixty miles an hour across the barely-paved road. The tanks had been left behind, were chewing that road up into a gravely mess at their own top speed a few miles ago.

"Just a few more minutes," Roeder's driver assured him.

* * *

"They're coming from behind us!" the hooded man next to Unitas snarled, turning around.

Yes. Headlights.

Oh, *shit*, thought Unitas. *The bastards had reinforcements a lot closer than we realized.*

The Klansman was already blowing a whistle. Unitas had to agree.

Those two in there are just shit out of luck, if they're not gone already. We're getting the hell out.

* * *

The Cheetah armored car was getting hot, which *had* to imply the boiler was heating up. And the men outside were getting very antsy; Perry had held them at bay with bursts from the chaingun so far, but how long before they dug out high-explosive grenades or simply brought in one of their already-activated heavy tanks?

"OK!" Ahle said. "Get your head down, because we're *going!*"

Perry braced himself. Then something occurred to him.

"This thing's in the maintenance shop."

"And?"

"You don't take things into the maintenance shop without a *reason!*"

"You don't take things through the closed front door of a maintenance shop without a reason, either!" Ahle yelled back, and hit the steam.

The car surged forward, Perry ducking behind the gun and its shield. Thin aluminum scraped hard, gratingly, painfully against the top of the Cheetah, and bullets slammed into the vehicle's armor. SS men on the other side of the door threw themselves clear.

"Shit shit *shit!*" Ahle yelled, and swerved hard.

Something big exploded behind them.

"Cover us! Aim for his vision slits! Aim for the commander!" she screamed.

Perry got up again, hunched over the gun's shield and hit the right pedal, rotating the tub in the direction of – *oh God*, he thought – the massive steam-tank twenty feet away. Thirty feet. Forty. Both of its two broad turrets were swiveling slowly toward the accelerating armored car, as Ahle shifted gears.

Perry raked the tank with fire, and he could *see* the sparking rounds bounce off. Oh, *shit*, he thought, but they were gaining speed, crunching over the multiple layers of razor wire.

"Flaregun," he said. "Gimme that flaregun for our pickup!"

"Later," Ahle snapped, and hard-turned the vehicle forty-five degrees right to keep from slamming into a tree. This area was almost a plain; smooth ground with a few copses of light trees here and there, a handful of bigger trees standing alone.

Ahle jerked the vehicle to the right, and a shell blasted dirt into the ground where they had been.

"We're on their twelve," said Ahle. "They can hit us, but we can outrun them. Heavy support tanks. Big boom. Great range. Not so great on accuracy."

She swerved and jinked the still-accelerating armored car

again. Another shell exploded twenty feet to their right.

"They have more of these *little* ones," Perry pointed out, breathing hard. Turning the chaingun around one-eighty, just in time to see the double-muzzle-flash of a second heavy tank.

One of the shells whistled overhead; the second hit not far ahead of them, and Ahle practically drove the armored car through the explosion. Dust and debris whipped Perry's hunched-over back.

"And *they* don't have to zag to avoid gunfire."

"Right," said Ahle. "You wanted that flaregun?"

* * *

Roeder turned the flasher one way and then another, repeating the same code: First company to the right, second to the left, go around. There was something going on at the other side of Joplin base, although the fight here – his track bumped over another hooded corpse – had mostly ended.

A purple flare shot up into the night sky. Followed by another.

Descending fast, a couple of miles away, came a sleek escort-class airship. Unlit. *Not* a friendly.

The Cheetahs' light chainguns wouldn't do much to affect the thing, not without tracers they didn't have. But the Tiger IIbs had guns *designed* for taking down airships, with the elevation to boot.

His own heavy tanks were miles behind. The ones belonging to the Joplin base, however, were very immediately handy.

* * *

"There she is! Go for it!" Perry shouted.

"I see her," said Ahle. The two-hundred-yard-away *Marlyville Zephyr* had stopped descending at about thirty feet, and a rope ladder had been thrown down. Perry could see men in the open hold, ready to ditch emergency ballast and leap their ship right up again.

Ahle changed course, aiming for the airship's rope ladder. Another shell, then another one, exploded around them.

A hundred yards. Seventy-five. Fifty.

We're going to make it, Perry thought, as the armored car decelerated.

Then the tail assembly of the airship exploded into burning fragments.

Suddenly without its steering, the airship began to turn on its axis.

The men with the emergency ballast released their loads, swinging the heavy lead-and-sand-laden sacks off and cutting their ropes. They impacted the ground as the airship shot up –

Another shell caught her high-amidships, and burning hydrogen blazed a fount into the sky.

"She's going down!" Perry shouted. "Avert!"

"What did you say?" Ahle accelerated as the airship, desperately releasing sacs of flaming hydrogen, began to descend.

Perry ducked into the turret, slammed the hatch hard behind him.

Another tank shell blasted somewhere close by. The flaming remains of the now-devoid-of-airworthiness *Zephyr* crashed down on top of them.

* * *

For a few moments, through Ahle's plexiglas-covered vision slit, all that she could see was fire. We're driving right into the inferno, she thought.

Hit the steam pedal. Increased speed.

Right *through* the inferno, she corrected herself.

Something burned behind them. Something exploded above them. Then they were clear, racing through the other side of the airship that had, in a few seconds, been reduced to a blazing skeleton.

Perry looked at her.

"That was our ride out," he said.

"Was. *This* is our ride out now," Ahle replied. "Tell me: Where?"

Perry thought for a moment.

"Hugoton. Fleming has to see those maps. We can trade copies of the shit to Lynch if he says so. Get 4-106 *next.*"

"We're on the wrong side of the Kansas state line," Ahle said. "And Hugoton's four hundred miles and change from *there."*

"Yes, but we're going to run into something first. Friendly airship. *Somebody.* Chances are best going that way. Got any better ideas?"

Ahle glanced at the compass, which read approximately south-southwest. She made a wheeling turn to the right. Turned back to Perry.

"No. But we're losing pressure. Get to the boiler."

* * *

Roeder was met by a seething, furious, icy-controlled Skorzeny, still coughing and slightly concussed. His rage seemed to cut through that.

"I want you to pursue them," he said.

"Some of our elements already are," Roeder said. "Stolen one of our vehicles, I saw. In the shop, I heard."

"Yessir," said the base commander, a Captain Metz.

"In the shop implies damage. What with?"

"Nothing serious. Her suspension took a hit from a mine that didn't completely go off. She'll drive just fine."

"*Damn it,*" said Skorzeny. "I want that vehicle destroyed. What do we have in the air near here?"

"Nothing closer than Columbia, last I heard, sir," said Roeder. "Nothing we can get at."

"Get them. Destroy them if you have to, take the documents intact if you can. But use everything you have, Major, and *stop them.* Absolute top priority. Critical One. *Stop them.*"

* * *

"They're in pursuit," Perry reported from the hatch. He could see formations of lights, miles behind them on the plains. Gaining? He couldn't tell. "Can you drive any faster?"

"I'm *already* driving faster!" Ahle shouted back.

That was true. The bumpy earth was racing below them, and the speed needle had to be pushing fifty if not past that. The wind blew hard against him, and the armored car kicked up a thick wedge of dust as they fled, the car bucking up and down under them.

Perry felt his ribs, where the bullet had hit. Sore, painful, bruised, but not broken. Thank God for kevlar.

"Angle south a bit. We want to hit the railway line."

He knew this part of Kansas, though. It was *empty*. Cattle country, farms and ranches. At night, they were unlikely to encounter anything. Unlikely to be seen by anything.

At least they had a head start.

"By the way," Ahle said, "just so you know, when I checked, we only have about half a load of fuel."

Oh.

* * *

"We're gaining on them, I think," Roeder reported to Skorzeny, who was sitting in the bowels of the armored car. About half an hour into the chase, headed west-southwest. "They're only a couple of miles ahead."

"Let me take a look."

Skorzeny, still coughing a bit – he was fucked up and his gut *hurt* from those punches, but damned if he'd let the major see that – took the commander's hatch. Roeder's sixteen armored cars, and the three remaining ones belonging to the base, and the one he was riding in, were sweeping across the plains in a line, racing each other as much as they were chasing the fleeing attackers.

Their searchlights swept across, too, occasionally catching the metallic glint of the now-enemy car. Too far for a lucky shot; the cars' tires were heavy, solid rubber that a single round from the one-inch chainguns wouldn't do much to, certainly not at this range.

Some of the cars' commanders had tried regardless, until Roeder had ordered them by flasher to knock it off.

Who are these damn people, anyway?

A black man, one had been. A black Southerner would never work with the Klan, so it had to be someone else. A Fed or an Imperial. Had the Feds gotten a clue? That could be *very* bad.

He'd have to interrogate the fuckers and find out. He'd already ordered Captain Metz to send his infantry through the scene of the fight, see if there were any enemy wounded who could also be interrogated.

At least he was having a smooth ride. The other vehicle had a busted suspension. The bastards would at least be uncomfortable.

And they couldn't run forever, and their obvious escape mechanism had been blown out of the sky. If they lasted far past dawn, Skorzeny was going to be surprised.

* * *

"I think I've figured out what's wrong with this thing," said Ahle, as the car bumped painfully across another rock. "The suspension."

"Very funny," said Perry, who was nursing a burned hand from a while earlier, when he'd been tending the boiler at exactly the wrong bump. *After* which he'd found the locker containing the gloves normally used by the car's engineman. "Very, very funny, Ahle."

He adjusted the boiler again to feed a bit more of the airship-grade petroleum-coal distillate into the engine, then moved back a bit through the car's narrow quarters, going for the aft hatch. That had a ring-mount that looked like it could hold a flasher or a detachable machine-gun; at present it held neither, but it was a closer viewpoint than the fore gun-tub.

He stuck his head through, getting used to feeling the wind lashing his back. They seemed to be gaining; the sweeping searchlights *definitely* seemed a fraction brighter. It was a little after five, and they'd been running for a very tense hour or so now.

"Gaining on us, I think," he reported. "Looks like

"I'm serious about the suspension. These things are supposed to normally have a *much* smoother ride."

"If we don't run into help soon, we're going to have a much *deader* ride," said Perry.

"Do you know exactly where we are?"

"Does 'somewhere in Kansas' help? Or maybe northern Oklahoma?"

"No," said Ahle. "Not really, no."

"Then just drive and hope this thing doesn't break down on us."

* * *

"Definitely gaining," Roeder said another half-hour after that. "Definitely. We're going to be approaching effective shooting distance soon. We'll shoot them to fragments and have them."

"You flashed my orders," Skorzeny replied. Not a question, or even really much of a confirmation.

"Yes. Destroy them. Take the stuff intact if you can, but don't under any circumstances let them escape. And kill the bastards."

"Right. It won't be much longer, sir."

"It better not be."

Roeder smiled. The thieves had the exact same model of APCs he and his men were using, of course, but *his* cars had full four-man crews, for one; driver, gunner, engineer and secondary gunner/flash operator. That helped a little.

What helped more was that the crews customized their vehicles a bit, and they *knew* the customizations and the invariable individual quirks of their particular vehicle. That added up to a little more efficiency from the boilers, and a little more speed from the engines.

Only a few percent more, perhaps another mile and change per hour, but at a couple of miles' range over the hour and a half it had been so far, it was going to be decisive.

* * *

The sun was beginning to rise in the east, backlighting the twenty pursuing armored cars. They'd drawn close enough, within a half-mile, that they were firing intermittent bursts; they were a line spread across the near distance, now, not just flashing lights that might have been on the horizon.

We're gone, thought Perry, as the marks on the hopper showed that the fuel was close to zero. There was what was in the engine now, plus about two percent more, and when that was in and burned...

They'd lose pressure, slow, and die. He'd tried a dozen stories in his head, but none of them fit. He didn't have Federal identification. He was officially a rogue Imperial, and Ahle was definitely a known pirate. And they'd killed at least one Special Squadrons man during the escape, not to mention sprayed

208

several others and beaten the crap out of one of their ranking officers.

There was no conceivable excuse they could use, and no conceivable way the SS would see fit *not* to simply execute them out of hand.

A week and a half ago, it crossed his mind, he would have absolutely agreed that they *should*. A pirate and a renegade with stolen documents and blood on their hands?

It felt different now. *She may be a pirate, but I'm not* really *a renegade!*

No time for excuses. *If we're going to die,* the Service officer's part of his mind said, *take as many of those bastards with us as we can.*

Very simple, when you came down to it.

* * *

Within a few hundred yards, and fire was striking home on the Cheetah regularly – not inflicting damage, but sparking off and making the hull ring. Making it dangerous for Perry to stick his head up without the shield of the front gun tub.

It didn't matter. There was no need for a man at the boiler; the last of the fuel was gone and Ahle's gauge was already showing a loss in pressure. Within a few minutes – ten, at best, if they put up an effective fight against twenty times their number – it would all be over.

Perry fired another burst at what he thought would be the command car, shooting through their dust trail and the rising sun, now visible across the endless plains.

A sudden noise to his left. Engines. Propellers.

An airship. Flying low, at a couple of hundred yards and getting lower.

Perry waved frantically.

"Pirates!" he shouted in the hope he might be heard, might be believed.

Was it just his imagination, or was the car starting to lose speed?

The airship continued to drop, on a clear intercept course for where they were headed. A rope ladder fell from it, swaying as it dangled.

Oh, thank God!

"Jam the pedal down and maintain speed somehow while we can," Perry ordered.

"I see him just as well as you," said Ahle, and proved it by adjusting course.

So could the pursuers. They switched their chainguns' fire from Ahle and Perry to the two-hundred-yard long airship's bulk. Even at extreme range, five or six hundred yards, they couldn't miss, and lines of sparks and dings clashed across the ship's colorfully-painted, dust-faded aluminum hull.

Perry laughed. They could fire all they wanted; at best they'd puncture a few hydrogen sacs. Without tracers, the armored cars' fire would be irrelevant to this airship.

Regardless, the ship fired back. A missile burst from amidships, trailing fire as it lanced out at the center of the line of armored cars. Two of them broke formation to avoid it. It hit the ground and exploded, sent a wild brown dust fountain into the sky against the sunrise.

Intercept! The ladder banged against the slowing armored car – they were down to three quarters or less of what their speed had been, now, and the Squadrons' cars were gaining *fast* – and Perry, bag over his shoulder, grabbed it, climbed. Ahle was immediately behind him.

"You two hold on tight!" someone yelled from the hatch above.

Perry hooked his arms around the sides of the rope ladder, planted his feet and held on for dear life. Chaingun fire continued to spark the gondola.

"Ballast *now!*" that same voice yelled. A voice Perry had heard before, although he couldn't place when.

Something rolled off the hatch, boxes and then barrels tumbling to the ground. The airship *jumped* with a sharp jerk, and suddenly they were fifty feet off the ground – no, sixty, seventy, and rising fast.

"Winch!" the man shouted, and the rope ladder, twisting and turning, began to be hauled up.

Below, the armored cars were frantically reversing, trying to get enough elevation to fire effectively. One of the commanders drew an automatic rifle and opened up wildly at the swaying, jerking, rising rope ladder. Lots of muzzle-flash, but none of the rounds came close.

The winch was drawing the ladder toward an open

trapdoor, up and into the airship's bridge.

A smiling man in a long brown coat was waiting there, pistols in his rig.

"Cap'n Perry," the man said. "Don't know if you remember me, being a high-level Imperial Vice-Commodore and all. But when Cap'n Nate Nolan tells you he's at your service, he *means* it. Your little operation bought us a new ship."

The balance woman in the dress and the spectacularly useless rig stood smiling next to him. This ship's bridge was – well, still a civilian mess, but neater and equipped with proper communications. Not up to Imperial standards, but an order of magnitude more advanced than the last bridge he'd seen this man on.

"Welcome aboard the *Red Wasp II*, Cap'n Perry. Heard you might have been in the area. Where did you say you wanted to go, again?"

"Hugoton," said Perry immediately. "This is a priority. They'll allow civilian transport as far as Dodge."

Nolan shook his head.

"In case you hadn't forgotten, Mr. Vice-Commodore, aren't you still a wanted man with bucks on your head? Not going to be seen to sell a friend out, I'm sorry."

"Just take me to Dodge and I can turn *myself* in. Report to Fleming."

"If you really insist," said Nolan. "But you're sure there's nowhere else you'd rather go?"

"We *were* sent to get that material," Ahle pointed out.

4-106, Perry thought. *I said I'd come back with my ship or not at all.*

And Lynch knew where 4-106 was. Or said she did. He could copy the material before giving it to her. Mail it to Hugoton, to Fleming; he had a couple of codewords that would reach him.

"Very well. Take us to the nearest place I can *wire* Hugoton," Perry said. "Any small town along the Dodge line should do, but keep us out of SS jurisdiction. And then take us back to New Orleans."

A smile spread across Nolan's face.

"The Free City, huh? Got some business to do there?"

"*Everyone*," said Ahle, "can find business in New Orleans."

Chapter Fourteen

The Great War, historians agree with practial unanimity, divides Early Modern history, defined as 1789 to 1881, from Modern, defined as postwar to present.

Where historians disagree on is when the Great War ended. Certainly its start is known - June 5th, 1881, when the Third French Republic declared war on Germany over the disputed territories of Alsace-Lorraine. Within a week, interlocking treaties - some of them secret until that point - had brought Europe into conflict, the two great alliances being the relatively modern Anglo-German powers (with lesser allies including Norway, Denmark, Holland, Greece and a wavering odd-man-out of Austria-Hungary) of the Great Alliance into war with the Royal Entente of Russia, France and Spain, their lesser allies including most of the rest of Europe.

It is beyond the scope of this work to discuss the ensuing warfare in detail, but the invention of the machine-gun had changed expectations considerably. Fluid, mobile warfare became bloody trench stalemate by midsummer, and what followed were years of grinding warfare between equally-matched powers.

The colonies were the first to show strain, native units rebelling when it became clear their home countries were too occupied in Europe to suppress those outbreaks. Other colonies, such as the generally-loyal Australians, were brought into the war more directly; the attempted Russo-Japanese invasion ofAustralia was a bloody failure, but the carnage wreaked by Tsarist troops during their brief occupation of eastern New South Wales remains a horrifying memory to this day.

But after years of fighting, social tensions at home surfaced, workers' movements demanding international unity and an end to the war. Many of the troops ordered to suppress the ensuing General Strikes mutinied, and by 1895 the war efforts had fallen apart. In the United Kingdom this was typified by the Revolt, as three years of bloody, vicious warfare between left-wing Commune and right-wing Royalist forces effectively destroyed the old - and Restored - Empire's heart for a generation...

From *A Young Person's History of the World, Volume VIII.*

"We found him playing dead," Captain Metz said to Skorzeny, gesturing at the wounded man strapped to a chair in the interrogation room at the Joplin base. He'd received cursory first aid, enough to stabilize the minor head wound that had knocked him unconscious.

"He'll *be* dead soon enough unless he co-operates," said Skorzeny.

The wounded man looked on with horrified eyes. He could see the implements on the table next to the chair. He'd been stripped naked and firmly manacled in, wrists and ankles. From the clothes and bearing, he was some kind of a dockside thug. But that could be faked.

Skorzeny turned to address the man directly.

"We can do this the easy way or the hard way, friend. One way or another, I'm going to learn who sent you and why."

"I don't know anything," the man pleaded.

Skorzeny picked up a sharply-serrated knife.

"Maybe you'll know more in a few minutes."

"No, really! I don't know anything! We were just sent in to do a covering operation, that's all I know!"

"A good start," said Skorzeny. "You may come out of this intact. Who were you covering for?"

"I" – the man's eyes looked to the table of implements and back – "I don't know."

"I don't believe that," said Skorzeny, and moved forward with the knife.

* * *

The man had lasted almost ten minutes, a little above average. Skorzeny, whose uniform was now spattered heavily with blood, nodded to First Lieutenant Schierbecker.

213

"Did you get all of that?" he asked his young aide. "How we applied pain visibly and *selectively*?"

"Yessir," said Schierbecker, who was looking a bit blanched by it all.

"You'll get used to this kind of thing. It's standard practice. If we'd asked him *nicely*, do you think he would have told us all about this woman in New Orleans he works for? Or this renegade Imperial named Perry or Parry they were taking in?"

"No, sir."

"What we're going to *do* about her is a different method. But first things first."

Skorzeny drew his sidearm, racked the slide, and shot the prisoner through the temple.

"Next," he said, calmly putting the Luger back in its holster, "we get on the line to our friends..."

* * *

The small escort-class airship, a narrow fighting vessel a hundred and ten yards long, nosed through the canyon where 4-106 sat, late in that afternoon. She flashed the proper code, which kept Pratt Cannon's crew – on a dismounted rocket launcher – from blowing her to skeletal wreckage – and came in.

A very short, rig-less man dressed in bright red from the toes of his thick-soled boots to the tip of his beret, jumped out. A brace of pearl-handled revolvers hung on a bandolier across his chest.

"Pratt Cannon!" he said to the guards. "Any of you know who Pratt Cannon is? I'm here to meet him. Him and somebody named Marko."

"Jebediah fucking Judd," said Cannon, coming forward. The two of them shook hands. "Thought the Sonorans got you last year!"

"Sonorans think a lot of things," said Judd. "Sonorans think too much, maybe. They got my *ship*. I got a new one, courtesy of some friends of yours. Just in exchange for a bit of work, is all. OK, a lot of work. But fuck it, new ship!"

"Somebody wanted me?" asked Marko. "You're my transport out?"

"I'm your transport out," Judd said. "Also got a few more

214

men." He took a harmonica from around his neck and blew a discordant blast.

A hatch of the slender airship opened and men piled out, carrying packs and rifles. They wore rough civilian dress, but from their bearing and the way some barked at others, they were obviously soldiers. Forty or so of them. The 4-106 crew eyed them warily; soldiers had never been good news for the likes of this lot.

"What's going on?" Marko asked.

"I'm just the delivery boy," said Judd. "But it looks to me like you've got a platoon of Texans for added security. Maybe my other man can tell you more."

The same Third Department man who'd taken the 4-106 documents a few days ago, appeared.

"New orders," he said to Marko. "You're off standby. There's been developments. I want you to take your crew and get moving."

"Where?"

"Taos, to begin with." A military town that marked the Republic of Texas' northwestern corner, right on the Sonoran border and not far from the Colorado line. "Further orders when you're in the air."

"You got a name, Third Department?"

"Call me Ivan. Now get your men together, and a dozen of these thugs, and move."

"Cannon, you stay here," said Marko. "You're in charge while I'm gone. The rest of you – you heard the man."

* * *

Fleming reviewed the telegram that had come to him from – Memphis – with greater and greater alarm.

Reached for his drink. Another sip.

There simply hadn't been time to teach many codes to the supposedly-renegade Air Service officer Perry. No more than a few ciphers for keywords that might come up.

The ones that appeared were bad enough. They fit into the picture he was gathering, cleanly. Too cleanly. *Hugoton. Texas. 4-106. Maps.* Although without *proof…*

Mind, he was looking forward to hearing the story from Perry himself. How he'd been gulled into attacking a

215

supposedly-friendly occupation unit's base. He supposed nonlethals had been used unless forced, but he also knew exactly how that pirate Ahle felt about the SS.

Did she sucker him that fast? I didn't have him as the type. Must have been some other reason.

Something from Lynch's end? More likely. He didn't know that woman's motivations.

Very bad news either way, he thought. He didn't have much in the way of resources; didn't have anything to speak of but a fragment.

May be time to send that fragment – named Moore – to Texas, though. Just to see if there was anything left to pick up.

Screw what had convinced the vice-commodore to attack the SS. He didn't peg the Service officer as a liar and he wasn't the type to argue with results.

Yes, he decided. *We send Moore with the last codes to Houston, to see if there's anything left of the network there.*

And as for Perry – there's not a whole lot we can do. We just hope he's wrong.

* * *

MI-7 Agent David Cornwell flinched as the heavy truck rolled past in the night. They were common enough on the Houston docks, of course, but he was in a state where everything and anything spooked him. Had been for weeks now.

Huddled in the laborers' rooming house, he ticked the reasons off on his fingers. Only blind luck had kept him from getting blasted in the initial attacks. Or busted in the following sweeps. Texan authorities weren't friendly to MI-7 or Imperials overall, with their support for the United States of America.

He'd had a private alley or two he'd kept open, despite that vainglorious idiot Fleming's insistence on all channels being shared within the agency. MI-7's encryption had been broken hard, that much he knew. The Okhrana here had been wiped out in response, but the Third Department were well and truly active. He hadn't thought those guys *operated* outside interior Russia!

They knew he was alive. They knew someone from MI-7 had escaped, and they were hunting him. His fieldcraft had assured him of that. They knew his drops. They'd busted his sources. They were getting close.

Texas was gearing up for something. Although he couldn't get the word out, although his sources had been busted, he could still see with his own eyes.

Reserve bases had been activated. There seemed to have been call-ups.

And the docks were gearing up to receive something big. Military shipments, from the number of soldiers around.

And, point five – his ticked-off fingers made a fist – he was sure, from his remaining sources, that some Russian big-shot was in town. The Priest. The Reaper. The Hammer. Conceivably the wheel behind all the wheels, Count Leon Trotsky himself.

Any of those would be bad news. Texas becoming a Russian client state would be very bad news, and that was where all the signs were pointing. Fleming had to know.

He had to get the word out.

He had to get himself out, if he wanted to live much longer.

He caught himself. Made himself breathe.

Breathe, David, breathe.

No. Pseudonym. He had to *be* that man if he wanted to make it alive through the tightened-up Texan customs.

Breathe, John, breathe.

Texas was gearing up for war. Not against the Sonorans, because a sweep against MI-7 would have been irrelevant and unwarranted in that case. Texas was gearing for war against the United States and expecting heavy Russian support, because why else that activity on the docks?

Yes.

Huddled on the laborer's bed in the dockside worker's room, MI-7 agent David Cornwell resolved to himself:

He *had* to get to Hugoton. Texas was gearing for war, and the Russians were backing them. As viciously blinded as MI-7 supposedly was, that only made his mission the more important.

Fleming had to know. Whatever the cost.

* * *

True to his word, the Third Department man whose real

name almost certainly *wasn't* Ivan, filled them in on the ride to fortified Taos, Province of Texan New Mexico. They sat – just the four of them minus Pratt Cannon, the dozen hired men were in the main cabin – in Jebediah Judd's large and well-decorated private cabin.

"The SS men taking their copies of the documents were attacked on their way back from Texas," 'Ivan' said. "Pinpoint strike clearly aimed at taking the reconnaisance and the analysis. Roughed up the emissary, didn't kill him."

"An Imperial response?" asked Marko skeptically. "I thought you Third Department bastards sacrificed the Okhrana's presence on this continent in *order* to blind Fleming's boys."

"We don't think so. We've identified the two as Captain Karen Ahle, known to the Texans as a pirate. Mostly operates on the Plains, but she's crossed borders; only flag she's never attacked is Sonora. And the other one as" – 'Ivan' produced one of the Imperial wanted posters of Perry – "Marcus Perry, late Vice-Commodore of the Imperial Air Service. Cashiered after losing a ship. *Your* ship, as it happens."

Marko's thin, skeptical smile became a wide, broken-toothed grin.

"Discordia at work! These chains of events!"

"These chains of events have given us a problem we can't explain. A renegade and an escaped pirate."

"Who did that attack for a reason," Ferrer said. Being logical. The implications went on. "Which implies you've got a leak somewhere. To tell someone those documents were valuable for some reason."

"Or at least interesting," Marko said. Giggled. "Logic doesn't fit into the real world."

"Worthwhile for whatever reason. Also worth a damn to the Imperials; Fleming may be low on assets, but he's going to reward whoever takes that shit to Hugoton. Maybe a pardon. Maybe a lot of cash. Perhaps reinstatement to his rank. These two were commissioned by a madam in New Orleans. Known as a high-level information broker. That's where you're going."

"By airship?"

"Not enough time. Special train, full priority to the eastern border. Faster than any airship."

"And then?" Rienzi asked. "We go kill this madam before

she can figure out who to sell the shit to."

"You, the goons you brought with you, and whatever assets you can sweep up on the ground at short notice, by which we mean immediately. We lost our old muscle there blinding the Imperials. You're the troubleshooters. Tie off this thread."

* * *

The *Red Wasp II* touched down at the massive Pontchartrain airship park, clumsily maneuvering onto a barge, deflating to negative buoyancy and tying down onto the barge's heavy, rusted iron stanchions.

"What business were you on, anyway?", Perry had asked Nolan some hours earlier.

The captain had shrugged, spread his palms.

"Bit of this, bit of that. We'd just dropped a load in Memphis when we got the tip about you."

"From who?"

Nolan shrugged. "Just something I heard in one of the bars, that you might be in a spot of trouble and headed the way you were. So we headed up that way ourselves. But, we'll find a cargo here. Take it" – Perry shrugged – "maybe to Dodge. If that's what you really want to do after this."

"Maybe we do," Perry had said. Thinking of 4-106. Thinking, *this man thinks he owes me and he's the closest thing we have to a trusted ally at this point. And he's got a ship.* "Or maybe you might want to think Denver instead. Or the Rockies. And take on a few more men who know how to crew a ship a short distance."

Now, as they tied down, a Port Authority motorboat coming in to collect the landing fee, Perry had a whole different set of problems. Their contact, Unitas, was gone, dead or missing; certainly the *Marlyville Zephyr* hadn't survived to pick him up as planned. Finding Lynch's hangout would probably be possible, but without a chip or an intro, how did they get in?

Ahle elbowed Nolan.

"They'll hit you up for a bribe, but don't pay more than twenty. Less than that and they'll get troublesome, though."

"Been here before a thousand times, cap'n. I don't have so much to hide as a real pirate. They're getting five plus the

219

docking fee."

The two port officials wore wet, dark-blue uniforms; one of them, the woman, had a cigarette in her mouth that had somehow managed to stay alight. Perry found himself sweating slightly – not just the heat – as the two looked them over; the wanted posters of him had had time to get to a lot of places. But nothing except boredom registered on the officials' faces as they exchanged signatures, paperwork and money.

I hate being uncomfortable around authority, Perry thought. Well, not for too much longer. Assuming Lynch *was* honorable – and after what they'd been through yesterday morning, she damn well had better be! – then in a couple hours, they would have the location of 4-106 and be off to recover it. This time three days from now, they could be sailing into Dodge with a hired crew, reputations restored and an honorable accomplishment on his record.

There are Wanted posters of me. He tried not to think of that, of the work it would take to scrub a deliberately-blemished reputation.

They boarded one of the several boats that had, on seeing an airship land, come along to take passengers or light cargo, and in a few minutes were on the docks proper, lost in a crowd.

"You go recruit some more bodies," Perry said to Nolan. "We'll meet you back at the airship. Don't lift until we're back. We *will* have a job for you."

"Mind if I pick up a cargo, if I find something?"

Perry didn't have the money, he realized, to personally charter this airship to the Rockies. Nolan might *have* owed him a favor, but after saving their lives, he didn't owe them much. And that ship would cost money to run.

"Go ahead."

* * *

The United States and Texas were by no means friendly, but there *was* peace and a reasonably open border. Getting across, with the sets of papers the Third Department had given them, had been easy, and from the border it was a very short train ride to New Orleans.

"We're going to need weapons," Marko said. "But that's not going to be so much of a problem; I have connections in

New Orleans."

"We need real firepower," said the leader of the dozen picked toughs Marko had brought from Colorado. A burly Irish brawler named Tate. "I heard of this L bitch. Real high-level, she is. You taking her down is gonna be trouble."

"Trouble's what we're for," said Marko. "But we're going to need men. Round up your connections. We have forty-five minutes."

* * *

A walk, through crowds and the ever-present sticky heat, took them into the French Quarter, in the direction of Denard's.

"She moves, I hear," said Ahle. "I've been to Denard's before, but she also owns several other places. And there has to be at least a couple nobody knows about."

"You're implying a woman with cause to worry about her own safety," said Perry. Although a woman capable of ordering attacks on Federal contractors just to get information – with *every* indication she'd done stuff like this before – was, yes, going to very rapidly make some powerful enemies.

"Damn straight. But they'll know where to find us at Denard's. They may even be expecting us."

They were. In fact, Unitas himself met them at the entrance to the place.

"Heard you were on your way," said the henchman. "Come in. The bosslady's in a meeting right now, but she'll see you in a few minutes. Care for drinks?"

"You know what I get," said Ahle.

"Of course. And a whisky for the Vice?"

"Sure." After the last couple of days, come to think of it, he *needed* a drink.

"Mr. Johnny?" A pre-teen urchin approached Unitas.

"Yeah?"

"Got word for you, Mr. Johnny. Urgent, sir."

"I'll deal with this," said Unitas. "You two can go in. The boss will know you're here."

* * *

Seated at a booth inside Denard's, Ahle and Perry raised

221

their drinks.

"To your airship," Ahle said. "And my crew."

"My airship. And may your crew have learned a lesson. You're skilled. Can't you find mercenary work somewhere?"

Ahle glared at him.

"Mercenaries are who killed my family. And a lot of others."

"An honest living, then," said Perry. "*Don't* tell me you're going to go right back to piracy."

"Honest piracy," said Ahle. She sipped on her rum.

"No such thing," said Perry. "Code or not."

"Maybe you can at least plunder outside Imperial spheres of influence? The Romantics and the Russians are a lot sloppier about their convoy protection, you know."

"And not as wealthy as the Imperial client states," said Ahle. "Bad governance has its drawbacks. They run things like the Feds run the South; brute force and corruption."

"At least consider it. I'd hate to see you hang after all of this."

"Maybe once I've done something about the Squadrons. Avenged my family. That was why I wanted your airship, you know. As a weapon against them. If they transferred to Texas... attack them en route. Or if they did renew the contract, sail straight into Columbia with that line-class and all those nine-inch tubes." Ahle's lips hardened. "Fly an Imperial flag. Hit their headquarters building. That Bavarian *bastard* Himmler works on the top floor."

"You've been researching this," Perry observed. Treason? Well, these people were involved with people *actively* scheming against the Empire, who had overflown Hugoton with *some* sort of nefarious purpose. His sympathies to them were more limited than they had been a few days ago... and besides, he'd seen a taste of what the German and the Italian units did in the South. Not treason, perhaps not even a whole lot more than disapproval.

He drained the rest of his glass to try to wash that thought from his mouth. Of course it was treason! The Hugoton maps weren't his department; 4-106 was. This woman had stolen 4-106.

"Oh, you think I'm bad," said Ahle. The flicker of a challenging smile was on her face. "Tell me, would the good people of London, St. John's, Dublin, Edinburgh, Sydney or Cape Town think I was so bad, if they knew what Himmler and his goons did to Wake Forest? The kind of thing Imperial policy is designed to *avert*, not turn a blind eye to?"

"The good people of the Empire can make up their own minds and vote accordingly," said Perry reflexively. "But – you were planning to take 4-106 not to sell its technology to the Russians, or its firepower to the Sonorans, but *purely* to make a one-sided attack out of personal vendetta? A one-way attack, too. You would have been blown out of the sky."

"A one-way attack would have been fine," said Ahle coldly. "If it inspired others. Himmler and his men are criminals and no more. When the law is corrupted, all you have is what men like you call 'vendetta.' I call it justice." Ahle drained the rum glass and put it down, a little harder than she might have, on the table.

"Miss L will see you now," said a flunky with a submachinegun slung across his chest. "Freshen your drinks before you go up there?"

"I'm fine," said Perry.

"Please," said Ahle.

The armed flunky produced a bottle of rum, filled Ahle's glass until – very near the top – she gestured for him to stop.

"Very well. This way."

* * *

There was an armed guard at the door to Lynch's office, which there hadn't been before. He saw the man leading Perry and Ahle in, recognized them and, without taking his eyes from Perry and Ahle, moved to an electrotelegraphic headset. Spoke something barely-audible into it. Received a reply. Stepped away from the door and opened it.

Lynch was leaning back at her broad, dark wood desk, hands clasped behind her tightly-coiffed hairdo.

"Good afternoon, Vice-Commodore, Captain," she said. "Thank you for coming. I see you have the materials I asked for."

"I have a request," said Perry, not moving to hand them over. "I'd like a copy of these." That was the best way to *not* indicate he'd already made copies and sent them to Fleming,

223

he'd reasoned a day ago.

"Oh?" Lynch didn't blink. "You think the information might be of interest to your boss."

"My boss is intelligence. I think everything is of interest to him."

"I think he already has copies," said Lynch evenly. "You've had the time to make and send them. But I'll indulge you, Vice-Commodore. Certainly."

Perry reached forward and slid the folders, and the chips, across the table to Lynch. She picked the folders – containing quite detailed maps and aerial pictures of the Hugoton area, he'd had plenty of time to confirm – up and looked at them.

He'd had the impression of a guarded, closely-kept woman. Therefore, the way her eyebrows shot up when *she* saw the maps, was... relevant.

"Oh my," she said after a few moments. "It... appears as though the loss of the *Zephyr* may have been acceptable after all."

Perry couldn't resist asking: "Does this fit into some kind of a picture for you?"

"It might fit into any number of pictures," said Lynch, recovering her composure. "You might talk to your boss Fleming about that. He and I are even now."

"Not quite," said Perry. If she thought she was going to get out of a deal that had nearly killed them... "You owe me a location. And that had better be correct, unless you want trouble from MI-7."

"MI-7 couldn't cause trouble to a pair of kittens right now. The information is correct as of a few days ago," said Lynch.

Something on her desk buzzed. As Lynch reached over for it, something outside – and not too far away – blew up.

"For once it wasn't a false alarm," Lynch said, drawing a pistol from somewhere in her skirt. Her other hand swept the SS maps and chips into a small bag.

Perry drew – the practice had paid off – his own gun. Didn't quite point it *at* Lynch.

"You owe me a location. Just to remind you."

"Oh, that." She slung the bag over a shoulder and flicked a piece of paper over the desk toward him. A map! With mechanitype-printed coordinates underneath. From the contours, the X appeared to be somewhere amidst mountains...

Gunshots. What were clearly gunshots, not far away. Unitas, followed by a flunky, pushed into Lynch's office.

"We've got a red alert, boss. There's a *lot* of them."

"Let's get moving, then." A glance at Ahle and Perry. "You want to come with us or not?"

Lynch's problems were her own, thought Perry, but whatever powerful enemies were coming to get her now probably wouldn't be too friendly to her guests either.

He had – probably – 4-106's location. Getting out alive was his objective now, and he couldn't imagine Lynch going in any direction other than safety.

"We're with you. Of course."

"Get moving, then. And when I say to fire on someone, you *kill them*. We know our own."

Lynch pushed at a panel in her wall, which slide aside to reveal a chipped-brick staircase going straight down into a dripping staircase. That became a passage, moisture oozing from ancient-seeming stones. Another flunky joined them as they ran down the passage, gunshots coming from not too far away. A second explosion.

Who is it attacking her?, Perry thought. It seemed entirely too coincidental. Right *now*, they were under attack?

"Along here." Unitas gestured to a sharp left turn in the damp underground passage. "This'll get us out of the area."

* * *

Ferrer had been briefed, fully briefed. He was in charge of a squad of these lowlife thugs – he had no other way to think of them, bottom-feeding trash – with the objective of cutting off one of this Lynch's escape routes.

The preliminary operation had been swift and sure, and Ferrer didn't know all the details of it. Marko had swept up a handful of Lynch's own goons, interrogated them, gotten one of her officers and put her to brutal torture. He'd heard the screaming, but it hadn't lasted long.

He supposed a man like Marko would know his way around torture devices. There'd been a time, before the knifework and the killings, that he'd have found that idea casually acceptable. Now he was seeing it – well, the state did still have to burn, right?

225

The state was evil, he reminded himself as he waited in the alley, looking at a brick wall that somewhere was apparently false. The state fucked you over. The state has to go.

"Look up, damn you!" he told the thugs. Ordered them. Raised his own submachinegun, *and can I really believe I'm holding one of those and supposedly ready to shoot?*, in emphasis. "They could come from anywhere, not just ground level."

Marko had briefed him, him and his trigger-happy assistant and McIlhan, well. The others didn't need to know so much, and Ferrer had been led to understand it would have been bad for their life expectancies if they did. The important thing was to keep this operation under control, Marko had said. Keep her from escaping with the information.

Well, he'd do his job at that, at least.

*   *   *

Another sharp turn, and in this underground labyrinth Perry couldn't tell how many there'd been at this point. Four, five, seven? Let alone the directions. Miss L had planned for survival, that was for sure.

Or her predecessors had.

That wasn't a particularly comforting thought.

Suddenly, in the cramped passages, they halted.

"We're about to come out," Unitas hissed. Over his shoulder was a heavy-looking backpack of his own. Containing information of what kind, Perry didn't *want* to know. "We're on the edge of the French Quarter. Docks district area. Follow me to the warehouse."

"And then what?" Ahle demanded.

"There'll be an airship," Lynch said flatly, as gunshots echoed through the tunnels. "You don't think I haven't *planned* for this?"

"Where does it go?"

"Out of here."

"That's not very specific," said Perry.

"Does it have to be?"

Before Perry could reply, Unitas pulled the lever that opened the door.

They were in an alley, was all Perry could tell, and there were goons there. Then the gunfighting began.

Ferrer had had orders. He'd had orders to keep the mooks between him and the enemy, if such enemy were to show up. But he was in charge, and didn't a leader have duties as well as responsibilities to go with the job? He wasn't going to let any human flesh stop a bullet for him, no matter how wasted and irrelevant that flesh was.

If the bullet was meant for him, it was meant for him. And he opened fire on the group, cocking his submachinegun as he'd been trained, methodically pointing it at the one with the heaviest weaponry – a liveried flunky with a light machine gun – and firing. All according to training.

Throwing himself to the side of the alley, according to training. Marko had drilled him hard.

The grenade hadn't been part of the training. A deafening overpressure that blasted his ears and his brain, *hurting*.

No.

Focus. *Focus damnit!*

Through the waves and the smoke – they must have let off smoke grenades, too! – firing. Focused on that liveried enemy with the machine gun, thirty feet away, shoot him down before the heavy weapon could deploy!

Around him, men were going down. It seemed to be happening in slow motion. They were falling, firing their pistols and their sawn-offs but falling regardless.

Ferrer fired another burst into the man with the machine gun. That was his focus, as the others around him broke and bolted. Follow training. Rules and discipline. The others didn't have machine guns. That one had a machine gun. Kill – no, *shoot down* was a much more comfortable thought – that man.

Explosions. Something tore Ferrer's head, and suddenly he was down on his face, kissing warm tarmac. The gun was out of his hands, he knew, because he couldn't fire it any more.

* * *

"This way," Lynch snarled. "They're onto us now!"

"I thought we'd fought our way past them!" Perry yelled back.

"Bullshit. That was a tripwire as much as anything else. They know where we came out, now, and they're going to be vectoring onto us everything that they have."

"Very well," said Ahle. "*We* have an airship. Want a ride? We're getting out our own way."

"I have my own airship."

Blazing gunfire came out of a side-street, no warning. Another of Lynch's flunkies was shot down. Unitas turned, hurled the sack of – documents? Not quite – an improbable distance into that street.

Blazing explosion.

"I'm getting the bosslady outta here," Unitas growled at Perry. "We've done your business. Come along or not."

"Safest not to," Ahle yelled at Perry. She gestured in a direction that appeared random, down an alley. "That way."

"That way," Perry agreed. He had the coordinates of 4-106, if the information fence knew them. He owed her nothing. Without a look back, he ran.

More shooting exploded behind them.

"Up!" Ahle gestured at a ladder. A fire-escape. They clambered up, up, to the roof of a cheap-looking warehouse.

"I don't think they noticed us," Ahle hissed. "These people, they stay on target."

"Who are these people?"

"Professionals."

* * *

"Holy shit," Rienzi was saying. "You nailed a whole ball of them."

Ferrer slowly found himself getting to his feet.

"You mean I'm not dead?" he muttered.

"Just a few cuts, boss. You killed a whole stack."

"One with a machine-gun?" He'd been shooting at that man. The best-armed man had been his priority, as per the general directions he'd been given.

You followed directions.

"You blew his guts out!" Rienzi exalted. Kicking a corpse. A machine-gun lay in the dust nearby.

Staggering, still disoriented, Ferrer went over. The dead man – gut-shot, he noticed, although riddled in the legs and shot in the face as well – had an elaborate jacket. He found a wallet in one pocket of that.

"What you doing?" Rienzi asked.

"I killed him," said Ferrer. "Ought to know who he is."

He'd taken a life. Him personally. Himself. There was bile in his throat, but you didn't hide from facts.

"Eh, just some fuckup. Your first notch, man."

"Philip Riordan," said Ferrer, reading off the state ID in the wallet. "Birthdate 10/22/1940."

"Don't get all sentimental, boss," said Rienzi, kicking the corpse again.

"Occupation, construction laborer. Funny. Should have said machine-gunner."

"You killed the fucker, that's all. And" – an explosion, a *big* explosion – "it looks like we just got the rest of them."

"It looks like we just got the rest of them," Marko said to McIlhan as the cabin of the formerly-ascending scout-class exploded.

"You sure that's her, boss?" asked McIlhan.

"Always the skeptical, logical Imperial bitch, aren't we?"

"Not afraid of you, crazy man. I want to fuck shit up just like you, and you know it. So, how you so sure we just killed this L bitch?"

Marko giggled.

"She's going to want to fly out, once she reaches the limits of her tunnels. Only so many places you can put even a scout-class. So we put the rockets in range – and when someone lifts under the shooting, we *know* it's got to be her. Everyone else in the warehouses and docks are keeping their noses down, not running, right?"

"So we got her?"

"You wanna stick around and sniff the corpses?" asked Marko. "Who else would be on that late, unlamented dirigible? We got her firm and good. Now, we just rocketed a dirigible out of existence over New Orleans dockside. You want to sniff, or you want to scram?"

Chapter Fifteen

Trotsky, Leon – Russian statesman

Born – 7 November 1879; Bereslavka, Ukraine (aged 84)
Present Position – Special Minister of State, Russian Empire

File Summary:

Despite coming from relatively low (kulak; upper-peasant) origins, Trotsky (original name – Lev Davidovich Bronstein) is one of the key figures in the Russian Empire's upper administration. Instrumental (as an organizer and field commander) in the Russian Restoration of 1917, he has gone on to be a close associate of three Tsars.

Positions held through his long career include heading the Ministry of the Interior, the Okhrana, the Foreign Ministry and the Third Department. He has held his present title since 1940; despite his now-advanced age, he shows no signs of mental deterioration or reduced energy. He is experienced, devious, ruthless, powerful, and is believed to be one of the very few people with the present Tsar's complete trust.

From MI-7 files; February, 1963.

"Finish loading that cargo already," Nolan said to the stevedores, who were manhandling wet crates marked 'Johannson' from another barge into the *Red Wasp II*'s hold. "Looks like we've got to move."

"Damn right you have to move," Perry said, glancing over his shoulder. They didn't *appear* to be under pursuit, but you never knew. Perhaps Lynch's enemy wouldn't be content with simply killing her, would want to sweep up her associates, too.

A mobile barge had drawn up along the stationary one the airship was moored to, and a human chain of shirtless, sweating stevedores were passing the crates up into the hold. It did look like they were almost done.

"You're not under active pursuit, are you?"

"Not as far as we know," said Ahle. "As far as we know."

"There was a fight. Someone shot down an airship that lifted from one of the warehouses. Is that what you were involved with?"

"No, it was a whole *different* major incident," said Perry.

Nolan shrugged.

"This can be a violent city. You see the stevodores don't give a damn."

"They're going to give a damn if bullets start flying around them," said Perry.

"No, they'll hit the deck, wait for the fight to end, and finish the job. At least if they want to get paid."

"We'll be on the bridge," Ahle told him. "Lift as soon as you can. He's right to be nervous."

On the bridge, Nolan joined them a moment later.

"Sorry, but a man's got to make a profit," he said. "Cargo of frozen crawfish. I was lucky to get it. We'll be stopping briefly at Dodge to refuel, if you want to get a signal off from there. But a straight run to Denver, after that."

"Not waiting for any convoys, I hope," said Perry.

"Convoy fees are a bit above my price range," Nolan said. "We kind of just hope to get lucky with the pirates."

"Like *that's* worked," said the balance woman in the dress.

"It's worked so far."

"Only barely."

"Ah, but it's worked! Mind, with a new ship like this – prettier, more capacity, although better in the way of self-defence as well, I *will* grant, thank you Mr. Vice-Commodore – we might look a bit more tempting to `em."

"We try to avoid the independents," said Ahle. "It's not so profitable. We don't have much use for crawfish."

"And we count on that, too," Nolan agreed. "The Code keeps things going. Can always buy the ship back, if we have to." A pause. "Although I'd rather not. Mr. Vice-Commodore, are we expecting any particular trouble?"

"None that I know of," said Perry. "Although the thieves who stole 4-106 will probably be defending it. Did you hire more men here as I asked you to?"

"Oh yes. And I guess there'll be a recovery fee for this big warship of yours, I hope?"

"We won't let an honest trader lose money on Imperial

service," said Perry.

"Or a not-so-honest trader, I gather," Ahle added, grinning.

"Honesty is an underrated virtue," said Perry. "Nolan, I gather you've had some shady behavior in the past, but that's the past. You'll do better for yourself as an honest man. Consider it a favor asked."

"Oh, I'm sure I will," said Nolan. "But it takes resources to be an honest man in these times."

* * *

"I killed a man," Ferrer was muttering when he met Marko and the others at the passenger terminal of an airship line. "I killed a man."

Marko clapped him proudly on the shoulder.

"The first of many, my friend! Isn't it fun?"

Ferrer restrained a retch. He was sick with himself and disgusted with the operation, but he had the feeling that saying so would go over badly. What had he gotten himself into?

The state had to go, the state was bad, but *killing* people?

"Not so much," he muttered. Thinking of the farm he was going to buy, and his nice little workshop in the basement. When this was over... and no more killing people. That was for damn sure. He'd have done his part.

Rienzi was working on his gun with a small blade, carving three more notches into the handle. Solidifying them.

"It's cheating if you didn't kill them with that particular weapon," said McIlhan. "Just so you know."

"Dead is dead. I killed them, didn't I? And this makes seven."

"You killed `em," said Marko. "That's what counts. Lives ended, threads cut sharply off."

"So what's next?" asked Ferrer.

"Back to Texas," Marko said. "Awaiting orders."

* * *

The *Red Wasp II* flew over bayous and then plains, through the night and then the sunrise. The wind was coming from the southeast and their engines were at full power; they were making good speed.

Perry was apprehensive about pirates, but they were overcrewed; Nolan had hired another nine men, acquaintances and referrals who he trusted. He'd also made a point of arming his new ship; the proceeds from Perry's action had been enough to also afford a pressure-gun and a pair of three-inch rocket launchers, enough – Ahle had agreed – to dissuade a lot of pirates. Nothing materialized anyway, and they touched down in Dodge late in the afternoon.

"You'd better stay in the airship when we refuel," said Nolan. "Last I was here, those wanted posters for you were everywhere."

"They don't check the ships themselves?" asked Perry. Despite fears for his own safety, a bit dismayed. No wonder so many fugitives and criminals could travel freely!

"Too manpower-heavy," said Ahle. "You saw how they try in the South, where they have the mercenaries in the jackboots. Feds can't do it everywhere and there's not enough Imperials."

That, Perry knew. His men *had* been known to do spot-checks of ships here and there, usually operating from tips that must, in hindsight, have come through Fleming's office. He'd always been under the impression that Federals and local authorities did more serious checks, going on board every airship, at least in shady towns.

He said as much to Ahle, who shook her head.

"Almost never, and you realize how little your Fed counterparts get paid?"

"You could bribe them off?"

"Quite easily."

From somewhere she'd gotten a bottle of rum, and was sipping from it as she lay back in one of the bridge's comfortable leather chairs. She offered the bottle to Perry, who shook his head.

"You sure? This is good stuff."

"I don't drink on the job."

"Technically you're not on the job right now."

Perry thought for a moment. Quite true.

He extended his hand for the bottle, took a sip. The pirate had been correct – it was excellent rum. He took a longer sip and handed the bottle back.

For a little while they sat on the bridge, as the sound came of coal being shoveled into the *Red Wasp II*'s bunkers. They exchanged the bottle a few more times before Perry, feeling a warmth in his stomach and a slight blur in his head, passed it up. Ahle kept sipping.

"You're worried, aren't you?"

"I'm relieved," said Ahle. "We just have to get your ship back and my officers are safe. And along the way, can we kill the bastards who murdered my crew?"

"I think Fleming would write you a bonus check for getting that Marko guy."

* * *

"You said Nate Nolan's in town," Rafferty asked his man at the Dodge airship park. It was Friday, after all, and he had a sixty-hour pass; he'd already started drinking, was a bit tipsy. The telegram had come to him, via the specialists' mess, a couple of hours ago.

"Maybe he is," said the clerk. Ran a thumb across his palm. "You owe me for that telegram, too."

Rafferty gave him a buck. The clerk was silent. Slightly annoyed, Rafferty peeled off another dollar and, after a pause, a third.

"Port 43-A," said the clerk.

"Give me a sip of that shit," Rafferty said to Duckworth.

Duckworth handed over one of the flasks he was carrying. Rafferty took a long drag on the whisky then turned back to the clerk.

"Thanks."

"Why are we doing this again?", Duckworth asked as the two began the long trek – looked to be about a mile – to 43-A, which was one of the further-out ports from the entrance.

"Because guys like Nolan hear things. Duh."

"Why do you give a shit about the Vice anyway? You just blew a day's pay on that damn clerk so you could *maybe* hear something."

"Not your money," said Rafferty. He drank again from the flask and handed it back to Duckworth. "Besides, what else'm I gonna do with it – gamble it away?"

"Vidkowski would say to put it into the five-percenters and save for retirement."

Rafferty laughed.

"They pay us so we can spend it. Come on, let's go see this guy."

"Why d'you give a shit about the Vice anyway?" Duckworth repeated as they walked.

"Because he's got into some action. High drama. Ian Fleming stuff. And I want to know what's going on. I *bet* you there's some covert shit going on."

"Richardson learns we're here looking for word on him," Duckworth said, "she's going to rip us *both* down to `shipman Third."

Rafferty shrugged.

"I been busted down before. So have you. Don't like it, go home."

Presently, they reached the port marked 43-A. It housed a larger and *much* nicer airship than the *Red Wasp* Rafferty had ridden on, and for a moment Rafferty wondered if the clerk had been mistaken. But the legend 'Red Wasp II' was clearly marked in foot-high, red letters near the front of the clean grey gondola. A refueling truck on rails was parked further down the ship, port fuellers busily shoveling coal in. Nobody else seemed to be around.

"Check the bridge first," said Rafferty, because it was closest.

* * *

"Oi!" came a voice. " `Ail the bridge an' all! Captain Nolan?"

Perry recognized that voice from somewhere. They were in Dodge. He'd known people in Dodge…

Yeah, and there were wanted posters of him in Dodge.

"I think he's supervising the fueling," he called back.

A second later, a man appeared in the doorway. Tall and lean, with messy brown hair, in Air Service uniform and —

"*Vice?*" demanded Specialist Third Rafferty. "*Vice Perry?*"

"Specialist Rafferty?" demanded Perry. A chill going down his spine.

Anyone from Hugoton would know about the reward. To get busted *this close* to success? *This damn close?*

No. They'd finish refueling soon. Lift. Retrieve 4-106 before a pursuit could be organized. Richardson and Fleming would delay it, make sure resources weren't available.

But Rafferty – and the man with him, Senior Airshipman Duckworth – did not look like bounty hunters who'd scored. Rafferty was grinning broadly – unless Perry was wrong, he was at least slightly drunk. Duckworth looked more sober, and there was an uncertain smile on his face.

"Vice, we was here to look for *information* about you. Didn't expect to score a face-to-face with you and the pirate our very selves!"

"Have a drink," said Ahle, offering Rafferty the bottle of rum.

"Don't mind if I do, cap'n," said Rafferty with a grin. He took a long swig from the bottle and handed it to Duckworth, who took a much shorter swig and stepped over to hand it back to Ahle.

Rafferty, still grinning like an *idiot* who'd scored, took one of the comfortable bridge chairs and planted himself in it. Duckworth was still standing in the entrance, looking uneasy.

"Come in, since you're here," said Perry. In the doorway, Duckworth could run and cause trouble. Seated – Perry didn't know if he could draw a gun on one of his own men, but...

I will get 4-106 back. This close, I am not going to fail.

Duckworth sat down.

"So where you been, Vice? And what're you doing sticking your head into the lion's mouth in Dodge, sir?" Rafferty asked.

He pulled a flask, took a drink, offered it to Ahle. The pirate captain took it, had a drink, handed back the flask and again offered her rum bottle.

"We've been all over the place," said Ahle. "Good of you two to show up. We could use men."

"Use men for what?" Rafferty asked eagerly. He took another swig from the rum.

"We only got sixty-hour passes," said Duckworth.

"You can stay. I'm going with the Vice wherever he says. *Told* you it was a covert operation, mate!"

"We might be back within sixty hours," said Perry. Or... well, what *else* was he going to do with these two?

Draw on them?

"Sixty, seventy, eighty," said Rafferty. "Worst they'll do is chuck you in the brig."

"Rip your props off," said Duckworth.

236

"Got `em back before, don't I? Vice, what's it you want to have us do?"

"We're going into the mountains," said Ahle. "Simple cutting-out operation. Take 4-106 back to Hugoton. Vice clears his name, I get—what I've been promised—and *trust me*, your commanders are going to look the other way at your coming back a bit late if it's in the missing airship."

"You got a lead on 4-106?" Rafferty asked. "That was the whole of why you ran, right? To track her down. Nobody steals a Denny-Neuvoldt without being pursued!"

"When we finish refueling," said Perry, "we're going straight there. And we really could use a couple more competent airshipmen to handle the trip back. You coming?"

"Oh, *fuck* yeah, sir. Coming with you all the way."

"Duckworth?"

"It'll be a lark," Rafferty insisted.

"You're a *fugitive*, sir," said Duckworth uneasily.

"He's one in name only," said Ahle. "You'll be up for a promotion or something if you help. We're coming straight back to Hugoton. And…"

"We ain't got a choice in the deal," Rafferty clarified.

"I'm sorry, but I don't think you have," said Ahle. "May as well make the best of it, Airshipman – Duckworth?"

"If you – if you really insist, Vice," said Duckworth. "But sir, you swear this is really legitimate Imperial business, sir? With respect, sir – I may cross the line now and again on minor disciplinary stuff, but I'm no damn traitor. Sir. Without meaning, sir, to imply, sir, that you might be. Sir."

"Of course he's no damn traitor, Ducks!" said Rafferty. "Any more than you or I am. He's an adventurer, is all, and now *we* get to be!"

"Now *you* get to be," Duckworth muttered.

Nolan came back to the bridge.

"You have guests?" he asked.

"Two of my old crew," said Perry. "Looking for you, apparently, and found us."

"Still a price on your head, ain't there?" asked Nolan uneasily.

"They're coming along, now," said Ahle.

Rafferty grinned. "Fuck yeah."

"When do we lift?" Perry asked.

"I was going to say: Fueling's done and that ice won't keep forever. Now, unless you have any objections."

"Now," said Perry, "would be good.'

"Jessie," said Nolan to one of his crew, "find these two a cabin for the night. Vice-Commodore, sir, we ought to be in Denver by mid-morning. Ought to find a few more men there. And from there, to take back your ship."

"To take back my ship," said Perry. "Ahle, hand me that rum. I think we can all drink to that."

* * *

"You get a good price for those crawfish?" Perry asked Nolan as they took off from Denver, a day later and with eight more men aboard.

"Prearranged contract," Nolan said exuberantly. "*Man*, I'm not used to those! Paid for the trip and then some – and then some more! Guaranteed, if we made it on time, which we did."

"So now we head off to 4-106," Perry said. "Right?"

"We don't have any other cargo; just your men and your mission. Your Governor is going to make it worth my while to help out, right? I've been promising these guys work and all, y'know..."

"I don't know how these things are arranged," said Perry, "but..."

"I do," said Ahle. "The men get paid fighting wages from lift, whether it was in New Orleans or here. A bonus if there *is* actually fighting, depending on how they individually acquit themselves, to be paid alongside another bonus on successful completion of the mission. Perry's boss in Hugoton will assure you of that."

"Fighting wages is what I've promised them," Nolan agreed. "Now, what about me? A favor is a favor and I owe you one, but I'm running an empty ship from this point and that's going to cost me."

"Fle– my boss will reimburse you for your costs plus a reasonable percentage," said Perry. "You have my word on that, as an Imperial officer."

"If you're still one, but you came across as a right gent that first time around," said Nolan. He extended a hand, which Perry shook. "We've got a deal, not as though there wasn't one

238

before. Now let's go get your ship."

Perry allowed himself another vision of triumphant return: Sailing into Hugoton – escorted, of course – with 4-106, touching down with his ship back and his honor restored. It was a beautiful sight and one he'd been sustaining himself on for over a week now.

And now they were finally off to make it happen!

"We've got a deal," he said, as he shook Perry's hand. That beautiful vision of finally, *finally* succeeding, still dancing in front of his eyes. "Let's go get my ship back."

* * *

"They should have done it this way *to begin with*," McIlhan said in a cabin of Jebediah Judd's streamlined red airship, as it followed the Mississippi north. It was a plain but comfortable passenger cabin with slightly worn brown leather fold-out seats and a presently folded-in pair of bunkbeds. Handcuffed to her wrist was a briefcase, identical in shape and contents to the one that the SS man Skorzeny had managed to lose. "No fanfare. Just ride a damn ship straight into Colombia."

Marko shrugged.

"People do what they do. They follow the archetypes. Soldiers must wear uniform and do military things, for example," he said.

Engineers, thought Ferrer, *must shoot people with machine-guns. Twenty-two year old liveried kids named Philip Riordan.*

He'd taken a life. The shattered face and body of the kid swam back into his mind, yet again.

"You alright, boss?" Rienzi asked.

Don't show weakness to these guys. Not even to that sick punk, Ferrer thought. Now he *had* killed someone, how Rienzi could actually enjoy the act – be thrilled by the same feelings that had been coursing through Ferrer's mind for the last day and a half – filled him with sick wonder.

"Yeah, I'm fine," he said.

Farm. Farm at the end of this; a nice little farm in the Midwest with a comfortable basement workshop. Grow crops and tinker.

That reminded him.

"Mr. Marko, do you have a moment?"

Marko gave a nod. A pause.

"You two, get out," Marko told Rienzi and Ferrer. When they'd left, Marko cocked his head.

"Having second thoughts about the killing, huh?"

Ferrer started – *is it so obvious?* – then shook his head.

"Liar. You'll get used to it. What?"

"My pay," he said. "I'd feel – a bit more comfortable if I – I know you've already given Pratt his first half. Do you think —"

To Ferrer's relief, the psychopath actually nodded.

"Of course," he said. "You'll have it shortly. Five thousand Imperial pounds. Should get you your retirement, eh?"

Ferrer nodded.

"With the other half, yes."

"Other half the same way as this," Marko said and giggled.

* * *

Alone in the cabin, Ferrer allowed himself to breathe again. This operation was a scary mess, and what if things *did* go really wrong? That they were traveling to Columbus in the first place was a bad thing – this Lynch woman had already fucked things up to some extent. If military strategy was anything like engineering, it involved analysis that took time, planning that took time. The SS were now getting the information they needed – for the necessary planning and analysis – some days later than they otherwise would.

He knew the schedule. He'd heard something about how SS units were *already* quietly leaving their stations in the eastern part of the state, moving to locations on the Arkansas border.

Columns of tanks and armored cars, truckloads of mechanized infantry in support, heading to where they would fuel up – and not arm, he supposed they were already armed, it was a part of their existing job – for their sweep toward the objective. Without specific plans for when they reached that objective, or if those plans had been made in a hurried way – then, yes, things were more likely to go wrong.

It's under control, he told himself. *Marko and his bosses are clever. They've planned things. They know what they're doing. They've allowed for these problems.*

The face of the man he'd killed, the twenty-two-year-old machine-gunner named Philip Riordan – *oh, why did I decide it*

was necessary intellectual honesty to learn his name? – swam back
into his mind. That had been the result of a problem, of
something going wrong. Of her boss deciding that she wanted
to know something that was emphatically none of her business.

What else, a small voice in Ferrer's mind wondered, *can go
wrong?*

* * *

The only place big enough to gather everybody was the *Red
Wasp II*'s cargo hold, an uncomfortable but empty grille. Perry,
who had been flying for eighteen years, still found it
disconcerting to have a grille under his feet, as opposed to a
solid footing where you *couldn't* see the ground under you.
He'd have preferred a briefing hall.

He'd have preferred a lot of things, but you dealt with what
you had. Twelve hours from now they'd be sailing proudly
back into Hugoton, and he'd again be able to put on the
uniform he'd comfortably worn for his entire adult life.
Squadron Thirty-One would know the truth, and...

"So, yeah," he told the eighteen assorted men – well,
fourteen men and four women – that Nolan had gathered up.
They were rougher than the norm, scarred and hardened, with
more than just the odd gas gun or .22 in their rigs. But not *bad*
ones; Nolan knew them all personally or by first-degree
reference, and Nolan didn't rate further down Perry's scale
than 'a bit shady at times'.

"We're going to be cutting out a stolen Imperial ship. We'll
make a pass over it to confirm she's actually *there*, then drop in
on top of her the way Ms. Ahle did. Take out what crew are on
the thing, being especially careful for a tall man with a
moustache – he's a dangerous one, I hear, and shoot to kill if he
comes in front of you. Lift, then head east. We'll be flying the
thing to the Imperial base at Hugoton, where you'll collect
your pay."

And I'll regain my honor.

"Mr. Vice-Commodore," said a sleek-looking woman from
Nolan's crew. Elegant, black-haired and rigless, and Perry
wasn't sure if she was actual crew or a longstanding passenger.
"Mr. Nolan says – from the map, we're about twenty miles
away. Half an hour. He says your men had better begin getting

ready."

Perry checked his watch: about half past three. Plenty of daylight in which to conduct the operation.

Nervous. Nervous like he'd never been on official service. He'd be going into action with men he didn't know, men who hadn't passed through any Academy, technical school or Service apprenticeship. Men who could be unreliable, who might be – Nolan himself was a bit shady when you got down to it! – little better than pirates.

The one person he *did* know under fire was an avowed pirate officer herself!

One who'd taken this very ship, with fewer people than he had right now. *Count your blessings. Ignore the nerves.*

* * *

Perry stood on the bridge as they made their approach. They were about fifty miles past the Front Range, the rather stark mid-Colorado border between the high plains and the Rockies. The ground below them was most definitely mountains, peaks rising higher at times than the *Red Wasp II* herself. Winds buffeted them, knocking the airship left and right faster than the crew could adjust. It was rough going.

"Coming up on the canyon now," said Nolan. They were flying high, about three thousand feet above the average ground level, although that varied hard with the rugged slopes.

"I can read a map," Perry snapped.

"Sorry, Mr. Vice-Commodore."

"No, my own apologies. I'm nervous. Not your fault."

"Fully accepted, then, sir. I can understand your nerves."

If Lynch was lying to me, after all of this…

Or if her information had changed… airships were eminently portable constructions. He could probably tell if 4-106 *had* been there, or at least if some airship had been parked in the location. But that would be useless.

The canyon was deep and relatively wide, according to the topographic map. According to what Perry could see with his own eyes as they approached it…

He went to the very front of the bridge, craning down to see directly below them. Looking for signs, looking for –

4-106!

He'd have recognized the triple-finned design anywhere, and the thieves had made no effort to disguise it. It was right there, in full bulk, sitting at the bottom of the canyon for the taking!

The relief was immense. *Lynch wasn't lying to me! It's there! The raid, all of this, was completely justified! My God!*

Until that point he hadn't realized just *how much* he'd doubted Lynch's word, how desperate he'd been to believe it. Now that it was proven true...

"We've got her!" he exalted. "We've got my ship! Turn your ship around, Nolan! Ahle, prep the boarding crew!"

He drew his own pistol. The .40 – lethal ammunition was most definitely called for in this case, and he *hoped* he'd get to use it against that moustached man who'd cut the rope!

Ahle had been conferring with one of the picked-up men, a guy of about forty-five with a black goatee and a rig loaded with weapons. Like Ahle – *like I should have thought to get*, Perry thought – he held a pair of binoculars.

"Like hell we do, Perry," she said. "You were looking at the ship. Did you look at the *location* at all?"

How was that relevant? Perry shook his head.

"Galvanny here" – Ahle gestured at the other man – "spent a decade as a US Marine officer. He saw the same things I did. There's at least three rocket batteries in the area, well-camouflaged but not invisible. I would bet there's a fighting reserve, and the people on that ship are *not* going to be taken by surprise for very long."

Perry looked at her. No. He *hadn't* been looking at the area around the ship.

She's lying, a part of his mind desperately wanted to believe. His mouth opened to repeat the order: *Go in.*

"The people who stole that ship have dug in and are guarding it well," Ahle said.

Galvanny, the former Marine officer, nodded in agreement.

"It's how I'd set an ambush. My money's on five rocket batteries minimum, if we can only see three."

"Perry, if we go into that with eighteen roughnecks – twenty including ourselves – then that trap will close on us, and we are all going to die."

"And our men are no fools," said Galvanny. "Some of them

243

in the hold, they'd have seen just what we did. Jackson was a staff sergeant in your own Air Marines, and I *know* he'd have noticed. If there were a hundred of us – sure, maybe. But we signed on to fight, not walk into an ambush. Pay or no pay, none of us are dropping into that shit."

"You're sure it's an ambush," Perry said. "Let's make another pass. Lower."

"Rocket batteries," said Nolan. "And they might decide to bring us down if we seem too inquisitive. No, sir. I'll take a certain amount of risk but I won't commit suicide."

"A hundred men," said Perry. "Even assuming we could find a hundred reliable fighters, this ship couldn't carry them all."

"I know where we can easily get a hundred – a hundred and fifty – men," said Ahle. "And combat-capable airships to carry them, and deal with those rocket launchers."

"I still say we go in," Perry insisted.

Rafferty shook his head.

"You might not trust the pirate, sir. But I'm an airshipman myself, and I seen the elephant a few times as you know. Classic ambush configuration, sir. I saw the same shit Cap Ahle and the former Marine did."

Rafferty – *was* an airshipman. A drunk and an incorrigible, but not disloyal and not incompetent. His judgment meant something.

"Very well," Perry found himself saying. "Where do we get a hundred and fifty men and combat-capable airships?"

"Cap Nolan," Ahle asked respectfully, "how are we on fuel?"

"Near full bunkers, ma'am. We topped up in Denver, as you'll recall."

"Very well," Ahle said. "Are you with me on whatever needs to be done, Vice Perry? So you can get your ship back?"

Perry nodded. Ceding command, for now. Shocked, but – you adjusted plans, didn't you?

"Captain," Ahle said, "set a course for the Black Hills."

Chapter Sixteen

Cordova's Armadillos: The real-life exploits of the world's finest mercenary unit, heroically serving Texas on our western frontier!

Interviewed live:

Commodore Jason Cordova, the *Lone Star* – as noble as the name of his own ship!

Captain Bill Snider, the *Scimitar of Silence* – scything down those in his way!

Captain Jennifer Atkinson, the *Squeeze* – until only blood drips from her enemies!

Captain Paula Handley, the *Vorpal* – swift death to those who oppose her!

Captain Richard Evans, the *Dread Wyvern* – on wings of death they fly!

Captain Peggey Rowland, the *Five Speed* – but her enemies' deaths come in only one: Fast!

HEAR the true-as-life discussions between the legendary airship captains, their banter and their battle talk!

FEEL the heroic attitude amongst the mercenaries who made Texas their home – the latter-day Spirit of the Alamo!

WATCH the combat actions that turned our tide in the Sonoran War! Plus five more that could happen – and might, as soon as tomorrow!

BUY the conjunctive novels, comics and rig accessories of our number one auxiliary unit, Cordova's Armadillos (tm), the Desert Heroes (tm) of the Sonoran War!

Texas Wire Communications Network
hyperkinematograph series promo, January 1962.

Early on in his ride, Agent David Cornwell had drilled, with his pocket knife, a tiny eye-slit in the side of the wooden packing crate he'd snuck into, quietly disposing of the well-wrapped drill bits the crate had formerly contained. It had been luck getting onto the train in the first place, with its international manifest.

Through it, as the northbound train clicked slowly along from Houston, he'd seen things. Occasional details that would have been irrelevant to most civilians, but he was a field agent who knew what to look for. Military convoys going north. A base he'd recognized, empty.

Texas was mobilizing. Texas was quietly but most definitely mobilizing north. And he was quite probably the last MI-7 agent left in the place.

The train had moved slowly, at one point being shunted aside for some hours on a siding. Cornwell had tried to sleep, but fitfully and without any real success. He was no longer running on nervous energy – that had burned itself out in the dockside boarding house, the last of it expended getting aboard this train – but on terror and urgency: *If they catch me, I am most definitely dead. Not exchanged, not now the Russians are clearly backing Texas. Dead, like everyone else in the station.*

That and the urgency. Very conscious that he was probably the last MI-7 agent alive in Texas. And the word about Texan mobilization north was word he had to bring. Hugoton was only a few dozen miles north of Amarillo. Texan activity, a new war, would be bad news for the United States; it was also a potential disaster, certainly a hard fight, for the admittedly impressive Hugoton garrison.

And with Russian support? There was only one thing the clearly-present Russians could hope to achieve from backing an invasion of the United States.

Hugoton has 93% of the world's helium reserves. Imperial warships, and quite a few *passenger* ships, ran on helium, which didn't burn, whose survivability in combat was infinitely better than flammable hydrogen. Simply *destroying* Hugoton would be an immense strategic victory for the Tsar. *Taking* it? *Russians* having access to all the helium they wanted, as their prize for backing the Texan invasion?

Nightmare scenarios danced through his mind, dimly aware that the train had stopped.

And then the nightmare became real, from the noises around him. Someone was in the boxcar. Someone was searching the crates.

We've reached the border, Cornwell thought. *And they're not fucking around.*

He reached into his jacket. If a customs inspector opened *this* crate, there was only one thing he could do. Whatever it took, he had to get to Fleming.

* * *

Heinrich Himmler was a surprisingly small man to Ferrer's eyes, given his reputation. Small, slim and mostly bald – what was left of his hair was tightly cropped, like his crew-cut guards – it was almost a challenge to remember that this man commanded fifteen thousand hard-bitten soldiers.

Almost. The security Marko, himself and the others had been through – everything short of a body cavity search, *despite* the letters from Houston and the Third Department with their enclosed photographs and detailed physical descriptions – made it hard to forget. Even in the commander's office, Ferrer could sense that they were being watched. The top-floor office was huge but Spartan, with extraordinary views but no decorations except for a suit of medieval Germanic armor and half a dozen swords.

"Ah, Skorzeny," Marko was saying. Ferrer vaguely recognized the man standing next to Himmler. "To deliver where you couldn't."

"Fuck you, gypsy."

"All your military song and dance, and it got you ambushed. Soldiers must soldier, eh?"

"I said fuck you."

"Gentlemen." Himmler's quiet voice held a certain cold authority. "Shut up."

Even Marko seemed to respond.

"Mr. Marko, you are here to deliver documents. Unpin them from your woman's wrist, if you would."

"The cuffs require two keys," said Marko. "You have the other one."

"Sepp," Himmler said to the other man with him. "Do it."

Sepp Dietrich, Himmler's deputy, was a big man in his sixties with a shaven scalp. He produced a small key from the front pocket of his starched uniform shirt.

Loreta McIlhan laid the briefcase on Heinrich Himmler's flat pine desk.

Marko moved forwards, put his key into the double-locked handcuffs first on McIlhan's end, then on the other end, then on the double-locked briefcase. All three clicked open.

Dietrich inserted his own key, starting with the briefcase. *Click. Click. Click.*

He stepped aside for Himmler to open the briefcase. He did, inspected the contents. Took the chips up and handed them to Skorzeny like a flunky.

"Get these to Tactical," he ordered. "We have limited time to plan the attack."

* * *

The moment Cornwell had been dreading finally arrived: a man with a crowbar opening the box he was hiding in.

Blinding light, relative to the near-complete darkness inside the packing crate. He looked up into the face of an overalled man in his early thirties. Thin face, and it looked like he was trying to grow a handlebar moustache. Pale blue eyes widened in shock.

I only have one chance at this, Cornwell thought, and pulled from inside his jacket.

"Who – what – what the fuck, there's a guy here!" the customs inspector was saying.

Cornwell shoved the money in his face.

"You get paid what, two thousand, two and a half a year? Here's four grand. You didn't see me. Count it."

Texan hundred-dollar bills. The customs inspector took the bundle of money. Inspected one closely.

"These are real," he muttered.

"Give me an address," said Cornwell. Going on reflexes and rote; he was scared out of his mind. "That's the down payment. You get the rest of the ten grand when I've cleared the border."

"Who are you?" the inspector demanded.

"Someone who can give you one and a half times that again if I clear the border."

The inspector slowly, painstakingly, going back a couple of times, counted the money.

"Holy shit. Four fucking grand. You're giving me four grand?"

Cornwell, in the crate, shook his head.

"What the fuck do you mean you're not? You just gave it to me!"

"I'm giving you ten grand," Cornwell said. "If you didn't see anything. If you missed this crate. Give me an address."

"You're not going to fuck me over. Ten Gs?" the clerk asked.

"Promise. Not going to fuck your country over, too. I'm gone, never to return. Promise you that."

The inspector reached into his own blue jacket, pulled a pencil and paper, scribbled something. An address, somewhere in Wichita Falls, Northeast Province, Texas.

Cornwell's heart leapt. *He's buying it!*

"Send it there, OK? You said *six more grand?*"

"Six more grand," said Cornwell. *I'm going to make it!* "Promise."

"Fuck it, even if you don't" – the inspector held up the money. "You gave me almost two years' pay right here. Holy shit. You say you *are* leaving, not gonna cause my country any more trouble at whatever you did?"

"Not a damn bit."

"Then I never saw you," said the inspector. He dropped the crate's lid back down.

Cornwell – he hadn't realized that he barely had, for the last couple of minutes – breathed.

I may have made it, he thought.

* * *

"Vice," Duckworth said nervously. "Do you have a moment? Sir?"

"Senior Airshipman," Perry said, looking up from the high, sparse plains they were flying over. "Of course."

"In private, sir, if you don't mind?"

Perry nodded. They got up and left the bridge, went to the small cabin Perry had been given. Plain and functional, like the rest of the airship, with a pair of folding bunks whose lower one was unfolded, and an unfolded seat next to a folded-in writing desk. Perry closed the door.

"What's up, Senior Airshipman?"

"Sir, I can't go to the Black Hills. Neither can Rafferty. He

249

got us into this – *you* got us into this, sir, with the highest of respect – thinking it'd be a quick run back and forth. Now we're going to consort with pirates."

Perry gave a nod. He was uncomfortable with the thought himself, very uncomfortable. Working with Ahle had been one thing, but directly enlisting the help of *active* pirates?

He, at least, was on a *legitimate* special assignment. Duckworth and Rafferty had been effectively dragooned into this, Duckworth apparently as much by Rafferty's stronger personality as any decision of his own. OK, so *he'd* been dragooned much the same way by Fleming, but he wasn't going to inflict the same crap on his men…

"And sir, I'm on a sixty-hour pass. It's already Saturday and I have to report Monday morning at the base or it's brig time. So does Raff. We need to get off this ship, sir. And…"

"And?"

Duckworth looked away, forced a sheepish smile.

"Sir, passage back to Dodge is going to cost money. Sir. And I make enlisted pay, sir. It might not be a big deal to you as a squadron commander, but – Vice Perry, sir, I can't *afford* to get back there!"

Perry nodded again.

"Very well. *That's* something I can help with." It crossed his mind for a moment to confide in Duckworth about his relief in actually having a solveable problem. Only for a very short moment: whether or not he was in uniform, he *was* still a Vice-Commodore of the Air Service who did not confide in enlisted men.

He took out his wallet and peeled off a fifty. Then, after a moment, another one.

"I'll have Nolan take us by Denver – we're still south of the place, I think. Fifty bucks is going to cover your passage to Dodge. You and Rafferty can go back."

"Thank you, sir. Much appreciated, sir."

* * *

"No," said Rafferty. "Like hell I'm getting off."

"That's *desertion*, Raff," said Duckworth. The airship had touched down outside Denver, hovering over a field near a main road with enough traffic that the two airshipmen should

250

easily be able to thumb a ride downtown. Or to Stapleton.

"Ain't desertion for another hundred sixty-eight hours after the pass expires," said Rafferty. "Until then it's just AWOL."

Yeah, thought Perry. Rafferty was the type who'd know exactly how far you could push the rules. But an order was an order.

"I'm not permitting you to go AWOL either," said Perry.

"Boss, we got more crew than we need at Hugoton, until 4-106 comes back. Now, Ducks can go back, that's a good thing, he can update the spooks on what you been doing. But I'm stayin' with you. Said I'd help you retrieve the big ship, and that's what I'm gonna do. Boss."

"Perhaps I misphrased," said Perry. "Specialist Third, that was not a request. It is a direct order."

Rafferty grinned.

"Under what authority, boss? You're officially a fugitive. Respectable Spec Third can't take orders from a busted fugitive, huh?"

There was a chuckle from someone on the bridge.

"He's got you there, Vice," said former-Marine-lieutenant Galvanny.

Perry sighed.

"OK, Specialist Third. Perhaps you can explain *why* you want to take brig time in order to come along. Or a court-martial, since there may not be guarantee we'll be back in a week?"

Rafferty grinned again, and cocked his head.

"Boss, it's an adventure. Joined the Service for adventure, din't I? Go into the heart of the Black Hills? Now, *that's* a story they'll be buying me drinks for ten years down the line! And Vice, think of it your way – you know I'm a loyal Serviceman, and you know I can handle myself in a fight. Don't you think *you'd* be a little better off with someone around to watch your back in the Black Hills?"

That *was* a point, although Perry didn't like it. He was supposed to send this man right back to his job! He really shouldn't have allowed him onto the airship to begin with, but there hadn't been any option, had there?

Allowing self-interest to overcome duty... but he didn't have the authority to kick Rafferty off the ship anyway.

But the captain did.

He looked at Nolan.

"Captain, I'd like you to boot this man from your ship. So that he *must* go back to Hugoton."

Nolan thought for a moment.

"Vice, I don't think that's a good idea. He's got a point– lot of men in the Black Hills would *love* the chance to crack an Imperial Vice-Commodore, ex or not. Story's gotten around, you know. Won't be anonymous. I think you could use a bodyguard."

"I have Ahle," said Perry.

"You could use another one. My money says Ahle is going to have to go places you won't be allowed. Vice, sir, with respect, I think he should come along and I'm not going to order him off my ship for that reason."

Bastard.

But if Nolan, too, thought he needed a bodyguard... perhaps it was something he could accept. He'd made every good-faith attempt to get rid of Rafferty, after all.

"Very well," said Perry. "You can stay. I am specifically *not* liable for your actions and I want it made very clear that I *attempted* to give you a direct order to follow Service rules. Understood, Rafferty?"

"Broken rules before an' been busted for `em," said Rafferty cheerfully. He touched the Specialist Third's insignia on his shoulders. "Always get me props back one way or the other."

"Raff, you're an *idiot*," said Duckworth.

"Probably," said Rafferty to his friend. "But I'm gonna be an idiot with a tale to tell."

"And charges to face when you're back," said Duckworth.

"Time enough to worry about `em when I'm back, Ducks."

"Duckworth, I'd like you to deliver this to proper authorities when you return," said Perry, handing the enlisted man an envelope. "The contents are to be considered extremely confidential. Is that understood?"

"Yessir. Who's proper authorities, sir, in this case?"

"Good point. Do *not* give it to your chain of command; this goes to the Flight Admiral directly. You will deliver it into the hands of either Flight Admiral Richardson or her personal adjutant. Nobody else, under any circumstances. It goes into your jacket now and does not come out until you are in the physical presence of one of those two people. Clear?"

252

"Got it, sir," said Duckworth. He went to the door of the bridge, prepared to jump down; they were still a good six feet or so off the ground, moving every so-often as gusts of wind blew the ship sideways.

"Sir? If I can say so – good luck with what you're doing, sir. I saw that stolen ship down there with my own eyes."

"And you don't tell a *soul* that," said Perry. "Everything about your little jaunt is confidential. Certain people are going to be watching for if you do talk. And it's more than brig time in that case – those people have powers that go well beyond Service regulations, am I clear?"

Duckworth nodded and his right arm twitched; he was restraining himself from a salute.

"Aye, sir. Well, good luck, sir." Duckworth looked down, then jumped from the ship.

"Next stop Red Cloud," said Nolan cheerfully. "Lift!"

* * *

Jebediah Judd's sleek bright-red airship – the *Red Ruby Robber* – had been tied directly to the roof of the seven-storey SS building in downtown Columbia, a privileged position. Around the edges of the roof, in fact, was manned heavy firepower – rockets and cannon – clearly intended to keep that position privileged.

For the last day and change, Marko, Ferrer, Rienzi and McIlhan had been waiting antsily in their cabins for the orders that were supposed to arrive. Now, the tiny, hyperactive captain in red pounded on the door of the cabin Ferrer shared with Rienzi. With him was Otto Skorzeny.

Marko and McIlhan were already out in the passageway.

"We finally got movement orders?" Marko was asking.

"You finally get the fuck out of here," Skorzeny replied.

From what Ferrer had seen, there was absolutely no love lost between the anarchist and the SS colonel. That was one reason the four were sleeping aboard the airship instead of taking the luxury-grade quarters Himmler had offered them. "Don't trust that uptight excuse for a commando fuckup not to be listening," Marko had explained curtly.

"About time," Marko shot back. Turned to Judd. "Where?"

"You have the orders, big man," Judd said. The little pirate seemed utterly unafraid of Skorzeny, maybe even considered him a kindred spirit in craziness. In the last day or so, through small-talk with Judd's engineering crew, Ferrer had *heard* a thing or two about Otto Skorzeny. Some of the shit he'd pulled over the years... even allowing for exaggeration, it was impressive.

A more honest form of action than what Marko had drawn him into. What he, Ferrer, had *thought* he'd be getting into at the start of all this.

"Gimme," Marko ordered Skorzeny.

"What, no please?" Judd asked.

"No thank-you, either," Skorzeny observed when Marko had the folder.

"Wire from Houston via New Orleans. Just came out of decryption," the SS colonel added. "Looks urgent."

"You know it's urgent," said Marko. Reading the orders. Nodding.

"Colonel, get the fuck out of here. Judd, lift immediately. We've got another loose end to tie off."

"I'll buy you a drink in Hugoton," Skorzeny promised Judd. "And" – with nods at Ferrer, McIlhan and Rienzi – "you guys too. Gypsy thief can buy his own."

"You can buy another ramrod to go up your ass," Marko muttered. "Shithead."

"Behave, gentlemen," Judd said. "Colonel, we'll be lifting immediately."

"For where?" Rienzi asked.

"Red Cloud, in the Black Hills. Pirateville!"

* * *

Cornwell's train had undergone a much less serious customs inspection on the US side of the Texan border; Cornwell's own box had not been opened and, from the speed of things, not many were. Before long they pulled into a town he recognized from pictures as Ft. Lawton, a major border outpost.

Finally some good news, he thought, getting out of the box. His legs hurt from the long concealment. There was an airship park in Ft. Lawton, and that park was a regular waypoint for the Imperial ships patrolling the border railway line that ultimately ran to Hugoton. He could get a train in any case, but he also had the option – if he was lucky – of riding an Air Service vessel.

I'm about due for some damn luck, he thought, as he carefully stepped through the wide-open boxcar door and began to head out of the airship park. *And with a bit more luck, I might even make Hugoton tomorrow.*

* * *

The yard workers weren't paid to pay attention to hoboes – not by their employers, at any rate, or at least the directives from management made other things a priority.

One man, however, had met a fellow in a bar a couple of weeks ago. On learning he was a yard worker, the man had bought his drinks for the rest of the night and said some interesting things about hoboes. A Federal agent, the yard worker had thought, or maybe organized crime. Either way, he'd said that some people he worked with would be especially interested to know about any hoboes coming from Texas.

That was silly, the yard worker said. Lately for some reason the Texans had taken to extra special care about outgoing customs inspections, and while they weren't *looking* for hoboes, a customs inspector would certainly kick off any he saw.

The Federal agent or mob man – from the yard worker's perspective there wasn't a whole lot of difference, but the guy *was* buying him drinks – had said that yeah, and thus we'll be especially interested in any who *do* get past the customs inspectors. Competition we don't like. Give us a call and there's a month's pay in it for you if we get him.

The yard worker had blown it off at the time, but he'd kept the card, stuffed in his wallet. And now – what was this? A hobo getting off a boxcar from a train he knew perfectly well had come from Texas.

More to the point, if that guy hadn't been shitting him – a month's pay!

He waved his flags to the man down the line: Hold – Back – Five – Minutes.

And, fishing in his wallet for the card, he ran for the office, where there was a telephone.

It had taken Cornwell a few minutes to find his way out of the yard and get his bearings. He'd never actually been to Ft. Lawton before, just seen maps and pictures of the place, and it took a short conversation with another bum – a *real* hobo, not a fugitive as far as he could tell – to get the location of the airship park. A few miles away.

Well, after days cooped up inside that damn crate, he could use the exercise.

Don't think for a moment, he told himself, *that you're home free. You're home free when you're physically on an Air Service ship or inside the Hugoton lines.*

To make sure, his hand reached inside his worn black-leather jacket, for the automatic .40. As he'd done a thousand times on that terrifying, informative ride north from Houston, his fingers slid along the body-heat-warmed steel of the gun.

This time he did something he hadn't bothered to do in the crate. He turned the safety off and chambered a round.

Nothing under his control was going to stop him from reaching the safety of Hugoton. If the worst erupted, the gun would keep things under control.

"That's him," said the offsider in the steam-car. He wasn't Third Department, just a locally-hired grunt whose other employers had included a couple of loan-sharks and the occasional smuggler. But the foreigner had offered him good money.

"We goin' waste him?" his buddy the driver asked.

"Put him six feet under," the offsider ordered, pulling a sawn-off shotgun.

Something in the amplified *chuff* of the passing steam-truck warned Cornwell; someone gunning an engine. He turned, drawing the gun.

A man was leveling a sawn-off shotgun at him.

Cornwell fired first. He was better-trained, a field agent,

and he was also more accurate. It was his bad luck that the gunman's finger clenched around the trigger in a reflex as the .40 slug tore through his skull.

Heavy shot blasted out into Cornwell.

The agent staggered, but fired again. If he was going down – *this close to success, damn it!* – he was taking one or two of these Okhrana bastards with him. He fired again and again, but the original gunman was dead, slumped across the window, and the driver was taking no chances with his own life; he'd floored the steam, his truck racing off.

Cornwell fell against the greasy industrial-slum wall, leaving a trail of blood with his body. His legs were limp; his chest was *hurting,* hurting terribly.

He had to get to the airship park. Miles away, but he had to get there.

They got me, he thought.

Yes. They had. But he could walk. His legs still moved. He could walk.

"Mister? Mister? You alright?"

A man – not a cop, just a passer-by. A passer-by, Cornwell realized, with a vehicle. A steam-truck, a delivery driver to one of these little factories.

A gasp, as the dismounted driver noticed the gun.

"I'm fine," said Cornwell, and stuck the gun in the driver's face.

"Nobody. Gets. Hurt. Get me to the airship park. Pay you. Don't I'll shoot you."

"Mister, you couldn't shoot a kitten."

Cornwell got to his feet, *forcing* himself despite agonizing screams of pain from his body. He'd been shot in the gut – at least one of those pellets had gone into his gut muscles. It *hurt,* and he could feel strength ebbing from his body.

He probably didn't have long.

Some chance was better than none.

"Wasn't. A. Request," he snarled.

"Airship park," said the man. "Well, I was going there anyway. Don't pretend to threaten me or it'll be the worse for you."

"Pretend to bribe you," said Cornwell, his left hand going for his wallet. There was still a few hundred, Texan currency that'd have to be converted, in there. He fumbled out a wad of

257

money and offered it to the driver.

"Just get me there."

The truck driver shrugged.

"Ought to get you to a doctor. You been shot bad, mister."

"You'll take me where I'm going."

* * *

The steam-car driver's friends didn't show up again – Cornwell had almost come to hope they *wouldn't*, that he'd get a free ride to the airship park – until they were almost there.

When they did, they came with a vengeance. Two sleek, low-slung steam-cars loaded with gunmen came screaming up behind the steam-truck without the slightest pretense of covertness.

"What the fuck did you get me into?" demanded the truck driver.

"Through the gates." Which were in sight. "Drive through the fuckin' gates!"

"That's illegal."

Cornwell leaned back in the worn leather seat of the truck and pointed the gun at the driver.

"I can't miss at this range. *Get me in there!*"

The driver gunned the engine, pushing steam, as someone in one of the tailing cars opened up with an automatic weapon.

"Who the fuck *are* you?" demanded the driver.

Cornwell could see an Imperial-grey airship – more than one! Looked like he was finally lucky, a wing of four! – in the airship park.

"Get me to the Imperial ships!"

Pursued by the two cars, they smashed through the lowered boom-gates of the airship park. Mechanics and stevodores dove out of their way.

"Next to that one! Now!"

The airships were fueling, but Imperial airships in territory that was still arguably South *never* fully powered down. Was it just Cornwell's wounded – dying? – imagination, or could he see crew moving to battle stations?

Heavy-caliber bullets cut into the steam-truck, lancing through, smashing the boiler.

"Fuck *you*," he murmured, as something struck him.

"I paid you. Get me there!"

"Can't! Lost pressure!"

The truck was slowing. Fifty yards from the nearest of the airships, across empty pads.

"Halt! All three of you, halt immediately or you will be shot!" came from one of the airships, an electrically-amplified loudspeaker.

One of the black cars heard the order too late, or ignored it. Boilers hissing, it moved in to block Cornwell's movement between his crippled truck and the nearest airship.

A missile blasted from one of the Imperial airships. Hit the car and practically vaporized it. Burning debris flew in all directions from its shattered hulk.

Now! Now is the only chance I'm going to get!

Bent double, crippled, staggering, Cornwell bailed from the truck and ran through the shredded wreckage of the steam-car, praying the airship crews wouldn't shoot him down. Instead, a door opened to him. He found himself on the ship's bridge.

Looking down the barrels of half a dozen pistols.

He dropped his own gun. Collapsed face-down, coughing blood on the airship's pristine stamped-aluminum deck.

"Who," an officer demanded, "the fuck are you?"

"MI-7," Cornwell coughed, barely audible.

"Who the fuck?" The officer leaned closer

"MI-7," Cornwell repeated. "Lift. And get me to Hugoton. I have urgent news."

"You been shot bad, agent," said the officer. "And we've got a convoy to protect coming out of here."

"Get here. And" – as Cornwell realized he'd made it, but he might not live long enough to reach safety proper – "get me a pencil and pad. I have a report to make."

"You heard the man," the fading Cornwell heard the officer shout. "*Lift!* And now!"

* * *

"He might live," the airship medic reported at Hugoton later that evening. "*If* he gets treatment, and gets lucky. But he was most insistent."

"On what grounds?" asked the base officer. "Get him to intensive care, of course."

"MI-7 agent," said the ship's XO. "Flasher command from Vice Begley said to go straight here because of this. Wounded, dying MI-7 agent."

"And your *point?*" demanded the irritated lieutenant.

"My point is this," said the XO, brandishing a blood-stained envelope. "This has what he knows. He said it's to get to Deputy Director Fleming *immediately.*"

"You flashed ahead," said a civilian on crutches, coming up. "I want that."

The man showed a card. Neither the ship XO nor the base officer had the time to look closely.

"Run it through the cogitator or take my word, lieutenant," said the civilian. "My name's Senior Agent Connery, MI-7, and I'm to *get* Cornwell's information to the Deputy. Immediately, as requested."

* * *

Ian Fleming put down his drink and re-read the last few lines of Cornwell's note. None of it was in the man's handwriting; it had been dictated by him to an Air Service ensign who was now in security isolation.

It was terrifying. It filled the last dots of a picture that, in hindsight, was all too clear.

"Shit," he murmured, as much to Connery as himself. "I was right."

"Sir, you wanted something?" asked Connery.

"Yes. I want a meeting with Flight Admiral Richardson, Brigadier Henry and the Governor. *Right now.*"

"Sir?" That was a substantial request, at 1 am. The governor had a reputation for going to bed early.

"Right now, Connery. You have half an hour to put me in a briefing room with those people. We don't have a lot of time. A day or two. At most."

"Sir, the governor will be asleep at this hour."

"*Wake him.* And scramble the garrison while you're about it. Unless you want to see Texas undo what's left of the Louisiana Purchase, *wake him!*"

Chapter Seventeen

Despite its neutrality in the Great War, the United States was drawn into the Collapse regardless, due to its government having made massive loans to the Alliance and its banks having made massive loans to both sides.

When the Collapse began and the governments to which those loans had been made, disintegrated, it became increasingly apparent that those loans would become default through borrower existence failure. The economic crash that followed began amongst the Gilded Age plutocrats but was not limited to them.

Social, regional and ethnic tensions compounded the Collapse, as the South took its opportunity to restart the Civil War - only to disintegrate within months under its own internal tensions. Indian groups re-surged to reclaim their land, while the cities became as violent as London, Berlin and Paris as the unwashed masses rose.

And unlike the educated professional classes of the United Kingdom, a meaningful number of whom were able to escape to isolated Newfoundland where they and their children would form the core of the Restored Empire, their American counterparts could only run west...

...where the Indian tribes were rising. The sensible tribal leaders, however, readily accepted the influx of once-American engineers and professionals, since they had ambitions of their own freedom...

From *A Young Person's History of the World, Volume IX.*

Perry's first sight of Red Cloud, at one thirty in the morning, was a shrouded nightscape, occasional street lights, fewer than there would have been in a legitimate city of the same size. Rumor had it that Red Cloud – which had for a few years, before the Crash had hit and the Lakota had come back to their ancestral lands, been named Custer – had a population of fifteen thousand. It didn't look half that size to Perry.

"Holy shit. This is me in the Black Hills," Rafferty was saying, a broad, excited grin on his face. "Joined the Service for adventure, never thought I'd get to see a place like *this*."

"Never wanted to," Perry muttered.

"Oh, you'll like Red Cloud," said Ahle. "It's not the shithole Deadwood is."

The airship park was large, much bigger than a town of fifteen thousand would normally have had, and lit well enough. A flasher instructed them to take any available slot; Nolan guided them into one that he said would be only a short walk from Port Control.

"Do we just walk in, or what?" asked Perry as they touched down.

Ahle shook her head.

"Not unless you want to get shot. Like I said, this isn't Deadwood. We wait for Port Control."

Three mounted braves appeared, wearing modern military fatigues and carrying sleek modern guns – two automatic rifles, one rocket rifle – over their shoulders. The man with the rocket rifle had three feathers in his headband; the others had one each. They dismounted outside the *Red Wasp*'s bridge.

"Welcome to Lakota country," said the three-feathered man. He raised an eyebrow when he saw Ahle. "Captain Ahle."

"Lieutenant," said Ahle.

"We heard about you. The black man must be Vice-Commodore Perry, of the Imperial Air Service."

"I am. Lieutenant, is it?"

"It's not often we get Imperials here in any form. And it looks like" – a glance at Rafferty's uniform – "we have two. Another deserter?"

"My bodyguard," said Perry.

"It's not often we get a full-grown lieutenant running our customs check," said Ahle. "Do you want to get on with it? We have business with the Kennedys."

"Very well. Anything to declare?"

"No cargo," said Nolan. "Not as though we'd object to picking one up."

"Twenty dollars, then."

Nolan raised an eyebrow. Steep fee.

"I'll cover it," said Perry, and paid the lieutenant. After a cursory check of the cabins and hold, the three braves rode off.

"So where do we go from here?" Perry asked.

"I have an apartment," said Ahle. "For that matter, Hollis lives next door. I'm sure he wouldn't mind if you crashed there. Given the *hospitality* you Imperials are providing him."

"We didn't come to Red Cloud to sleep," said Perry. "We came to hire men and get resources so that we can take 4-106 back."

"And that might take a little while. Get some rest and we'll work on it in the morning."

* * *

Perry had expected a raucous, drunken parkside district – Dodge City's Boot District only more so, since Red Cloud was *known* for pirates. That element probably existed somewhere, but the street Ahle took them down was quiet, clean and orderly; two- and three-storey office buildings, houses above the mostly-closed storefronts. The three taverns they passed were quiet and subdued – conversation, not roistering.

"Not the town I expected," said Rafferty. "Where's the fun part?"

"A few blocks over," said Ahle, gesturing in the direction Nolan's mercenaries had headed. "This is officer country. And businessmen."

"Red Cloud has *businessmen*?" asked Perry.

"Sure. One in four of these offices we're passing belong to insurance companies," said Ahle. "What do you *think* happens to ships that get taken?"

"The insurance companies have *offices right here* for buying 'em back?" Perry asked incredulously.

"Of course. It's easier for all concerned. And there are independent brokers for the un-insured ships. Banks, too. You know, it's not totally uncommon for an owner-operator to lose his ship, come here looking for a cheap replacement, and buy his old ship back – with the loan money coming from a deposit made by the pirate who took his ship in the first place, stashing the money he got for its sale."

"You're joking."

"I'm speaking from personal experience. Pirates have to invest their money somewhere, those who make it. The local economy is the easiest place to. In here."

* * *

A little to Perry's surprise, Ahle didn't take him up into the two-story building. Rather, she took him in and down two flights of stairs, to a foyer where a doorman in a brown-and-grey uniform waited behind a desk.

"Captain Ahle, ma'am," he said. Another Lakota, from his complexion.

"Philip. Good to see you again. These two are Imperial Vice-Commodore Perry and Specialist Third Rafferty."

"Sir. Sir," the doorman nodded.

"I'm coming home, for now. These two will be borrowing Hollis' apartment. Anyone comes to see them, send them to me. Understood?"

The doorman nodded. Perry, from his read of the directory, was noting that this seemed actually quite a respectably-sized apartment building; two storeys up but four down, twenty-four apartments in total. Two thirds of them underground.

"Thank you, Philip," said Ahle. "Vice, shall we go downstairs? Here's a key."

* * *

Lieutenant-General (retired) Sir Charles Lloyd, Governor of the Hugoton Lease, was a big man of about seventy, with a thick, well-groomed white moustache and a few thin wisps of white hair remaining. He wore the insignia-less remains of a red and gold regimental dress uniform, and he did *not* look happy.

"This had better be *good*, Fleming," he growled. "By which I mean *critical*. It's two in the morning. This could not have waited five hours?"

Fleming met the Governor's glare directly.

"This can't wait another thirty minutes, sir. We have at best seventy-two hours in which to prevent not merely the loss of this territory but—"

"Hold on," the Governor interrupted him. "*Merely* the loss of Hugoton?"

The others in the sparsely-appointed conference room had similar skeptical looks. Those were Flight Admiral Richardson and Brigadier Henry, Richardson's ground-forces counterpart. Their personal aides and the Governor's private secretary, a handsome twenty-five-ish lord named Warren Buff, who wore a monocle and an immaculate, elegant black suit. Fleming's own aide, Connery, stood in the background, leaning on his crutches but ready to present the supporting materials that had been hastily run off.

"Yessir. The loss of Hugoton may in fact be unavoidable. Gentlemen, Flight Admiral, we are facing perhaps the biggest power play the Russians have attempted in a generation. Their intent is not merely to destroy Hugoton; it is to undo what remains of the Louisiana Purchase."

The Governor looked at him.

"You're insane, Fleming. The Russians would never dare. How *would* they?"

"Hold on, sir," said Richardson. "Deputy Director, you wouldn't have called us into this conference at this hour – nor exceeded your authority by waking every soldier, Marine and airshipman on this garrison and bringing the place to orange alert – unless you were prepared to justify that statement. If the Governor will permit you to, please do."

Fleming looked at the Governor.

"Go on," he muttered.

"As you all know, my organization has been systematically destroyed over the last month. We've taken out the Okhrana presence on this continent in return, but that wasn't a coincidence.

"This spy war now appears to have been staged *deliberately*. The leak that triggered it may have come directly from St. Petersburg with the specific purpose of initiating this mutual destruction. Because the Russians could afford to sacrifice the Okhrana presence on this continent for enough gain. Through a stroke of luck and some sacrifice, sir, we've determined that the Russians also have a *Third Department* presence in North America.

"The Russians could afford to ultimately lose their Okhrana network here. They have other eyes. Not as plentiful nor as

265

effective, but they exist. While we're blind.

"Why would the Russians make this sacrifice to blind us now? Because I have also confirmed that a sizable Russian force has either landed in Houston or will do so very shortly. Multiple divisions of fighting troops. Logistical and support structure. Meanwhile, Texas has fully mobilized."

"You're drunk," said the Governor flatly. "The Russians are never going to directly invade the United States. That would mean open war with us."

"No, sir. They're not. But they can provide logistics and support inside Texas, thus freeing up Texan troops and resources for the invasion. They can go to the Sonoran border, thus freeing up a number of Texan divisions from security there. Lyndon Johnson has made repeated threats against the United States; the Russians have given the capability to act on them.

"The Russians have already shipped arms to the South; there's going to be another rising, set to begin at any time. West of the Mississippi, Texans are going to sweep north up the plains, possibly as far as Canada – their entire army, with what the Russian logistics will have freed up, will make mincemeat of the Department of the West."

"Hold on," said Richardson. "Texas may attack the United States. They're not going to attack *us*. Russian backing or not, they're not going to risk open war with the Empire."

"No, Flight Admiral," said Fleming. "They are not. A Germanic mercenary unit called the Special Squadrons, which would have been hired or confirmed by the Russians quite recently, is going to do the dirty work of wiping out Hugoton itself. Or taking it; I imagine Russia's motive behind this play is to take this Lease for themselves, and with it most of the world's helium."

"Special Squadrons," muttered Brigadier Henry. "I know of them. Light division-strength. They would – they would pose a threat. Except that Richardson's squadrons should chop them to shreds."

"Richardson's squadrons would have their own problems," said Fleming. "The Russians would have hired air support; mercenaries, possibly even the Armadillos – those guys switched contract to someone unspecified about a month ago, and this is big enough for Trotsky to have hired the best. The

Squadrons will be covered when they attack us, I can assure you."

"You're serious," said the Governor. Slowly he tapped tobacco into his pipe, lit it. Nobody objected to the pungent smell. Nobody spoke as Governor Lloyd slowly inhaled, then exhaled a cloud of smoke in Fleming's direction.

"You have evidence that can back this theory," he said finally.

"Yes sir," said Fleming patiently. "This is the conclusion I've drawn *from* that evidence."

"That the Russians have forged an alliance with Texas, that Texas is gearing up – as we speak, you say – for an invasion of the Plains that will give them everything between Deseret and the Mississippi, as far north as Canada. And Hugoton, through this mercenary unit you've mentioned. These units."

"Their biggest power play in a generation," Fleming repeated.

"Very well, Deputy Director. I trust you've notified Denver and Washington of this."

"Forty-five minutes ago, sir. I've also prepared messages to Edmonton, St. John's and Nassau, urgently requesting reinforcements. Give the word and they'll be on their way."

"Do it."

"I have an idea of our strengths in the Caribbean and Canada," said Richardson. "And their readiness. Flight Admiral Lubbock and Vice-Marshal Henshaw are stretched thin as it is. It'll be days before they can send meaningful reinforcements, and more days for those to arrive."

More long moments of silence.

"I'm not sure which is worse," said the Governor's aide, Buff. "Losing Hugoton, or the Yanks losing their West. That would cripple them. Reduce them to a third-rate power, if they went on to lose the South. A few Northeastern and Midwestern states, an independent Confederacy that I'm sure the Russians would back..."

Fleming nodded.

"Leon Trotsky has his flaws, I'm sure. He's never to my knowledge lacked ambition in his plans. And this one..."

"This one seems foolproof," said the Governor.

Fleming slowly shook his head.

"Sir, I have a solution to the invasion. Trotsky will still win, but a substantively lesser victory. We can save the Yanks, at least."

"Explain it."

"Texas is not under any circumstances prepared to engage Imperial troops directly," Fleming said. "As it stands, they can accomplish this by simply avoiding Hugoton and letting the deniable mercenaries do their work. We have the time – we *may* have the time – to make the invasion impossible for them."

"How, Deputy Director?" asked Brigadier Henry.

"You're not going to like this, Brigadier."

"I don't like any of this, Deputy Director. What are you proposing?"

"Get to the point, Fleming," ordered the Governor.

"We have – the Yanks have – good and sufficient railways along the Texas border. We take the Hugoton garrison units and disperse them along the border. Visibly. Right now. A platoon here, a troop there, an airship over there. There will be no point along the United States border with Texas that the Texans will be able to breach without engaging Imperial troops. We inform the Texans of this, and make it clear that if they *do* engage, it will mean all-out war with the British Empire."

"We'd bury them and they know it, Russian logistics or not," said the Governor.

"That's a gamble," said Richardson. "And you're omitting a critical point here, aren't you, Fleming?"

"No, Flight Admiral, I am not," said Fleming. "I'm perfectly aware that this response would by necessity strip Hugoton of almost all its defenses. We might otherwise have been able to defend the place. We're going to have to sacrifice the Lease."

Fleming had actually expected the room to explode in shouting, at this point. The silence unnerved him for a moment and he stepped it into it himself.

"Trotsky would have foreseen this response of ours," he said. "Either way, he wins something big."

"Give the movement orders," the Governor said. "I hate this. We're sacrificing Hugoton; even if we keep the territory, it will take *years* to rebuild the wells and the facilities."

"Which the Russians are counting on, yes. Besides, Lord Governor?"

268

"Yes?"

"I have a few field agents left," said Fleming. "Including" – a nod to Richardson – "your Vice-Commodore and his pirate. It's distinctly possible – it's happened before – that one of them might produce some kind of a miracle."

The Governor of the Hugoton Lease steepled his fingers. "Then let's just *bloody* well hope one of them does, then."

* * *

Perry had slept uneasily and was having an early breakfast with Ahle and Rafferty, in Ahle's apartment, when the knock came at the door. It was a two-feathered Lakota sergeant.

"Yes?" Ahle asked.

"Captain, Vice-Commodore? Joseph Kennedy, Jr. will see you. Right now."

* * *

The *Red Ruby Robber* touched down at Red Cloud early that morning, receiving a berth and paying the landing fees.

"We've got another loose end to tie off," Marko had explained on the way. "Wipe out a potential problem before it can arise."

"Someone we get to kill?" Rienzi asked eagerly.

"Someone *I* get to kill. Judd don't need to know about it. He's got orders to lift fast and hard the moment I'm back. You three stay aboard the ship."

"You mind if I ask who?" McIlhan asked.

"You three ain't leaving the ship," Marko repeated, "but you may as well know. But Judd and his crew don't need to, clear? Ever heard of the Kennedys?"

Grinning, Marko raised the sniper rifle.

Chapter Eighteen

ARMADILLOS RETURN TO ACTION

The legendary mercenary unit Cordova's Armadillos, who saved our skies over Alberquerque during the Second Sonoran War, are reportedly under new contract.

"We found another employer who'll pay a hell of a lot more for just one job," said a crewman of the *Vorpal*, who refused to be named. "Maybe after that we'll go back to Texan employ. Maybe not."

"Been too long since we've heard gunfire off of a sound stage," corroborated an officer on the *Dread Wyvern*, who again refused to be named.

While their departure is to be missed, the elite airship squadron's action is only to be understood: units of their grade can't be reasonably expected to endure peacetime conditions indefinitely.

Without a doubt, when their adopted home needs them again, they will answer our call.

For the time being, the identity of their new employer remains unknown... but we are sure the seven Armadillos will carve their name as much into that employer's legend as they have ours...

Editorial News section, *Houston Chronicle*. February, 1963.

Marko had been to Red Cloud before and knew his way around. More to the point, Okhrana intelligence had apprised him of the Kennedys' routines. The younger sons were less predictable – John Francis, especially, as head of the family's intelligence and covert operations, traveled around a lot and might have been anywhere at any time – but reliable intelligence, as relayed in the orders, gave him a good idea of the pirate king's behavior.

Joseph Kennedy and his crown prince, Joe Jr., rarely left the Black Hills these days; it was the administrative center of their operations and it wouldn't do for the big bosses to be too far from it.

For the most part, they ran things from the legendary underground fortress called the Black House, but they found it politically convenient to circulate every so-often, usually midday, usually around the Liberation Park area in the center of Red Cloud. There were taverns and an open fencing market there, and the Kennedy father and son seemed to spend an hour or so a day circulating there, shaking hands and slapping backs.

Typical fucking politicians, thought Marko, heading that way. *I'll enjoy killing them.*

* * *

"You'll enjoy meeting them," Ahle was saying, as she, Perry and – he'd insistently tagged along and the Lakota hadn't stopped him yet – Rafferty rode in a well-escorted steam-car toward Liberation Park, at the center of the Red Cloud business district.

As well as the Lakota sergeant who'd come to their front door, there was a lightly-armored combat vehicle that led the way, and six horsemen riding alongside and behind them. Perry couldn't be sure whether the excessive security was respect or paranoia; *are we especially honored guests, or not-yet-declared prisoners?*

Ahle didn't seem worried. Rafferty was thrilled.

"We're actually going to see the fucking Kennedys!" he was saying. "In the Black Hills. Ducks and Vidkowski aren't gonna believe me when I tell `em about this shit!"

Perry couldn't resist the snipe: "Vidkowski is a good airshipman who obeys orders, Specialist Third."

Rafferty grinned and shrugged.

"Vidkowski never has any fun. His idea of it is attending a church service or something."

"While your idea of fun involves a splitting hangover the next morning, Specialist?" Ahle asked.

Rafferty shrugged again. "Just part of the price. By the way, cap'n, get started early?" He offered a flask.

"Don't mind if I do, Specialist," she said, taking a sip. "Not bad rum. Where'd you get it – thought you ran out last night."

"One of Nolan's engineers. Turns out she couldn't play poker worth a damn," Rafferty grinned. "Vice, you up for

271

something to take the edge off?"

"I'd order you to stop drinking if I could," Perry growled.

"Fair enough, boss, but you know you can trust me not to get too impaired when there might be action imminent. How about you, two-feather?" – a gesture at the Lakota sergeant driving the steam-car.

"Catch me in ten hours, Imperial," the sergeant said without turning around.

"Oh yeah? Where?"

"Buckner's. First three are on you."

"Holy shit," Rafferty exalted. "First *five* if you insist. I'll drink with Lakota pirate studs any day!"

"Hold a sec," said the driver coldly. "I'm no pirate. Let's make that clear."

Rafferty spread his hands.

"Sorry, man."

"I am a sergeant of the Lakota Nation. I am not a pirate. There is a distinction."

"Which they take seriously," Ahle added. "Rafferty, apologize more seriously to the honorable sergeant of the sovereign Lakota Nation."

"Sorry for the misunderstanding, sergeant," said Rafferty a little more seriously. "Honorable sergeant, if that's what you like."

"Apology accepted, Imperial. The invitation's still open if you're interested and available, but I don't drink on duty. Should you?"

Rafferty moved to take another swig from the flask. Perry slapped it down.

"Put that back where it came from, Specialist."

"And here we are," said the driver, outside a single-storey building that looked like it might have been carved from obsidian. Perry guessed that much of it was underground, like so much of the rest of Red Cloud seemed to be. "Welcome to the Black House."

* * *

There were two layers of security, one at the entrance – where Perry, Ahle and, since nobody seemed to be stopping him, Rafferty, were frisked before being allowed onto a slow

272

elevator with three rifle-toting guards in plain khaki and the same Lakota sergeant who'd knocked on Ahle's door and driven them here.

Perry couldn't tell how far underground they were – it might have been twenty feet or a hundred – when the slow elevator opened. More well-armed men in khaki – uniforms, Perry supposed – stood waiting for them.

"A more detailed search, Captain. Vice-Commodore. And" – to Rafferty – "who the hell are you?"

"Specialist Third Rafferty, mate. Of the Imperial Air Service."

"My bodyguard," Perry explained.

"You're under the security of the Kennedy organization here," said the senior man, who was clean-shaven, heavily moustached and forty-ish. "Your bodyguard can wait outside."

"Mate-" Rafferty began.

"He's with me," something made Perry say. Assuming his old tone of command; *I am a Vice-Commodore of the Imperial Air Service!* "He comes with me."

The senior man paused for a moment.

"He's a good man," said Ahle, to Perry's surprise. "It won't hurt anyone, and it'll make the Vice more comfortable, if he comes in."

"You're personally vouching for him, Cap'n Ahle?"

Ahle nodded. "Yes. I will."

"Very well; you can come in. Imperial officer, you first."

"Just go with it," Ahle hissed.

Not that he'd ever met Her Majesty Victoria the Second himself, in person, but he'd heard stories about the security that even respected Imperial officers had to go through before doing so. From what he'd heard, this was worse.

The serious men in khaki had him remove his coat, boots and – saying something about how it contained metal – belt. They took the .40 from his shoulder-holster with a noise about how they'd return it when he was done. The knife from his right boot. His wristwatch, his wallet and the locket with Annabelle's portrait that he wore around his neck.

Then they ran him through a magnetograph, a new piece of technology – only recently introduced to Buckingham Palace, and Perry was *surprised* they had one here in the Black Hills – just to make sure. It rang, a small bell.

"Got any coins, Vice?" one of them asked.

Perry checked his pockets and found about a dollar's worth of small change in one of them. Meanwhile, another man was – intrusively! None of his business! – examining the contents of his wallet.

"You'll have them back with your weapons," the man said, taking Perry's coins. "Now, please step back through the machine and then put your hands above your head."

What followed was a comprehensive frisking, the pirate king's men making *absolutely certain* Perry wasn't carrying a – wooden or ceramic? – blade on him.

Then, having inspected his boots and belt, those were returned to him.

"You can go through," said the man in charge. "Fly on; the boss is ready."

Jeez, thought Perry. *Imagine a world in which people do have to go through this before they fly.*

At least Ahle and Rafferty had to go through the same indignity, Rafferty growling as the men confiscated not just an – illicit! – pistol from him, but three knives and two flasks. Ahle was carrying a pair of guns herself, plus a flask and more than one knife, but seemed to take the indignity in stride.

"Very well. Ms. Lincoln will see you now," said the chief guard.

Not a Kennedy personally?

The guard saw Perry's look.

"Their private secretary. You've been admitted. Now wait."

* * *

It was only a few minutes, sitting in a comfortable waiting room with more of the Kennedys' khaki-clad personal security watching them – but yesterday's editions of the *New York Times, Washington Post* and *Boston Globe* available for the reading.

If that was a gesture of power, thought Perry, it *was* one. To get those would have required an airship to steam through the night, daily, just to bring those editions. But he resisted the urge to actually look at them; that might have implied weakness in front of the stern-faced, black-haired woman who was apparently the Kennedys' personal secretary.

274

Ahle seemed impassive, as though she'd been through this procedure a few times before. Perhaps – probably – she had. Rafferty couldn't stop grinning, to the point where Perry saw fit to give him a sharp backhanded slap on the thigh.

"Knock it off. This is serious."

"Yessir," said Rafferty, and at least wiped the grin off his face.

"You're my bodyguard," Perry snarled in a harsh whisper. "Act like it."

"Boss, there's the guard you can see, and there's another one in that slit up there; mirrors and magnification most likely."

What guy?, Perry wondered and looked up. There *was* a small slit in the ceiling, which he hadn't noticed before. Could well have been magnified mirrors through it.

OK, so the insolent fucker is smarter than I gave him credit for. Not that I thought he was dumb.

"Keep that up," Perry replied in the same low whisper, "and I may just allow you those drinks with the Lakota sergeant."

"Right now you're payin' for `em, sir."

Perry fought to control a smile. What could you do with cases like this man?

"Maybe I will, if you get the chance."

Intelligence out of the Black Hills had to be worth something, right?

* * *

The stern-faced woman looked up from her board.

"Captain Ahle, Vice-Commodore Perry, the Vice-Commodore's bodyguard? Joe Sr. and Jr. will see you now," she said.

By this point, Perry had almost expected a throne room. Pirate *kings*, after all, he'd heard them described as often-enough. Including by Flight Admiral Richardson, a couple of times, and informally in at least one of MI-7's – Fleming's, damn that bastard! – briefings. He'd anticipated literal thrones, like Her Majesty's, inside a large audience hall with a rug leading up to it on which supplicants could comfortably bend their knees in rightful abasement.

"The scourge of the West and a damned pestilence elsewhere," Richardson had once called the bald, clearly-aging eighty-ish man and his late-forties son, a handsome man with dark, slicked-back hair.

Josephs Sr. and Jr. sat on comfortable chairs behind a large desk, which Perry had no doubt included built-in cogitator screens and keyboards. The room was comfortable and well-carpeted, perhaps three times the size of Fleming's or Richardson's offices; clearly designed for accommodating large audiences, whole groups of people.

And yes, there were a few trophies on the walls of the well-carpeted room. The eagle standard of a US Army regiment sat next to a pair of propellors, with plaques below – unreadable given Perry's ten-foot distance and momentary time – probably telling the stories of their actions. A certificate of some kind sat next to the propellors. Similar decorations on the other side of the room.

"Captain Ahle," said the younger man, Joseph Junior, getting to his feet. His father didn't, and Perry realized that that man wasn't in a chair but a wheelchair. "It's good to see you again."

"Good to see you, Joe," said Ahle.

Her voice, Perry noted, didn't convey an inch of the apprehension that he himself felt. This seemed like routine business to her.

"Vice-Commodore Perry. Thank you for your visit."

"Thank you for seeing us, Mr. Kennedy." It felt like the only appropriate response.

"And Airshipman Rafferty. I applaud your nerve coming in this far."

"It's good to be here," said Rafferty. He advanced on the desk drawing something –

A notepad.

"Mr. Kennedy, Mr. Kennedy, my mates aren't gonna believe this unless you sign here," he said before Perry could intervene. "Your autographs, please."

"Excuse my — "

Rafferty advanced across the carpet of the spacious office and shoved the pad in front of Joe Senior.

"Excuse my subordinate's *insolence*," Perry snarled.

"Well excused," said Joseph Senior. He drew a pen.

"Rafferty, is it? Let me guess, Jim Rafferty?"

"George, sir."

"Well, Airshipman—"

"Specialist, sir."

"Specialist George Rafferty, here's something for you to show your mates in the enlisted mess." Joseph Senior scribbled something onto Rafferty's pad, finishing it with a flourishing signature.

"And here you go," said Joe Junior, writing his own note.

"I can only apologize," Perry snarled, before being cut off.

"No need," Joseph Senior waved him off. "But this is a large room for the five of us; meant for groups, not small meetings like this. Suppose we with business to do withdraw to the working office."

"With business to do," Perry said, glaring at his Specialist Third.

"With business to do," agreed the pirate king. He leaned over to what must have been a mike. "Bill, you around? Entertain our other guest, will you? Bring a bottle or two."

Joseph Junior got up, moved to – yes, it *was* a wheelchair – wheel his father through the unobtrusive back door of the main office.

"Mr. Rafferty, if you'd stay here," Joseph Junior requested before he turned. "Officer-level business to discuss, I'm sorry. Our assistant chief of intel, Mr. Bill Colby, will entertain you while you wait."

"Don't he report to John Francis himself, Mr. Kennedy?" asked Rafferty.

"He does. But wait here, please."

"Damn straight! Sir!"

* * *

The inner office, which Joseph Junior gestured Perry and Ahle into, was much smaller and more comfortable. Undecorated except for a couple of mechanitype printouts on one wall, it contained a single broad desk.

An elegant blond woman rose to her feet as the two entered.

"Miss Lynch," said Ahle, recovering from her surprise a moment earlier than Perry.

"Thought those bastards had killed you," Perry said. Not that he was *glad* to see the information-fencing bitch, but – he supposed – it was nice to know she'd lived.

Enemy of my enemy, and all.

And she did give me the location.

But how–?

"Oh, it was simple," Lynch said, smiling. "By the way, please sit down."

Both Perry and Ahle glanced at the Kennedys before doing so. Joe Junior nodded.

"Make yourselves comfortable," said Junior. "The other room is for the big audiences."

The seats were padded and well-appointed, with leather armrests. Yes, thought Perry, this was a room for serious business.

"Very simple story," Lynch stated.

"Hold on," said Joseph Kennedy Jr. "Now you're in our private *sanctum sanctorum*, if you will – are you hungry?"

"I'm fine," said Perry. "We were just finishing breakfast when your Lakota henchman called."

"Not quite our henchmen, but close enough that the point's irrelevant," smiled Joe Junior.

"Care for a drink, then?"

"Not at this hour," said Perry. "But thank you."

"Rum," said Ahle. "Lynch knows my favorite."

"We do," came a disembodied voice from the ceiling.

"So how the *hell* did you survive?" Perry demanded of Lynch. "We *saw* that airship explode."

Lynch shrugged.

"A pretty sight, wasn't it? I paid enough for the spectacle."

"You weren't in it?"

"I was in a sealed basement two blocks away. That ship was unmanned, and the launch crew had orders to bolt immediately. The shooters had their own assumptions. Twelve hours later, Unitas and I boarded a different ship. Is that all you wanted to know, Vice-Commodore?"

"No," snarled Perry. "You could have warned us that 4-106 was well-guarded."

Lynch shrugged.

"You didn't ask."

Joseph Senior interjected, with a cough, as a khaki-clad

female assistant brought in a glass of rum for Ahle: "I think I know why you're here, Vice-Commodore Perry."

"To get my ship back," Perry said. "Ahle says you have the resources. I'll pay for them, on Fleming's account – I won't pretend you don't know who he is."

Senior smiled, as Ahle sipped her rum.

Perry sighed.

"You can afford a fortress like this and security like you have. But *don't* tell me money's of no account to you."

Senior and Junior looked at one another. Was it Perry's imagination, or did he see eyes rolling?

"We'll do it for free, Vice-Commodore. At your convenience within twelve hours, an assault company of my men will descend upon 4-106 for you and return your airship."

"All we ask," Junior added, "is a favor in return."

Perry, guarded: "And what's that?"

"An introduction," said Joseph Senior.

Ahle was silent, but Perry could see she was smiling thinly. Had she anticipated this? Was this all part of some plan of *hers*?

"To Ian Fleming," Senior went on. "And through him, to the Governor of the Hugoton Lease. We understand he carries plenipotentiary authority."

He gave enough of a pause that Perry saw fit to fill it in:
"He does."

"Very well," said Joseph Kennedy Junior. "He must, by now, see the same picture we do. Our friend Markell over there" – a gesture at the woman to his side – "has enlightened us on a few things. He'll be interested."

"I have sources inside Texas," said Lynch quietly. "Including a few extreme deep-cover. All of that information came with me to the Black Hills."

"Suppose you enlighten *me*," growled Perry, "as to what the hell is going on?"

* * *

When Lynch and Kennedy Junior were done, Perry found himself slowly shaking his head. A Russian play for all of the West? Impossible! Merely to destroy Hugoton? Still implausible! This was a stolen airship and no more!

But here were credible people in a room that had required

279

paranoid-level security to get to, saying…

And all the pieces fit together. He'd wondered more than once why the Special Squadrons would want tactical maps of Hugoton. He'd blundered into something *much* bigger than he'd expected.

"I'll have another rum, please," said Ahle to the room. "And bring the bottle." Under her breath, to Perry: "This is serious shit."

"While you're about it," Perry raised his voice to whoever was monitoring the room, "I'll have a triple Scotch. Glenfiddich, if you have it."

"Glenfiddich twenty-one coming right up," came a voice back.

"So," Joseph Junior asked, "are you willing to accept our assistance, in return for getting our emissary a direct introduction to Deputy Director Fleming?"

Perry nodded. Fleming would be able to spare ten minutes to talk to a pirate; it probably wouldn't be the first time for that shady bastard, either. Maybe he'd even enjoy it.

But in this light…

"What do you want to talk to him – to the Governor – about?"

"That would be for them to discuss," Joseph Junior said. "Do you give us your word of honor as an officer of the Imperial Air Service that, once we have secured your airship and returned it to you, you will endeavor to the best of your abilities to fulfill your side of this bargain?"

That was an easy question. The harder part was giving his word of honor to a damn *pirate*!

No. Not so hard. Ahle was honorable enough, and the Kennedys – he'd heard a lot of bad things about them, but rape and needless killing – much killing at all, really – had never been among the rumors.

"You have my word of honor as an officer," Perry told the man and his father. "But what you were just saying – you *mean* that? I've heard that that bastard Trotsky thinks big, but *that* big?"

"I mean every word of it," said Lynch. "Deal with it, if it's within your scope. Maybe there's even something you can do about it. Deal with the facts, Vice-Commodore."

"Deal with the facts," Ahle agreed. "The lives of my crew

depend on it. I'd appreciate this. Please."

A khaki-uniformed flunky came in with a tray carrying more, and a filled-to-the-brim tumbler of Scotch for Perry.

Russian invasion of the West? Hugoton falling to the Tsar? Best-case if the Governor's smart and reacts in time by throwing out the entire garrison – including Thirty-First Squadron! – *to extreme risk? The Hugoton Lease merely destroyed?*

He threw back the triple Scotch in one elongated gulp and gestured to the flunky, who wasn't yet out of the room, for more.

"Joseph Senior. Joseph Junior," he said. "Miss Lynch. I'm not authorized to deal on my own, of course. But" – a gulp, as the flunky returned with more Scotch; he reached for the tumbler like a lifeline – "I should be able to put you in touch with my superiors. Get me my airship back and I will."

"I *thought* we had a deal," Joseph Junior smiled.

Chapter Nineteen

...in conclusion, this novel is utter trash even by the dismal standards of 'alternate universe' technofiction. John F. Kennedy – the pirate family's little-known *second* son, what happened to Joe Junior? – as President of the United States? Impossible heavier-than-air flying craft? Fidel Castro not playing baseball, but *President of Cuba*? Gigantic rockets on their way to being based out of that island, which we are supposed to believe have the range to hit *Florida*? With magic 'nuclear' warheads, somehow derived from Curium and the Marseilles Catastrophe?

'The Cuban Missile Crisis' is solid one-star garbage, although we can expect David Oglivy's legions of barely-literate fans to lap it up regardless. Some of them, no doubt, are so ignorant that they will consider its events real.

Pauline Kael, *New York Post Review of Books*, December 1962.

The Hugoton base was in total, unprecedented motion. Airships loaded with men were taking off; special trains had been ordered, more infantry piling aboard them. Tanks slowly rumbled east, followed by vehicles containing mechanics and support crews. Other support personnel loaded trucks, boxcars and airships with everything that could be stripped and moved.

"Never thought I'd see the day," Swarovski muttered to Martindale as a human chain of enlisted men passed boxes up into *Johnstown*'s hold. "We're getting ready to lose Hugoton? This is *crazy*."

"Ought to strike them first," said Commander Ricks. "Mercenaries. I hear the SS are good, but we could put a dent into them."

"You heard what the hag lady said, sir," said Swarovski. "Just wish we could go off with you boys."

Another airship took off, cumbersomely because it was loaded to capacity with Air Marines. As it lifted, it began to slowly rotate – heading west for some point along the Texas border.

"Yeah," said Ricks. "Swarovski, Martindale, I don't envy your crew. I understand someone has to stay behind until the end. Hope they have a plan to get you out at the *very* end."

"We'll find something," said Swarovski with more bravado than he felt. "Richardson's a fanatic, but she's not dumb. We'll survive."

"You better," said Ricks. "Mind, if you guys want to come aboard the *Johnstown*, I can promise you I won't notice until we're safely up."

"Do admit, I envy that idiot Specialist Rafferty," said Swarovski.

Yesterday evening, Senior Airshipman Duckworth had come back from somewhere, his lips tightly sealed. Rafferty was still missing, AWOL at this point. The interesting part was how Duckworth had gone straight to the Flight Admiral's office and demanded an audience.

That was something a Senior Airshipman would *never* do on his own – there was a chain of command that went through his department head, his ship captain, and Ricks as Thirty-First's acting squadron commander. Jumping that chain was serious business, and Duckworth wouldn't have done so without very, very good reason.

Reason such as specific orders from someone even higher on that chain.

Like Vice Perry.

Duckworth hadn't said anything, and his response to direct questions had been "Sir, I was ordered by the Flight Admiral personally not to discuss my last forty-eight hours. She said, sir, to take it up with her if you had a problem. Sir."

An absolute non-answer, and Swarovski wasn't crazy enough to tangle with Admiral Richardson. But a non-answer like that implied specific, serious information that Duckworth had been forbidden to talk about. The fact that Rafferty had been with Duckworth and chosen – or been forced – *not* to return, was equally telling.

Swarovski's own theory, and he'd have bet money on this, was that the two had run into Vice Perry somewhere in Dodge City. He'd left, done something with them, and sent Duckworth back to report. Possibly with the very information that had caused Command to bring the entire Lease to orange alert last night, and then issue the movement orders that were being followed now.

Warrant Brooks, a tiny woman who was the *Johnstown*'s senior ship NCO, drew herself up in front of Ricks and saluted. Ricks returned the salute.

"Loading complete, Warrant?"

"About to be, sir. And that's the last of it."

"Very well. And everyone's personal possessions are on board?"

"Yessir."

"Orders are to lift ASAP once loaded. We're going to Louisiana."

Ricks turned to Swarovski and Martindale.

"Good luck, boys. Take care of yourselves."

"You too, sir," said Martindale.

A few minutes later, the *Johnstown* – the last airship of Thirty-First Squadron, carrying its acting commander – began to rise.

"That's it, Swav," said Martindale. "Just us left. Is there anything more god-damned pathetic than an airship crew without a ship?"

"A Lease without a garrison," Swarovski said. He understood the reasoning, but *damn*.

"You've got a point," 4-106's XO said. "Come with me to the officers' mess, will you? Let's get a drink while we still can."

* * *

Otto Skorzeny drew himself to attention and saluted.

"Final orders, *mein Fuhrer*."

"At ease and bring them in, Otto," said Himmler.

"Just came out of decryption," Skorzeny explained, handing his commander a folder.

"And you read them first, no doubt. Hence your uncharacteristic formality."

Skorzeny grinned.

"I thought so. Well, you can summarize them for me. I assume they're orders to move out."

"Yes. With an update. The Imperials have gotten wise to something. They're redeploying their own troops along the

284

Texas border. Meanwhile, the Americans are moving everything they can south. Too little, too late. But Texas is not going to fuck with the Imperials."

Himmler gave a terse nod. That had been anticipated; it was a logical reaction, to set up a tripwire. Texas would overrun the Imperials easily, but public reaction through the Empire – at seeing four Imperial battalions wiped out – would mean open war.

The Imperial public would not necessarily support a full-scale war to retake the West, not against a Russian-backed power. They'd certainly support a war to avenge the deaths of several thousand men, and Texas wouldn't last a month against the full force of mobilized Imperial power.

"So Johnson's calling it off."

"Third Department says he's in conference, now the reports are coming in. The Imperial Ambassador to Texas has made it very clear that an attack on Imperial troops *will* mean open war."

"Doesn't affect us so much," said Himmler. "We're mercenaries; we're deniable. Do we have the go order or not?"

"Sir. We're to move out immediately. Expected arrival time is tomorrow afternoon. Destroy the Dodge City refineries, move into Hugoton itself. Kill everyone they've left behind, destroy every structure, then – well, run south into Texas."

"Status on our air support? Not as though we'll need it, against an undefended base."

"We're to have a squadron anyway. Cordova's Armadillos. They're our personal transit out, for that matter."

"Good."

"Yes."

Privately, Skorzeny had his doubts about whether Texas would be such safe asylum. Oh, they'd get across, but Imperial pressure for the heads of the troops who'd destroyed Hugoton – and killed a number of Imperials in the process – might result in their being handcuffed before too long. It was fine, from Skorzeny's perspective, for the grunts to get thrown to the dogs, but he was going to make damn sure that he, his personal cadre and the Squadrons' top officers would be safely in South America before that could happen.

"So we're to move out immediately?" Himmler confirmed.

"Yes."

"Very well. Convey final authorization. And get moving."

* * *

Governor Lloyd's office took half the seventh-storey top floor of the Hugoton Lease's tallest non-industrial building. Until a few hours ago it had been extravagantly appointed, as befitting an Imperial governor, with mementoes of nearly six decades of distinguished service across the globe. Now it was mostly bare floorboards and a few heavy pieces of furniture that had been judged immovable given the time and resources available.

A pair of overalled workmen at one end of the room were busily disassembling a suit of medieval armor. At the other end, around a massive, now-bare, oak desk, a small conference was taking place.

"I'm not leaving," the Governor said. "While even a few of my men remain – or even while they don't. A captain goes down with his ship and a Governor is not expected to survive the destruction of his Lease."

"Lord Governor," Brigadier Henry repeated, "they're not going to take you alive and exchange you. I've *met* Heinrich Himmler; he's as cold a sadistic bastard as they come."

"They're not going to take me alive," the Governor said. "I stay, and that's final."

"Very well, Lord Governor. In which case I'm also staying," Henry said.

"You're going to Tulsa. We've had this discussion."

"And I assumed, Lord Governor, that you were leaving. Some of my men are remaining here. I'm remaining with them."

"Brigadier, we've had this discussion." The Governor raised his voice. "Buff, I want you to assign two of my bodyguards to Brigadier Henry. They are to escort him to Tulsa and report when he has arrived."

"Sir," said his aide.

"Richardson?" the Governor addressed the Flight Admiral.

"I have a personal airship. I'll be staying until the last moment, myself," said Richardson. "But no, I don't intend to die here."

Ian Fleming came into the office, not bothering to knock.

286

All four – the Governor, Richardson, Henry and Buff – looked up. The spymaster's arrival could only mean bad news.

"What?"

"Lord Governor, we just got a wire out of Missouri. SS units are beginning to leave their stations and cross the Kansas line. It's starting. ETA about thirty hours from now."

"Very well," said the Governor. "We have that time in which to move everything that can be moved. Richardson, you have a plan for getting your last crew out?"

"Civilian airships," said the Flight Admiral. "I'm not leaving a highly-trained ship crew to die here. But they'll stay until nearly the end, to help with evacuating what we can of the ground facilities."

Governor Henry clasped his hands behind his back, stiffly turned to look at the forest of wells and refinery stacks visible from his high window. Scattered across the grassy plains, they went into the distance. Dozens of them, and those were just the ones in this quarter. Together they produced the helium that Imperial power depended upon.

How long would it take to rebuild them, once they had been destroyed? Two or three years *minimum*, had been the most optimistic estimate. That was two or three years in which the Empire would not have helium, two or three years during which the Russians would have an incomparable edge if they chose to go to war.

Damn.

* * *

At the military airship park outside of Amarillo, Texas, seven legends met. Two clicking kinematographs recorded the event.

Word was that the general invasion was being cancelled. Imperials covering the border.

Can't fuck with Imperials, the Texan officers were saying. It'd mean open war. Couldn't survive that. Not against the British Empire itself.

Captain Paula Handley shook her head in contempt. There was *nobody* she couldn't fuck with. History had made that clear. Those who went up against Cordova's Armadillos died. Simple. Didn't matter whether you were Brazilian, Argentine,

287

Sonoran, whatever. Imperials were supposedly the best in the world, but to Handley they were just another addition to the list.

The Armadillos were mercenaries. They were deniable. And they were elite.

You mess with us, you go down burning.

"We move in twenty hours," Commodore Cordova was saying. "You hear the plan? Wing chiefs, report."

Handley was the first to speak.

"Evans and I" – a nod at Richard Evans, commander of the *Dread Wyvern* – "go over to Hugoton. We kill everything that moves and any threats, but save the real fun for the following ground troops. We remain on station in case trouble arrives. If it does, we destroy it."

Cordova nodded.

"Peggey?" he asked.

"The *Five Speed* and Meier's *Pith and Vinegar* make haste to Dodge City," Captain Peggey Rowland reported. "We shoot the crap out of anything that might lift and any anti-air defences, then await the main force, shooting down anything that comes within range."

"Meanwhile," said Cordova, "Jennifer, Bill and I go to west-central Kansas, link up with the ground forces we're covering, and make sure *nobody* comes in from above and fucks with us. We've all got that clear."

What happened next was well-rehearsed cinematography. A Texan camera clicked as the seven captains laid their palms down on top of each other, in the center of a small circle that had only been widened slightly, to make room for the cameraman.

The royalties were generous, after all.

"Armadillos?" Cordova asked his captains.

By now it had become slang amongst teens in Texas. The response was trademarked.

"Armadillos *Yeah!*" they shouted, throwing their flat palms high into the air.

"You have a day for final prep," Cordova ordered. "Now get moving – and get ready to destroy anything that flies into our paths!"

Another, this time unscripted, cheer. This time as always, Handley thought, they were going to obliterate any enemies moronic enough to bring themselves into range.

"Armadillos *Yeah!*"

* * *

"Hurry," the Army sergeant was saying, trying to keep the panic out of his voice. "Onto the train. It'll take you to safety. Come *on!*"

Annabelle Perry wasn't worried about the general panic around her; she'd seen it before, in Gibraltar, and things had come out fine. In the end, the Army, the Navy and her husband's Air Service would always take care of things. It was her responsibility as an officer's wife to keep things stable in the meantime.

She was more worried about her husband.

She and the children, one of their hands clasped in each of hers, found their way onto the third-class passenger carriage. It was going to Dodge City, where command – her husband's CO, Flight Admiral Richardson herself, an hour ago – had personally assured the group senior officers' husbands and wives that they'd be safe. A hotel in downtown Dodge, away from the industrial districts the enemy might threaten, to stay until the danger passed and relief came.

Your job, the Flight Admiral had said to the senior officers' partners, *is to keep the others calm and remind them of the truth of Imperial inevitability.*

To that end, Mrs. Perry thought as she sat down with Ernest and Maria, each of them carrying their own small bag of well-traveled goods, it seemed that the Army sergeant was being most disgraceful and completely inappropriate.

We're not going to lose. This will be a temporary inconvenience at most.

Marcus will make sure of that.

Wherever he is.

* * *

Liberation Park was a broad park in central Red Cloud, one face of the square looking out onto small Stockade Lake. The other three faces – and most of the lake-facing side, with waterfront cafes – were crowded with the inns and storefronts

289

of Red Cloud's business district, and there was an open-air market in the park itself; intangibles like ships and whole cargoes changing hands over storefronts. Runners, mostly young Lakota teenagers, went back and forth between those vendors and their cogitator-fed higher offices in the downtown buildings.

It was Wall Street in miniature and, despite its contribution to overall chaos, Theron Marko would have destroyed the entire scene in a moment if he could have. Right now he crouched on the roof of one of the taller buildings overlooking the park, looking down the scope of a .303 rifle.

He'd have destroyed the whole bustling place in a heartbeat, but right now his sights were aimed more specifically. He'd seen Joe Junior – with an aide wheeling Joe Senior, and a fourth man discreetly tagging along behind them – go into one upscale bar a couple of minutes ago. Shaking hands as they went in.

Typical fucking politicians.

They had minutes to live.

* * *

Lynch was fishing for information. And trying to get them drunk.

Ahle, thought Perry, was already well on her way. If she wasn't there already. But she'd kept the conversation primarily to irrelevant subjects, although they might have been of interest to the madam anyway. Right now she was describing a raid in the Rockies, perhaps a year ago. It sounded as though it might end badly for a rival of hers.

Lynch was listening, although not too eagerly. Doubtless she'd heard this kind of thing before. Perry was keeping his mouth shut. The Kennedys themselves had gone for what Joe Jr. had referred to as their "regular tour."

Rafferty was still off with their man Colby, doubtless getting drunk and exchanging stories. Well, he couldn't do much about that. He just hoped the Specialist wasn't getting *too* smashed, although his hopes weren't high.

"So then what?" Lynch asked Ahle.

This had to be as pointless an exercise for her, Lynch, as it was for him, Perry. But Joseph Jr. had said it would take some time to assemble a fighting force big enough to firmly defeat what was probably aboard 4-106. May as well wait here.

* * *

Marko saw the slight disturbance at the doorway of the tavern the Kennedys had gone into.

Calming himself, he aimed the rifle to eye-level.

A man wheeling a man – Joe Senior! – came out. Followed by, shaking hands again with the bouncer as he left – a man who looked like – yes, was – Joseph Junior.

Theron Marko pulled the trigger.

He was six hundred and forty yards away.

He'd once killed a Royal heir from three times that distance.

Joseph Kennedy, Junior's shattered brains blew through the back of his head.

Marko refocused his scope on the helpless man in the wheelchair. He looked to be struggling to get up.

"Oh, *no* chance, oligarch," Marko murmured under his breath. "*No fucking chance,* oligarch."

Another trigger-pull smashed Joseph Kennedy, Senior's brains into leaden jelly.

And now, Marko thought, *to get out of here.*

For the first few seconds after the shot, he'd known perfectly well since childhood, you stayed motionless. The immediate temptation was to bolt, but the fact was that the victims' surviving friends would now be scanning around for movement.

Instead, you didn't move at first. Then you moved slowly enough to not draw immediate attention.

Outside line of sight, of course, you bolted.

* * *

It was actually halfway up the external fire-escape that Marko encountered Kennedy's men – dressed in street clothes, but their alert demeanor and the fact that they were ascending a fire escape at 11:30 am would have alerted Marko if their half-drawn handguns hadn't.

He slashed the first man's throat with a left-handed knife

291

swing.

The second had time to draw his gun.

Good, are we?

Marko killed him anyway, slashing his throat open in a backhanded swing from his first thrust. A second slash practically removed the goon's gun-hand, blood fountaining from the severed wrist.

A third stab would have ended Kennedy's goon's life for good right away, but Marko didn't have the time for mercy. Or much interest in the concept.

He shouldered the already-dead fucker aside and continued his dash down the fire-escape, heading for the airship park.

* * *

"Lift!" Marko shouted, jumping through the bridge door of the *Ruby Red Robber*. "Lift, damn you!"

Jebediah Judd, on the bridge, knew better than to argue.

"Lift, my men!" he shouted. "Ditch ballast and lift, boys!"

The *Ruby Red Robber* jumped.

"Stop immediately, lifting airship!" came a powerfully-amplified voice that could only have been Port Control.

"Evade `em," Marko ordered.

"Harder than it looks," Judd shot back.

Shit, thought Marko. *I blew away both of the top Kennedys.* "Just do it!"

* * *

Perry still wasn't drunk, although Ahle was probably close to it, when Joseph Kennedy Junior wheeled Joseph Senior back into the personal office where Lynch had been attempting to pump him for knowledge. This time, a half-dozen-strong squad of khaki-clad escorts came with the two pirate kings.

As usual – damn it – Lynch was the unsurprised one.

"So it happened? I warned you they'd try," she said.

"Fuck you, Markell," said Joseph Kennedy Junior. "Thanks to you, both Felix and Marv are dead."

"Better your body doubles than you," Lynch said.

"*And* we're out half a million in pension endowments to

their families," Senior hissed.

"Be glad," Lynch replied evenly, "that you're alive to write the checks. Where *were* you anyway?"

"Attending to paperwork in the other offices," Joseph Junior said. "There's always notices to review, checks to sign, so on. You've been there."

"Sir, a report," said one of the khaki flunkies. He handed Joseph Kennedy, Junior a handset on a cord.

"Yes. Kennedy Junior. Uh-huh. Roger that. Acknowledged," Junior said, and gave the handset back.

"What was that?" Perry asked.

"That was Port Control," said Kennedy Junior. "The man believed to have been the attempted assassin – who killed two of our bodyguards as well; they were moving to anticipate him before he got *into* position – escaped aboard a ship. Weapons were fired at him; too late. They missed."

"They get a picture of him?" Perry asked.

"Nobody who got close survived," said Junior.

"A tall, broken-toothed murderer," said Lynch. "The same man who wiped out my organization in Louisiana. As I *did* warn you he might try here."

"The same man who stole 4-106," muttered Perry. "*That* bastard."

"Trotsky's troubleshooter, no doubt," said Lynch calmly. "I wouldn't have realistically expected that man, given the scale we're dealing with here, to use any but the best."

"Dispassionate, aren't we?" snapped Junior. "For a woman who lost her organization due to machinations she didn't realize she was messing with."

"Realistic," Lynch glared back. "Given circumstances. My hard lesson was your free information, Kennedy."

"Two good men died because of that data," snarled Joseph Senior from his wheelchair. "Given our pair of bodyguards, *four.* But we'll continue in Lynch's 'realistic' vein and stay on-point. Vice-Commodore."

Three pairs of eyes focused on Perry.

"Your enemies just proved their seriousness," Joseph Senior went on. "They – he – beat the precautions we'd have taken had it been ourselves, and not just body doubles."

"If you thought they were fucking around before," said Joseph Junior, "they aren't now."

"Those people were competent to begin with," said Lynch. "It was my mistake for thinking they were Hoover's amateurs."

"So do you want your airship back or not?" Joseph Senior asked Perry,

"Any time, pirate. Any damn time."

"The company's ready," Senior snapped back. "Go fetch it. And keep your part of the deal we made."

"If your men get me my ship back" – Perry glared at the elder pirate king – "then I'll do my part of your deal."

"John Francis is back," said Kennedy Senior. "We have three airships ready, and a company assembled. He'll be leading the recovery operation."

"They're your men so he can lead it," Perry said, "but I insist on accompanying. This is *my* airship. Ahle and Rafferty too, if they wish."

"That's fine," Senior said.

"When do we leave?"

"The men are boarding the ships now. They'll be ready to leave as soon as you join them. We have a car ready."

"Let's go," Perry said to Ahle. "It's time to take my ship back."

Chapter Twenty

We, of course, were not the only ones who had somewhere to go; the Russian royal family could follow others disdained by their own people into the frozen wastelands of Siberia.

Unlike previous dissidents, however, the Tsar and his court did not have the good manners - 'courtly manners', of course, having been oxymoronic in those times - to stay there. The Tsar's son, Nicholas II, crowned in 1890 in Vladviostock, began gathering strength from Siberian clans and Cossack factions.

Backed in the cities by firebrand young reactionaries such as Lenin, Bukharin and Trotsky, the Russian court returned in February of 1917 in what is generally known as the Russian Restoration.

This is not generally considered to have been a good thing for Imperial interests.

From *Events in a Cynic's Lifetime*, Baron Oscar Wilde, 1930.

"I have your money," Marko said to Ferrer, handing him a wallet. There was a sick grin on his face. "We're heading for Amarillo. Don't bother me until we're there."

Marko spun on a heel and went into his cabin.

Ferrer, relieved, went into the cabin he shared with Rienzi, unfolded his bunk and sat down on it. It was good to have the money; five thousand Imperial pounds, enough in itself to buy a decent farm. That was twenty-five thousand United States dollars at the present exchange rate – enough for a couple dozen acres, a small house and to get a start on furnishing the workshop. The other half would get him a *good* workshop and leave enough for a comfortable retirement.

No more running from pirates. No more shooting people. This is my one blow against the System. I'll have done my part.

He opened the wallet.

Inside there was money, yes. A five-thousand pound

295

Exchequer note – that had been shredded to the point where it was barely recognizable.

What the fuck?

He flipped the shredded mess out onto his bunk, examined it closely. Maybe if he carefully glued it back together? Was this some kind of a challenge?

No. It was some kind of a sick joke. Marko had clearly cut up at least *two* Exchequer notes; there were double pieces, pieces missing.

What. The. Fuck?

Part of Ferrer wanted to go out into the corridor and pound on Marko's door *right now*, demanding an answer. But the terrorist had specifically ordered that he wasn't to be disturbed until Amarillo. And a confrontation would get him shot, or worse.

What. The. Fuck?

"The other half the same way as this!" Marko had said.

Sick bile rose in Ferrer's throat. He wasn't going to be paid for the operation. Maybe he wasn't even going to survive it. People like Marko, that sick *bastard*, enjoyed killing people.

Another sick bastard came into the cabin right now; Pete Rienzi.

"Killed four men, he did," Ferrer's assistant giggled. "Wish I could have been there. What's going on?"

"I've been paid," Ferrer growled.

Rienzi glanced at the shredded mess on Ferrer's bunk, and laughed.

"Knows how to do a joke, don't he?"

Ferrer kept his mouth shut.

You bastards.

* * *

Perry stood with Ahle, Rafferty and the Kennedys' handsome, boyish-looking second son on the bridge of a family-owned airship called the *Viking*, as it lifted from Red Cloud's park. The hold and the cabins of the airship were crowded with men; forty of them, another eighty on the two other airships coming with them.

They were escort-class fighting craft; this one, Perry identified as a *Fuego del Gato* class, built in quantity across the

296

Spanish Empire from about 1950 until a few years ago. Not a top-line ship, unless the Kennedy engineers had made substantial modifications to it, but certainly serviceable.

"Captain, Mr. Kennedy," reported one of the signalmen. "Other two say they're ready to head out."

"Tell them to follow," said the ship captain, a slender ponytailed woman named Ahle. She glanced back to Kennedy, who nodded in confirmation.

"Helm, you know what to do."

"Let's do this thing," Rafferty said.

"Yeah," said Ahle. "Let's finally fucking do this thing."

* * *

Pratt Cannon sat in the captain's cabin of 4-106, which he'd appropriated for his own use after Marko had left. On a fold-out table in front of him were the guns he'd just finished cleaning; there was also a watch, which said it was three minutes to eight. Almost time for him to supervise the change of guard shift.

The Ranger platoon had their own schedule, and their prickly asshole of a first lieutenant had stubbornly refused to obey Cannon's orders, or even to coordinate very much. Cannon had considered shooting the fucker – that was usually his first reaction when someone bothered him, kill the bastard and see if the platoon sergeant would be more reasonable – but Marko had specifically ordered him to behave himself around the Texans. Plus, Texas Rangers were hard men, not to be fucked with lightly.

They were being useful enough anyway. Running patrols around the local area on the ground, although so far they were yet to encounter anything. The others had removed six of the nine-inch rocket launchers and set them up around the edge of the canyon.

Cannon's own men, the fifty-two crew, had been divided into three guard shifts. By the unstated agreement with the Texans, the Texans were essentially handling area security while Cannon's men were in charge of the ship itself. All fifty-two slept aboard it – there were more than enough cabins – but at any given time, a third of them were stationed in the rig house on top, the bridge of the ship – that was where Captain

297

Caine liked to hang out – the aft station and a few of the missile bays along the side.

Eight o'clock. Time to make sure the new shift was in place. Kick some ass if they weren't.

Tomorrow they'd lift for Hugoton and join Marko in the attack.

* * *

The *Viking* and Kennedy's other two ships had moved fast through the afternoon, the sunset and the night. Faster, actually, than Perry had thought a *Fuego del Gato* was capable of, but it had been years since he'd read those specs and aftermarket engineering rebuilds were common enough anyway.

Now, all lights off except for dim shrouds on the bridge, they flew by moonlight through the Rockies, three large, dark shadows full of tense men. It was one thirty in the morning and they were about half an hour from the objective.

"Over the plan one final time," Kennedy said to the lieutenant and his four squad leaders, as Perry and Ahle looked on. "Lieutenants Gosford and Jones drop their men in across the outer area, take down their outer perimiter. We know they have rocket launchers; those are Gosford and Jones' responsibility. We're the center element. All clear so far?"

The three men and two women made noises of agreement.

"Taking the airship itself is our responsibility. Squads A and B, you're landing on top of the ship. Subdue whoever you find there, rappel down and meet us inside the ship. Squad D, you're landing immediately behind the ship; make entry and move from aft to fore. I'm going in with Squad C, Lieutenant Wyclef, and our Imperial friends. We land around the nose of the ship and move on the cabin, going aft and linking with D. And the rest of the platoon, when they get down. All clear on that?"

There were nods and noises.

"Perry, Ahle, are you fine with your part?"

"Yessir," said Ahle.

"Vice-Commodore?" asked Kennedy. "It's your operation, although I'm in tactical command. Any last-minute objections to the plan or your place in it?"

"None I can think of," said Perry. *That I'm working with pirates* crossed his mind, but not heavily. He was getting 4-106 back; he was finally getting 4-106 back!

High altitude, wearing steerable rectangular assault `chutes, they dropped. Kennedy was first, cradling a submachinegun. Perry moved to be next, but Lieutenant Wyclef politely pushed him aside as his men jumped, pair after pair.

"Boss said you're not to incur any undue risk, sir" Wyclef said. "You're his – their – ticket to something big."

"B Squad!" shouted a sergeant, and ten more men jumped from the stationary airship.

"Go now if you insist," Wyclef said.

"I insist," said Perry, and leapt.

A few seconds of freefall, and then the ripcord ran out and the parachute opened. Below them, spread out, was the canyon. 4-106 hidden in there, vaguely discernible from a mile up.

Perry's weapon – an Imperial-issue Sterling submachinegun that the Kennedys had provided – was slung across his back. He gripped the steering cords of the `chute and aimed down for the nose of 4-106, light wind buffeting him as he descended.

We have the equivalent of a company of Air Marines, he thought. *This time we can't fail.*

About time.

* * *

Ahle had jumped a moment after Perry. Now, bursts of automatic fire rang out from around the site as her feet touched dirt. She shrugged away her parachute and drew her two revolvers. Lethal ammunition; lethal ammunition was most definitely called for in this situation. They were going up against the bastards who'd killed her crew.

As she began to run for the bridge, following Kennedy, Perry and the Kennedy Organization squad, lights started to come on across the massive airship. The bridge first, then running lights, the missile bays, everywhere. Dark figures, moving back and forth, appeared silhouetted in the bridge. It looked as though someone was panickedly just pulling switches.

An alarm on the ship began to wail – a deep, penetrating noise. *Thrummm. Thrummm. Thrummm.*

She was under the cover of the airship's gondola now, running for the cabin, overtaking a pair of Organization troops. One of them paused to raise his battle rifle to his shoulder, aiming for the figures on the bridge, but then the lights there went out.

"Follow me!" Jack Francis shouted, a few steps ahead of her.

Ahle had no intention of doing otherwise. She ran.

* * *

What the hell is going on? thought Pratt Cannon, a revolver in one hand as he stood on the bridge of 4-106. He'd killed the lights on the bridge, was tempted to blow away the *moron* who'd turned them on in the first place. But then the fucker had shown the good sense to hit the alarm.

They were under attack. That much was clear. Dark figures were coming toward them, looked like about a squad's worth. But flashes of gunfire – around the rocket positions and the Texan camp – implied more in the area. And panicked messages had already come through from the aft station, and the rig station on top.

Concerted attack from a meaningful force.

Who could have known this location?

How can I react?

Or escape?

Not much time. They were in a canyon, but Cannon hadn't lived to see forty-eight without good planning. There was a narrow path up, about two hundred yards southwest of the aft end of the airship.

And there were men coming at him, *right now*, and he had to deal with that threat first.

"To arms! Guns up and – repel boarders, you lot!" he shouted as another of the crew stumbled half-awake into the bridge. A middle-aged woman, half-dressed and bootless but her rig was on and there was a gun in there.

"Wha's happening?" she asked.

"We're under attack, fuckup," Captain Caine snarled. "Arm yourself and fight back!"

Jack Kennedy ran for the ship, his submachinegun – a pistol-grip .355 with a now-extended folding stock – raised and ready. He'd originally led the attack, but a three-man fireteam of the squad had overtaken him. Yeah, they'd want to protect their boss.

Shooting going on all around as the Texans were overwhelmed.

It was dark, the heavy gondola of 4-106 obscuring even the night's faint starlight.

"Attack!" shouted the corporal of the fireteam ahead, pushing up the lowered staircase into the airship's bridge. His men followed.

Shooting on the inside. A man in buckskins, two pistols drawn and handling them like an expert. One man's, then the corporal's, body fell backwards, out of the airship.

Kennedy was next, although he could tell the Imperial Vice-Commodore and his bodyguard were a moment behind him. He lunged up the airship's folding staircase and into the bridge, firing as he went.

For a moment he faced his enemy, a tall man in buckskins with a pair of long revolvers.

Time slowed for a moment.

"Johnny Kennedy." The man in buckskins recognized him. Raised his guns toward Kennedy's face, correctly assuming body armor.

"Johnny Kennedy," said Kennedy, whose gun was already raised. A burst of .355 lead took the man through the face.

He crumpled, brains blown out the back of his skull.

"We surrender!" shouted one of the other crewmen, as the Vice-Commodore and his bodyguard piled in behind them. A submachinegun clattered to the floor. Three other weapons followed, and hands reached for the ceiling.

* * *

Rafferty lowered the Service automatic and looked at the

prisoners. Kennedy was already covering them; more elements of the assault squads were coming in, going through the ship.

A Kennedy man came back, herding three more prisoners into the bridge. They looked shocked and only half-awake; *typical pirate riff-raff*, he thought.

Well, he was a Service career away from being that kind of riff-raff himself. *But*, he thought proudly, *I'm* Service *riff-raff.*

"Don't touch the controls," Vice Perry was snarling. "Or I'll blow your worthless heads off. Keep those hands up in the air where I can see `em or it'll be the worse for you."

The Vice seemed disappointed not to have gotten to kill anyone, was clearly itching for the chance now. Rafferty didn't envy the poor bastards on the other end of his gun.

Ahle seemed equally pissed as she helped Perry cover them. Her crew had been murdered en masse by this lot, and the rapid surrender had denied her a chance at revenge. As four more prisoners, one of them in his underwear, were pushed onto the bridge, the pirate captain tensely caressed the trigger of one of her guns.

Guys, Rafferty hoped to telepathically convey to the now-a-dozen prisoners, *don't try anything. Don't get smart, either. You guys are in deeper shit than you begin to realize.*

* * *

Captain Caine made himself breathe. Deeply, as he continued to talk. He knew exactly how deep in shit he presently was, and he wanted to live.

Routine operation blather. Johnny Kennedy, and that nasty black guy who was apparently an Imperial officer, could know it all. About how that crazy black-clad guy with the broken teeth had made them fly over Hugoton.

"Look, I'll fuck with Imperials," he pleaded to Kennedy. "*You* guys do. It's part of the business. But – Mr. Kennedy, I'm sorry. If I'd realized that these were friends of *yours*, Mr. Kennedy."

That didn't seem to impress the black Imperial officer, whose gun twitched in Caine's direction. Hastily he moved to apologize.

"And I've never hurt Imperials, sir. Mr. Commodore, sir. Maybe traded shots with them a few times, but... sir, I was

Code through and through. Never killed a man in my life to my knowledge."

"Get back to the point," the black man coldly ordered. "The bastard went to the Black Hills. Where was he going to go from there?"

"Don't know," said Caine. "We were just supposed to prep the bird – this bird, sir, Mr. Commodore and Mr. Kennedy – for departure at six this morning. He'd know." A gesture at Cannon's smashed corpse, which nobody had bothered to move from where it lay.

"Would have known, that is. He'd have told us where to go."

"I didn't do nothin'," put in one of the other prisoners. "Code pirate, Mr. Kennedy. Good Code woman, always followed your rules and shit. Like the cap'n said, if I'd known we was goin' up against *you*–"

"Shut up," the black Imperial ordered in that disconcertingly – frighteningly, given the circumstances – upper-class-English accent of his. "You shot down two Imperial ships and murdered my friend's crew. Tell it to a judge."

* * *

My friend's crew, thought Perry, realizing what he'd just said. Well, Ahle...

She was a damned pirate and the bitch who'd originally stolen 4-106 from him. If she hadn't, none of this operation would have been necessary.

And she was small fry, another part of Perry's mind came back. She's honorable in her own way, she has legitimate grievances – *her family was murdered by second-degree Imperial proxies!* – and she's saved your back more than once.

He was an Imperial officer. How could he be friends with a pirate?

How could he *like* John Kennedy, as he was finding he did. The man had a certain boyish charm, could tell a story well, and knew his work.

The man would make a fine Imperial officer, he thought.

For that matter, so would Ahle.

But he had more urgent matters to attend to. Bigger things

were going on than a lost airship. Much bigger things. Hugoton itself was under threat; perhaps the entire West.

"Get these trash off my bridge," he ordered Kennedy for the first time. Reports had come through, a few minutes ago, confirming that 4-106 was solidly under Kennedy's control. A group of – twenty or so – Texan prisoners were being herded just now into the space in front of 4-106.

"You heard the Vice-Commodore," Kennedy ordered the prisoners. "Get off his ship. Join your Texan friends over there."

"One *hint* of funny business and you're all dead," Ahle snarled.

"Wasn't us who killed your crew, cap'n," one of the prisoners pleaded. "That psycho in black was who did it."

"You were party to it," snarled Ahle. "And you killed a bunch of *his* compatriots, anyway. Just give me the excuse..."

* * *

Perry leaned back in his seat on the bridge of 4-106 – *mine again!* – and looked up at John Kennedy. Ahle was comfortable in the XO's, Martindale's seat, sipping from a canteen of rum. She'd offered Perry some, but he'd declined; the euphoria of finally, *finally*, after all this hell, having his ship back, was not something he needed alcohol to enhance.

His again. He had his ship back.

And there was work to do.

John Kennedy came back to the bridge. "*Red Wasp* coming in now," he reported. "Your prize crew's ready to take over. But I've a question for you."

"I'm listening," said Perry. The man had gotten his ship back; he'd listen to *any* proposal from him.

"You're going into some action, Vice. Some of these men are trained in the operation of ship weapons. Right now you only have enough crew to fly that ship and only barely that; you can't fight her. You want to be able to fight her?"

They *were* heading into action, thought Perry. Whatever he was going to find in Hugoton when he got there, it was going to be bad.

But there was a certain lunacy to the idea of taking a line-class airship right into Hugoton, with all the weapons stations manned by pirates.

Hadn't lunacy been the defining state of his existence for the last two weeks?

Yeah, but there were still precautions you could take.

"I'll consider that," he said. "But I'll want them disarmed and stripped. Hideout weapons too; Ahle and Nolan's men will see to that. They obey my orders and submit themselves, in advance, to Imperial custody."

Kennedy opened his mouth to say something. Perry – *on the bridge of my ship again!* – waved him down.

"To my knowledge, none of these people has committed a criminal offence, and they've done the British Empire an invaluable service. They won't be held for very long and the evidence doesn't exist to try them, let alone convict."

"Very well," said Kennedy. "I'll ask for volunteers. And now we go to Hugoton; it's time to do your part of the deal. I'm meeting with Ian Fleming at the man's earliest convenience, and Governor Henry at *his*."

"If we were in London," said Perry, "I'd do my best to introduce you to Her Majesty herself."

* * *

Nate Nolan sat personally at – the late – Sub-Lieutenant Kent's communications station. He'd made up a line of bullshit about how Perry could use any available crew and for the money…

Perry had handed the captain a sheaf of hundreds on the spot. He'd already paid Nolan for the rest of the job, and given him more money – fighting wages, as originally promised – to distribute to the others.

"Gina reports boilers hot, Mr. Vice," reported the scavenger captain.

"We loose?" Perry, now at the helm – *my beautiful new ship, again!* – of 4-106, asked Ahle.

"Loose as a Deadwood whore."

"Then lift in three, two, one," ordered Perry.

It actually took a few more moments than that; it was only a makeshift crew, after all. But a few seconds after Perry's command, buoyancy reached positive and the warship began to lift.

"Next stop, Hugoton," said Nolan happily.

"Next stop, Hugoton," repeated Perry as the canyon walls began to slide past them.

John Kennedy, at Swarovski's Weapons station, grinned.

"Next stop, Ian Fleming," he said.

* * *

Skorzeny's command car drove through the night across the Kansas plains, the speedometer holding down an even thirty-five miles an hour; the highest practical long-range speed of the Tiger IIs, IIas and IIbs in the division.

It was the second time since the Special Squadrons' formation that the entire organization had been brought together in one place. The sight – the lights of hundreds of tanks, armored cars, battalion command cars and fighting vehicles – was impressive. Three miles wide as they kicked dust through Kansas, the division-sized formation with its headlights, searchlights and spotlights dominated the night.

We're twelve hours from Hugoton, the SS colonel thought. *And the Imperials have scattered their garrison across the border. There's nothing there to stop us.*

A pity. It looked like they were going to do a painless wrecking job on the place, trashing facilities, wells and refineries without more than token resistance.

He'd have almost preferred a good fight.

Chapter Twenty-One

Part of the Imperially-guided reconstruction of North America involved Texan independence. Maps were redrawn to create the Hugoton Lease, essentially granting the Southwestern quarter of Kansas to Imperial control, for the sake of the helium reserves there...

From *A History of North America*, Winston Churchill.

Early in a clear-skied late-March morning, the *Ruby Red Robber* touched down at the military airship park of Amarillo, Texas. Coming in, Ferrer had seen seven brightly-painted airships, but the signature jet-black ship of Commodore Cordova was what really gave him the clue.

Cordova's Armadillos. Like anyone media-literate, he'd heard of those guys and their previous feats. The Russians had hired *them*? Oh, God was Minister Trotsky serious.

They're killers like anyone else in this line of work, he tried to tell himself.

Still, he was impressed.

"4-106 should be joining them within a few hours over Hugoton," Marko told him, Judd, Rienzi and McIlhan on the bridge as they landed. "I'm about to make a final report. Then we'll join the Commodore" – a gesture at the jet-black, four-hundred-yard fighting ship they were parked beside; at this distance Ferrer could clearly make out the florid lettering *Lone Star* on the nose of its gondola – "and the SS as they make their final approach. Any questions?"

Nobody had any.

You bastard, thought Ferrer. *I was doing a good job for you. Why did you stiff me?*

You're as bad as Federal Electric.

"There'll be burning and fire and explosions!" Marko exalted. "The South's already going up, and soon Imperial power will do the same!"

And replace it with people like you? Ferrer thought.

Bile returned to his throat, but he kept his mouth shut.

"Detach and lift!" came over the wire. A crewman on Paula Handley's ship relayed the command to her. It was ten thirty in the morning.

"Detach and lift," Handley ordered.

The usual slithering noises. *The Vorpal*, and Rick Evans' *Dread Wyvern* half a mile away, began to ascend.

"To Hugoton," she ordered her XO – and husband – Brad, at the helm. "To kill everything that lifts."

Damn, was it going to be good to be back in a fight again.

Although from all she'd heard, it was going to be more of a turkey shoot.

Damn, she corrected herself, *will it be good to earn combat pay again. Instead of just appearance fees and media revenue.*

"Adjusting course," Brad Handley reported, turning the wheel. A moment later: "On course."

The *Dread Wyvern* fell in next to her as they headed for the Hugoton Lease.

* * *

Fleming stood in Governor Lloyd's all-but-empty office.

"Governor of Mississippi assassinated," he reported. "Federal airship base in Biloxi, Louisiana under rocket fire. Georgia statehouse bombed. Two dozen lesser incidents; the Southern States are exploding. Reports were still coming in when we lost communication."

"We lost communication?" demanded the Governor. Although he'd been anticipating this.

"SS must have finally cut the wire. We're still in communication with Dodge, but that's it."

"So they're coming, Ian."

"We know they're coming," said the spy. "Sir, if I may respectfully suggest you get yourself the *hell* out of here?"

"You may not," Governor Lloyd snapped. He'd had this damn conversation enough times, hadn't he? "Although you may entreat my aide again, if you wish."

"I'm not leaving," Warren Buff said. He was dressed as for an evening in Mayfair, as always, and Lloyd respected the young man's spirit. And his style. If not his intelligence. "Not unless the boss goes."

"Your Lordship's family will be deeply upset if you're killed," Fleming said. "*When* you are. The SS aren't known for their mercy."

"I signed up for a Colonial assignment," said Buff. "I accepted the risk, sir. I will live with it, *sir*."

Lloyd smiled thinly.

"Why are *you* remaining, Mr. Fleming?"

"Duty as long as practicable," Fleming snapped. "Besides, who says I don't have a way out?"

Governor Lloyd decided not to ask. He didn't want to know, and the man would probably conceal it anyway. *Of course* Fleming would find a way to survive.

Fleming's injured aide, Connery, pushed his way into the once-well-appointed office.

"Deputy Director?" he called from across the large room.

"I'm here," said Fleming.

"Lookouts reported. Just now," said Connery. "They've been spotted. Incoming airships."

"It's starting," said Fleming.

* * *

The two line-class mercenary ships, one bright red and the other a striking lime green, flew over Hugoton two and a half hours before the Special Squadrons – given their known capabilities and anticipated speeds – had been scheduled to arrive.

Flight Admiral Janet Richardson watched dispassionately as the lime-green ship shredded, with a single missile broadside, her personal transport. Its cannon began to work on the other two civilian ships, which had been hired in Dodge for the purpose of getting the remaining Air Service personnel out of Hugoton.

The bright red ship – Richardson could not be remotely bothered with a scope, and could have cared less for the names of the supposedly-celebrity enemy – fired a wave of missiles into the first civilian airship and then, as it lifted and desperately attempted to turn, the other.

Both went down in bright flames, amplified all the more by the darkly-overcast day, as storm clouds gathered above them.

That's it, Richardson thought, as the junior officers and enlisteds who'd expected to leave aboard those ships, went to pieces around her. *I suppose we die here.*

To Richardson, who as a twenty-year-old ensign had seen four of her classmates – and best friends – die over Berlin, it was a mere detail. Her present rank and the famous action in which she'd won it, her present rank and the offer of a knighthood that she'd refused – *Charles, Marie, Jennifer and Gordon had never lived to earn those* – had been a later byproduct.

Janet Richardson had considered herself dead since 1939. The remaining details were just that, as her adjutant cried out: "What do we do now?"

"We die here," Richardson responded reflexively with the obvious.

Just details.

* * *

"We're dead," Senior Airshipwoman Hayden was saying. "Our ticket out just went boom. We're gone."

"Not necessarily," Vidkowski said. "There's horses left. And a few steam-cars. And the railway. Maybe we can do something."

"If you have to" – Lieutenant-Commander Martindale appeared, his own sidearm drawn – "you'll die fighting. With those crazy Army sons of bitches."

About a hundred volunteers from the Army garrison – Vidkowski had heard something about bonus pensions being granted by executive order from the Governor – had stayed. A mishmash of various units, but their job was to put up a fight. To not let Hugoton go down without some kind of resistance.

Nothing more than maintaining Imperial honor, thought Specialist Second Ernest Vidkowski. A worthy objective, but not one *he'd* signed on for.

And their way out had just been blown to flaming trash.

Very well. If he was going to die, he'd die as he'd lived.

As an Imperial airshipman.

"Mr. Martindale," he shouted.

Lieutenant-Commander Martindale turned.

"Specialist Second Vidkowski."

"Gimme a rifle, sir. They're coming and our way out is shot

to crap. I'll do my bit."

"You'll get one," the lieutenant-commander snapped back. "We all do our bit. For Imperial honor, if nothing else."

Captain Peggey Rowland and her ship, the *Five Speed*, flew over grassy Kansas plains toward Dodge City, flanked by Shirley Meier's *Pith and Vinegar*. The light line-class ships flew straight, under the darkening clouds.

As they approached the railway line, they saw a train. A long line of tankers and – mostly – boxcars, making haste out of Hugoton, racing east ahead of the oncoming storm.

Too bad, thought Rowland.

"Signals, tell Captain Meier the obvious," Rowland ordered. "Helm, you know what to do."

"Aye, ma'am."

* * *

The *Five Speed*, paced on the other side of the railway line by the *Pith and Vinegar*, matched speed with the train from Hugoton and then descended to obliterate it.

Six-inch missiles lanced out, pounding into the engine and the tankers.

Those went up in blazing fireballs. The *Five Speed*'s experienced helmsman slowed the ship to a crawl, following the train.

As flames and thick black smoke boiled into the sky from the wrecked engine and the burning tanker cars, Rowland slammed missiles, cannon fire – and, as she drew closer, descending to three hundred feet – 30mm Gatling bursts into the powerless train.

"Next stop Dodge City," she murmured, as something in one of the boxcars went up in a blazing pyre. "If they fire on us, kill them. If they lift, kill them. If they *can* lift? Kill them."

* * *

Otto Skorzeny grinned as the flasher reports came in.

He could see perfectly well from his own maps, of course. They were approaching Dodge City, which itself was an hour

311

and a half away from Hugoton.

"Destroy everything that pumps or moves," came the flasher orders from Himmler's own command car. "We are now in free-fire mode. Kill everything."

* * *

"Sir," Fleming reported to Governor Lloyd. "We've just lost contact with Dodge. More of those Armadillo bastards must have cut our wire."

"Then they must have cut our wire," said Lloyd calmly – pleasantly? "We have a job to do, Mr. Fleming. We die well."

* * *

The two brightly-colored line-class ships had been comfortably holding station, at about twenty-five hundred feet relative, above Hugoton for about twenty minutes since they'd destroyed Admiral Richardson's *White Lightning* and the two civilian ships.

Presumably waiting for more trouble to erupt, thought Lieutenant Swarovski, cradling the semi-familiar US Cavalry carbine. He'd kept it over the Army rifle he'd been offered. He and the rest of 4-106's crew, and the fifty or so ground crew, who had been disassembling and packing the last semi-portable material from the air base, were milling around the flight pads. Taking care never to congeal into clusters so big that the hovering Armadillo airships might bother to fire at them.

Soon, Ensign Hastings had informed him a few minutes ago, they were due to move into defensive positions against the SS. A final stand.

Swarovski would have desperately appreciated a final drink. A final hand of cards or spin of the roulette wheel. He'd joined the Service because Pater had required him, as the fourth son of an aristocratic family, to make his own way. He'd chosen the Service because neither salt water nor rigid Army discipline had appealed much to him. And an airshipman got to see the world, right?

But, very well. If he was going to die here on this rig-filled ugly Kansas plain, he was going to die here. A man couldn't always have what he wanted.

Sudden cry out.

"Someone's coming!"

Yes. A new speck on the northern horizon. A big ship, Swarovski could make out.

He raised his binoculars for a closer look.

Oh shit.

He recognized that ship, unless he was very wrong.

He'd flown on it. Briefly been its weapons officer.

DN 4-106.

Hope.

"Oh shit," came Specialist Singh's voice. "She's flashing the bastards. She's with them."

* * *

"We carry Theron Marko," Perry told Nolan. "We request loudhailer distance from senior present airship. Wish to convey intelligence."

"Got it the first time, Vice," said Nolan.

A short pause.

"But repeating the flash now. Hold on – the red fucker's responding."

"Go on," said Perry. Tense. He looked at Kennedy. "Acting Weapons, you ready?"

"Primed and loaded on all stations," John F. Kennedy reported.

"Says to come in," Nolan went on. "They know who your Marko is, apparently. Message is, 'We're listening'."

"Get as close as we can," Perry ordered Ahle, who was at the helm. "And then on my order" – to Kennedy – "destroy them."

* * *

Captain Handley was a little confused, watching through a monocular scope as the big line-class moved to rendezvous with them. Hadn't Mr. Marko, the apparent Russian agent, been aboard the *other* airship?

Covert operations be damned. That shit confused her.

But she'd also been told to expect an airship matching this

313

one's description, designated 4-106 as this one was. She put down the monocular.

"I still say we kill them," Brad muttered from the helm.

"You say to kill everything, dearest," Handley replied.

The airship designated 4-106 was moving to within loudhailer distance. A couple of hundred yards away, half its length and two thirds the *Vorpal*'s.

"Engage loudhailer," Handley ordered.

"Loudhailer engaged," reported the crewman. "You have the speaker."

Handley reached for the mike.

"Mr. Marko," she said pleasantly. Her words were amplified by loudspeaker over two hundred yards of airspace to the massive – *damn, that's an Imperial line-class* – airship across from her. "What can I do for you?"

The answer came in an upper-class Imperial accent.

"You can jump, mercenary."

Trailing fire, a dozen missiles followed.

* * *

At effective point-blank, even the relatively untrained missileers on 4-106, handling heavy nine-inch launchers that were all but completely unfamiliar to most of them, couldn't miss. The twelve rockets slammed into the *Vorpal* before anyone aboard could begin to react, twenty-five pound warheads detonating along the cabin and the lower edge of the gondola.

One of them scored a direct hit on the airship's engine hall, which was armored but not well enough to withstand nine-inch missiles. Bright yellow secondary explosions erupted as one, then another, of the boilers blew out.

Another rocket smashed into the *Vorpal*'s aft battery, a revolving cannon mount. The battery was obliterated and its stock of ammunition began to cook off, another wave of secondary explosions.

One detonated amidst empty crew cabins, sending a rain of flaming junk down toward the plain.

The other nine rockets hit along the edge of the gondola, detonating along its thin kevlar armor. Burning shrapnel cut through the airship's hydrogen-filled bags, setting them ablaze.

In seconds, two thirds of the *Vorpal* was an inferno, riggers and crew beginning to bail.

The flaming wreck began to drop – slowly at first, but faster as her hydrogen burned or escaped, the fires spreading – toward the grassy plains of Hugoton.

* * *

"Engage his friend, and *now!*" Perry snarled, as the shattered *Vorpal* went down in flames.

"Miss," Kennedy reported from the Weapons station. "Hit, and that's a good one – got her fins!"

"Who?"

"Aft station," said Nolan before Kennedy could. "That pressure-gun of yours" – Halvorsen's, Perry thought, and Hastings' – "did a job on them."

"Bring them down before they can repair it," Perry ordered.

* * *

"Enemy civil war?" Specialist Singh asked as the bright-red airship went down burning.

As a missile volley at point-blank would do to you, yeah, thought Swarovski. Those missiles hadn't just lanced the mercenary's gondola; at that range they'd been more than able to aim precisely and the *Vorpal's* engine room had taken at least one, possibly two, direct hits. He'd seen it go up.

He tuned out Lieutenant-Commander Martindale's shouted orders for men to round up the survivors and get them into custody. 4-106 had just fired – ventral and tail guns – on the lime-green mercenary.

Looked like at least one critical, too.

"Don't know," Swarovski replied to the Specialist. He didn't lower his binoculars as 4-106 closed in for the kill on the *Dread Wyvern*, who appeared to have lost steering control. "But it looks like good news."

* * *

"Missile Ten reloaded and ready," Kennedy reported finally.

"Slackers," Rafferty remarked. "An *Imperial* crew'd have taken thirty-five seconds. Not eighty-five."

"At this point," Perry said, "I don't care. Full volley, Weapons. Blow them out of the sky."

Guns – fore, ventral and rear, since 4-106 had turned broadside to the crippled *Dread Wyvern* – had already been pounding at the airship, making sure her disabled steering fins stayed that way.

Now 4-106's twelve missile batteries opened up. The dozen-strong nine-inch missile broadside smashed into the *Dread Wyvern*'s aft.

The steering had been hurt a moment ago by a lucky hit from 4-106's surprise attack. More pressure-gun and cannon fire had all but destroyed the tailfins and started a small fire. Now, twenty-five pound high explosive loads tore apart the *Dread Wyvern*'s aft third, and set alight most of its remainder.

The second of Cordova's Armadillos followed its sibling down in flames.

Perry smiled. This was his job; this was him *doing* his job aboard the finest airship he'd ever commanded.

John Kennedy coughed.

Fair enough.

"Nolan, flash base," Perry said. "Tell them we're coming in."

* * *

The returning airship – formerly Vice-Commodore Marcus Perry's 4-106, Ian Fleming had recognized from his own data – had come in. Flashed the enemy ships saying he was a friendly. Claiming to be Theron Marko, although Fleming had doubted that.

The captain of, at least, the bright-red *Vorpal* – Paula Handley, if he remembered correctly – hadn't had the same information Fleming did. She'd allowed 4-106 to come within loudhailer distance.

And been thoroughly blasted out of the sky by a full broadside at effective point-blank. Gunnery – lucky shots? – had crippled its lime-green friend's – the *Dread Wyvern*'s – steering. A minute later, a second concerted missile volley had destroyed the *Wyvern*, too.

"What the *hell* is going on there?" Governor Lloyd demanded.

"Lord Governor" – the aide, Buff, had a pair of binoculars affixed to his eyes, following 4-106's flasher as the line-class warship descended – "it sounds – Lord Governor? As though..."

"Go on," the Governor snapped.

"Vice-Commodore Marcus Perry says he's back."

Fleming and Connery looked at one another.

"With his ship," Buff went on. "And he wants an audience with the Deputy Director. Right now."

"You heard my aide," the Governor snapped. "Get down there."

The two spies were already moving.

* * *

"That's *Perry!*" Swarovski repeated to Specialist First Singh.

"Says he is, sir," replied the communications woman.

"It makes sense, Lieutenant" said Martindale. "Who else would have shot down those puffed-up merc bastards?"

"He brought the ship back," Swarovski muttered. "Holy fucking shit. I *told* you he was on covert assignment, Jules!"

"Who gives a damn, Swav?" Martindale shot back. "Let's go say hello to him, shall we?"

"You're the boss, sir," said Swarovski. The two, followed by Singh, Vidkowski and a crowd from 4-106's crew, ran to intercept the descending 4-106.

* * *

"Perry's back," Commander Ojibwa reported to Richardson, lowering her binoculars.

"I can read a flasher," said the Flight Admiral tonelessly. "Tell him he did a good job, will you?"

"You're not going to greet him yourself, ma'am?"

"I don't need to bother him. It looks like he wants to talk to somebody else."

From across the pads, Richardson could see Deputy Director Fleming making haste toward the growing crowd of airshipmen waiting to greet the Vice-Commodore. Flanked by his pair of aides, Fleming was moving fast.

"He flashed for *him*," the Flight Admiral repeated. "Not me."

But beneath the hag lady's always-expressionless demeanor, Ojibwa thought she saw the ghost of a smile.

Chapter Twenty-Two

The cornerstones of the Restored Empire were laid on January 1st 1901, the first year of the new Empire, when the Second Decree was passed unanimously by the Houses of Commons and of Lords.

Alongside the absolute rights to individual cross-border movement and group/regional self-determination granted by the Curzon Doctrine, the Decree made other elements foundational to Imperial law and identity going forwards, primarily a legal indifference to matters of 'personal morality' such as homosexuality and full House of Commons voting franchise to all literate adults of majority age within the Empire's dominions.

"The greatest day in Imperial history," Baron Oscar Wilde said on the floor of the House of Lords. "You will forgive me for not cracking the usual joke."

From *A Young Person's History of the World, Volume X.*

"Looks like they want a speech," remarked Ahle from the helm, as 4-106 landed. Meeting them at the bridge were a crowd of cheering airshipmen.

"There's seven Armadillos," said Rafferty. "Vice, you only killed two of `em. Five more around somewhere."

"And the others won't go down as easily," Ahle added. "We had surprise this time. And luck."

"But first," said John Kennedy from the Weapons station, "you swore as an Imperial officer to make an introduction."

Perry nodded at the pirate.

"I did, at that. And I will. Looks like he's coming to us. But give me a moment."

Perry keyed the loudhailer mike.

"Crew of DN 4-106," he said into it.

The words echoed, amplified, across the bare concrete

landing pads and through the mostly-abandoned Hugoton base.

"Thank you for waiting for me," Perry went on. Why *had* these guys stuck around – some exigiency of evacuation logistics? Although it was obvious that a shipless crew would be last on the list to get out – "I look forward to taking you under my command once again."

Another cheer rose at that statement.

"For now, we have urgent work to do. Prepare yourselves for action."

"Looks like your MI-7 boss is here," said Nolan.

"Drop the door," Perry ordered. "Let him in."

* * *

Ian Fleming looked John F. Kennedy in the face, on 4-106's bridge, and smiled.

"Mr. Kennedy," he said. "I won't ask why you're aboard our prodigal airship. I will apologize for not being able to offer you a drink."

"Oh, I can make up for that," said a Specialist Third in his late thirties, offering a flask. "Drink with Mr. Fleming would *add* to the adventure."

"Another time, Specialist," said Fleming.

"You probably don't have a lot of time," said Kennedy. "So I'll get to the point."

"You wouldn't have put your head into my noose without one," agreed Fleming. "So yes, please."

"Colby's information says your Governor is the type to remain around. Is he here?"

Fleming considered prevaricating, but only for a brief moment.

"He's here."

"I want to see him. Vice Perry?"

"Deputy Director," said Perry, "I promised Mr. Kennedy an audience with you and – I know it's not within my authority – with the Governor if you could swing it."

"I can probably swing it," said Fleming. "Suppose you tell me why."

"I'll tell *him* why," said Kennedy. "Fifty of my family's men are here as hostages – manning this ship's weapons and rig stations. I've returned your airship when I could have easily kept it for ourselves. I think that's enough of a good-faith gesture to start the conversation."

"I can't begin to guess why the Josephs' obvious emissary would wish to speak with the Lord Governor," said Fleming slowly. "So I'm going to emphatically recommend that an audience be granted."

"Thank you," said Kennedy. "I'm unarmed, although I expect you to verify that. I'm here to talk."

"Once we're inside," Fleming said. "But Perry? Your ship already has a crew. Replace your pirates with them, will you – and join us."

Kennedy reached for a mike on his console.

"All secondary crew," he ordered, "surrender yourselves as planned."

"Join you?" Perry asked.

"With the Governor," said Fleming. "You organized the introduction. He's your problem."

* * *

Heinrich Himmler smiled broadly as his outriding tanks blew another oil well into a geyser of flames.

They were approaching suburban Dodge City.

Three hours, now, from Hugoton.

* * *

Perry followed Connery, Fleming and – having been quite thoroughly searched by Fleming and his aide – Kennedy – through the stairwells of a mostly-abandoned Government Tower. Ahle tailed them, clearly itching to speak to Fleming herself.

He could guess why.

They reached the seventh floor. The Governor's last remaining aide, an immaculately-dressed young aristocrat, stood outside his office.

In twenty months stationed here, Perry had only been inside that office twice; once for his official welcome to the Lease, the second time for a personal commendation. Both had been formal audiences, not personal meetings.

321

"Holy hell," said the aide, "that's John F. Kennedy."

"A pleasure to meet you," said Kennedy, extending a hand. The aide shook it, clearly shocked.

"Mr. Buff, this man requires an audience with your boss," said Fleming. "Urgently."

"He's still inside, Mr. Fleming," said Buff. "I guess I can let you through."

"Your Empire may thank you," said Kennedy, as they passed in.

* * *

The Governor's office had been stripped of everything that could easily be moved, but to Perry's eyes that only gave it a stark simplicity fitting the man's rank.

After all, Flight Admiral Richardson's office was like this normally, wasn't it?

"And who is this fine fellow I hear I've been urged to meet?" the Governor asked.

"John Kennedy," said Fleming. "Joseph's son. And younger brother."

"The pirate kings? And what would *they* want? To gloat?" demanded the Governor.

Perry stifled an interruption. He *wanted* to be back with 4-106, prepping his crew for the desperate battle to come. But he was curious as to what would happen here. John Kennedy had gone well out of his way to put his head deep inside the lion's mouth for a reason.

"No," said Kennedy. "I'm here to offer you a deal. We can save your Lease from destruction. If you grant us a few concessions."

* * *

Governor Charles Lloyd couldn't believe he was hearing this insanity.

Here comes pirate prince John F. Kennedy personally, known from Fleming's briefings to be the family's second son and chief of special operations, attempting to negotiate something?

Remember the fact, the Governor told himself. *The SS is*

coming. Her Majesty will thank you for any actions you take to save the Lease in the face of this disaster.

Any.

That gave him room, didn't it?

It depended.

"You're pirates," said Lloyd. "How in damnation do you claim you can save the Lease against what's coming?"

* * *

"Trotsky's man attempted to assassinate my family heads for a reason," said Kennedy, as Perry looked on. "There are two effective powers on the Plains; Imperials and the Kennedy family. Successfully killing the Josephs would have perhaps caused enough disruption as to render *us* powerless against what was to come."

"The invasion was cancelled the minute we deployed along the border," said Lloyd. "Now all that's left is the destruction of this denuded Lease."

"Which I can prevent," Kennedy repeated.

"How?" asked Fleming and the Governor simultaneously.

"My family went to full mobilization eighteen hours ago," said John Kennedy. "Every ship we have an interest in, every debt we're owed, every pledge we've been given. And everything the Lakota can send. We can stop the SS."

"I don't believe it," said Governor Lloyd. "Vice-Commodore, what do you think?"

Perry swallowed hard.

"Lord Governor? I won't outright contradict Mr. Kennedy on that statement, sir. His family commands resources."

"Resources *here*?"

"Mr. Lloyd," said Kennedy, "I'll make the deal plainer to you. You keep your part of the deal if, and only if, we save Hugoton."

"Suppose we make a deal with your pirates," said Lloyd. "What would you want?"

Kennedy's mouth became a smile.

"Legitimacy. We want Imperial law to recognize the Code."

"You want piracy legalized?" said the Governor. "Like hell."

Kennedy shook his head.

323

"We would be fine if piracy remained a crime. Just not a capital one, or one with *too* long a prison sentence. Let's say, five years minus the usual reductions for good behavior and whatnot. If the perpetrator is a known Code pirate."

"I'm not going to abandon the law for the sake of saving my Lease. Rape and murder are crimes that deserve hanging, not wrist-slaps!"

"Rape and murder aren't engaged in by Code pirates. We make sure of that. Crimes committed alongside piracy, you can punish as you see fit – we'll even assist you. I'm referring to the act of piracy in and of itself. If the perpetrator is a Code pirate, you do not hang them solely for piracy. You can imprison them for up to five years. That's it. Rapists and murderers have never, do not, and never will, come under our protection."

Governor Lloyd was silent for a long, long moment.

Then he nodded.

"Mr. Kennedy, I will make this policy and recommend its ratification as Crown policy, *if* you deliver on your promise and save Hugoton."

Kennedy extended a hand. The Governor, after a pause, shook it.

"In the presence of these witnesses," Kennedy said, "we have a deal."

"We have a deal," Governor Henry slowly agreed.

"Now" – Kennedy spoke to Fleming – "get me to a flasher. We don't have much time."

* * *

From the roof of Hugoton's Government Tower, Kennedy – assisted by a pair of Army communications personnel that one of the Air Service ground officers had picked up from the garrison stay-behinds – carefully aimed the heliograph, checking against a compass. Fleming, Connery and Buff hovered watching in the background.

"There," said Kennedy. "No – another quarter-degree. Now. Corporal, are you ready with your binoculars?"

"Yes, mate."

"Yes *sir*, Corporal."

"He a sir – Mr. Lieutenant, sir?"

"For now," said the Air Service lieutenant, "he's a 'sir' if he wants to be. Get to it."

"Yes, sir. Sir."

"Transmitting," Kennedy said, and began to flash.

A tense few moments.

"Sir," reported the corporal. "We got a response. Acknowledged, he says. No – acknowledged and conveying, sir."

* * *

From one temporarily-assembled field heliograph station to another, Kennedy's message flashed north until it reached a field command post about seventy-five miles away, on the Kansas plains. There, nine combat airships and a bobbing flotilla of three dozen pirate ships sat low, amidst heliographs pointed north and south, east and west.

Joseph Kennedy, Junior was in command on the ground. With him were Bill Colby and Joseph's youngest sibling, Ed.

"Mr. Kennedy, sir" said the senior flash officer – a uniformed Lakota lieutenant. "Looks like you got a reply. Blue four, sir, he says. Hugoton."

Blue four. That was Jack's prearranged code for 'we have made an acceptable deal.'

Joseph fought to restrain the euphoria that rose in him.

Legitimacy! My God, legitimacy!

"Very good, Grey Eagle," he replied, hoping he could stay calm.

Legitimacy at last, if we can win this thing!

He and the family had taken on ridiculous odds before. And won.

"Reply," Joseph Junior ordered. "Acknowledge. Your other flashers can spread the word. We have some new Imperial friends."

"My God," Colby said. "Jackie fucking did it. I owe that fucker a grand."

Ed Kennedy produced a flask.

"Wouldn't you say this calls for a drink?"

* * *

"New message, sir," said the Army signals corporal. "Says,

325

'Acknowledged Joseph. Relaying and lifting.'"

John Kennedy nodded.

"So they're coming?" the Air Service officer asked.

"They're on the way," Kennedy said.

* * *

Captain Shirley Meier of the purple *Pith and Vinegar*, with Captain Peggey Rowland of the sky-blue *Five Speed*, had arrived over Dodge City about forty minutes earlier. Challenging them on station had been a Federal, United States Air Force, wing of four large escort-class airships, presumably – Meier had thought – hastily deployed out of Amarillo.

One of them had bolted upon seeing the two Armadillo ships arrive. Meier's second signalwoman had reported flasher communications between the largest of the Federal airships and that one – 'Come back, you coward!'

The coward, at least, had lived.

The *Pith and Vinegar* and the *Five Speed* had split wide over downtown Dodge as the remaining three Federals had turned to engage.

Cannon chewed back and forth across the four miles of intervening sky. Neither really, among the wind-blown, slightly bobbing, airships, got lucky. Four miles became three. Two and a half. Two.

The Federals came on in a close trio, only a few hundred yards apart. Below them were the Dodge railyards and industrial district – targets of convenience anyway, although the SS would be coming soon enough. Smokestacks reached toward the sky; cracking towers and storage silos.

One and a half miles.

"Turn," Meier ordered. "And broadside."

Eight nine-inch missiles blasted across the sky at the Federal formation, which itself was beginning to turn in response, to show a broadside to the mercenaries.

Rowland had thought the same thing. Another broadside followed – twelve six-inch missiles, as Meier knew full well.

Two of them scored hits, one on the nose of a Federal airship, another amidships. Flaming bags were jettisoned into the sky, riggers sprayed foam, ballast was ditched. The airships survived easily. Another bag was jettisoned as a tracer from one of Meier's pressure-guns went home.

Angling toward one another, the two Armadillos and what remained of the Federal wing had met over industrial Dodge City at the range of a mile and a quarter.

Missile volleys blasted back and forth.

Meier felt her ship hit, didn't need the rig officer's report – the falling as burning hydrogen bags were unleashed, the recovery as inert lead bags were correspondly released.

One of the Federal ships began to burn. She fought as she fell, a final ragged volley going out as she descended in flames toward the cracking towers and smokestacks of the Dodge industrial district.

A mile.

Meier could see that she was scoring hits, but the other two weren't catching fire. Helium birds, then. She'd heard of those – fought one, once, over Chile. You had to expect helium from an Imperial ally.

There were ways to deal with helium.

"Missiles, aim for the cabin," she directed her weapons officer. "Guns, pound away. They don't have an indefinite supply."

The weapons officer looked at his captain as though her brains were granite.

"*Duh*," he pointed out. "Our missileers have already figured that out. Aiming for cabin. Is free fire authorized?"

Duh herself. That meant, could each battery fire as soon as they were loaded without waiting for the others.

"Free fire authorized," Meier said. "Just bring those Federal *impediments* down."

* * *

"There's a fight going on!" ten-year-old Ernest Perry exalted from the window of the hotel room. "Those two Armadillos – it's the real Cordova's Armadillos, Mother! I can *see* the purple and blue ones – are attacking the Feds right above us!"

"Get away from the window," Annabelle Perry ordered. "I told you this before, Ernest! *No*, Jeremiah! You are not to join him!"

"No, you are not to!" snapped Christine Dorsett, the wife of

Thirty-Second Squadron's commander, Vice-Commodore Jody Dorsett. "Tripp, get away from that window right now!"

They were in a top-floor, executive-grade, hotel room on the edge of Dodge City's industrial and business districts; some perhaps-foresighted entrepreneur had built a six-storey hotel on the edge of the two neighborhoods.

Some *idiot*, Annabelle thought – not for the first time – had assigned the higher-ranking Imperial officers' partners the 'better', top-floor rooms of the place. Lieutenants' partners and children occupied the safer, lower-storey rooms.

Tripp Dorsett moved away from the window. Ernest, being the brat he was, refused to. "Holy crap, Mother! They just scored a hit on the *Five Speed*! Fires – no, they jettisoned a sac! And one of the Feds is going down! And the other's turning to – oh, no he just got hit, he's descending – scored another good hit on the *Five Speed* as he's down, now he's leveled – no, cannon fire is cutting him up! He's going down!"

"Get away from the window, I said," Annabelle repeated, moving to physically wrench her son from where he stood exalting.

At the *enemy's* victory. Didn't he realize that the colorful, photogenic Armadillos were working against Imperial interests this time? Were fighting the allies of their father's Service?

"So we've lost," said Christine from one of the luxury suite's two king-sized beds. "They own the skies over Dodge now."

"The Armadillos *never* lose, Mom," said Tripp.

"They're the *bad guys*," said Ernest. "They better lose. Or Father will shoot `em to shreds when he's back!"

"Your father," the wife of Thirty-Second's commander said slowly, "might not be coming back."

A glare from Annabelle kept her from going further. But for a mutter: "I wouldn't get my hopes up, is all."

* * *

"Dodge City is ours," came across the flasher from Meier to Rowland, as the last Federal ship crashed flamelessly somewhere amongst the corrals and abbatoirs of the eastern cattle district.

"Shall we begin trashing the place?" Rowland flashed back.

"Shall we?" Meier had replied, as the *Pith and Vinegar's* missiles lashed at a petroleum refinery.

* * *

Perry relaxed in the command chair of 4-106.

"Preparing lift," he said into his command mike. "Final check, confirm."

"XO confirms," said Martindale. "Checks?"

"Engineering and rigs, fully crewed, sir," came Lieutenant Vescard's voice over the bridge loudspeakers. "Boilers hot and check."

"Weapons, fully manned, sir," said Lieutenant Swarovski. "All twelve missile batteries. All guns loaded and check."

"Helm is check," said Ahle from that station. "But you knew that already, Perry."

"Communications?"

"Communications are check," said Nolan, from the station that would have properly belonged to the deceased Sub-Lieutenant Ross. Two specialist-grade enlisteds sat to his right. "Ready as according to your protocol, Mr. Imperial, sir."

"And it looks like we have ground clearance," said Ahle.

"Very well," said Perry. "Lift and turn for Dodge. It's time for Trotsky's mercenaries to learn some Imperial discipline."

Chapter Twenty-Three

One by one, starting in Canada, the capitals of the Imperial colonies - except for India,which had become hopelessly fragmented - re-pledged their allegiance to Parliament, Crown and the Restored Empire.

Retaking the British Isles themselves, expected to be a bitter fight against the populations of the Communes, began in November of 1908 with an unopposed landing in the Hebrides, followed by incursions into North Scotland.

Initial resistance was high and deaths included the commander of one Expeditionary Force, Major-General Douglas Haig, known for his innovative tactics, care for the lives of his men and insistence upon leading them from the front...

From *A Young Person's History of the World, Volume X.*

"Commander SS, respond and confirm," Commodore Jason Cordova's communications officer flashed the vicinity of where the SS command cars would be. Center of the broad phalnax as it advanced. A small, built-for-speed escort-class ship was already hovering high over the general vicinity; Captain Judd and a couple of Russian agents. He'd met them earlier; the observers.

"Commander SS here," the command car's communications officer flashed back.

"Thirty minutes from Dodge; two hours from Hugoton," said Cordova's ship. "Let's do our jobs, shall we?"

"Let's kill some things," Himmler responded as they approached Dodge City.

* * *

Dodge was burning. Or at least, that was how it appeared to Perry, as 4-106 came in on the industrial cowtown from the west-southwest.

No, not completely burning. Just the northern industrial parts, although the fires were spreading. *Somebody* – and, with a glance at the bright-purple and sky-blue shapes hovering above what had been an airship park, it wasn't hard to guess who – had done a proper job on the place. They'd laid waste to the easy targets across the northern industrial district, blowing distillation and cracking plants into red pyres that spewed thick black smoke up into the cloud-laden sky.

They'd gone over the airship park and smashed a dozen freighters, whose captains had been too dumb, faithful or stubborn to flee, into skeletal wreckage. More black smoke roiled into the sky as those ships burned. A couple of other wrecked ships lay – not burning, must have been Federal helium birds – in the south, having crashed among what Perry knew to be a residential district. The flickering remains of another ship had fallen onto some slums abutting the Boot District.

So you killed a few Feds, Perry thought. *Big deal.* By his understanding, none of the Federal squadron based out of Amarillo was bigger than escort-class. The two enemies were light line-classes, as opposed to 4-106's little-above-medium size for the type.

And now I'm coming for you, Perry thought. *Before you can do any more damage. Before you make another run over whatever might be left of the industrial district. Before you can kill any more innocent people.*

His wife and children were somewhere down there, damnit! Although probably in a business district hotel, an area that didn't look like it had taken much damage. But if the wind changed and the fires spread in that direction...

There were two of the bastards. Blue and Purple. He outweighed them, although not by very much. The Armadillos, Perry thought, were merely legendary.

I, *on the other hand, am* good.

"Wonder if we can authorize colored kill-marks," Swarovski said.

"Two down, two more *going* down," said Martindale.

"Engage," said Perry.

* * *

"Says they're Theron Marko with urgent information," Captain Meier's communications officer reported as the big line-class drew closer to Meier's purple *Pith and Vinegar*. "They request permission to come within loudhailer distance."

Meier shook her head.

"I know they told us to expect that ship, but that Marko guy's aboard another one. This guy should have an identification code. Ask them for it."

* * *

"Tell them 'password'," Ahle suggested.

"That captain should have coughed it up," Perry growled. "He was spilling his guts once he realized who Kennedy was."

"Maybe he didn't know. He said the dead guy in buckskins was the boss."

"Any other guesses?" Perry asked the bridge.

"Yo ho ho, sir?" Swarovski suggested.

"Surrender and you might live?" Martindale put in.

"I'm with 'password',Vice" said Nolan.

"As long as we keep them talking," said Perry. "Actually – tell them we've got it, but it's not for flasher communication. It'll be the first thing we say by voice."

* * *

Nice try," said Meier. "Comms two, tell Rowland 'engage wide'. That thing's back under Imperial control."

"Imperial?" asked her helmswoman.

Meier shrugged. "Could be Federal. Maybe another firm. Hostile anyway."

"Tell 'em anything?" the senior comms officer asked.

"Yeah," said Meier. "My first response."

* * *

"'Nice try'," Nolan reported. "And it looks like they're splitting apart."

"To engage," said Martindale.

Right now the two enemy airships were about four miles

away, perhaps half a mile apart and a mile up. The wind was behind Perry at about twenty miles per hour, but smoke patterns from the burning city indicated that that might not be a constant. There was a maelstrom down there, and it'd be doing all kinds of things to the air currents.

Splitting was 101-level tactics; maneuver to engage at right angles so that *one* of your ships would be crossing the enemy's tail or nose.

There was a 201-level counter to that. Perry had a postgraduate degree.

Ahle was already lifting the ship. She glanced at Perry with one eyebrow raised.

She has at least a bachelor's herself, Perry remembered. The Sonoran Aerospace Academy was supposed to be pretty good, and she'd had legitimate combat experience before going pirate.

"The purple one," Perry said.

"*Si, capitan.*"

As 4-106 steadily rose – you wanted to gain height in an engagement like this, because it was easier to fire down than up – Ahle turned the wheel to starboard, in the direction of the purple *Dread Wyvern*. With considerably more speed than a 450-yard line-class was supposed to be capable of, she handled the thirty-degree turn.

"Anything more you want said to `em?" Nolan asked.

Inappropriately – a Signals officer wasn't expected to initiate bridge communication unless reporting an incoming. And there was a console button for that. *Speak when you're spoken to,* rose in Perry's mind.

Not very hard, or harshly. Nolan as a civilian volunteer couldn't be expected to know Imperial bridge protocols. And besides, there *was* something.

Annabelle's somewhere down there, Perry thought. *With the children. And Ernest knows flasher codes. Maybe they're watching.*

"Yes. Flash this slowly, understand? Tell them 'Vice-Commodore Perry sends his regards'. Slowly, as I said."

* * *

"I said to get away from the window!" Annabelle Perry snapped at ten-year-old Ernest.

333

"Mother! The big ship the pirates stole from Father, it's definitely hostile to the Armadillos! Looks like she's moving to fight them."

"And what if a stray shot lands *here*?" Annabelle demanded, getting ready to pull her son physically away from the open window he'd planted himself against.

"Mother – our ship's flashing them again. Just let me see what he's saying, *please*?"

"You have ten seconds to get away from that window," Annabelle said.

"'Vice – Commodore – Perry – Sends – His – Regards', Mother!" Ernest shouted. "It's *Father*!"

"It's *Marcus*?" Annabelle demanded. And ran to the window herself.

* * *

"Vice-Commodore Perry," said Captain Rowland to her bridge. "That a name we should know?" Vaguely she remembered an intelligence meeting, one of the senior Imperial officers. Supposed to be meticulous, careful and detail-oriented.

"If he's messing with us," said the weapons control officer, "we'll know it from the obituaries tomorrow."

Rowland brought back her memory of the briefing. For now, she'd assume they *were* facing a careful guy. Thinking about how best to use that.

"Just some Imperial," the weapons officer repeated.

"And Imperials don't deserve respect," Rowland agreed. Too much like Sonorans in their focus on technology rather than spirit, when spirit was what won fights. "So we won't send those."

"Aye," said Comms.

"But we ought to say something," Rowland went on. "Condolences, I think. Advance condolences to his family."

* * *

"Cute," said Perry coldly. Because his family probably *were* down there, quite likely watching from an upper floor of some hotel when they needed to be in a fireproof basement. Maria was the sensitive kind and probably scared - viscerally he wanted to comfort her; intellectually he knew perfectly well that the appropriate reaction was to destroy the source of the threat.

But Ernest, too curious for his own good, would likely be glued to the window, and Annabelle paralyzed with trying to stop him.

He nodded firmly.

"Lined up a string of technically-not-curses befitting the Service but giving `em hell," said Swarovski. "Say go, sir."

Perry shook his head.

"Exchanging trash-talk with movie-star mercenaries isn't befitting the Service and we've done enough of it. I think I have better people we can talk to."

* * *

"E-R", Earnest Perry read the flasher, with his nose pressed to the window. "N-E-S-T. Ernest!"

4-106 was tilted upwards, rising fast, buffeted and pushed higher by the flames it was above, heading on an intercept course for the bright-purple airship, which was also rising, the other one closing on it like halves of a vice. A grey shape several thousand feet up, but the bright flashes were unmistakable.

Ernest whirled. "Daddy flashed me! *He flashed my name, E-R-N-E-S-T spells Ernest!*"

That *had* to be for them, thought Annabelle. Since that airship *had* to be commanded by Marcus now, who would have some idea where the Staff idiots would have put them. And of course, coming from an airship's flasher, Ernest was taking it like literal Word of God.

"And he hasn't stopped, dear," Annabelle Perry pointed out.

The airship was still flashing.

"Away," said Ernest.

"You missed the 'safer.' Safer away."

"From - that - window - end"

Marcus, I love you.

Ernest turned, a *broad* grin on his face.

"Father flashed me personally from his command ship!"

335

"And you saw what he said?"

"Ernest, safer away from the window," said Ernest, firmly turning his back on it. Heading to where Maria was sitting against the wall, hands over her eyes.

"Father's fine," Ernest told his seven-year-old sister.

"How do you know he's fine? You haven't spoken to him."

"He seems to have got his missing ship back and come to fight the pirates," Annabelle said. "He gave them his regards - and then he flashed Ernest!"

"Underground," Ernest insisted, pulling Annabelle toward the door. "Come *on*, Father said to with his flasher!"

Annabelle Perry hated the wives who wore their husbands' rank - or the husbands who wore their wives', rarer but not unknown - on their sleeve, tried to pull it on the other spouses. She had not so much as earned an ensign's commission in the Service; she had no right to wave Vice-Commodore's rank.

And she wasn't going to wave that rank now, but the squadron commander's wife also had responsibilities. To take care of the enlisted crew in the lower floors and the basement - give them some encouragement, set a careful watch on those fires and draw an evacuation plan in case they got too close...

A final glance over her shoulder saw 4-106 still rising fast, closing in at a right angle on the bright purple airship amidst smoke and flames from the burning industrial district.

God, I love you,Marcus, Annabelle thought.*Win this one. Come back to me, please.*

* * *

"They've been planning this for a while," said Perry as the ship rose, the gap from the sky-blue *Five Speed* closing to within a mile on their twelve, visible through wisps of boiling black smoke from the firestorn below. The *Pith and Vinegar* closed on their five, a little further away, only intermittently visible through the smoke from a furiously burning refinery.

"They'll have gathered some idea of what kind of a man I am - that I'm going to fight carefully and logically." Perry smiled thinly.

"A careful and logical man would run away when he's outnumbered two to one, outclassed in firepower by about one point eight to one," said Ahle, probably speaking for the whole

336

ship.

"I didn't say," said Perry, "that I was going to prove their intelligence right. Besides, we have a job to do." He outlined the plan.

"You're crazy," said Nolan.

"You forgot the 'sir'," said Perry. "Now, Comms, your part in this – start talking again. Random two-letter code groups."

"There's no friendlies nearby, sir," said Nolan.

"They don't know that. Give them something to worry about, take their mind from what we're *really* about to do to them."

* * *

4-106 flew through the smoke above Dodge City, kicked and buffeted by heat columns, the wind behind her as she rose on a T-bone course for the *Five Speed* as the *Pith and Vinegar* closed in at a right angle. Soon they'd be within missile range; the *Five Speed* would be in a position to turn and broadside Perry's nose.

If 4-106 turned to face *Five Speed* with a broadside, they'd be exposing either the vulnerable nose or tail - without being able to shoot back with missiles - to the heavily-armed *Pith and Vinegar*.

You didn't need an Academy commission to know it was a bad situation.

* * *

"What's he doing?" Airshipman Gilford asked as the purple airship closed on them. There was another ship to their twelve, that they had to be *racing* toward. Was Vice Perry *trying* to get them killed, were those rumors true about him being a traitor? Fires below would be a hell of a thing for a man to jump into…

"Have a piece of gum," said Rafferty, chewing on his own. The grin hadn't left the Specialist Third's face since he'd returned on the newly-recovered 4-106, and from what Gilford had been able to gather so far, there was reason for that - Raff had done some *crazy* shit.

He took the gum.

"Attention all stations," came Lieutenant Swarovski over the ship intercom as, buffeted by the winds behind them,. "Here's what you're going to do..."

By the end of it, Rafferty was grinning even more widely than he had before. He clapped Gilford on the shoulder.

"We got this one."

Something impacted 4-106. Missile hit. They were closer to the ship on their twelve than Gilford had thought.

Those flames below. The whole industrial district of Dodge City burning. Not to mention the airship park, the Boot District, everything you could see if you looked down.

It would be a hell of a thing for a man to have to bail into.

* * *

"*Yes*, nose return fire!" Swarovski shouted.

"Damage report, sir!" said Martindale.

"Report," said Perry. Calmly, his veins ice.

"Four hits. Fore port fin damaged. Lost six sacs, nose compensated. Aerodynamics affected perhaps five percent."

"We going to turn and engage that fucker," Nolan asked plaintively, "or just let 'em give us another volley right down the gullet likethat first one?"

The hissing vibrations below their feet began to jerk slightly; pressure-gun fire opened fire, one ball after the other firing at the smoke-darkened sky-blue airship that was now within a mile and a half, closing very fast to a mile.

Engines thrummed faster as 4-106 picked up speed, redlining the boilers.

Perry imagined the *Five Speed*'s missileers, mercenary trash for all their noisy celebrity, frantically reloading, calculating, aiming. They'd get a second volley. Maybe a third.

They wouldn't get off a fourth, not in the time they had left.

"Estimate her at a mile, sir!" reported one of the bridge crew.

Perry turned to Nolan.

"We follow the plan, Signals." Then to Ahle: "Prepare to turn."

* * *

338

Followed by the wind, 4-106 turned on her axis as the sky-blue airship came within a thousand yards; nine hundred, eight hundred, pushed hard by the wind and rocking, bumping back and forth from the unsteady fire-driven air currents below.

Another salvo of missiles from the *Five Speed* hit as it turned, some of them going wide. Others tore into the airship's kevlar and aluminum plating, ripping apart sacs; ballast was automatically dropped to compensate, and the airship stayed as level as the firestorm-driven currents allowed.

As 4-106's tail gun brought to bear, more fire poured into the *Five Speed*, wild shots but also hits, explosions amongst the gondola setting hydrogen bags alight. Ballast fell from her, too, and riggers danced to release flaming bags - some quite low, requiring the release of ones above before they could catch light and the burns spread - into the smoke-filled sky.

* * *

What *was* that insane Imperial doing, Captain Rowland thought, as a nervous crewman reported point after point of minor damage and 4-106 drew closer.

Four hundred yards. Less than the *Five Speed's* own length. She could see missilers, nine-inch, and the coming broadside was going to *hurt*.

But then what? He'd only get one, with the wind blowing into her like this. Side-on collission.

"He's crazy," Rowland's exec murmured from the helm. "He's an Imperial. He's supposed to be-"

"Men crack," said Rowland. Raised her voice, spoke into the microphone.

"All hands! Prepare to repel boarders!"

* * *

"Missiles," Perry said calmly to Swarovski, "you may fire. Ballast, release when they have."

"Missiles free. Kick their asses, boys!" Swarovski cried into his microphone.

"Weapons," said Perry mildly, "we've *spoken* about appropriate language on the bridge."

339

"You heard the chief," said Rafferty. "Do it."

Standing clear, Airshipman Second Gilford hit the trigger of the already-aimed nine-inch missile launcher. Flaming backblast blew through their bay;the missile streaked out, along with eleven others, toward the huge sky-blue airship.

"Starboard side," Rafferty yelled, bracing himself for what was about to happen. "Come on!"

A half-assed third volley of missiles crossed 4-106's from the *Five Speed*, mostly wildly fired as that ship's crew raced to draw cutlasses and prepare pistols. One shot hit the gondola, destroying four bags; ballast ditched automatically to compensate. There was no risk of fire with the inert helium bags; *only* those four had to be ripped open, not the dozens that a similar hit might have cost a hydrogen bird.

Another missile scored a lucky direct hit on one of 4-106's engines, blasting it - and its propeller - into whirling debris. A piece of the shattered propeller lanced up and ripped through two more hydrogen bags.

In his engine-hall station, Vescard swore as the report came in.

"Tell Bridge and reroute power," he ordered Warrant Second Rodgers.

"Already rerouted. Telling Vid now," said Rodgers.

The *Five Speed* wasn't nearly so lucky. Missiles exploded along her gondola - not the series of direct cabin strikes that had smashed the bright-red *Vorpal* a couple of hours ago, but bad enough regardless. One hit did rip open a section of the cabin, hitting crew cabins and a missile bay; one missileer, stunned by the blast and teetering over the space where his balance had been, lost his balance and fell.

The revolver, which he'd drawn against the anticipated boarders, dropped faster as that missileer yanked his parachute's cord and hoped the flames wouldn't get him; a moment later another man came past, a rigger knocked off balance by hits above.

4-106's other eleven missiles slammed into the *Five Speed*'s gondola, ripping apart hydrogen sacs and turning sections of the aircraft into brief infernos as her remaining riggers dashed to release hydrogen.

And then 4-106, still being swept broadside on what would have been a collision course, *jumped.*

* * *

Every man aboard had been expecting it, as almost a metric ton of inert ballast dropped from the ship. The kick still came as a surprise, the deck of the airship surging up toward them as the ship jumped a hundred feet in a couple of seconds.

"She'll be right below us, sir!" Vidkowski reported - "Now!"

"Away," Perry ordered curtly.

Another half-ton of ballast fell from 4-106. Unlike the ton from before, this load was *not* inert.

* * *

Four hundred pounds of blazing, ignited thermite fell onto the top of the *Five Speed*, ripping through the airship's thin kevlar-aluminum armor in fractions of a second and falling through her gondola, lighting waves of bags as, burning at four thousand degrees Fahrenheit, the loads tore through the Armadillo airship like drops of molten steel through tissue paper.

Riggers screamed and one recent recruit saw the writing on the wall, checked his parachute and bailed.

The rest were longer-term Armadillos who believed the legend, and most of them had been at Alamogordo the day they'd become one. They'd fight on regardless.

As 4-106 released helium bags to drop again, and her starboard-side missiles came to bear on the cripped and burning *Five Speed*, it was noble futility.

* * *

"Get 'em, boys!" came Weapons Officer Swarovski's voice into the starboard-side missile bay.

"My turn," said Rafferty, and hit the missile they'd loaded and timed earlier.

Twelve more twenty-five pound, nine-inch missiles streaked out at the *Five Speed*.

* * *

Airships had a lot of buoyancy, and fighting airships kept plenty of refillable sacs and hydrogen cylinders in reserve. Damage like the *Five Speed* had taken could have been repaired - if the three strikes had occurred with minutes between them, rather than seconds.

With only a few seconds between the point-blank missile barrage, a bombload of thermite and a second point-blank barrage from the other side, the *Five Speed* had no chance. Experienced riggers realized this, as did the rig officer, who called a report into the bridge and then raised one of his paddles to wave in the pattern that meant Abandon Ship.

Below, on the bridge, Rowland cursed under her breath as more reports came in, feeling her ship begin to fall as the hydrogen that kept her flying, burned or was jettisoned.

Others on the bridge were looking at her, waiting for her to make the call. They were brave, not stupid, and they knew what it meant when a ship began dropping like this.

"Abandon ship," she muttered. Raised her voice again: "We'll fight again another day! Abandon ship!"

* * *

From a mile and a half away, Shirley Meier on the purple-gondola-ed *Pith and Vinegar* had watched in shock as the Imperial's suicide charge had become an improbable, daring, deadly leap-frog of Peggey's ship. Parachutes now bloomed as the wreckage of the *Five Speed* started to fall from the sky.

"They took hits," Meier said aloud. That much was apparent; the Imperial's sleek, shape was battered now, her armor pitted from chaingun damage, her maneuvrerable form that much less so.

"We'll finish those dirtbags off, then," said Borean, her helm officer. "Fuckers."

"Turn to engage," said Meier. "Weapons free to fire at will. Take them down."

* * *

Cheers sounded across 4-106 as the burning wreckage of the *Five Speed* slowly fell out of the sky, through smoke plumes and up to where a lick of flame from a refinery stack licked her, brought her into the flames. Her crew in parachutes around, steered for the least flames and the best safety.

"Good job,crew," Perry spoke through the intercom. "But there's another one left, and we're going to have to fight it out with her. Every serviceperson will do their duty."

* * *

"Fire at will," came Swarovski's voice over the intercom to Rafferty and Gilford. They could see incoming missiles from the bright-purple ship, their trails of fire coming toward them.

Mercenary trash, thought Rafferty with pride, as he and Gilford loaded a missile into its tube. Careful - yep, looked about nineteen hundred yards.

"Bay clear? Fire!"

* * *

As rapidly as their crews could fire them, missiles ranged across the smoke-filled sky between 4-106 and the *Pith and Vinegar*, the two ships angled just off broadside to each other, slowly closing; nineteen hundred yards, eighteen hundred, a mile between them.

Secondary weapons - spinners, cannon, pressure-guns and chainguns - opened up as their operators took chances, aiming for lucky hits at extreme range. One of the Armadillo riggers was killed, a direct hit from a pressure-gun round taking him through the chest and tumbling his smashed corpse off the airship and into the fires below.

The airships buffeted by fire, updrafts pushing them up, kicking them around. It made aiming of missiles hard, and more went wide than not.

Others hit. A pair of nine-inchers from 4-106, one of them fired by Rafferty, exploded dead on the center of the *Pith and Vinegar's* gondola, blasting through the kevlar and setting thirty-some bags on fire at once. Riggers raced to the scene, spraying extinguisher and releasing the catches that sent burning bags loose.

A missile hit 4-106 near her already-damaged nose, striking a support strut whose structural failure slashed through nine helium bags as it, already under pressure, failed. Another one hit near a tailfin, narrowly avoiding major damage but blasting open three more helium bags.

* * *

"We're hurting them," said Perry, putting his scope down and walking back to his station. His own ship was taking damage, was definitely being bloodied, but the mercenary ship was smaller and it was only a matter of time.

She had three more friends accompanying the SS, of course.

And as she began to disengage east, Perry wished he had time to land for repairs. Or even better, time to go back to Hugoton for *real* repairs.

The SS was coming. They didn't have that time.

"Pursue them. And ready the Marines."

* * *

Second Lieutenant Herbert 'H' Jones of the Imperial Air Marines was a small man with a big grin. He'd chosen to remain at Hugoton with the last of his men in the hope of seeing the action he'd joined up for; twenty-two years old he hadn't yet, and he'd wanted to his entire life.

As he came onto the bridge he drew himself to attention and saluted the Vice-Commodore.

"At ease, Lieutenant. You and your sticks ready?"

Jones usually commanded a platoon, but he had two four-man sticks now, two thirds of a squad.

"Absolutely, sir. Whatever you need done, the Air Marines will handle. Gung ho, sir!"

The Vice-Commodore explained what it was. Jones' grin

344

became a massive one.

"Any questions?"

"No sir."

"Dismissed. You'll be ready to drop in five minutes. Any problem with that?"

"Gung ho, sir!"

* * *

"Deputy Rig Officer Brown's dead, ma'am," came the damage report to Captain Meier. "And they've closed to within half a mile."

Something shook; the *Pith and Vinegar* began to slowly turn to port. The bridge damage officer turned, shouted something into his microphone.

Meier didn't need to hear the response; it was obvious they'd just taken a bad hit on the steering.

Fleeing wasn't going to work any more. At least they were away from the flames, getting over the eastern Dodge cattle districts. Below them were pens and abbatoirs, not refineries.

And the Imperials had just made her decision for her, *forcing* her to cross their T. Really, there were worse positions to be in.

"Port-side missileers load and engage. They caught us; let's see if they can swallow us."

* * *

"They're turning to fight," Martindale reported. "I estimate them at eleven hundred yards."

That was close, for the huge airships. Definite pistol range, if not the sword range you often got. Of course, leapfrogging the *Five Speed* had been point-blank.

"Turn to starboard ourselves," Perry said after a moment. The port side had taken more damage. "Let's take them down."

"Oh, and sir? We're about to be over the cattle yards. Release the Marines?"

"Tell Jones they can jump any time."

* * *

Missiles lanced from 4-106, blasting out at the enemy airship as Jones jumped, his men behind him - free fall in light kit, just a combat load augmented by some electrical guns, from the ship armory, that they'd been told would come in handy for this mission.

The wind was coming from the south, not the west; only some of the massive smoke from the burning oil district was around here, but the fires were clearly spreading and there was more of a wood smell to the smoke than there *had* been.

Jones had goggles, didn't care.

Freefall, loving every moment of it. A glance up showed missiles streaking through the sky at the enemy ship, who'd had the class to turn and fight like a real airshipman did - and Jones had *been* there, only as a passenger but still - he'd have a tale to tell his mates in the O-Club about that leapfrogging maneuver the Vice had pulled on the other ship.

Focused down again, on the cattleyards that filled the eastern part of Dodge. Sheds, pens and slaughterhouses, and the cattle seemed agitated; they could smell the wind.

At two thousand feet he hit the ripcord, his parachute opening. His other lads had done so earlier, as they were supposed to; he wanted more precision himself.

He selected a rooftop, corrugated iron above what might have been a cowboy bar or something. Brought up his legs as it drew closer, closer - flat square rooftop, then a three-storey drop, but if the other side of the building was anything like the side he'd come from, there'd be a balcony to break his fall.

Impact! He curled into a roll across the cool iron of the rooftop, turning vertical motion into horizontal. Knife came out of its sheath like he'd practiced a thousand times; cutting the cords, rolling, stretching a leg out to arrest the roll with a good two and a half feet to spare before the edge.

And the muzzle of a gun less than a foot from his face, was the next thing Jones noted.

Carefully he raised his hands, looking past the muzzle of the gun to see that it was a revolver. The man behind it was a tanned, hard-faced type in a cowboy hat who'd come up a ladder from the balcony.

"You're trespassing," the cowboy said.

"Terribly sorry," said Jones.

"Keep one of your hands where I can see it. Have the other

one drop that battle kit with your rifle. We got a dozen armed men in here, including Deputy Colson. He'll take you into custody un-til such time as the Imperials can exercise their pre-rog-a-tive and take you fuckers in for trial."

"Hold up a moment. You think I'm one of those fuckin' mercs?"

The cowboy grinned.

"Imperials look to be winning that fight up there, don't they? Don't see *them* jumping."

Jones glanced up at the battle, which had moved northeast a bit with the wind. As he watched, 4-106 took another couple of hits, pieces of something flying off. But the purple merc - that one was definitely taking the worst of it, burning in a couple of places - another geyser of flame bloomed as he watched, ant-like riggers running to take care of it.

"Imperials always win," said Jones. "And you don't recognize my uniform, do you?"

"Ain't Imperial Army or Air Service."

"Imperial *Marines*, cowboy. Gung ho Marines, and we got a job to do we could use a few cowboys to help us with..."

* * *

A couple of minutes later, Jones was in the common room of the cowboy bar whose roof he'd landed on, holding a glass of cold beer he had no intention of drinking, while three dozen cowboys - and a sheriff's deputy - listened.

"Of course, we'll find some way of compensating the owners for the cattle," said Jones.

"All these ones are branded," said an older cowboy. "So you want us to *start* a stampede?"

A couple of Jones' men had found their way into the bar, were standing at the edge of the crowd with weapons ready.

"That's what I'm saying."

"These beef are spooked already, with all the fire happening. Getting `em going won't be hard," said the older cowboy. "The question is, *why*?"

"You," Jones pointed at the cowboy who'd initially tried to arrest him. "When you were up on the roof, you see any smoke coming from the east? Dust, rather?"

"Some big cattle drive," said the cowboy. Thinking for a

347

moment. "*Big* one."

"Not cattle," said Jones. "That's an armored division coming to finish the job those mercenaries started, and then go on to wreck Hugoton. That's hundreds of armored vehicles on the way."

The room exploded in shouting; *they hadn't heard?* was Jones' thought.

"So our job is to stop them. Vice Perry up there is getting ready to fight their air support, and word is that there might be some assistance coming from the ground, too." Jones didn't consider it wise to mention that the assistance would come from pirates, who were an ongoing cattle-rustling nuisance to the ranchers.

"Down here, we're thinking that a few ten-thousand cattle stampeding into their faces might slow 'em down a little as well," Jones went on.

"And your Governor, he'll pay market price for any we lose?" said the older cowboy. "Count the double-Bar L crew in!"

About half the men in the bar agreed and nodded.

"You know how to ride a horse, Lieutenant? Rounding the cattle and steering 'em west is going to work a hell of a lot better if you do."

"Played polo at Eton," said Jones happily.

"Then we'll saddle you up." The double-Bar L rancher turned to the others in the common room. "Boys, let's get this stampede started!"

Chapter Twenty-Four

...progress through a United Kingdom that had only bitterly been given up in the late 1880s was rapid, more so than expected once the initial hurdles had been overcome, as many of the impoverished residents of the former Communes happily re-pledged their allegiance to legitimate rule.

The Provisional Government of the Irish Free State declared its membership of the Restored Empire in early March of 1909, subject to full and equal treatment and an acknowledgement of Catholic legitimacy. This was confirmed by an overwhelming margin in a general plebescite a year later.

The last serious resistance to the Restoration ended on March 22nd, 1909, when the Allied Midlands Communal Council surrendered. Its chairman, revolutionary general and one-time technofiction writer Herbert George Wells, disappeared and is believed to have been killed in the last of the bitter fighting for the industrial cities...

But the forces of the Restored Empire always have excelled in tough fights, and continue to as of this day...

From *A Young Person's History of The World, Volume X.*

Perry didn't bother to watch the burning *Pith and Vinegar* crash; his scope was pointed across the plains to the east, and at the leading-element armored cars that were starting to become visible. Three airships, side by side, flew above them as the beaten and battered 4-106 slowly turned to face east. A smaller fourth one flew much higher above the center of it.

"Sir, we have time to land just briefly?" Martindale asked. "We could really stand to make some field repairs."

"I don't think we have time," said Perry slowly. "In your opinion, Lieutenant-Commander - could we do much in ten minutes?"

Martindale thought for a moment.

"I doubt it, sir. Nothing the riggers aren't already doing."

"Then we'll stay up. Helm, keep the eastern heading and accelerate us to half speed."

"Aye," said Ahle. A minute later: "We've definitely taken damage. Handling's not *bad*, but it's not what it was before the fight."

"And *what* a fight!" said Swarovski. "Four of the Armadillos! *We killed four of the Armadillos!*"

Perry allowed himself a smile.

"Duty and service, Weapons. Honor and reason. They trump grasping arrogance any day."

"You think we'll have to take on the other three?"

"We're going to kill the SS first," said Ahle, grinning. "Only got to do that in dribs and drabs before. Now there's *all* of them *coming right to us.*"

"Flashing us," Nolan reported. Yes, flashes visible from the center of the airships above the SS. In the foreground, groups of shapes, three thousand feet below and only a couple of miles out, were sharpening into individual vehicles; armored cars and steam-trucks, throwing their own plumes of dust. Behind them fighting vehicles, tanks, self-propelled artillery, ordered in four loose formations across a front maybe four miles wide, a command battalion at the center of it. They were starting to split, the command battalion taking the northern course, to go around the burning center of Dodge City.

"What are they saying?"

"Don't know - the Armadillos are using some code."

Commodore of the Armadillos probably asking for a status report, then.

"Tell Cordova his people are dead or in custody," Perry said. "Then flash the command group. Himmler has one chance to turn his division around and head into Texas. At this point they're not culpable under Imperial law. If they come further, they will be."

"Got it, sir," said Nolan.

"They have one chance to turn around," Perry repeated.

* * *

"*What?*" Judd asked his signalwoman. The *Ruby Red Robber* was the fourth ship, high above the SS as they made their approach toward the burning city. "You sure you got that right, Mary?"

"I been known to fuck up before?" Mary demanded. "That guy there says he's an Imperial, he's taken care of the other Armadillos and he's got the balls to stand up in front of an entire armored division and tell 'em he's going to spank 'em if they don't go home like good little boys."

"He didn't say all of that, exactly," put in McIlhan, grinning.

"Amounts to that."

"That's the airship we stole, too," said Ferrer, putting the spyglass down. "4-106 - they must have found and retrieved it."

"Discordia!" Marko said, and laughed. "We stole it and now Skorzeny's jackbooters will kill it! And then we all get paid, and go home!"

Without his seeming to think about it, a knife appeared in Marko's hand, danced across his knuckles, flew into the air and fell before he dropped it back into whatever wrist-sheath it came from.

Ferrer could imagine it drawn across his throat. Sickness, bile, anger.

"I'm going to take a rest," he said. "Be in my cabin."

"Engineer's just queasy about more blood being shed!" Marko laughed.

The laughter followed Ferrer out of the bridge.

* * *

"Himmler here," Nolan reported. The flashes had come from the vehicle at the center of the command group. "Fuck you, Imperial. Say your prayers."

"Sir!" reported one of the bridge lookouts. Pointing north.

Airships appearing on the horizon some miles away - rising, drawing closer. *Lots* of airships.

Perry raised his scope, saw - everything, and dozens of it. Merchantmen with their self-defense weapons, purpose-built escort-class ships and the *Vulk*-class he'd heard was the Kennedy flagship, a current-build Russian line-class warship the Kennedys had acquired somewhere.

Alongside it were - the biggest swarm attack he'd ever

351

seen. Spring-powered blimps, big captured merchant carriers, easily a hundred real ships and probably more.

Flashes came from the *Vulk*. Five very simple words: "Don't," Nolan reported. "Fuck. With. The. Kennedys."

Ahle turned to grin at him.

"Helm, take us down. We're going to engage their lead elements."

From below, a sound - a rumbling sound. Smoke, kicked up.

Cattle, stampeding east, cowboys riding among them. With his scope Perry could see a few of the riders wearing dusty Imperial uniform; a small man on a black horse turned to wave up at him; that *had* to be Lieutenant Jones.

Thousands - no, tens of thousands - of head of cattle from the Dodge yards, charging head-on into the SS.

"Or the cowboys," Perry remarked.

* * *

On the bridge of the *Vulk*, John Kennedy watched dispassionately as more missiles fired down into the SS. Cattle were running amuck - clever trick, that Imperial Vice was uptight but no moron - among the SS, disrupting their vehicles' maneuvers; the eighty-ton Tiger IIs and seventy-five ton IIas and IIbs, with their rocket variant, weren't going to plow straight through thousand-pound, fifteen-hundred pound beef.

Disrupting them and making them easier targets.

They'd rounded up everyone in the West who owed the Kennedys a favor or could be asked for one, at short notice. That meant almost everyone - there were *sheriff's* aircraft here, and militia. One company of Nebraskan State were deploying now in a ranch hamlet to the north, some men setting up anti-tank weapons while the others dug defenses, filled sandbags.

The plan was to attack around the edges, picking away. Leave the south open, let them run south into Texas if they wanted to; the objective was *save Hugoton*, not *destroy the SS*. At a certain level of casualties the mercenaries would run away, and that was fine.

* * *

352

"Flasher message coming in from the south," Nolan reported. "Imperials, the Admiral's there personally."

"What is it?"

4-106 was angled slightly to port, the damaged ship firing at will on the SS vehicles below. They were reacting themselves to something their scouts had encountered south of Dodge City.

An explosion caught Perry's eye below, as one of 4-106's rockets hit an already-damaged tank, blew its turrets in the air.

"Another one down!" Ahle exalted from the helm, pumping one fist in the air. "*Fuck you,* Heinrich!"

"Admiral says she's got the rest of the garrison and about two thousand locals from Dodge. Forting up to make it harder for them to pass south. Digging and building a line of forts with makeshift anti-tank guns and rockets."

* * *

Heinrich Himmler, in his command tank - a monstrous Tiger IIb with its huge airship-grade rocket launcher taken out to provide some planning space - got the report at about the same time.

"Imperials and locals digging in south of the city," his senior comms officer reported. "Chain of little forts we'll have a hard time busting individually. Close enough together that we can't go between them, extending south."

"South's out, then. What do you think, Dietrich?"

The SS' burly second-in-command nodded.

"We go through. We fuck these pirates, punch through and complete the job."

Except that the pirates were on *all sides* now, slowly chewing up his personal army, and a collection of Plains locals - *that problem was supposed to have been tied off!* - were digging in to the north, too, building a firebase that would make it impossible to pass through those suburbs.

"We go through," Himmler confirmed. "Fuck them. We go through."

He turned to the comms officer.

"And tell them I'll *personally* execute any soldier who fails in his duty to me at this time."

* * *

Sheriff's Deputy Sergeant Joe Danhauer sighted his rifle over the makeshift barricade. Since they'd dropped in, courtesy of a Kennedy-run airship, twenty minutes ago, he and the half-dozen Kearney deputies that consituted their town's part of the Nebraska State Militia ready reserve had been alternately digging and shooting; sharp anti-tank trenches, the dirt packed hard into collapsible boxes that were a wall against incoming fire. When packed three-deep the solid two-foot cubes were supposedly able to withstand a direct hit from anything short of the tanks' main gun, and three were packed in front of him now as he - fired!

The Tiger II's commander, standing in his hatch and gesturing possibly to subordinates - probably not just commander of his own tank - fell forwards onto his machine-gun.

Another burst of machine-gun fire stitched the impromptu barricade. An armored car running past, fully buttoned-up except for the gunner behind a shield that bullets sparked off of.

Norris, next to him, was loading an anti-tank rocket launcher.

No time to think about how the hell Nebraska's Adjutant-General had been in bed with the Kennedys all along, had some kind of deal. But it did explain why none of the organized pirates had ever raided towns like his, something he was thankful for - a you-don't-try-too-hard-to-pursue-us-and-we'll-leave-your-own-residents-alone kind of a deal that apparently translated to active support in a shooting war, now the Kennedys had called in everything to support some kind of deal they'd made with the Feds and the Imperials.

Norris fired his launcher, not being too careful where the backblast went. The rocket streaked toward an armored car.

The Feds and the Imperials approved of this; Danhauer wouldn't have gone into combat without that solid assurance from Captain Atchison. The Feds probably approved only because the Imperials said so - nobody in Nebraska had any doubt who was in charge there - but nobody cared much, because rumor had the Imperials telling the Feds to back out of Nebraskan affairs a few times, too.

354

"Got that one!" said Norris, pumping a fist in the air.

Yes. An armored car was on fire, men bailing out; riflemen and a machine-gun from Danhauer's barricade opened fire on them, and at least one didn't get very far after he'd hit the flat, cover-less ground.

Other SS vehicles returned fire, and Danhauer shoved his deputy back into cover as a fusiliade went over his head.

"Of course," said Norris, breathing hard, "don't need a rocket launcher to set something on fire; *I* can start a fire by rubbing two ice cubes together!"

"Shut the fuck up," Danhauer said, "and fight."

* * *

High above the fight, Ferrer watched tiny vehicles circling, minuscule explosions blooming. Pirates seemed to be mobbing the three brightly-colored airships, while the big Imperial one kept its focus against what seemed to be the SS' main drive to pass north of Dodge.

I'm fucked. I've been working with a lot of violent criminals and I'm fucked. I made a mistake, I'm not going to change the world like this or even get a comfortable retirement, and that psychopath Marko is probably going to kill me when I'm no longer useful.

Yeah. Well, he could do something about that *now*, couldn't he.

And perhaps he could make amends for that poor kid he'd killed, for the part he'd played in killing others.

Resolved. He got up, checked his gun. Work to do.

He'd always been comfortable with work.

* * *

Second Lieutenant 'H' Jones waved the cowboy hat in the air; the rancher had given it to him, saying if he was going to be doing cowboy's work, he ought to be wearing at least some of a cowboy's outfit.

Cattle running everywhere at this point; he and his men had the role of keeping as many of them pointed east - now, northeast, to interfere with the heavy armor's movements - as possible.

In the other hand to his hat was the stun device, which

355

didn't stun cattle but worked magnificently to inflict a bit of pain without actually hurting them, to keep them moving.

A couple of big bulls had gotten a bit tired, had stopped to snack on some brush. With his knees Jones steered his horse toward them, zapped one on the rump with the taser. Then on the flank, aiming them in front of a SS Tiger II wheeling around.

The Tiger II's main gun fired - up at one of the circling-everywhere pirate airships. This airship was a bad excuse for a semi-dirigible blimp, a few hydrogen sacs held in place with netting, crude engine belching black steam as one of the pirates threw high-explosive grenades down.

The shell missed and one of the pirates yelled something, hurled three grenades at the tank. One hit, bouncing off the light roof armor - the tank was zipped up, most of them were by now against the sheer volume of fire coming from above and around - and doing no apparent harm except for - when the smoke cleared - trashing the coaxial gun.

And maybe doing something through the driver's visual slit, because the tank stopped - got going again after fifteen or twenty seconds, but maybe that was the time it took to get a dead or wounded man out of the driver's seat.

Jones slapped his cowboyhat against the horse's flank, kneed the animal toward a couple more cattle that had slowed down, charging the taser again.

"Ride `em, cowboy!" he yelled, as one of his men passed by.

* * *

Inside Marko's cabin, in one of the evil clown's bags of tricks, Ferrer had found what he was looking for - two of them, in fact, with the appropriate accessories. Guilt at invading the space was mitigated by anger, not only at Marko but at himself, for being drawn into this *murderous* scheme to hurt *how many* innocent people, people just like him, people just as fucked by the corporations as him.

"Ooooh jeez," came a voice from behind.

Rienzi was standing in the doorway. Ferrer couldn't keep the guilty look off his face, couldn't pretend for a moment that he was legitimately in the cabin.

Fear rose through him, but he'd been terrified before. It was controllable.

"You are going to be *so fucked*," Rienzi smirked. "Marko is going to cut your fucking lungs out when he learns you've been going through his shit."

"You like to kill people," said Ferrer, keeping the fear down. Engaging the incompetent psychopath on his own terms, something told him, was a bad idea.

But some men you couldn't reason with.

"Maybe I'll get to kill *you*," said Rienzi.

"Maybe you will," said Ferrer. "Draw."

"What the fuck?"

"I said draw, quick boy," said Ferrer, and drew his own gun.

Rienzi was reaching for his when Ferrer shot him - once, twice in the chest, and then, as the body fell, once again in the head because he only *thought* Rienzi had neglected his kevlar.

That murderous little punk had bragged about how much fun killing people was, Ferrer thought as he picked up one of Rienzi's boots and pulled the body into their cabin. Shoved it under the lower bunk. The murderous little punk had talked constantly about how enjoyable it was to end lives, and it had disgusted Ferrer from the start.

But under certain circumstances, the engineer had to admit, the act *could* have a certain satisfaction to it.

* * *

Skorzeny pointed from his armored car. "That looks like the weak point," he gestured to Schierbecker. "Signalman, flash that to the *Fuhrer*. Everything directed at that point."

The point in question was a cluster of ranch buildings about two miles north of the Dodge city line, where industry met plains quite sharply. A unit of pirate troops - the Lakota battle standard indicated what type of a unit, hit-and-run guerilla raiders who kept the Feds off their land by hitting supply lines and long-range raiding of logistical points, not farmers used to defending fixed positions.

That was evident by how they'd relied on the - now trashed wreckage - buildings for cover, hadn't thought to dig much in the way of anti-tank defenses. The position bristled with anti-

357

tank guns and rocket launchers, but it wouldn't withstand a concerted attack; a company of Tigers would crush it easily, let alone the division. That would open a gap, but...

The SS wasn't used to this kind of fighting. The simple reality was that they were a counterguerilla force, not a conventional armored unit, and their thirty years of institutional experience had been primarily against Klan-type irregulars; the last really organized action had been the fighting around Raleigh in 1944, nineteen years ago.

As if to confirm his thoughts, another Tiger went up in flames, hit by that monster of a stolen-back Imperial ship that seemed to have an endless supply of missiles for pouring in.

This was going bad fast. The SS was reeling and Heinrich was kidding himself if he thought they still had much of a chance.

He said as much to Schierbecker, who nodded. Wouldn't do for a promising young first lieutenant to agree too loudly with any criticism of his Fuhrer, even if it *was* the Fuhrer of an organization being steadily destroyed.

"*Fuhrer* says he'll try," said the signalman. Skorzeny could see Himmler's command group and, yes, red-tinted flashes - the filters meant certain commanders, the red meant priority to *all* commanders - said that he was directing attention.

Nobody seemed to be listening.

Tell him that if he doesn't try harder, Skorzeny thought but didn't say, *he may as well not bother.*

* * *

"That's the command group," said Martindale. "See the signal propagation, the flash repeaters?"

"See the black airship right above them, holding station and repeating?" asked Ahle. The last of Cordova's Armadillos, Commodore Cordova himself. A ship the equal of 4-106, and less damaged from the fighting. Burning wreckage around the path of the command group had shown why everyone in the sky had learned to keep a very, very wide berth.

"See him go down, then," said Perry. Ahle wanted to engage the SS commander directly, wanted that more than anything else, and it was time to give the pirate what she wanted. Not to mention the tactical benefit: cut the head off, and the rest of the snake might just give up.

"I get to engage? Do we turn to engage him?" Ahle asked eagerly.

"Weapons?"

"Sir?"

"Hold fire. We're loading up for the black one."

"Aye, sir."

"Helm? Turn to engage as desired."

"Aye *sir*," said Ahle.

* * *

"We're getting flashed," said Judd's signalwoman aboard the *Ruby Red Robber*. "SS commander says he wants a ride out. That Imperial bird's engaging his air support and he's no longer comfortable. Wants to direct the battle from up here."

"As he should have been all along," said McIlhan.

"They didn't expect such a fight. Wouldn't have one if not for that fucking Imperial son of a bitch *who should be dead like the Kennedys*," said Marko. "Punk."

"It safe to go down and get them?" asked Ferrer. So far the *Robber* had been mostly unmolested, well above the fight at nine thousand feet relative, because the pirate horde was clearly dedicated to stopping the SS. A couple of venturesome attempts had been beaten off with the ship's defensive rockets, although a couple of pesky idiots were circling at a distance.

I'll enjoy cutting your cowardly throat, thought Marko. Although maybe he'd just let the fucker outlive his usefulness, with another couple of slashed-up banknotes to remind the weak who was strong.

"This ship's *fast*," said Judd. "We'll nip down, pick up Himmler and Dietrich and a couple of their people." He began issuing orders; dropping heat, the airship began to descend.

Below, Marko could see 4-106 exchanging rocket volleys with Cordova's black *Lone Star*, other pirates taking advantage of the opportunity to circle in and nip at the heels of the Armadillo commander. That battle would last a few minutes, at least.

Then something - no, *two* somethings, in close succession - exploded inside the *Ruby Red Robber*.

The ship's rapid descent stopped. Reversed.

359

The little pirate in crimson cursed, turned the wheel. Shouted orders.

"Steering's gone, totally gone, boss!" someone shouted back. "And-"

"And buoyancy control's gone, too, you don't need to tell me *that*!" Judd yelled. "Get a repair team to *fix* it, then!"

One of the bridge crew dashed off. Followed by Ferrer.

Good, make yourself useful, thought Marko. "Fucking logic man."

* * *

Eight-inch rockets punc hed into 4-106, exploding invisible geysers of helium. 4-106's rockets pounded back, producing torrents of fire that riggers dashed to put out. Burning hydrogen sacs filled the air. Below them the SS had turned to laager, their assault halted; some individuals had broken south amidst the stampeding cattle, running already for the Texas border where they'd be safe. A lot of people seemed to simply be watching the duel between 4-106 and the *Lone Star*.

Which 4-106 was winning, but barely. *Lone Star's* crew really was as good as the Texan media had made them out to be, thought Perry.

Almost up to Imperial standards.

* * *

Ferrer came back onto the bridge as the *Ruby Red Robber* continued soaring up into the air. Feigning panic, although in actuality strangely calm. The bombs he'd taken from Marko's supply had been placed exactly as they should have been, gone off exactly when they were supposed to. One thing with engineering, you always knew how proper components would act.

Marko bought his feigned panic. One thing with people, he'd learned from that psychopath; they always saw what they expected to see.

"Steering completely gone," he reported.

"*Shit*!" Judd snarled.

"Buoyancy too. And we're on fire."

Rising up, ten thousand feet or so relative now, and - yes,

the ship began to list sideways and drop.

"Then we bail," said Marko. "Fight again another day."

"I got us parachutes," said Ferrer, eagerly - but not too eagerly. Handed one over.

Marko strapped it on. Judd and the other crew were already wearing theirs; the signalwoman pushed open the downward-facing door of the airship, which was now tilting at almost a forty-five degree angle, and hurled herself out.

Judd followed.

"What are you waiting for?" asked Marko, heading for the door. "Let's get the fuck out to Texas."

* * *

Lone Star tilted sideways, sideways and up, making her cabin vulnerable to 4-106 as she descended. Flasher signals W-F, W-F, W-F came from the fore station - its aft had been destroyed - and someone waved a white flag from the bridge.

"Nolan, general broadcast," said Perry. "Armadillo is now a captured enemy and will be treated with mercy."

"And what do *we* do?" Ahle asked.

"Weapons? Ship is now under helm command."

Ahle's teeth bared.

"Weapons," she said. "See that cluster of SS vehicles in the center of their laager? The command IIb in particular?"

"Aye, ma'am."

"Destroy it."

A moment later, two thirds of a dozen rockets lanced out at the center of the fomation. Only eight of 4-106's launchers remained functional, after the hard fight with the Armadillos.

Only three of their rockets hit Heinrich Himmler's command tank.

Only one would have been needed.

* * *

In freefall, maybe ten feet apart, the air whooshing deafeningly around them as the burning *Ruby Red Robber* fell past behind Marko, Ferrer shouted to the anarchist:

"Thought you'd appreciate the parachute — "

"Cowardice has its uses!" Marko grinned back.

Ferrer continued: "Like I appreciated my pay!"

It took Marko a moment to comprehend.

Horror on his face, turning to a snarl as he desperately pulled the ripcord.

The parachute cloth unfurled - as torn and slashed shreds of fabric, a few of them crudely re-sewn together like Ferrer's money had been. Fabric confetti spreading into the air above him.

Ferrer grinned.

"You fucker."

Even then, Marko almost made it. Snarling and yelling and somehow pushing against the air, he flipped toward Ferrer, who yanked his ripcord reflexively.

His parachute blossomed open above him, arresting his fall with a sharp yank. Marko seemed to drop past him.

Twisting and contorting desperately, he screamed all the way down.

Chapter Twenty-Five

Refoundation Day: 23rd April, 1909.

Not coincidentally the accepted death-date of St. George, Patron Saint of England, Refoundation Day is the day the Union Jack rose again over London as Parliament and the Royal Family officially returned after nineteen years of exile.

Although unofficial efforts had begun almost as soon as the notional street fighting of the Imperial Return had ended, London began to be rebuilt, and would soon take her place again as a world capital of commerce and culture.

The surviving leaders of the Communes, amnestied months earlier, were officially pardoned in return for their re-pledging loyalty to the restored Crown...

From *The Imperial Almanac: A Primer for Young Boys and Girls.*

The SS was fleeing. On foot – the parachute had been steerable but not very – Ferrer picked his way through the destroyed armor and milling cattle to where Marko had hit the ground. There was money in that greatcoat of his, a lot of money, and Ferrer intended to have some of it. The pay he'd been promised, at the very least.

His gun was drawn, but still he didn't see the steam-bicycle until it was coming to a halt five feet away. Skorzeny swung his big body off the pillion, over the sidecar, and smiled. His assistant Schierbecker looked on, his pistol not *quite* drawn. Skorzeny's was.

Ferrer took half a step back and angled himself to where he figured he could take at least the Special Squadrons colonel down, if not his aide.

"It seems we have about the same idea regarding his operating funds," said Skorzeny, eyeing the tattered remains of Marko's parachute. It was a prettier sight than the splattered remains of the man.

"Maybe we do," said Ferrer evenly. He eyed the bike's sidecar. "And maybe you can solve a problem. Half of it, if you can get me out of here."

"There's three of us; three shares," said Skorzeny, while Schierbecker looked on. "You get a third and your ride."

Ferrer angled his gun hand slightly more toward Skorzeny. He didn't want a fight and a third would be plenty, but he was done taking shit from people.

"You guys can split sixty percent," he countered. "And you get it out of that mess, give it to me. I'll mind it until we're somewhere safe we can count."

A wide grin broke across Skorzeny's face. "Or you'll take a knife to my parachute, huh, engineer?"

"Maybe I will," said Ferrer. "If you cheat me."

"Forty-sixty if I get it out," said Skorzeny. "I'll deal with that."

He bent into the jellified mess that had been Theron Marko's long coat. The grin left his face for a moment, but came back when he dug out the wallet and tossed it at Ferrer, who caught it with his free hand.

"That piece of shit had it coming a *long* time, engineer. Tuck it safe and get in."

Still a little wary, Ferrer stashed the wallet on the inside pocket of his vest; he'd made sure Skorzeny hadn't had a chance for some Marko-esque sleight of hand, although he didn't think the SS man was that type.

Skorzeny climbed back onto his bike; Ferrer folded himself into the sidecar and Schierbecker headed the vehicle south.

Money, thought Ferrer. Money for that farm, and the experiments he'd wanted to do for a long time. About deliberately amplifying electromagnetic interference and using it as a form of communication...

* * *

McIlhan climbed onto the back of the SS vehicle, cursing. That jumped-up kaffir piece of shit... Marcus Perry, his name had been. Was. For now.

"You on tight, bitch? You owe me that fuck when we're safe," said the corporal commanding the armored car.

"Fuck your brains out," said McIlhan, not meaning it. She'd

stick a knife into him first. Fucking *Marko*, that would have been fun.

And she'd never get her chance, now, thanks to that shithead Ferrer, who she was pretty sure had had something to do with Marko's parachute failure. Certainly from how he'd been right there when it happened, which was good enough evidence for her.

I'm going to fuck you up, Imperial shithead Perry, she thought. *And you, Ferrer.*

"Willy, get us the fuck out of here," the corporal told his driver.

Yeah, I'm running now. But watch both of your backs, I'm going to get even.

* * *

Ahle and Perry met the Governor of Hugoton, Ian Fleming and Admiral Richardson in the Governor's restored office, an unofficial-official meeting because Perry and Ahle had spent the past couple of days at the Imperial office in Dodge, Perry with his wife and children.

Fleming was doing the talking in this meeting, and he got straight to the point.

"For a man who hated the idea of working as an undercover agent," he said to Perry, "you did an excellent job as one. Hugoton might have been saved without you, but perhaps not. Your contributions - have been communicated to Her Majesty. And she sends her thanks."

"Directly," said the Governor, reading from a purple telegram sheet. *Directly from Buckingham Palace?*

"Vice-Commodore Perry is to be commended on his actions as described, which shall by Our direction be rewarded with a place on the Honors list," he read out. "Her Imperial Majesty, Victoria Elizabeth the Second."

Perry found his mouth slightly open. The Queen *herself*, noticing - honoring - him? And an Imperially-directed place - that meant an Order, that probably - almost certainly - meant a *knighthood.*

"Except," said Fleming.

Except. Perry's heart, from its glorying heights - *Sir Marcus!* How Pater and Mater would be proud! - sank. There was

365

something solid and awful in that Except.

"Ahle, you've avenged your family," Fleming turned. "What do you have in mind now?"

She shrugged. "Go back to being a Code pirate. You've confirmed Marko's death; when you free my crew we'll be on our way."

"Committing crimes against the Empire's law," said Fleming smoothly. "Perhaps I should break my word. What's a pirate without a ship, anyway?"

"I have assets in Sonora. We can buy a new one."

"Had assets," said Fleming. "Your accountant, Sciapella, made a deal in exchange for her freedom. She's under a new name, now, and my black accounts are that much richer."

"That *bitch!*" said Ahle, then slowly made herself calm down. "She had no way of knowing I'd come back; I'd have done the same in her shoes. That bitch stole my money! *You* stole my money!"

"Oh, she got a piece of it," Fleming smiled. "But yes, you're a pirate without a ship, without money, without employment - or, to be frank, without a cause. How about a new one?"

Ahle cocked her head.

"That bitch stole my money and you got it. Give me some of it back and we'll talk."

"I was thinking a new purpose, a new cause, not a new fortune."

"Fortune and cause can go hand in hand," Ahle shot back.

"I like the type of idealist whose primary ideal is money," said Fleming. "The depth of the Imperial Treasury means I can depend on them."

"So what's your cause? Can I go after the last of the SS? Texas isn't going to care so much about arresting them given that they didn't really fuck with Imperial property, just tried to. No public outcry. You could use black agents like me for that."

"Or we could use them to create peace in the South. A lasting peace, not dependent on mercenaries. A South in line with the Curzon Doctrine - either a part of the USA or a free Confederacy, allied to the Empire on its own terms."

Fleming displayed for a moment, his own purple telegram paper.

"Lord Mountbatten and Her Majesty have been communicating with me most firmly on this matter.The South is rising again, as they did in 1861, 1889, 1929 and 1944. This time, Her Imperial Majesty has said in no uncertain terms that" - he showed the purple telegram - "she is fed up with it. Victoria Elizabeth wants a peace, a lasting peace, and has directed Imperial assets in North America not to crushing the present revolt but to ensuring there will *never* be another one."

Ahle was silentfor several long moments. Perry could see she was trying to suppress a faint smile.

"To make sure nobody *ever* does a Wake Forest or a Raleigh again?"

"Yes."

"I'll help with that." A heartbeat. "If you pay me."

"I'll pay well," said Fleming. He turned back to Perry. "And the two of you work well together. You know the reward for a successful job."

"You said - a knighthood."

"And a promotion, Commodore with fast-track to Admiral," said Richardson. "I agree with this."

"4-106 was, officially, never recovered," said Fleming.

"Never named, either," said Ahle.

"Off the record, I think her crew have gotten to know her by the serial number. She'll stay 4-106, as an off-the-books asset of *mine*," said Fleming.

Richardson gave the spy chief a not-too-friendly look. Clearly they'd had words about this earlier. Probably some of Fleming's discretionary funds - if he'd kept only half of the money Ahle and her crew had made, there'd be a lot - had contributed to his winning this particular argument.

"You, too, are deniable, and are probably more useful that way. For now."

"You - can't keep me a spy," said Perry weakly. But not just Commodore down the line, but *Sir*... that was something to look forward to. An incredible reward, that knighthood, and if Fleming wanted him to do more to earn it... he would.

"You two will be going to Atlanta," Fleming said. "To meet with a man named King. You served us well in the West, Marcus. You'll hopefully soon do the same for us in the South."

Sir Marcus. Commodore.

"It's partly a request," said Richardson. "You do have the option of refusal, if you object strenuously enough. But Her Majesty has expressed her gratitude for your service, and would appreciate further."

God. Damn. It, Perry thought, but his mouth spoke anyway. "I will do my duty."

THE END

For more great books, go to
www.henchmanpress.com

Made in the USA
San Bernardino, CA
03 February 2016